BOUNDARIES
WITHIN
Book I

HOLLY A. KELLISON

authorHOUSE®

AuthorHouse™
1663 Liberty Drive
Bloomington, IN 47403
www.authorhouse.com
Phone: 833-262-8899

Published by AuthorHouse 02/14/2023

ISBN: 979-8-8230-0089-5 (sc)
ISBN: 979-8-8230-0088-8 (e)

Library of Congress Control Number: 2023902248

Print information available on the last page.

This book is dedicated to my Mom (1947-2022).

CONTENTS

PROLOGUE

If death comes for everyone at some point in their life, why can't it be swift? Why is there intense pain until the utmost end for some? Was it some sort of karma collecting on a debt? Tess knew her suffering came with nothing but karma for the things she had done in her life. As she lay on the marble floor trying to catch her breath, she couldn't, as she was drowning in her own blood. Tess was being granted exactly what she served to others.

Unable to speak, her hand reached out for Colin. All she wanted was for him to hold her until she died, and her suffering was over. Death couldn't be too far away at this point. Feeling his warm hand grasp hers, she held tightly as if the joining of their hands would somehow heal her. Yes, she still had some hope of surviving. Coughing up the warm, sticky liquid, which she knew was blood, darkness within her peripheral vision was closing in quickly. Tears slipped from the corner of her eyes, as Colin rolled her to her side draining some of the blood from her mouth. A piercing pain burned through her back and felt like an explosion in her chest, making her eyes wide with the agonizing pain.

As he laid her back, she caught a moment of air that was quickly replaced with blood, again. Where was the reaper, she wondered as her eyes rolled back, then focused on Colin again as he was saying something. The words were incoherent for the most part, but she did hear him tell her to fight. What did he want her to do, fight death, the reaper, the Almighty? If it was her time, short as her life may have been, she couldn't stop it, nor could she have stopped the bullet that pierce her back. Shot in the back! Whoever did this couldn't even face her head on. Too bad she wouldn't survive to execute her revenge.

Feeling her body relax, her hand slipped from Colin's, and her eyes began to close as the darkness filled in the remaining bit of her vision. Finally, the pain and the struggle disappeared.

CHAPTER 1

One Year Earlier

Dominic Markenna stood six feet tall with perfect dark brown hair and piercing green eyes. Morgan Kellas stood beside him, thinking how attractive he was in a smooth, dangerous way. Then again, so was she. Their conversation about financial investment easily flowed the last time they'd had dinner together. Dominic owned his own investment firm, and Morgan was a self-employed financial investment counselor to a very select population. Tonight, she wasn't there to counsel him; she was simply there because they had clicked a few months before when he ran into her near the elevators at his work. She'd had a meeting with a client that day—at least that's what he thought.

"Morgan," he whispered in her ear. "You look beautiful tonight."

Smiling, she leaned up, and kissed him tenderly. Intimacy always softened a man. "You've told me that twice now."

"I'm very tempted to just skip this whole thing and take you home with me." He kissed her hand.

"Just make an appearance." Standing in front of him, her hand brushed over his black silk tie. "Then we can slip away."

"I suppose you're right." Gently, his hands ran softly over her bare shoulders. Dominic loved how her dark hair was straight tonight and hung like silk down her back.

"Of course, I am." She grinned. "One thing I know how to do is work a crowd."

"That is not the only thing you know how to do," he said with a mischievous grin.

"Shh." She put a finger gently to his lips. "That's our secret."

Dominic took her hand and walked her gracefully into the ballroom. It was a black-tie affair, and he was dressed accordingly. Morgan, his girlfriend, wore a long, sleeveless, body-curving dress that matched his tie, making her stand out from all the other women. With her hand in his, they made their way around the room. Their appearance seemed to last much longer than he anticipated and by the time they were able to leave, it was well after ten.

As he drove them to his home, he took her hand and kissed the top of it. Tess was a woman that he could easily spend the rest of his life with. Aside from her beautiful looks, she was highly educated, graceful, and classy with a quirky edge. None of that compared to her passion in the bedroom. She knew what she wanted and had a subtle way of telling him, which made their lovemaking extremely intense in the most desirable way. What stood out to him the most was how he fell in love with her in such a short time.

"Morgan," he spoke her name softly as his hand rested on her hip when they walked into his bedroom.

"Yes?" Tess turned to him.

Running his hand over her cheek, he kissed her. "I'm completely in love with you."

Morgan looked down for a moment and then up at him. "Dominic ..."

"I know." His finger ran along her jawline. "You said falling in love with you was dangerous emotionally, but I can't help the way I feel."

Morgan let a tear fall, and Dominic wiped it away. "I like what we have, Dominic. I don't want to lose that."

"We won't. I like what we have too, but you must realize that this will progress into more—and it will happen sooner rather than later."

"I know." Taking a slow, deep breath, she ran her hands over his shoulders. "Just take it slow with me. I'm not used to letting anyone ... in."

"I know." Wrapping his hands around her body, he easily pulled her close.

The passion Dominic felt when they were together was the most extreme feeling he had with a woman in quite some time. Tonight, they went slow, caressing and kissing every inch of each other's bodies. With his history with women, he knew he must find a way to keep her because at this point in his life there had been only one other woman that he loved to this degree but lost her and he wasn't having that happen again.

They spent half of the next day together since Morgan said she had a dinner meeting with a client in the evening. Dominic did not have any issues with that, as he had to take care of some business as well. The background check he ran on her when they met had come back clean. Nothing illegal or immoral popped up. Raised by her mother, a single parent, Morgan had no idea who her father was. With her mother passing away two years before, Morgan had no living family. Dominic wished he would have been an only child. It would certainly have saved him many headaches and lots of money.

At about seven o'clock, the car came for her. She was ready, as always. Climbing in, she closed her eyes as the driver took her to the private airstrip. After spending three months with Dominic, she found herself enjoying her time with him much more than she should. She knew she was breaking her first rule: never get emotionally attached when working, but she couldn't control these feelings for him.

Sitting on the bottom step of the stairs up to the private jet was her favorite man. Colin McGowan would certainly take her mind off Dominic. She loved this man and his bad-boy look. His hair was light brown and short, and it didn't look like he'd shaved in a few days. When the car stopped, he waited for her to get out, knowing he liked to watch her.

When the driver opened her door, her long legs came out first. Noting they were bare and tan, he stood up with a smile. Tess popped her head out of the car returning the grin. He whistled low when he saw the small red dress she was wearing. It hugged her body and fell midway down her thigh.

"Tess." Colin walked over, giving her a slow and sultry kiss, then a hug.

"I've missed you," she told him with a smile. "I hope we can wrap this up quickly. I want to come home. I've been with him too long, and it's becoming emotional."

"I had a feeling." Simply holding her close, he drew in her sensual aroma. "It feels like I haven't seen you in months."

"You haven't," she answered. "Just us—or is Jack here?"

"On the plane," he apprised her.

"At some point this weekend, we need to talk," she told him as they stood before each other. "Just you and me."

"As long as you're not leaving me." His hand caressed her cheek. "I've missed you too."

Tess grinned, touching his face looking into his brilliant blue eyes. "I love you."

"I love you." He tilted his head slightly and kissed her softly.

Colin took her hand, and they walked over to the plane. Tess headed up the stairs first, but she stopped midway and turned to him. He was only one step below her, making them eye level. Putting her hands on his shoulders, she leaned in and kissed him slowly. Colin's hands came around her back and moved over her hips. Easily he picked her up, and feeling her legs wrap around his waist, he finished carrying her up the stairs. Walking over to Jack, he set her down on his lap and went back to the pilot to confirm their destination.

"Hi, Jack." Tess's arms wrapped around his shoulders.

"Hey, beautiful." Jack kissed her forehead as his hand slipped under the hemline of her dress and rested there. "I don't like you sleeping with him."

"I don't like you sleeping with other women." Tess shook her head in frustration and got up with a sigh, sitting in the chair across from him.

Colin walked back and took a seat beside Tess instantly feeling the tension. "What is the issue this time?"

"I told her I didn't like her sleeping with him." Jack shrugged. "I don't trust or like him. I don't even like this job."

"Then why are you doing it?" Tess asked. "Every job is optional. Isn't that what you tell me?"

"I do it because this one is important to you." He looked her dead in the eyes.

"Yes, it is." She nodded, pulling her small purse out from across her shoulders. Opening it, she took out a USB memory stick and handed it to Jack. "I have all the information we need. I've memorized the code on his safe, and I have the key swipe to get into the building. You two figure out your end, and we can finish this."

Colin looked at Jack with his eyebrows raised. "Thoughts?"

"Nope." Jack sighed. "None of my thoughts are nice at the moment, so I will just shut up."

"Damn. You make me angry, Jack." Tess walked back to the galley and poured herself a glass of water. "Why does this bother you this time? It never has before."

Colin sat back simply listening to them bicker. The tension strained between the two more and more as of late. This solidified his feeling that everything was about to change between the three of them.

Jack shook his head. "I honestly don't know, but it bugs the hell out of me. I know that you have sex with other men, and it has never bothered me until this guy. Just call it a bad gut feeling."

Tess sat back down and leaned forward, taking his hands in hers. "I can't believe you said that. Don't talk to me like I'm a whore because you know better. Dominic is a job—that's it. I trust you and Colin more than anyone else in the world, and if this is bothering you this much, I won't do it anymore. We need to wrap it up in the next few days—or he will think something's up."

"Fine." He nodded with a sigh. "We will put it together tomorrow."

Tess squeezed his hands and sat back as Colin took her hand in his. Putting her head against his shoulder, her eyes closed. She'd had very little sleep for the past week and wanted a nap before they landed. The flight was only an hour and a half. It didn't take long for sleep to come, as her body shifted and breathing slowed.

"You never talk to her that way. You know she doesn't sleep around.

What's going on, Jack?" Colin asked, thinking she may be asleep, but possibly not.

"We can't keep doing this," Jack explained.

"You need to be a bit more specific. What exactly?"

"Sharing her." His eyes dropped to Tess.

"I know," Colin replied with a long sigh and glanced out the window.

"I love her," Jack easily stated. "This thing the three of us are doing has been crazy fun, but I am coming to the point where I want more—and I know I can't have it. I need to step away because everyone knows she belongs with you. I don't want our friendship messed up because of this. You're my best friend and have been since high school. I don't want that to change. I am closer to you than my own brother, and I can't lose that."

"Our relationship won't change," Colin stated firmly. "I can't speak for her—you know that."

"I know." Jack nodded. "After this job is done, I'm doing an overseas mission with Gina and Harper for six months. Your father has been talking to me about running the security division with the company, and I am seriously thinking about doing it."

"You should. He asked my opinion a while ago about that, and I thought it was a great idea. I know the contract work needs to end. My father wants me to start working regularly at the firm so he can cut back."

"Well, maybe this is just the beginning of changes for all of us." Jack shrugged.

"It is said that nothing ever stays the same," Colin noted.

Tess opened her eyes, looking at Jack. Hearing the conversation, she had very mixed feelings about this ending with him. Her relationship began with Colin—and he was very gracious in letting her bring Jack into their bedroom—but she loved them both.

Jack saw her looking at him. He knew that she'd heard the entire conversation, and he was okay with that. "Don't just lay there staring at me. Speak your mind."

Tess sat up and looked at Jack. "I miss you already," she whispered.

* * *

It was after two in the morning when Tess crawled into her bed. She just had to hope nothing went wrong on Colin and Jack's part, and then she could go home tomorrow. It was easy getting into Dominic's office and the safe. The information she needed was tucked nicely inside. As she took what she needed, she left a little something extra for Brian. After she was safely out of the building, she called Colin and gave him the address they needed to take out the chemist and the product. It all went very smoothly—even though acquiring the information took her nearly three months.

For three months, she dated Dominic Markenna. Internationally, he was known as a fierce businessman, but he was gentle and kind with her. Then again, she wasn't business—she was pure pleasure for him. Admittedly, he was a great lover with incredible stamina and deeply passionate. Dominic would kiss her neck just like Jack would, which was one of the desirable points for her. And his hands were well versed with her body. Just thinking of him that way began to get her aroused. Knowing nothing like that was happening tonight, she tried to push it from her mind and get some sleep.

Twenty minutes later, there was a soft knock at her door. The clock on the nightstand was flashing three in the morning. Tess got up with her 9 mm to see who it was. In the back of her mind, she was hoping it was Colin or Jack, knowing she would get this sexual appetite fed—at least for the night.

"Morgan," a man's voice said softly.

"Dominic." She opened the door, looking oddly at him. "What are you doing out so late? Come in."

"I'm sorry I didn't call." He came inside and pulled her in for a long hug after she shut the door and locked it. "I needed ... you."

Tess let him hold her, and she put her arms around him. A few minutes passed before he loosened his grip enough to kiss her lips. She could tell he was in need of something, and she was hoping it was just sex. He lifted her tank top, pulled it over her head, and dropped it on the floor, then slid her shorts down. His mouth left hers and began that trail down her body and between her legs.

Tess didn't think she could maintain her balance with the crazy pleasure he was giving her. "Dom …" Her voice trailed off as his tongue hit the sensitive spot. "Ooh…"

Dominic knew when she came when her whole body shuddered, and she nearly lost her balance. As he stood up, she began undressing him as his lips met hers.

"I want to make love to you," he whispered, kissing just below her ear. Then, picking her up, Tess wrapped her legs around him as he entered her. "Mmm," he mumbled softly, walking over to the sofa. Laying her down with him on top, he kept a continuous slow motion with his hips.

"Domin …" her voice trailed off as he rendered her speechless with pleasure.

"I love you, Morgan," he interrupted as his lips met hers.

When her body tightened, her legs gripped his waist, holding him deep inside her for a moment as she peaked.

Dominic waited a few moments, simply kissing her lips slowly, before he picked up his rhythm again.

Tess smiled as her hands rounded his shoulders.

"Think you could do it again?" he asked with a grin.

"Yes, just let me be on top?" she asked.

Without objection, they changed places. Tess came one more time with him, and he held her in his arms for a few minutes before she laid with her back against his chest and their legs intertwined, both fully expended.

"Thank you." Dominic kissed her shoulder.

"For what?" she asked. "Orgasms? I should be thanking you."

"No, for letting me in and not being a bitch," he explained. "I needed you tonight, and you let me in. Most women I know wouldn't have done that. They would have been kind of bitchy for waking them up."

"I'm not most women," her voice was soft.

"I know." His hand ran down the curve of her hip and back up to her waist.

"Are you going to tell me what brought all of this on?" she asked.

"My brother was killed tonight," he answered with a sigh. "He was the last of my father's family that I speak with."

Tess turned over to face him, putting a sympathetic hand on his cheek. "I'm so sorry."

"It was his own damn fault. He was making this synthetic drug. It was illegal and dangerous, but he wouldn't stop. The house blew up, killing him and four others that I know of."

"You're not part of any of this, are you?" she asked as a knot settled in her stomach.

"I originally bought the house. My name is on it, but I let him live there. I guess that would make me part of it. I've covered for him all his life and bailed him out of more situations than I can recall. When I got the call that he was killed, I was almost relieved to think I didn't have to cover for him anymore. The things he did reflected on me, which made me angry because everything he did was illegal."

"Is this going to fall back on you in any way?" Had she pegged the wrong Markenna for the job, she wondered?

"I don't know why it would." He shook his head as he thought about it. "It better not. This was his deal—not mine. Why?"

"I can't have things like that trickle into my world. I would lose my clientele."

"I won't let this touch you in any way." Gently, his hand caressed her cheek. "I will protect you from this—I promise."

"I'm sorry. I don't mean to seem so selfish at a time like this."

"Don't apologize for being concerned about your business." His finger easily moved a wispy strand of hair that fell and covered her eye. "I'm concerned for mine too, but I am really concerned about you having another orgasm right now." He kissed her again, slowly, as his hand slipped between the wet folds of her legs.

＊ ＊ ＊

Tess woke around nine. Sometime in the early morning, they had made it into the bedroom. As she thought about the night before, she breathed out slowly. The sex, the orgasms, and the kisses were incredible. Quietly, she got up while he was still asleep. She took her robe and her cell phone from the chair in the corner and went out on the balcony.

"Tess?" Colin said knowing her private line. "What's wrong?"

"He showed up here last night around three—and he's still here," she alerted him.

"Brian has a warrant for his arrest. Do you want me to send him there?"

"I think I made a mistake with all of this." She rested her forehead on her palm. "His brother was the chemist."

"Too late now to change the rules in the game. We're in the bottom of the ninth."

"Okay." She sighed. "I will research this after I get home. If I made a mistake, I must fix it."

"Fine," he answered, releasing a deep breath a little irritated with himself that he trusted her to do all the research on this job herself. "I'm calling Brian to tell him he's at your place."

"Give me ten minutes first. Please." Hearing the slider open, she changed her tone. "Thank you, Mr. Landis, for understanding. I will see you on Thursday ... okay ... good-bye." She ended the call and turned to Dominic. "Good morning." She walked over to him. "Hope I didn't wake you?"

Dominic slipped his hands around her, giving her a kiss. "No, you didn't. I hope you're not canceling any clients because of me."

"I had an appointment at one o'clock today, but I just moved it to Thursday. I want to be here for you today." She pursed her lips with her hands on his chest.

"I love you," he said with a small kiss.

"I love you too." A lump caught in her throat as she realized the sacred words she just spoke.

Dominic grinned and kissed her a bit slower.

Is it possible, she wondered, to love more than one man at a time? Or three?

"What is that for?" he asked, wiping a stray tear from her cheek. "Love is a good thing."

"Love has always come at a high price for me," she replied, biting on her lower lip.

"Well, it's time that changed for you." His hands cupped her cheeks, and he kissed her deeply. "I want to marry you."

Tess was speechless, and her heart raced knowing time wasn't on their side.

"Dominic," she spoke softly but firmly, taking his hand, walking him back inside. "You need to leave. They are on their way to arrest you. If you leave now, you can get out of here before they show up. Please, Dominic."

"What? How do you know this?" he asked confused as his forehead scrunched in confusion.

"A friend of mine works for them." She was sort of telling the truth. "He knows I have been seeing you, and he called me to let me know they were coming to arrest you."

"For what? I haven't done anything?" Confused, he took his shirt from the chair and put it on.

"I don't know," she lied. When the doorbell rang, she froze, and her breath escaped.

Dominic walked over and put his hands around her waist and felt her hands come around his shoulders. His lips dropped to hers for a long, slow, deep kiss. There was another knock, but they didn't part. When someone yelled, "Police," they kept kissing. Tess jumped a little when the door was kicked in, but Dominic held her tightly.

"I love you," he whispered in her ear.

"I love you," she answered as the chaos ensued.

"Dominic Markenna," Brian Marks stated his name as an officer cuffed him, but he didn't take his eyes off her. "You're under arrest for financing the international sex trade of minors."

"Are you kidding me?" Dominic's look of complete shock confirmed to Tess that she had it wrong the whole time. "Whatever this is, it's bullshit."

Brian walked over to Tess after they took Dominic out of her apartment. "You should get dressed and come with me—if you want to keep your cover."

"Brian, I think I made a mistake," she whispered. "It's not him. It was his brother."

"Tess, the evidence was found in his safe."

* * *

An hour later, Tess was in an interrogation room. She crossed her arms and stared straight ahead. Brian had not been back in since he put her there, and her patience was thinning.

Another ten minutes passed before the door opened and a plainclothes cop walked in with Colin following. "Your attorney is here." He left the room and closed the door behind him.

"Come on." Colin motioned for her to rise. "We're leaving."

"Colin," she began not wanting to leave until she spoke with Brian.

Colin got right up in her face. "You argue with me right now, and I will have Brian find some trumped-up charge to keep your ass in here. I swear to God, Tess, keep your mouth shut until we get out of here."

Tess got up and followed him out of the precinct without saying a word. They walked over to the car that Jack was waiting for them in.

As Colin opened the door, Brian ran down the stairs. "Tess, wait a sec." Knowing how influential Colin and Jack could be, Brian took her arm, and they walked out of ear shot. "Look, I know you've been working on this case for a while now. What changed your mind in six hours?"

"He came to me after he found out his brother was killed, and he started talking about all the illegal things his brother has done over the years and how he has always tried to cover it up for him. The house is in Dominic's name, but Dimitri lived there—not Dominic. I swear, Brian. He wasn't lying."

"How do you explain the evidence we got?" Brian asked but he already knew the answer.

"I planted it," she admitted softly. "It's all bullshit."

"Damn it, Tess." He ran a hand through his hair. "Get out of this city, and don't come back. I will handle this. I will get in touch to let you know how it all shakes out."

"Thank you." Tess gave his hand a squeeze. "If I don't hear from you in forty-eight hours, I'm calling in a favor."

"That's fine." Brian nodded knowing she was unaware of the larger picture and the favor would be from him. "You may need to since the evidence you planted is almost airtight."

Walking back to the car, Tess got in the back seat without saying a word to Colin or Jack.

* * *

A week later, Dominic was released from custody. All the charges were dropped.

Brian escorted him out of the building and spoke only when they stopped on the bottom step. "A little advice for you."

"And what would that be?" Dominic asked.

"Morgan Kellas got your release, but there was a price both of you must pay. You can't contact her or look for her. She comes from a very affluent family. She had to ask her father to pull a few strings. In return, she agreed to not see or speak with you again."

"Her name's not Morgan is it?" Dominic sighed deeply.

"No." Brian shook his head. "You must stay away from her, son. The men in her family are very protective. Dominic, trust me on this."

"Noted, Uncle Bri'," Dominic acknowledged, turning to get into the taxi, but stopped looking back at Brian. "Don't ever do this to me, again. You owe me ten-fold."

Brian nodded and watched Dominic get into the taxi and leave.

When the taxi dropped him off at home, he walked slowly up to the front door deep in thought. It wasn't until he was nearly two feet from the steps that he saw her on the stoop behind a well-manicured bush. She was not dressed in her usual high-end clothes. Instead, she wore shorts, a tank top, and a zip-up hoodie. There was very little makeup on her face which he preferred as she looked just as pretty without it.

Sitting beside her, he put his arm around her shoulders, pulling her close. "You're defying the stipulation of my release." He kissed her temple as tears slipped from her eyes.

"He can't revoke what he already called in." She wiped her eyes dry. "I left my phone at the hotel so they can't track me. And the hotel is about four hundred miles away. I rode the bus here. That was an experience I hope to never have again."

Dominic smiled. "The charges were bullshit. You didn't have to do what you did. I would have figured a way out of it. I usually do. I have a great team of attorneys."

"No." She shook her head. "You were set up, and the evidence was planted."

"How do you know this?" he asked curiously if she would admit her part in this charade.

She wiped her eyes again. "Don't ask. I can't tell you."

Dominic sighed. "Why does your background come back as you were raised by your mother, but that Brian guy said you come from a wealthy, dangerous family?"

"My parents were murdered. It's not something I carry around on my dossier. A friend of my mother's took me in, and he is very wealthy. It's just not something I like to tell everyone. I have my own money. I don't need the family's name or finances. And there are a few mercenaries in the family."

"Were you … am I like a … job? Was it supposed to be me—not my brother?"

"I didn't realize the chemist was your brother until you came to my place that night." She sighed. "My sister overdosed on that drug he made. I wanted the drug off the street and the maker … dead."

"You thought I was the maker?" A small chuckle slipped from deep within as he failed chemistry in college.

"At first, yes. But when we spent more time together, I realized it couldn't be you."

Dominic shook his head, stunned. "This is your … thing. You set all this up, didn't you?"

Tess sucked in her upper lip, nodding slowly.

"You're the mercenary or whatever you're called?" The thought was unfathomable, and he wanted clarification.

Again, she nodded.

"Unbelievable." He closed his eyes. "I fell in love with a killer."

"I won't apologize for what I am." Tess sighed holding firm on who she was.

Dominic stared at her, unbelievingly.

"My intent was not for you to fall in love with me," she whispered.

"Yes ... it was." He instantly disagreed. "That's how these things work, isn't it? What you mean to say is that you didn't mean to fall in love with me."

Tears surfaced in her eyes.

"How is it that I still love you?" he asked, taking her hand in his.

"I wasn't lying when I said I loved you." Tears finally spilled from her eyes.

Dominic nodded. "I know."

"I'm so sorry," she whispered. "I warned you when we first met not to fall in love with me."

"You can't control who you fall in love with. It just happens, and it doesn't matter your name, who your family is, how much money you have, or if you're a saint or a killer. If there's that connection, it's going to happen. Your father or guardian, whatever he is, doesn't get to dictate who I can be with or who I can love. And you shouldn't let him do that to you either." Dominic leaned in and kissed her lips softly. "I love you—regardless of all this—and I am going to keep loving you even if you leave because I know you love me too. No one can take that away from us no matter how many miles are between us. I think we should go inside and take a long, hot shower together. I need to get the stench of the government off me. And then we will make love until you decide to leave." Dominic stood, taking her hands, and pulling her upright. "I've got to ask what your name is?"

"Tess," she answered.

"I love you, Tess." Dominic gently kissed her forehead.

"I love you too," she replied, kissing his lips softly.

Tess stayed for four days before she rented a car and drove back to the hotel. Dominic vowed to find her one day—even though she told him not to. Knowing once she was back in McGowan territory, Dominic would simply become a sweet memory.

The long drive gave her entirely too much time to think. She knew she needed to get out of Virginia and back to Colin. That way, the feelings she was having for Dominic would go away because they were overwhelming. Deep inside, what she truly desired was the peacefulness of Carina's home in Maine.

Walking into the hotel room, she wasn't surprised to find Jack waiting for her on the bed. Tess stared at him for a long time. Something about his look made her trust him the very first time she met him. Besides that, his caramel skin, brown eyes, and perfectly innocent smile made him irresistible.

"Do you have the plane—or are we flying commercial?" she asked, pursing her lips otherwise she would smile.

"I have the plane," he answered, spinning her phone in his hand.

"Well, let's go," she sighed, snatching her phone from his hand. "I only came back to pick this up. Where's Colin?"

"Atlanta. He's trying to keep his father from calling in another favor." Jack stood up and stretched.

"I had to tie up some loose ends." She stood before him. "You know I screwed this one up, and I had to fix it."

"I don't think you messed up. I think you called it dead on. Where you messed up was when you let emotions in. T, anybody but this man. Please?"

"It's done," she told him. "I had to close this with him—and that's exactly what I did. I promise you."

Jack reached over and kissed her forehead.

"Why can't Colin treat me the way Dominic did or the way you do?"

"One day, he will get it right with you," Jack stated to give her hope. "He really does love you."

"Mmm." She raised her eyebrows. "Sure."

Jack shrugged, having no answers for her.

"Jack." Tess put her hand in his as they walked to the car.

"What?" He stopped walking and faced her.

"When do you leave on the mission?"

"Eight days." He sighed knowing exactly what she wanted. "Why?"

"Can you take me to Carina's?"

"You know what will happen if we go there." He ran a hand through his hair in frustration. Leaving her was already difficult and now they would be spending even more intimate time together.

"I need it." Unable to stop the pending tears, she squeezed her eyes closed, but it didn't work.

"You don't make saying good-bye to you easy," he told her.

"I hate good-byes. It seems like everyone is leaving except me."

Jack hugged her tightly. Pulling back but keeping her in one arm, he made a call. "Hey, Gran," he began. "Is my room available?"

"Well, Jack," Carina smiled. "I just had the last guest check out. The next one isn't due until the following weekend. House is empty. When can I expect you?"

"It'll be Tess and me. We are on our way from Virginia. We'll be there in a couple hours. Don't hold dinner for us though. We're going to eat on our way."

"Sounds good," Carina replied. "See you when you get here."

Jack ended that call and made another.

"Hey, Jackson," Colin said after one ring.

"I have someone here for you to talk to." Jack handed Tess the phone.

Tess took the phone and walked a few steps away. "Hi," she spoke softly.

"Tess, I wasn't sure if you were coming back this time."

"I told you I had to fix what I messed up." She paced as she talked.

"I know. I just wish you would have said something instead of just taking off. If you don't want to tell me, at least tell Jack so I know you're okay."

"I'm going up to Carina's for a few days. And then I'll go to Savannah to say good-bye to Harper and Gina. After that, I will be back in Atlanta. Perhaps we can have that talk I wanted to have a couple weeks ago."

"I will actually be in Savannah two days before they leave." He looked at his calendar on the desk. "Father wants to have a family dinner before they go overseas. Want to drive back together?"

"Since I live with you, that would make the most sense." She smiled, needing to be close to him. "Want to meet us at Carina's?"

"I would love to, but I can't." He sighed knowing she wouldn't like that. "I have a meeting with the attorney tomorrow and then a dinner meeting with some new client my father wants to bring in."

"Okay." The disappointment was evident in her voice.

"Tess." Colin turned away from his desk and looked out the window at the city. "It won't always be like this—I promise you. I just need to figure out this whole business thing. It's not easy stepping into my father's shoes at his company."

"Colin, it's okay," she tried to assure him. "I understand. Maybe I should find myself a real job."

"Please don't. I couldn't imagine having to work around both of our schedules. With one of us still flexible, at least we can make something work."

She smiled to herself. "Honestly, I don't want a nine-to-five job. I like randomly surprising you."

Colin laughed, remembering one of her surprises a few months before when he was working at the office.

He'd been working late all week, and he'd hardly seen her. On a Friday afternoon, she showed up when he was in a meeting with two of the company's attorneys. Tess bypassed his assistant and walked into his office. She was wearing one of her dresses that hit just above her knees and five-inch heels. Her dark long hair was silky smooth, and she looked amazing. Colin lost his voice for a moment as she stood before him.

"Gentlemen." She smiled at the two other men in the room. "I need to borrow him if you don't mind. I'm certain no one is dying, so whatever this is can wait."

After Colin gave them a nod, the two men nodded and left without muttering a word.

Tess shut the door, locked it, and turned to Colin. Walking back, she ran her finger down his tie. "I've missed you," she told him, softly touching his lips with her finger.

Colin let her finger trace his lips as he watched her eyes. He knew he'd been working too much lately, and she had been neglected.

"I'm sorry," he whispered, bringing his lips to hers. His hands slipped around her waist, over her bottom, and up her sides.

"I can only entertain myself for so long. Then I need you."

"Well, you have me now."

"Can I have you for the rest of the day?"

"Let me check." He kissed her soft lips, then buzzed his assistant. "Anything urgent for the afternoon?"

"No. You had an eleven o'clock tomorrow, but I changed it to Tuesday."

"So, I am clear from this moment until Monday morning?"

"Yes, sir," she replied.

"I will be leaving the office and won't be back until Monday."

"Got it," she answered and hung up.

Tess smiled as he took her hand, kissing the top of it. "I'm all yours. What would you like to do?"

"Go home," she answered. "We can make love, eat, swim—and repeat all weekend."

"You don't want to go anywhere?" He wanted perfect clarification for this weekend.

"No." She shook her head. "We go all the time. Let's just go home and not answer the phone. I just want you … uninterrupted."

Colin pulled her into his arms. "I love you."

Tess smiled. "I love you too."

Colin smiled at the memory, loving those little moments with her. "Tess, I know I don't say it often, but I do love you very much."

"I know you do." Tess handed the phone back to Jack.

"Hey." Jack turned away from her to talk to Colin.

"So, I'll see both of you in Savannah this weekend?" Colin asked not liking the fact that she didn't tell him she loved him as well.

"Yes." Jack kept his voice low. "She asked to go to Carina's. She started crying when she asked. There's something off with her, but I don't know what it is."

"I noticed last weekend," Colin added. "Just take care of her like you always do. I can't go up there this week. I have too many meetings in the next few days."

"You don't have to explain it to me," Jack reminded his friend.

"I need to go. My cousin's buzzing me. I'll see you in Savannah this weekend."

"I'll catch you later." Colin ended the conversation.

Jack switched the call over to his cousin. "James, what are you doing?"

"I'm heading to Carina's. She said you were on your way there too … with a pretty girl."

"I am." Jack put his arm around her shoulders and pulled her in for a hug.

"Can't wait to meet your protégé," James chuckled amused that it has taken this long to meet her.

"I bet." Jack smiled knowing his cousin always knew more than he let on. "See you in a few hours."

Jack ended the call and slipped the phone back in his pocket. "Are you okay, T?"

"Yep." She nodded. "Who are you going to see in a few hours?"

"James," he answered. "My cousin. He will be at Carina's."

"Okay." Tess shrugged. "Is he good-looking like you?"

Jack laughed and shook his head. "You can make that determination yourself."

Tess grinned, already knowing what his cousin looked like.

They arrived at Carina's bed-and-breakfast around seven. The three-level, 5000 square-foot house had an amazing view of the harbor. There were eight rooms, not counting the master suite that Gran had on the main level and the private suite up on the south end that no one was permitted to enter. If she was full, Jack didn't mind her using his room for the guests.

Tonight, it was just Jack, Tess, and James. Walking down the hall, he saw James coming out of his room on the south side.

"Hey." Jack walked over to him.

"Jackson," James said his name as they hugged. "How's life?"

"Absolutely crazy," he replied. "And yours?"

"Perfect." James smiled.

"I think if you put a woman in the mix, it wouldn't be so perfect. It would be more like mine—absolutely crazy." Jack grinned.

"Ah, so it is a woman that has you messed up." James laughed. "And I would bet it is Tess."

Jack nodded. "There's been this sort of thing between us, and it is coming to an end. I love her, but I can't keep doing this. I want more, and she truly belongs with Colin."

"That's why you're doing this overseas thing?" James inquired.

"Yes." He nodded. "It will just be easier if I leave for a while."

James nodded, not knowing why his cousin would have put himself in the position he was with Tess. "You know I always keep an eye on her."

"I know." Jack rested his hands on his hips, looking down with a sigh. "I'm glad you're here."

"You know me. I work off gut instinct. Harrison was fine, so that left you and Gran. When I talked to Gran, I knew it was you. Take me to meet her. You know I've waited years for this."

Jack found Tess and Gran in the great room, which had a two-story ceiling height. Floor to ceiling windows face the east, which lent to a magnificent view of the Atlantic ocean. On the north side of the room a large fire roared in the fireplace, making everything cozy.

Jack took Tess's hand and helped her upright. "This is my cousin, James."

"Hi," she spoke softly. "Nice to meet you."

James smiled. After years of watching over her, it was the first time he had met her up close and in person. Well, at least in her memory. She was beautiful now as she was the first time he spoke with her all those years ago. "Hello," he began, foregoing the whole handshake formality and hugging her. "I feel like I've known you for years."

Tess smiled and looked at Jack.

"He's harmless, at least to you, I promise." Jack sat down with Tess on the couch.

James sat in a leather chair across from them next to Gran.

"Are you Jackson's girlfriend?" James asked bluntly.

"Yes." Tess looked at Jack. "Right up until he leaves on his mission—then it will be over."

Jack squeezed her hand.

"Just like that?" James asked.

"Just like that," she replied.

"It's like you have an on/off switch," he mused.

"Don't you, Mr. Cordello?" Tess smiled. "Being who I am, did you really think I didn't know who you are?"

"I said nothing to her." Jack put his hands up in defense.

"Impressed." James grinned knowing Tess McGowan was a very smart woman on the streets and on paper.

"Jack and Colin aren't the only ones who do research." Tess leaned her head against Jack's shoulder. "You do have a secret that I haven't figured out yet."

James smiled. "Yes, I do. One day it will be presented to you, and I promise you will be nothing short of stunned—in a good way, I think."

"Great." Her eyes widened. "I love surprises in my life like a bullet in the head."

James laughed. "I like you even more in person."

They all chatted casually for the next hour. Eventually, Gran excused herself for bed, leaving the three of them alone.

"How long are you two staying?" James asked as he stood.

"Only three or four days," Jack answered. "Tess can stay longer, but I must pack for the mission and deal with my finances for the next six months. How long are you here?"

"Three or four weeks," James answered. "I need to fix some things around here for Gran. All my business is wrapped up for a while, so I'm free to help her do some repairs. Anyway, I'm heading up. Tess, it was a pleasure meeting you."

Tess stood up, giving him a hug.

"I'm sure we'll be spending more time together while you're here," he noted.

"Good night, James." Jack gave him a hug and watched him walk away. Finally, his full attention was directed back to Tess. His hands slipped behind her neck, and his lips found hers soft and ready. When he felt her hands under his shirt, he knew what she wanted. "I'm sorry I was such an ass last week."

"It's okay," she replied softly. "I know you're trying to push me away to make it hurt less when you leave."

"I'm sorry." He kissed her again.

"I know you say I belong with Colin." She moved her hands slowly to his chest. "But what if you're wrong?"

"I can't take you from him. He loves you more than he loved Kate, and that nearly destroyed him."

"What about you?" she asked.

Jack grinned. "I will always have you right here close to my heart."

Unbuttoning his shirt, he showed her the tattoo of the cross pounded crookedly into a mound of dirt. There were several dog tags hanging from it with names of men he had lost over the years. She had seen it many times.

"Look at the base of the cross," he told her.

When she looked closely, she saw her initials and a tiny heart next to it.

"How long have you had that there?" She ran her finger over her name.

"A while." He kissed her.

"I never noticed."

"And neither will anybody else." He gave her a long, deep kiss. "This is something that we will have between you and me—and never anybody else."

✳ ✳ ✳

Tess woke the next morning curled up to Jack. She liked the smell of him, a mix of pure man with a little bit of herself. She kissed his shoulder as a wave of nausea rolled up in her throat. Jumping out of bed, she ran to the bathroom.

"Tess?" Jack called out to her as he got out of bed.

"Don't come in here," she replied as he walked in and knelt beside her. "Go away. You don't need to see me vomiting."

"I've seen worse," he reminded her, pulling her hair up in her large clip as he had seen her do many times.

"I must've eaten something off," she muttered, resting her forehead on her palm as she leaned over the toilet.

Jack lifted her head up, pressing his palm on her forehead. "No fever."

Tess looked up at him, and they both had the same thought at the same time.

"No way." She laughed, shaking her head.

"You could be." He shrugged. "The only birth control that's 100 percent is abstinence."

"No." She kept shaking her head. "I've had that implant for three years, and it's good for five. Besides, my period is supposed to start … oh hell."

Jack grinned, helping her up. While she brushed her teeth, he climbed back into bed and waited for her.

Looking in the mirror, Tess rested her hand on her stomach, imagining the unimaginable. She wouldn't even know who the father was at this point. Shaking off the thought, she went back to bed.

Jack wrapped her up in his arms. "If you are, you'll tell me, right?"

"Of course, I would. Let's just hope this is all a coincidence—and we don't have to deal with that."

"That would certainly put a new twist on our trio." Jack kissed her.

"I know. I'm going to miss you." Her hand ran softly over his cheek.

"You can call me," he reminded her.

"Wouldn't that sort of defeat the purpose of you leaving in the first place?"

Jack laughed as he thought about that. "I suppose it would. Last night was very … passionate."

Tess smiled, running her hand over his shoulder. "Did you like it?"

"I loved it." He kissed her again.

"I think it's time to eat and then repeat last night." She moved her leg on top of his.

Jack rolled on top of her. "I think we need to repeat a little bit of last night, then eat, then run through the entire process again."

Her breath hitched as he entered her. "I think … I think I love the feeling of you inside me."

"Mmm." He moved his hips slowly and kissed her wanting lips.

Tess rubbed the length of his back, his hips, and his shoulders with her hands. Time slipped by as they enjoyed the deep sexual passion between them.

"Jack, let me be on top," she whispered.

Without hesitation, they changed positions.

Tess dropped her head back as she took in all of him. Feeling his hands cup her breasts, she knew she would be climaxing quickly. This was, by far, her favorite position. "Jack, come with me," she breathed looking down at him.

Jack put his hands on her hips as they moved in a steady motion. It didn't take long before her body began to shudder. When she came, his body reacted to hers, joining in the heightened moment.

"I can't move," she breathed out slowly.

"Good. I don't want you to." He ran his hands from her shoulders over her breasts and back to her hips. "You feel so damn amazing."

"You do too, always." She looked down at him with a smile. "I love you, Jack."

"I know you do." His hand ran over her cheek. "You know I love you."

"I can't stand these emotions that feel like my insides are ripping apart," she confided as she laid on top of him.

"It'll get better for you when I'm gone." His hands ran over her back in an easy caress.

Lifting herself up on her elbows, she nipped soft kisses on his chin. "Why does everything have to be so complicated?"

Jack shrugged. "We made this complicated. Maybe if we had met first, it would be different, but we didn't—and Colin's not letting you go."

Tess took a deep breath, resting her chin on his chest. Jack was right: Colin wasn't letting her go. It was as if they were tethered together with an invisible wire. He always gave her room to explore herself and her sexuality once she was ready, but in some unusual way, Colin always controlled it. Jack was the only other man she wanted to be with until she met Dominic.

Closing her eyes, she thought of Dominic and his charming grin, dark, wavy hair, and gorgeous green eyes. It was a bit refreshing that he wasn't related to the McGowan family in any way, and he wasn't Colin's best friend. Deep down, she knew she fell in love with Dominic, but there was no way she could ever let anyone know. His life would be over if Colin or Jack knew how she felt about him as they were a little possessive. Tracing his lips with her finger, she brought her eyes back to Jack's. "What's your plan?"

"I want to do this mission, come back, and focus on a legit career. I accepted the job Jonathan offered me."

"Great—now you'll be working all the time too," she replied with a pout.

"You're sounding rather spoiled at the moment," he noted.

"I know. I'm sorry. I feel like I'm losing everybody." Tears filled her eyes.

"You're not losing me. We're just not going to be sleeping together anymore. You've got to let me go, baby." Gently, he wiped the tears from her eyes. "If you're holding on, I'm going to hold on even tighter."

"I know, but it's really, really hard." Her voice cracked before she could continue. "You're my best friend. You know all my secrets."

Jack laughed and rolled them over, so he was on top again. "Yes, I do. Don't forget that. I won't be gone forever, but I need to go. Otherwise, this will never stop between us—and it needs to. Don't think it's easy for me to leave either. It's the only way I know how to do this. The McGowan's are as much my family as they are yours, and I will lose them if I stay."

"I know," she admitted. "I've run every possible scenario through my head over and over, but I come up with the same thing."

"I love you and leaving you in a couple days is going to be one of the hardest things I've ever done." After kissing her again, he sat up on the edge of the bed. "Let's go eat and then spend the rest of the day in bed."

Tess grinned and shook her head.

✳ ✳ ✳

Tess leaned against the railing and looked out over the bay. It was raining, so the view was obliterated by the clouds, but she still found it beautiful. She was wearing Jack's flannel shirt since she didn't really bring cold-weather clothes. If she really wanted, she could go into town and buy some, but she didn't really want to. Jack was leaving tomorrow, and she needed to decide if she was heading back to Savannah with him or staying a bit longer. Currently, she wanted to stay because she didn't want to say good-bye to Jack.

When she heard footsteps, she didn't turn around and was surprised when James leaned on the railing next to her. "Hi."

"What's that look for?" he queried.

"I thought it would be Jack," she answered.

"Sorry to disappoint you." He grinned, not sorry at all.

"It's not that. Unexpected is all."

"What are you thinking about?"

"Jack," she answered, looking out at the sea.

"Are you going to miss him?"

"Would you miss your gun if it was taken away?" she asked.

"I wouldn't let it be taken away," he stated firmly.

"I imagine everything is black and white for you?"

"Most things." His gaze was also drawn to the view.

"I wonder what would happen if I never went back, and I started over somewhere else." She swiped a wandering tear away. "Would Jack not go if I asked him to stay? Would that be completely selfish of me? Would he be willing to walk away from that family if I asked him to?"

"Jack may as well be my brother. We damn near grew up together except when his mom moved them to Savannah for those few years when he was in high school. You're not going to ask him to stay; you're going to let him go. You must. And you're not doing it for yourself; you're doing it for him. That family has been so good to him, and he loves all of them—even if his one fault is having Colin McGowan as a best friend. You can't take that family from him, as it will divide him from them if you choose him over McGowan. You should know by now that Colin McGowan is damn vindictive when he doesn't get his own way. I'm not going to let my cousin be hurt—or worse—because of you."

"Thanks," she replied sarcastically.

"I guess that did come out a little harsh. It's just that you're not who Jack is supposed to marry. I know you don't want to hear something like that, but my gut tells me you're not it."

"Am I not good enough for Jack in your mind?" She inquired.

"No, it's not that." He shook his head, frustrated as he knew he wouldn't explain this correctly. "I can't explain my gut instinct. All I know is that it's always right."

Tess looked at James. "Do I dare ask how you know so much about them and this?"

James smiled. "You know what I do for a living, so you know I am damn good at my research—and that is just for the jobs I do. Now, if you will, imagine what I would do for my family."

Tess smiled and nodded, understanding.

"Let Jack go tomorrow and stay. Gran's making jam. I'm sure she would love to have your help."

"I already planned on staying," she answered. "I will say good-bye here. I don't want to do it with the whole family around. I do love him very much."

"I know." He nodded, staring out at the sea. "Just not enough. I also know that you think you're conflicted about this, but you're not. And you know that deep down."

There was a comfortable silence between them for a few moments before Tess looked at him with a grin.

"What?"

"Why was your nickname Cord?"

James smiled with a slight laugh. "Well, you know you have a certain style with your work?"

Tess nodded.

"In the beginning of my career, I … eliminated people by coming up behind them with this thin cord. I was strong, so it was an easy, silent way to kill."

"Do you still use that technique?"

"No. That nickname was from a long time ago." He shook his head. "I learned the art of twisting a man's neck with my bare hands instead. Honestly, I like that better. If I don't have a weapon or something catches me off guard, my hands are their own weapon."

"Show me sometime?"

"Sure." He shrugged thinking it was easy, at least for himself. "Jack didn't teach you that?"

"No." She shook her head. "Just hand-to-hand with the quick punch to the throat, knife in the heart or liver. You know, moves that incapacitate or kill."

James grinned understanding that Jack taught her basic maneuvers that she perfected. "You like this place?"

"Yes, I love it here."

"I own it." He leaned against the railing taking a deep breath.

"Really? I thought it was a collaborative effort between Jack, Harrison, and you."

"The three of us make sure Carina's financially secure, but this house is mine. I only own one other, outside of Chicago, but this is where I come to get away from work."

Tess grinned. "Me too."

"Glad I could be so accommodating for you." Glancing at her, he slightly grinned as she was still that adorable sixteen-year-old that he spoke to that fateful night.

"I love it here." She shrugged taking in the view. "And I love Carina. She's everything I imagined a grandmother would be."

"Happy to share my grandmother with you. She is great." He nodded in agreement. "You know, now that you're not doing any contract work with them, you should do a few with me."

"I would only do it if it was a hit. I don't want anything where I play a part and seduce a man."

"Oh no." He shook his head. "I don't do stuff like that. My work is very specialized—extractions and assassinations—and I hear you are an excellent sniper shot."

"I'm not bad, I guess." She shrugged knowing she was very good at hitting her target.

"Modesty." He grinned. "That's a good thing. I don't have anything right now, but if something comes up, I'll call you."

"Okay." She stretched. "I guess I'm unemployed now. Wow, what a weird concept."

"You could get a real job."

"*You* could get a real job," she threw back.

"I do have a real job." He glanced at her. "My company saves people and eliminates the bad ones."

"That's what I do. So, what's the difference between you and me?"

"The difference is that you can't keep doing this work while you're pregnant. You know the physical demands. How are you going to be six months along, laying on your stomach as bullets are being sprayed inches above you?"

"Why do you think I'm pregnant?" Tess asked awed that he even said something like that.

"I've known you since you were sixteen." He stared at her. "You're different, emotional. That's not you. What changes a woman your age? Pregnancy."

"There you are." Jack walked up to them, pulling Tess in for a long hug. "I've been looking for you—either one of you."

"We were just talking about you," she said with a smile eyeing James.

"Great." He rolled his eyes, taking her hands in his. "I'm running into town. Come with me?"

"Okay," she quickly answered with a nod. "I should get some clothes I suppose."

"Sure, if you want." Jack held her hands out, looking at her in his shirt. "Although I think you're pulling off a whole new sexy look."

"I'm leaving you two to your whole whatever you want to call this." James patted Jack on the shoulder and went into the house.

Jack leaned down and kissed her slowly. Their lips parted, and their tongues found each other immediately, intensifying the kiss.

Tess's hands rested on Jack's hips as his hand wrapped around her back.

After a few minutes, Jack stopped kissing and wrapped her up closely in his arms. "Lord, I'm going to miss you." He closed his eyes and simply held her.

Tess wrapped her arms around his waist and hugged him for a long time. She wanted to absorb every moment that she could because she knew it was quickly ending.

✳ ✳ ✳

The next day, Tess sat on the bed and watched him pack. He didn't have much since he lived scattered, like herself. Most of his things were at Colin's house in Atlanta or his room at Jonathan's home in Savannah. He sold his condo in Atlanta, knowing he was going to be making a change of some sort in his life. At the time, he wasn't certain about the change, but now he knew.

When he was done, he pulled out his phone and took a picture of her.

"I look like hell," she told him, shaking her head.

"No, you don't." Sitting beside her, he tilted her head to his, and snapped another picture as he kissed her softly. "I will save this one forever."

"And what will your wife think of that?"

"Doesn't matter." He pulled her down on him. "Whomever I end up with will know that you are very special to me, and I will always love you."

"I love you, Jack," she told him as a tear slipped from her eye for the millionth time today.

Jack rolled to his side, wiping her tears with his thumb. "I wish I could pack you up and run away with you."

"James said we couldn't do that."

"Did he?" Jack grinned knowing his cousin could see the bigger picture as his own judgment was clouded for the moment.

"Yes, he said it wasn't fair of me to ask you to do that because your loss would be greater than just walking away from me," she shared.

Jack leaned over and kissed her slowly, softly. His hand wrapped around her back as hers went around his shoulders, and one hand rested on the base of his neck. They kissed for a long time with their legs intertwined.

James knocked on the door, and even though they were intimately absorbed, he spoke. "Pilot's ready. We should get going."

"I'll be there in a couple minutes." Jack looked at Tess.

"I'll be downstairs waiting," James told him and walked away.

"Walk me to the door?" Jack asked.

"If you want me to," she replied, trying her best to stop crying.

"I do," he answered with a kiss. "Come on."

Jack rolled away from her as Tess got up on her side. She wiped her tears, knowing there would be more regardless. Jack picked up his duffel and took her hand. Together, they walked down to the front door where James was waiting with Carina.

Jack dropped Tess's hand to give Gran a hug and a kiss on the cheek. Turning back to Tess, he sweetly touched her cheek, and rested his forehead on hers. "I'm going to miss you," he said softly.

"I will always love you," she whispered.

Jack gave her a long hug. "James is wrong."

"About what?" she asked, wiping her eyes.

"My loss is greater walking away from you than anything else in the world." And after one last kiss, he walked out the front door.

James drove them in silence for the first couple miles. At one point, he rested an understanding hand on his cousin's shoulder. "Are you okay?"

Jack wiped his eyes dry. "Yes. I'll be fine as soon as I can get busy doing something else. Loving her is so … intense. I can't even explain it. It's unlike anything I've ever experienced with any other woman."

James smiled.

"Why are you smiling?" Jack asked.

"Because you love her. You didn't love the other women—that's why it is different with Tess."

"Take care of her please," Jack stated rather than ask. "And don't sleep with her."

James smiled. "I don't plan on it, and if I did, I wouldn't tell you.

And you always know that I keep an eye on her. I'm going to fly to Atlanta with you."

"You don't have to do that," Jack told him.

"My plane—I'll do what I want." James smiled. "Besides, I want to know how all of this got started between you and Tess. I've got to know what I'm dealing with."

"You might as well know that she may be pregnant." Jack sighed, looking straight out the front window.

"I know." James gave him a glance. "I wasn't sure if you knew."

"How do you know?" Jack shouldn't be surprised but he was.

"I know that girl inside out," James reminded him. "You know how long I've been watching her."

"True." Jack sighed. "Will you please tell me if she doesn't? We spent a lot of time together in the last three months while she was working on the Markenna case. Colin doesn't know."

"If you think Colin McGowan doesn't know that you two have spent a lot of time together, then you're not as smart as I thought you were, Jackson."

Jack sighed. He knew James was right: Colin knew everything Tess was doing, whether he was with her or not.

CHAPTER 2

Carina kept Tess occupied in the kitchen canning jam. She liked cooking and learning new things. Everyone she cooked for loved her food. Most of the basic skills she learned from Gina while she finished her last two years of high school, and she learned more after she met Carina.

It was well after four in the afternoon before James resurfaced. He walked into the kitchen and kissed Gran on her temple and then walked over to Tess and did the same thing. He grabbed a bottle of water from the fridge and an apple from the bowl on the counter before sitting down. "Smells good in here, ladies," he said between bites. "Gran, do you have plans for dinner?"

"I have bingo tonight." She glanced at him as she and Tess finished labeling the jams. "You two are on your own. There are leftovers in the fridge and lasagna in the freezer if you want to heat it up."

"Oh," James stated, disappointed. "Tess, do you want to go out and grab a bite?"

"No," she answered softly. "I want to finish up here, crawl into bed, and be depressed."

James laughed. "That's not happening. Finish whatever you're doing—and be ready to go around five. I'm hungry."

Tess looked at him sideways, shaking her head in frustration.

Surprisingly, by five o'clock, she was ready, and James was waiting for her in the great room. "You clean up well and rather fast," he noted.

Tess wore a pair of black jeans, boots, and a simple button-down blouse and cardigan. She brushed her hair and put it up in a bun and didn't put on any makeup. "You don't look so bad yourself," she remarked with a half grin.

"I know." He shrugged modestly. "We have reservations at a lobster joint in town. It's very good. Let's go."

As James drove them into town, their conversation was simple and light. Jack told James to keep her mind occupied because over the years, Jack would watch her get depressed about simple things. Sometimes she would stay in bed for days, and he didn't want that to happen when he left.

After the waiter took their orders, Tess asked, "Is there any other family that you and Jack have besides Carina and Harrison?"

"No." James shook his head. "They've all died except my father. He took off when I was a kid. That is why my mother moved us in with her mom. I was raised by the two of them. When my mother died, Carina was all I had besides Jack and Harrison. Even though we're scattered in Chicago, Georgia, and here, we're still close. It helps having your own private jet. Harrison has his company jet, and Jack seems to get the McGowan one whenever he needs it. So, we all get to see each other often enough."

"Jonathan treats Jack like one of his own—like he does with all of us." Tess smiled. "He's a good man, and he's been a good father for all of his wayward children."

"I can't imagine what it was like for him to take on three teenage girls after having raised two boys." James shook his head.

Tess smiled. "He did good, considering."

"Why did you get into the contracts business? You have a business degree from one of the best Ivy League colleges," he reminded her. "You could write your own ticket anywhere with that."

"The business degree helps me manage my finances." She grinned, looking down for a moment. "I liked the contract work up until this last job. I'm good at … detaching my emotions. I like turning it off. When I'm in the real world, everything is so emotional."

"Just flip the switch. Everything is so much easier when you turn it off."

"That's easy to say." Shaking her head, her eyes connected with his. "But I want to love and be loved. And you must allow yourself to feel emotions to love. Don't you want to love a woman with the incredible passion that you only get from loving someone fiercely?"

"I've never loved a woman like that … yet," he confided.

"Just wait until you do. It makes everything so much more intense— in a good way, especially in bed." Jetting her brows upward, her mind quickly thought of Colin and the intense passion they shared.

"In our conversation yesterday, I'm sorry if I came across as an ass."

"It's whatever. Not easily offended." She shrugged. "Not too many people will say it like it is to me. Colin says people are afraid of me because I'm quiet and reserved. I'm mistaken for being a bitch."

James smiled knowing the truth. "I know you love Jack."

"Yes." She nodded. "I've always loved the men I've been with."

"And how many has that been?"

"Just three," she admitted easily.

"Jack, Colin, and …?"

"Nope." She shook her head. "Just an investor."

"Come on." He tried to coax it out of her, but she simply shook her head. "Well, you do realize you don't have sex with anyone who has less than a seven-figure account?"

"How do you know the investor is that successful?"

"Just a gut feeling." James raised a brow.

"Well, what does that tell you?"

"Colin has a very tight leash on who you sleep with," he stated knowing she needed to open her eyes and realize how controlling Colin was with her.

"Wow. I can't determine if I should be offended by that comment or not."

James smiled. "Just an observation. I know you don't sleep around, and it took you a very long time to ... deal with what Robert Monroe did to you. I just never thought you would end up in bed with McGowan."

"I can talk about my relationship with Jack." She pursed her lips. "But I can't talk about my relationship with Colin. It's not something I can put into words."

"Do you want kids someday?" he asked, dropping the McGowan conversation as the waiter brought their food.

"Someday," she replied with a shrug. "I don't want any kids until I have stability in my life with a man I'm in love with who is in love with me. That foundation must be solid before I have children."

"That's probably what everyone says."

"Probably. What about you?"

"I will have to quit the contract work first, and I'm nowhere near done doing that yet," he answered. "However, if you wanted to have my children, I would make an exception."

Tess laughed. "I would say that will never happen, but with the way my luck goes, who knows."

"Geez, you say that like it's a bad thing."

"It would be so out of the box for me to end up with you." She shook her head as she thought of that scenario.

"Why?" he asked.

"Because." She tilted her head. "I've been with your cousin, and I love him. Don't you think that would be weird?"

James thought for a moment and then shook his head. "No."

Tess shook her head with a grin and continued to eat.

They talked and laughed through the rest of dinner. James kept her mind off Jack, and that was his goal. He found her to be fun, flirty, and witty. And he loved her dry sense of humor.

They arrived back at the house after nine, and Carina wasn't home yet.

"Want to see the best place in this house?" he asked.

"Sure." She shrugged thinking she had seen all of it already. "Let me just get a glass of water. Want anything?"

"No, I'm good." He shook his head.

Tess was back in less than two minutes and he had her follow him upstairs. They walked down the hall to a room at the end.

"This is the one room I've never been in," Tess softly stated before he opened the door. "Jack always said it was his cousin's room, and you didn't like people coming in here."

"No, I don't." He opened the door and took her hand. "The rest of the house is open to whomever, but my room is not public. I only share with people I like."

"Are you saying you like me?" Tess grinned with a slight tilt of her head.

"You're growing on me. Come on in." Walking her inside, he watched her look around.

The room was at least seven hundred square feet, including the master bath. It housed a king-sized panel bed, a sitting area with a sofa and a leather chair, a dressing room, a Jacuzzi tub, and a double-headed walk-in shower surrounded in stone.

"This is amazing," she told him as she walked around.

"When I bought it, I wanted a space that was just mine. I wanted a place where I could go when I was done with everything out there in the other world that I work in. This is my calm, my peace."

Tess realized how much she completely understood him.

James had waited years to meet her, knowing they would click. He walked over and caressed her cheek. When he saw her eyes fill with tears, he pulled her to him and held her gently.

"I'm sorry," she whispered, pulling back, and wiping the tears from her eyes and cheeks.

"Nope." He put his hands on her shoulders. "You don't have to apologize to me. I do understand, believe it or not. I saw the way Jack was with you. You can be sad for a few moments."

"Just a few moments?"

"Yes," he answered. "Jack would be pissed if I let your sadness linger. Let's sit."

They sat on a sofa that faced the massive corner windows. James picked up a remote and pressed a button that opened the shades. Even though it was dark, she could see the lighthouse, which must have been a mile or so away, and the moon lit up the sky enough to make the tall trees shadow the ground.

"I love the view from my room in the early morning." He walked over into his dressing room where he changed into lounge pants and a long-sleeve Henley and grabbed a shirt and pair of sweats for Tess. "Here you go," he said, tossing them to her.

"Thank you." She went to change in his dressing room as he sat down on the sofa with a throw blanket. When she came out, he laughed a little. "It's a little big, but it's this or naked."

"I know it gets chilly in this house at night," he admitted, tossing half of the blanket to her when she sat down. "You can sleep in here tonight. I have a feeling that if I let you sleep in Jack's room you would cry all night—and I can't have that."

"Thank you for being so nice to me," she sighed, pushing the tears back, again.

"If you're considered to be with Colin McGowan, how did this all get started with Jack?" James asked with a raise of his brow.

Tess smiled, remembering eighteen months ago. "Rio. We had just finished a job with a big payday, and Colin rented a place on the beach for a week. We had huge parties. It was fun. The first couple of days, there was a lot of flirting between Jack and me. When it was happening, I always watched Colin for some sort of reaction—and he seemed to encourage it. One night, tons of people were at our place, music loud, drinks all night long, and Jack and I were dancing. I saw Colin watching us, drinking his scotch … and then it happened. Jack and I kissed, and Colin seemed to like watching. He came up behind me and asked if I wanted them both, and I said yes. He smiled at Jack, Jack took my hand, and Colin took the other. We went to our room with a bottle of Hennessy. It's been the three of us for a year and half. It's usually just one on one unless there's alcohol involved."

"Damn," James bemused with a stunned grin. "Jack adores you. Why Colin?"

"I don't know." She shrugged. "Colin and I just have this thing. I can't really explain it. He's like a part of me that makes me complete."

"Personally, I think he's an ass—arrogant and cocky."

Tess smiled. "I know that's what people say, but he's not like that with me. We can fight like crazy, but he's not mean to me like I've seen him be with others. I love him deeply."

"At least someone does." James smiled.

"Change of subject," Tess sighed. "Tell me about some of the jobs you've done."

"Hmm. A few years back, my men and I went down to Nicaragua for an extraction …"

James shared that story and two others before he noticed she was trying her best to not fall asleep.

"Come on." He scooped her up and carried her over to his bed. After tucking her in, he kissed her forehead and went to see if Carina was home yet.

✳ ✳ ✳

It was dark and eerily silent when Tess woke up with an incredible pain in her lower stomach. Rolling over to get out of bed, she cried out in pain.

"What's wrong?" James asked instantly, sitting up, turning on the light.

"Oh my God!" she said through gritted teeth. "The pain—this pain is terrible. Somethings wrong."

James was up and around to her side of the bed within seconds. When he pulled the covers back, his eyes widened when he saw the blood as Tess was holding her stomach, curled in pain.

"Let me call the ambulance." James grabbed his cell and called 911. After he had the ambulance coming, he ran downstairs to wake Gran so she could get the door.

"James!" Tess was rolled up in a ball and unable to move. Tears streamed down her face. "It hurts so bad. Make it stop—please!"

James gently placed his hand on her face. "Tess, just breathe slowly in and out. Focus on me and just breathe. Control the pain. I'm sure Jack taught you how. The ambulance is on its way. They'll be here in a few more minutes. Just breathe through it. If I could take the pain for you, I would."

James could hear the sirens in the distance. "They're almost here, baby." Wrapping her in a blanket, he scooped her up and carried her downstairs.

Carina opened the door when the ambulance pulled into the drive and James brought her out to them.

"Please call Colin," she breathed out as another wave of pain surfaced.

"I will," he stated.

The paramedics put her on the gurney in the back of the ambulance and took off with sirens blazing.

James ran upstairs, changed into his jeans and another shirt, slipped on his shoes, grabbed his phone, and ran back out the door.

✳ ✳ ✳

James woke the next day to voices in the hallway outside of Tess's room. He had fallen asleep in a chair, which was extremely uncomfortable, and was in desperate need of a chiropractor. It wasn't until he stood up and stretched that he noticed who was talking with the doctor in the hallway. Glancing over, in the bed, Tess was still asleep.

Colin McGowan walked in, held out his hand to James, and shook it. "Thank you for calling me," he spoke, looking at Tess.

"They say you are the one she's supposed to be with, so, I figured you should be the one called." James eyed the man as he wasn't entirely sold on the idea of liking him to any degree. The man stood about his six-one height with hair like his own in color, but perfectly cut as if he'd been the barber in the last few days. His frame was solid, strong just like his brother's as was the dark blue eyes. Then, for a very slight moment, James felt almost sorry for the man knowing what Colin's own brother did to him years ago.

"Did Jack also say what a pain in the ass I am to her?" Colin asked with a slight grin.

"No. Jack didn't have to say that." James shook his head and smiled, perhaps a small bit of him would like him. "Everyone already knows."

Colin chuckled, walked over to her bedside, and took her hand.

"Since you are here, I'm going home to get some decent sleep and shower. You can stay at Carina's since her next guests don't arrive for a week. The rooms are ready."

"Thank you for everything." Colin humbled himself for a moment knowing James took care of her when it should have been himself.

"Call me, please, if anything changes," James asked, heading to the door. "Let me know when they release her, and I will pick you both up."

"Okay." Colin nodded.

"You should know." James turned back around before he walked out the door. "You are the one she wanted me to call."

Colin looked down at Tess as James walked out.

A few hours passed, and Colin was simply staring out the window at the small town. Just beyond the town was the vast sea of blue. The day was clear, for the moment, but the weather could change quickly on the northeastern coast. Hearing a slight mumble, he glanced back to Tess as she was beginning to stir.

The love he felt for her was deeper than she realized, and he knew it was his fault that she was unaware. Yes, she knew he loved her, but she just didn't know to what extent. After the Markenna job, he was done with her sleeping with other men, including Jack. If she wanted to be with him, everything else had to stop: the contract work, her long trips away, and Jack. It was time she chose who she really loved and wanted to be with because he was done sharing.

When her eyes opened, he sat on the edge of the bed and held her hand. Her gaze was blank, and she seemed confused as she looked around the room.

"You're in the hospital," he finally stated in a soft voice. "You lost the baby—the baby I didn't even know you were carrying."

Tears fell from the edges of her eyes as she looked away. "I didn't know for sure. And I felt like this was a conversation we needed to have in person if I was. Did I do something wrong?"

"No, Tess." Colin's eyes filled with tears. "The doctor said it just happens sometimes, and there's nothing you could have done to prevent it."

"I'm sorry, so sorry," she cried as big tears overflowed and ran down her cheeks. "How far along was I?"

Colin knew why she was asking. "The doctor said about eleven weeks."

Tears continued to slip from the edges of her eyes. She knew the baby was either Colin's or Jack's since she hadn't been with Dominic that far back. "I must've done something."

"Honey." He leaned close to her face, running his hand over her cheek. "It's not your fault." Colin kissed her lips gently and wrapped his arms around her shoulders, holding her tightly as they both cried silent tears.

After a few minutes, Colin sat back up and wiped a few more of her tears away.

"Jack?" she asked.

"I called him on my way up here. If you want him, he will come up."

Tess stared blankly for a few minutes and then shook her head slowly. "No." She sighed. "As long as he knows. I promised him I would tell him if I was."

"Well, he is aware of what's happened. I will call him later to let him know you're okay."

"I can't say good-bye to him again," she admitted, tears still falling.

"I will talk to him for you." He ran his hand over her hair. "Remember when you said you wanted to talk to me, alone, a week or so ago?"

Tess nodded knowing they never got to have that conversation.

"Was this what you wanted to talk about?"

"No." She shook her head. "I didn't even suspect this until four days ago when I got sick in the morning. I wanted to talk to you about us."

"And what about us?" he asked curiously.

"I wanted to get back to us," she answered honestly.

Colin leaned over and kissed her softly. "I was just thinking about that before you woke. I just wasn't sure if you would want that exclusiveness with Jack or me."

"It's always been you," she reminded. "I love Jack deeply, but you … are in my soul. I don't know how else to explain it. You're the one I want to call when something happens—good or bad."

"I've loved you since the first time I kissed you on the dock at my father's house in Savannah. Do you know that?" Colin ran his hand over her soft cheek.

"You remember?" Tess was rather surprised he remembered that little detail.

"I remember more things than you realize." He raised his eyebrows. "I know I work a lot and you feel … neglected. I will try to work on this. I struggle with that balance as you are aware."

"I know your work is important, but there are times when we'd go weeks without seeing each other. That's when I would just leave and do other things. I will not sit around waiting for you," she told him pointedly.

"I know, and I wouldn't want you to." With her hand still in his, he kissed it again. "I will figure out a balance somehow."

"Lay with me?" she asked with a yawn.

Colin took off his shoes and wrapped her in his arms as his mind traveled back to the summer they met.

It was the middle of June, and the sun was hot and muggy. Colin had heard that the book-smart, athletic twin was going to be at his father's place in Savannah for the summer. Tess was in between her junior and senior years of college, taking a break. He'd already met the other one, six months before, in Chicago. Rumor had it that they were night and day, yin and yang, and rarely spoke to each other. All of it made him curious, and he had to meet this one.

Walking into the kitchen, he dropped his bag on the floor as his cell phone rang. Pulling it out, caller ID revealed it was his father.

"Yes, Father?" he answered unamused, knowing another lecture was coming.

"I heard you went home for the summer." Jonathan took a deep, purposeful breath.

"Yes. I can still come home, can't I?"

Jonathan laughed. "Of course, you can. It's just been a long time since you have, and I'm going to get straight to the point. Tess is there this summer. Don't play with her emotions, don't mess with her head, and don't make her another notch. I swear by the grace of God if you do—"

"Dad . . . wait," Colin began. "I won't do any of that. I promise. I don't need another notch. I need to find a wife. And you told me she was smart, beautiful, and could knock me on my ass when needed."

"I wasn't meaning that she was your wife material," Jonathan closed his eyes fearful of this potential union. "Son, she's been through hell, and it took years to get her where she's at today. Don't hurt her, please."

"I haven't even met her yet," Colin defended.

"But you have a reputation," Jonathan reminded him.

"I know. I would like to change that reputation if people would give me a chance. I'm not twenty-five anymore, Dad. I don't want one-night stands. God knows, I've had more than my share. Will you just trust me this time?" Colin tried to defend his previous playboy lifestyle.

"Do you know how nervous this makes me?" Jonathan asked.

"Yes, Father." Colin turned around to find a beautiful woman listening to his conversation. "You didn't tell me she was this beautiful."

"Colin—" his dad began again knowing he was losing his son's focus.

"I have to go now." Colin was mesmerized by this woman. "I'll talk to you later, Dad."

Tess was wearing cut-off shorts that rested low on her hips and a bathing suit top. Her skin was golden, and her hair, although it was in a ponytail, was dark brown and streaked with lighter shades of gold from the sun.

As he stared at her, she took off her sunglasses and perched them on her head with a smile. "Hi," she mused, knowing he was checking out her body.

"Hello, I'm Colin," his voice soft, still lost in her beauty.

"I gathered." Having seen his picture in Jonathan's office, she nodded as he held out his hand for her to shake. "I'm Tess."

When she shook his hand, Colin could feel the warmth of her skin, but it was her eyes that hooked him. They were sky blue, like the waters in the south seas. The other twin didn't have eyes like this. Even though the twins were identical, he barely saw any resemblance.

"Did you hear all of that conversation?" he asked.

"Yes, pretty much." She nodded and walked past him to get the iced tea from the refrigerator.

"Shit," he mumbled.

"Don't worry." She grinned. *"Would you like some tea?"*

"Please." He nodded, standing on the other side of the counter. *"Don't worry about what?"*

"Don't worry about your reputation with me." She handed him a glass of sweet tea. *"I already know it. And can I just tell you, in advance, if you're thinking about getting me into bed with you, keep thinking because you will have to buy a new bed with no notches before you get me into it. And even then, your chances are still very slim."*

"Damn." Colin smiled. Never had he met a woman that spoke to him with such regard, most just wanted his attention. *"I've not met a woman that's straight with me as you are."*

Tess nodded. *"I've been through too much to not say it straight. Besides, you're Jonathan's son, and he's been wonderful to my sisters and me. And if I can't be honest with you, who can I be?"*

"So, Tess." Colin took a sip of the tea. *"Shall we try the whole friend thing ... first?"*

Tess grinned. *"First? What makes you think there will be anything beyond that?"*

"Just a gut feeling. To have a woman stand up to me and not just drop her panties and spread her legs ... is very refreshing." Colin spouted wondering what her reaction would be from that comment.

"You know the only reason women do that is so you will either knock them up so they will have a tie to you and get your money or get you to marry them in the first place so they can have access to your fortune. You see, those are the ill-educated women who need to realize that to have power over a man, they need to be educated themselves, make their own money, and have some self-worth. Otherwise, you won't respect them. It will just end up being another one-night stand or perhaps two, but you'll tire of the beauty and desire of a woman who has a brain between those ears and not just a vagina between her legs." Tess shot her brow up as she sipped her tea.

"Damn." He grinned, loving the directness of her already.

"And I know you have a double major with one of those being in

psychology." Her eyes met with his. "That was my minor. Don't try to pull any of that shit with me. It won't work. Friends?"

"Absolutely." He smiled, raised his glass to hers, toasted.

"Will you be here all summer?" she asked.

"That was the plan. I can work from here. Dad knows that I wanted to take a break and reevaluate my life a little."

"Well, it'll be nice to have someone else here." She shrugged. "It's very quiet when Jonathan and Gina aren't around. And Harper is pulling a full schedule at the college this summer."

"Want to go to the beach?" he asked. "Growing up here, I know all the good local places where there's not a lot of people."

"Sure." Tess gave him a nod. If nothing else, she found him amusing.

Colin held Tess in his arms as they lay in the hospital bed. It took a month for him to work up the nerve to try to kiss her, but he remembered it vividly. He had never wanted to kiss a woman so much in his life.

It was the middle of July, and they were fishing off the dock one evening. Tess had just caught her first fish and was as excited as a child on their birthday.

After he unhooked the fish from the line and put it in the cooler, he rebaited her line and washed his hands. Tess cast out the line with a smile still fixed upon her lips. And that was when he walked over to her, placed his hand on her hip, and kissed her gently. He felt one of her hands rest on his chest, and when he felt the other one around his shoulder, he was a bit relieved that she didn't pull away.

Thinking back, that kiss seemed the last for a while. He also remembered the fishing pole that she dropped into the water when her other hand came around his shoulders. A smile rested upon his lips with that memory.

It was a very slow start for them, and how they ended up where they were now was a blur to him. Colin wanted to get back to the beginning—when it was just the two of them and they were very happy together.

CHAPTER 3

Almost One Year Later

Tess sat at a bistro table outside a small café on the corner by Matthew Taylor's office. She had been watching him for about three weeks and wanted to meet him, but she didn't want to come across like she had been stalking him. What made her a bit nervous was the incredible physical attraction she had to him. Matthew had short, dark hair, amazing dark blue eyes, and skin that she knew would tan well if he ever wore anything besides a suit. Standing about six feet with broad shoulders, he kind of reminded her of Colin. Maybe that's why she was attracted to him.

The past year with Colin had been great for a while, but then things went back to the way they were before. For some unknown reason, he just couldn't seem to find the words to give her hope that he loved her like she loved him. Three weeks before she left Atlanta, she told him had commitment issues and needed to figure them out—or she wasn't coming back. Thus far she had, conveniently, not answered his multiple daily calls since she left. It was time he missed her for a change.

Mathew Taylor was a name that she overheard Colin say every now and again. So, when she packed a bag after her fight with him, she decided to check out the man for herself. It took a little digging around; it was as if the man didn't exist eight years ago. Intrigued, she decided she would get to know him and see if she could find out why his life only began eight years before. But after three weeks of watching him, she decided he was just a normal man. She should probably leave him alone, but he was so attractive. Perhaps one night of sexual indulgence with him would curb this desire in her. It was a great fantasy she created in her mind, but she knew she wouldn't do it. After the Markenna incident, she had no desire to manipulate any man at this point in time; it was easier to just live in her fantasy.

Needing to shake off her continuous wandering thoughts, she called the hotel to set up an afternoon at the spa. Self-indulgence was not something she was accustomed to. She liked to think she was simple, didn't require attention, and didn't really want attention, but she did like a good massage.

Wanting to go back to her suite, she stood up and accidentally dropped her phone. The cover popped off, shattering the front screen. Sighing, she knelt and began picking up the pieces. Wearing a body-hugging shift-type dress and four-inch heels, she was careful about the way she knelt. As she gathered two of the pieces and was going for the third a man kneeled beside her, picking it up and handing it to her.

Looking up, she couldn't help but smile. "Thank you so much."

"You're very welcome." Matthew Taylor took her hand and helped her up.

"Tess," she said her name with a smile gazing into his gorgeous blue eyes.

"Matthew." He looked at his hand holding hers. "I'd shake your hand, but it seems I haven't let go of it yet."

"I …" She looked at her hand in his and smiled. It surprised her to find he had a very slight accent that she couldn't quite place, but it reminded her a little bit of Dominic's. And when he smiled, she nearly melted, feeling like a sixteen-year-old girl with a crush.

"Here. Let me put your phone back together for you." Matthew released her hand as she gave him the three pieces. "I must tell you that I've noticed you around here the last few weeks. You're hard to miss. You're incredibly beautiful if I may be so bold."

Tess felt her cheeks blush. "Thank you. Admittedly, I've noticed you too."

Handing her the phone, he spoke. "This is going to be very forthright, considering we just met, but would you like to go to dinner with me tonight? I don't see a ring on your finger, so I am assuming— and I know I shouldn't do that—that you aren't married?"

"No, I'm not married." Tess couldn't tame the smile on her face. She looked down for a moment to calm her nerves, then back up at his handsome face. "I would love to have dinner with you."

"Perfect." With a slight nod, he grinned. "Seven o'clock?"

"Yes," she answered. "Let me give you my number in case you need to cancel."

Matthew took out his phone. "You can give me your number, but I can guarantee I won't be canceling."

As they exchanged numbers, Tess told him which hotel she was staying at.

"Are you in town for a while?" he asked.

"I was thinking about leaving, but maybe you can change my mind," she suggested as her eyes held his.

"I'm certainly going to try." Matthew gazed intently at her glass blue eyes. "Walk with me for a few if you don't have prior engagements?"

"I don't." She placed her hand on the inside of his arm when he held it out for her. "I was just going to spend the afternoon at the spa, but I don't have to be there until one thirty."

"Perfect," he stated. "Could I interest you in a glass of wine in my office … if that doesn't sound really weird?"

Tess laughed a little. "As long as your office isn't in a basement and only if the wine is red."

"Red? Really?" Peculiar, he glanced sideways at her.

"Yes."

"That's my favorite," he admitted. "I promise we will be going up and not to the basement." Matthew mused, guiding her through the doors of the high-rise.

"What do you do?" she asked as they got on the elevator.

"Financial and management consulting and a little investing." He grinned with a quick raise of his eyebrows. "I know it sounds very exciting."

"Actually, yes." It was her turn to grin knowing he wouldn't expect what was about to come out of her mouth. "I have my MBA in quantitative finance."

"Which school?" he asked.

"Columbia," she answered.

"I was MIT with finance and management. My father wanted me to go to Columbia, but I didn't want to live in New York." He shrugged with a grin as the bell dinged for his floor. "After you."

"I didn't venture too far away from school when I was there," she noted. "I wanted the education—not a social life. Besides, I was very quiet back then."

"And now?" he asked before they got to his floor.

"Still quiet. I'm a good one-on-one person. And if there's something I want, I'm not afraid to go after it."

"Nice." Matthew smiled as the doors opened.

Tess stepped out onto a high-end executive-level floor. With his hand gently on the small of her back, he guided her past reception and down a long corridor with several other offices to a corner office. He stopped at his assistant's desk for a moment. "Anna, please hold my calls. This way." Matthew walked Tess through the double doors and closed the doors behind him.

"This is very nice." Tess walked over to the windows to admire the corner view of the city and the lake beyond.

"Thank you." He went to the mini bar in the corner and poured them each a glass of red wine and stood by her side. "Here you go."

Tess took the glass then a sip. "This is really good."

"Do I look like the kind of man who would serve anything less than the best?"

"Nope. You strike me as the kind of man who likes his lifestyle a certain way and will do whatever he has to do to maintain it."

Matthew nodded. "I guess I do. Are you in the city on business?"

"No, just running away from my life." Tess eyed him carefully, having an unusual sense of instant trust between them.

"It can't be that bad," he surmised.

"No, probably not." She smiled unconsciously, glancing at the glass in her hand. "Just at a crossroads and not certain as to my next step except for dinner with you tonight."

Matthew wondered what her life was really like. Was she happy? What was she running away from? "Which reminds me, is there any food you don't like?"

"Sushi," she answered without any hesitation.

"Noted. That's not my favorite either. I was raised on meat and potatoes."

"I'll eat shellfish and salmon, once in a while, but sushi just has a taste that is icky." Her nose scrunched at the mere thought of sushi.

Matthew laughed. "If one doesn't like sushi, it is generally the seaweed that they don't have a taste for. There's a steakhouse on the lakefront. I'll make our reservations there."

"Perfect."

They chatted for an hour about random topics. Tess trusted him even though she had just met him, which was unusual given her past. Matthew was smart, handsome, and very sexy. The attraction she had to him was undeniable. "I need to get going." Tess stood.

"Okay." He stood with her. "Thank you for coming up here and talking with me."

"Thank you for asking." Noting she stood dangerously close to him.

"Can I kiss you?" he asked softly without hesitating.

"No one has ever asked before—they just did."

"They should have asked." Matthew's hand caressed over her shoulder.

"Yes," she replied, looking at him a bit nervously.

Matthew slipped his hands behind her neck with his fingers in her hair and placed his lips upon hers. They were soft, full, and willing.

Tess felt her knees want to buckle, and an odd swirling was in her stomach as her hands rested on his waist. Slowly, the kiss deepened, and she brought her arms around his shoulders and his wrapped around her waist, pulling her close to his body. Tess wasn't certain how long the kiss lasted, but she didn't want it to stop. A man hadn't kissed her like this for a very long time.

Matthew pulled his lips back first, resting his forehead on hers. "I could kiss you forever," he whispered, kissing her again.

Tess nodded slightly, feeling tingly all over.

Matthew kissed her, again. "Do know that I will be thinking of you until we meet tonight."

Tess grinned and felt her cheeks flush. "I'm going to be so late."

"Wait a moment." He walked over to his desk and buzzed his assistant.

"Yes, sir?"

"Can you please have Henry bring my car around and let him know he will be taking Tess to her hotel," he apprised his assistant.

"Absolutely," she replied. "Will you be leaving as well?"

"No, but I will be escorting her down." Hanging up, he walked back over to her.

"Thank you," she said as he took her hand.

"For what?" he asked as they walked to the office doors.

"The car and driver," she answered as they walked to the elevators.

"You can use my car and driver anytime you want—as long as they are bringing you to me." He grinned as they stepped into the elevator.

Tess smiled as the elevator doors closed.

Matthew held her hands mesmerized by her beauty. "You are so beautiful."

"I feel my cheeks flush when you say that." She looked down for a shy moment and then back up, before leaning to him for another kiss.

At some point, the elevator doors opened for a couple people. Matthew reluctantly pulled his lips from hers and looked at them. "I would highly suggest that you take another elevator." He turned back to Tess after pressing the button for the doors to close. Instantly, his lips went right back to hers until they were on the ground floor.

"It's going to be a very long afternoon," he sighed as they walked across the lobby.

"I know," she agreed.

Matthew's car was right in front, and Henry was holding the door open. Before she got in, Tess turned back to him with a soft smile. "Thank you for the wine and conversation," she spoke softly.

"You're welcome," Matthew replied. "I will see you at seven."

"Yes. Have a good afternoon." Tess slipped into the back seat.

With a smile, he closed the door. Matthew watched the car until it was out of sight before he slowly walked back up to his office. Tess was the first woman he had found himself drawn to since Sarah left a few years before. She was beautiful, smart, and educated. This one was different he could tell already.

Tess took a deep breath and looked in the mirror after she dressed. She had the hotel salon put long curls in her hair. Usually, she liked to do her own hair, but since she had already had a massage, mani-pedi, and a facial, she might as well let them do her hair. It draped nicely down the center of her back, and she liked it this length. Her makeup was light with very neutral colors. There was a strong disdain for heavy dark makeup, simply because it reminded her of her twin, and she didn't want to look anything like Taryn.

Wearing a slim-fitting dark blue dress, she turned herself in front of the mirror, making sure it looked perfect. The hemline was just above her knees, a respectable length, she thought.

Picking up her phone, she called Jack.

"Tess?" His voice answered almost instantly. "Are you okay?"

"Of course, I am." She smiled at his protectiveness. "Why is that always the first thing everyone asks me?"

"There's something wrong. It's in your voice," he noted.

"Matthew Taylor." She took a deep breath.

"What about him?"

"What do you know about him?" she asked.

"All I'm going to say is there is bad blood with Colin and Matthew." He sighed, closing his eyes. "I know you're mad at Colin, and if you're looking to really piss him off, this would do it."

"Jack." She hesitated a moment before continuing. "I met him earlier today. He asked me to dinner tonight."

Jack couldn't help but laugh. "Well, hell, then go and have fun. He is a good guy despite the issue between him and Colin. If you find what you're looking for with Matthew, take it and don't look back. I want you to be happy."

Tess's eyes filled with tears. "You made me happy."

"Tess." Jack hung his head.

"Jack, I'm sorry." Her voice was soft. "I try not to go there with you. It's just hard."

"It's hard for me too, and it's been a year." He shook his head.

"Complete change of subject," Tess began. "I dropped my phone today. It's not working very well. Can you send me another or, better yet, can I be a normal person and go to a store and get a new phone?"

"No, you cannot be normal." He smiled to himself. "You know the rules, and you know why. I'll have a new one sent to your hotel in the morning. Toss your other one in the suitcase, but don't throw it away. I'll need it back."

"Fine. I should go," she said, disappointed that she couldn't be like normal people. "I love you, Jack."

"I love you too, T."

Tess dabbed the tears that threatened her eyes, gave herself one more look over, and walked to the balcony. As she looked out at the city, there was a knock on her door. With a deep cleansing breath, she walked across the room and opened the door.

Matthew was standing before her with a single red rose. "For you." He handed it to her. "Have you been crying?"

Tess looked up and smiled. "What makes you say that?"

"Your eyes are a little red," he noted.

Tess smiled, shaking her head. "There were tears forming, but I didn't cry."

"I don't like that." He ran his hand over her shoulder. "What can I do to make it better?"

Tess grinned. "You're already making things better."

"You look absolutely gorgeous." He slid his hand down her arm.

"Thank you. Come in, please."

"This is like your own apartment." He walked into the living room.

"I guess." She looked around. "Maybe that's why I like being here …
my own space."

"You don't have your own place where you live?"

"No." She smiled. "I stay with the family. The house is huge. We get
to have bodyguards and all sorts of fun stuff like that."

"Then how are you in Chicago without a bodyguard?"

"Cell-phone tracker." She shrugged. "I don't mind. Sometimes it
makes me feel safer. I tend to wander. Let me grab my shoes, and I will
be ready."

Matthew walked over to the balcony and looked out over the city.
He wanted to get to know her better, but she always seemed evasive
when they talked about family. How could he judge, he didn't care to
talk much about his either?

"Ready," she announced, walking back into the living room with
her shoes on. "Why are you smiling?"

"You're beautiful," he stated, again.

Tess leaned over, meeting his lips with hers. It was another slow,
sensual, lingering kiss. Both needed the passion that was so strong
between them.

"I have something for you." Matthew gazed into her eyes and pulled
slightly back.

"You didn't have …" her voice drifted off as he pulled out a small
box from the inside of his jacket and handed it to her. Tess opened it up
to find a large diamond on a thin silver chain. "This is beautiful. Thank
you so much. You shouldn't have."

"I wanted to," he told her with a shrug.

"And what if you decide I'm a lunatic?" She handed the necklace to
him to put on her and held up her hair.

"I'm damn confident that you aren't." Matthew clasped the necklace
and resisted the urge to kiss her neck.

Once it was clasped, she turned to him for approval. "Well?"

"Perfect," he said, giving her another kiss. "We should get going."

"Okay." She took his hand, and they left the suite.

They arrived for dinner promptly at seven-thirty. Matthew had reserved a secluded spot with a view of the lake and a bottle of his favorite red wine. The conversation flowed effortlessly between them just as it did earlier in the day.

Tess really enjoyed hearing him talk about his company. She knew he loved his work and had built a very successful business with a stellar reputation.

After a couple of hours and two bottles of wine, they walked down the street to a cozy piano bar. They sat in a secluded corner and drank more wine.

"Tell me about your parents," Matthew asked, wondering if she would share.

"I don't remember my real father. My mother said he was killed in an auto accident when I was three or four. She went through many men until she married a DA in Los Angeles when I was about ten. Our life after that was parties, cocaine, alcohol, and strange people in and out of our house all the time. They were murdered when I was sixteen. And sadly enough, it was probably the best thing that ever happened for my siblings and me."

"I'm so sorry you had to grow up that way." He squeezed her hand.

"It was bad, but they got what they deserved—and they never caught who did it. My sisters and I ended up with a great man who had known my mother from college. He took us all in and finished raising us as his own."

"And look at you now," he stated with a smile.

"Yep." She smiled back at him. "I believe people come into our lives, or we go into theirs, for a reason, a purpose. I don't think anything is by chance. I believe that we were supposed to meet, and I don't know why, yet, but we were supposed to. Please don't think I'm weird for thinking that."

"I feel the same way. Let's get out of here," he suggested.

"Okay," she agreed, and they stood up. "I think I may have had a bit too much wine."

"I think I have too." He slipped his arm around her waist. "Good thing I have a driver."

Their lips connected and parted as each tasted and savored the other. After a few minutes, Matthew looked at her. "Can I take you home with me tonight?"

Tess nodded slowly and put her finger to his lips when he wanted to kiss her again. "This is not a one-night stand."

"No." He shook his head. "I don't do those."

Tess smiled, and they walked out the door.

It didn't take long before they were at Matthew's. As they walked in together, Tess set her purse on the table in the entryway. Matthew hooked his arm around her waist, drawing her close to his body. Their lips feverishly found each other in a need stronger than either could control. Tess's hands untied his tie, and her fingers began to unbutton his shirt. Matthew's hands slipped under the hemline of her dress, pushing it up a bit, and then he pressed her body against the wall, picking her up. She wrapped her legs around his hips, and their kisses continued.

"You're not wearing any panties," he whispered between kisses.

"I don't like panty lines." Her hands reached down and unzipped his pants.

"Oh my god," he breathed out. "You're going to be the death of me."

Tess felt him find his way into her. She swore she stopped breathing as the amazing feeling of him paralyzed her. Her hand reached down to steady herself on the table next to them, but she hit it too hard, knocking her purse on the floor. She brought her arms around his shoulders tightly and continued to kiss him as he brought her closer and closer to the edge. Her mouth left his as she neared the climax. Matthew knew he had her almost there. And when she crested over that edge, her whole body tightened, and she held her breath.

"Breathe, T," he reminded her softly as she contracted around his pulsing cock.

Tess opened her eyes and smiled just as she went over.

Matthew came right behind her. Then rested his head on her shoulder, and neither moved for a long moment.

Her legs were still wrapped around his waist when he looked up at her and smiled. "That's not exactly how I planned that happening," he stated, and she kissed him.

"Maybe not, but that was a great spontaneous moment." And she kissed him again.

Matthew reluctantly set her down and brought his hands up, kissing her slowly with a deep desire for more.

"Let's move this out of the foyer at least," he suggested.

They both noticed her purse on the floor. Matthew bent down and picked up her 9 mm.

"Should I be worried?" he asked.

"No." Tess shook her head, noting how comfortable the gun settled in his hand, and picked up the other things that had fallen from her purse. "I'm a single woman who travels all over by herself. I believe in protecting myself."

"Are you a good shot?" he asked.

"Excellent. I never miss my target."

"Mmm." He reached out his hand to her. "I may be falling in love with you, Tess."

Tess stared at him when he said that, and all words seemed to escape her.

Matthew bent over, kissing those lips that he loved. Her arms came around his shoulders, and he let the kiss linger.

Then, she stepped back. "Matthew, I haven't … well … I'm trying to say that I have a terrible track record with relationships. Honestly, I've really only had one, well maybe sort of two, and … I pretty much walked away from him when I came here."

"Why did you leave him?" he asked curiously.

"He seems to have commitment issues." She bit the inside of her mouth.

"His loss is my gain," Matthew wrapped his arms around her waist again. "I can assure you that I have no commitment issues."

Tess tilted her head up to his lips. Kissing him felt so good, so natural.

"Come on." He locked the door, placed her gun on the entry table, and guided her into the bedroom. "Let's do this a little bit differently this time."

＊ ＊ ＊

Tess woke in the morning to the smell of coffee. The shades were still closed, and Matthew was not in the bed. After a long stretch, she got up. Picking up his white button-down shirt from the night before, she smelled the fragrance of him that lingered. Putting it on, she rolled up the sleeves, and buttoned a few buttons to hide the necessities. Then, she ran her fingers through her hair, wishing she had a hairband.

Matthew was at the kitchen table, shirtless, with the paper when she walked in. Seeing her, he put the paper down, took her hand, and pulled her onto his lap. "Good morning," his voice low and sultry.

"Good morning," she replied with a smile as her finger traced the outline of the wing of a raven tattoo that draped over his shoulder. The rest of the bird wrapped around his shoulder and across the shoulder blade. "What does the raven symbolize for you?"

Matthew pursed his lips, then sighed. "I was at a really low and bad point in my life, and I had gone to a cabin, in the middle of the wilderness in Idaho to get my head on straight. The first day I showed up, there was a raven perched on the railing of the deck just watching me. I didn't think much of it at the time. Every day for three weeks, this raven showed up and perched itself where I could see it, whether in the house or while I was outside. I finally looked up the meaning of this raven showing up like this and it said that they show up when one needs guidance. I certainly did back then, and as odd as it sounds, I began talking to the bird every day when I saw him. When the day came a few weeks later, and he didn't show up, I knew I was ready to go back to Chicago and begin a whole new life. Which I did. What's interesting is that the day I signed the lease for my office, there was a raven perched on a tree outside of the leasing office when I walked out. I gave it a smile and thank you and it flew off. I knew I was heading in the right direction, and he confirmed it."

Tess was awed by this explanation of his tattoo and ran her tongue over her lower lip before she spoke. "That is incredibly symbolic. I truly love it."

Matthew kissed her lips softly. "I like you in my shirt." His fingers undid a couple of the buttons.

Tess watched his fingers. "If you like me in it, why are you unbuttoning it?"

"Because I like what's inside of it too." He slipped his hand inside the shirt so he could caress her breast.

"Mmm." Tess closed her eyes, enjoying his touch.

"I hope you don't have plans for today," he murmured between kisses on her neck.

"I was going to fly to Maine," she answered.

"I hope I changed your mind last night." Matthew kissed the soft curve of her jaw.

"Umm. I'm not quite sure. Maybe a repeat performance will jog my memory?"

"Oh." He nodded slowly, then grinned. "We can repeat all of that over and over if needed."

Tess smiled. "I'm staying, but we can still repeat last night over and over."

"We will." Matthew kissed her one more time before gazing into her eyes. "I thought we'd go sailing. If you like that sort of thing?"

"I'm going to say yes even though I have never really sailed before. I don't think a rowboat counts."

"No, it doesn't." He moved his hand from her breast to her leg. "It's been so hot lately. I've wanted to get out on the water for a while, but I haven't given myself a good enough reason to take a day until now."

"You have your own sailboat?" Enthusiastically, her eyes widened with a big smile.

"Yes." He raised his eyebrows. "Something I took up in college."

"This will be fun. I love trying new things."

Matthew loved the genuine smile on her lips.

"I need to go to my hotel for some clothes and a bathing suit," she apprised him, standing up.

"No problem." He slipped his hand behind her neck as he stood beside her, pulled her to his body, and kissed her deeply. "I could kiss you all day long."

Tess smiled and kissed him again, wondering why Colin couldn't be like that.

CHAPTER 4

Three months passed rather quickly, Tess thought as she read a book on Matthew's sofa. It felt like they had been together for years. Matthew gave her everything she wanted in a relationship that Colin didn't. She loved Matthew, but in her heart, she still loved Colin too. There had been no communication between the two of them since she went to Chicago, and she had declined all his calls. She didn't even touch base with Jack; she knew he would track her phone to find her. There was no communication with anyone else in the family. She wasn't sure how to combine the life she was creating with Matthew with the life she had in Georgia. Avoiding it altogether seemed to be working out very well.

A knock at the door jolted her back to reality. Tess thought that was kind of odd since all visitors were to be announced. She put her book down and went to answer it with her 9 mm in hand. Looking through the peephole, she swore under her breath before opening the door. Colin stood before her with a displeased look upon his face.

"You can't be here," she told him and went to close the door.

"Matthew is in a meeting with his attorney," his voice stated flatly as his hand stopped the door from closing. "Therefore, I can be here since you won't take any of my calls."

Tess stepped aside as he let himself in. Colin briefly scanned the apartment and turned back to her. "There are two ways to do this, Tess."

He looked down for a moment and back up to her eyes. "Come with me now so we can talk—or I will go talk with Matthew."

"And tell him what?" She crossed her arms.

"That we are married," he stated, curious of her reaction.

Tess smiled and then sort of laughed. "If you're going to tell someone we're married, there better be a damn ring on my finger—or I will hurt you."

"You've already hurt me." He looked seriously into her eyes. "Get whatever you need, and let's get out of here."

Tess looked at him for a moment, then got her shoes and purse, and headed out the door with him knowing she didn't really have a choice. As always, Colin had a car waiting downstairs. The driver took them to a private airstrip outside of the city where he had the company plane. There was very little talk between them during the drive. When she saw the plane, she looked at him.

"What are you thinking?" She shook her head. "I don't want to leave the city."

"I know you don't." He got out of the car and held his door open so she could get out.

"You can't do this!" Her voice thundered.

"I can—and I am." He leaned in the door, looking at her. "You won't answer any of my calls; therefore, you leave me no choice. Get out of the car—or I will drag you out kicking and screaming, and nobody around here will stop me. You know you brought it to this."

After pausing a few seconds, she reluctantly scooted out of the car and walked over to the plane. She sighed deeply, having no idea where he was planning on taking her. They used to be spontaneous before he began working for his father, but then his free time was quickly consumed.

Taking two steps up the stairs, she turned to him. Colin stopped on the step behind her, which brought them eye level. She went to say something, but the words wouldn't come out. Colin held her eyes firmly with his, and when he saw them begin to fill with tears, he wrapped his hands around her waist and pulled her close. She buried her face in the nape of his neck as tears fell from her eyes.

"Come on, T," he spoke softly. "I don't know why you make me be such an ass."

"Defense mechanism." She wiped her eyes. "Because you hurt me all the time."

Tess turned from him and headed up the stairs. They took seats beside each other toward the back as the copilot closed the door and went back up to the cockpit.

Colin handed her a tissue, and she wiped her eyes dry as the plane left the ground.

"Where are we going?" she asked as he slipped her hand into his.

"Your favorite place," he answered straight faced.

"I thought you didn't like it there?" She eyed him.

"It's not all about me." He pursed his lips and closed his eyes before looking at her again. "You told me I had commitment issues before you left, and you're right. I did. I do, but in the past three months, I realized how much I've missed you and how much I love you. I want you to come home … with me."

Tess smiled and unhooked her seatbelt so she could face him. "I like how you have me in a plane so I can't just walk away from you."

"There are some things I do plan knowing your reaction," he reminded her.

"It took you three months to come for me?" Her head tilted as she shook it.

"I honestly thought you would come back. You've always come back. You've never stayed away this long," he reminded her.

"I've never had anybody love me the way he does," she told him as she held his eyes.

"Yes, you did," he stated. "You do. I always have. I just didn't know how to show you or tell you." Colin stood up and paced in the walkway. "I didn't know what I was doing to you until Jack, literally, popped me one in the face. After what happened with Kate, I turned that part of my emotions off. I didn't want to ever feel the way that I felt when I saw her and …" Colin turned away from her. He hadn't ever talked about what happened with Kate with anyone—not even Jack. If he wanted Tess, he knew he would have to share.

Tess took off her shoes and sat cross-legged in the oversized chair. "Colin, this is that life-changing moment for you. Tell me what happened or take me back to Chicago."

Sitting in the chair before her, he held her eyes as he spoke. "Three days before our wedding, I caught her with my brother. So, I shot her."

"You shot her? Wasn't that a little extreme?" Her eyes were wide with surprise.

"No." He shook his head in defense. "Not at the time. I wanted to kill my brother, but I couldn't. She was the next best one to kill."

"And you've talked to no one about this? Not even your dad?"

Colin shook his head. "Nope. I dealt with it in my head. I shot her and told my brother to stay out of my life."

"Why did he do that? I'm sure there's a reason," she asked.

"He told me from the beginning that she was after me only for the money." He smiled remembering the dozen or so times his brother tried to warn him. "I didn't believe him even though he was very persistent. I was very stubborn about it. What better way to get me to break off the engagement than by finding her with him?"

Tess looked sideways at him. "Your brother was just trying to save you from a gold-digger?"

Colin nodded.

"And you haven't talked to him since?"

Again, he nodded.

"You are such an ass," she muttered. "Do you know what this has done to your father?"

Another nod.

"Fix it." She gestured with open hands. "Apologize."

"I will," he stated. "This is like a twelve-step program for me. You're the first and most important step. I've not done well by you, and I need to fix us before anything else. If I can't fix us, then nothing else matters."

Tess took a deep breath and slowly released it. She had loved him for years—never to get it back until now. Matthew showed her how much he loved her, and he said it every day. There was no doubt how she felt about her. If she left Matthew to go back to Colin, would it be a forever love or would she be risking the forever love with Matthew? "Loving you has been such a one-way street. Why do you think I brought Jack into our bedroom?"

"Why?".

"Because every other man in this world gives me what I truly want, except you. And you are the only man I want it from." Tears fell from her eyes.

Colin leaned forward, taking her hands in his. "T, I want you to be happy—genuinely happy—and I know that we can be together. I don't want to be with anyone else. I've no interest. I love you, only you."

She had waited a very long time to hear those words, but she wasn't sure if it was enough. "I don't … even know what to say at this moment. I've wanted you to love me for years, and you decide to do this now? When I'm with someone else? Damn it, Colin." Tess stood up, letting her hands pull away from his. She walked back to the galley for a bottle of water, took a drink, went back, and stood before him. He took the water she offered and set it in the cup holder. Tess brought her hands to his head, looking down at him.

Carefully, his hands wrapped around her legs, and he rested his forehead on her stomach.

"Colin," she began softly. "I love Matthew. He has given me everything you were afraid to give me."

Colin raised his head as she dropped to her knees before him.

"However, you've always had my heart," she said with tears in her eyes. "Stop fucking with it, and just love me."

"I promise you, Tess." Colin cupped her cheeks. "I will love you the way I should have been loving you from the beginning." Colin pulled her onto his lap and kissed her slowly—with purpose and love.

They arrived in Aspen a few hours later. Colin had another car waiting, and they drove twenty minutes to the home by the river. As soon as she got out of the car, she walked to the back of the house to admire the view of the river. She loved it there. It was always green and beautiful and peaceful.

Colin went in through the front door with his bag and the one he had packed for her. Most of her clothes were at his home in Atlanta, and he figured he would pack her a bag because the only way he was getting her out of Chicago was by surprise. After he set their things down, he walked to the backyard, knowing exactly where she was. She was standing at the edge of the lawn, looking at the river. The water flowed rapidly, and a cool breeze blew through the tall trees. She was everything he wanted in a woman, in a lover, in a best friend. And he nearly lost her; in theory, he could still lose her.

Walking up, he slipped his hands around her waist and kissed her cheek.

"Isn't it beautiful here?" she asked knowing it was more how she felt then him.

"Yes, it is. I know how much you love it here, and I was getting tired of wasting money on renting it. I bought it for you." He held out the keys for her.

"Seriously?" Her mouth dropped open, and he placed the keys in her hands.

"It's in both our names." He shrugged. "I wanted it to be just yours, but without you present, I had to add mine. Hope you don't mind."

Tess smiled, shook her head. "Don't think this gets you off the hook."

Colin laughed and kissed her again. "It's got to help at least a little bit."

"Maybe a little." She hugged him. "Does it come with everything that's already inside?"

"Yes, as is." Slipping her hand into his, he brought it to his lips to kiss. "Let's go check out your house."

"I finally have my own home." She glanced at him with a half grin.

"I love you, Tess." He wrapped his arm around her shoulder and kissed her temple.

✳ ✳ ✳

Tess walked into the living room to find Colin was working on his laptop after they settled in.

"We should head over to the store," he suggested as he finished an e-mail to his assistant. "I'm almost done here."

"I need to call Matthew first," she told him. "I don't want him to worry."

"When you're done, we can go—or just eat out. Whatever you want to do." Colin took an uneasy breath knowing their future was still in the air.

Tess walked out of the room before she pressed the connect button on her phone.

"Tess?" Matthew said her name as soon as the call connected.

"Hi," she spoke softly. "I'm so sorry I didn't call you sooner. This is really the first chance I've had." She walked out the back door and closed it behind her.

"It's fine. You're calling me now. Is everything okay?" Matthew was relieved just to hear her voice, worried that she wasn't at home when he got there.

Tess felt tears coming, and she tried to shake them off. "Not really. I'm in Aspen, and I think I will be here for a few days at least."

"Okay. Tess, is there anything I can do for you because you sound like you're crying, and I have an uncomfortable feeling about you and me."

She sat on the lawn. "I'm sorry. It's just family drama. There's a reason I didn't call them or visit them in the past three months. I love you."

"I love you too," he repeated. "T, if you need me, I can be there as fast as my plane will fly."

"Thank you." She smiled to herself knowing this was going to break his heart and hers. "This is something I caused, and I have to fix it. It's just something that is very emotional. I truly hate dealing with that type of stuff."

"I wish I could help you." He ran his hand through his hair. "I am here if you need me—at any time."

"I know. Thank you. I need to get going. I love you," she told him knowing the future was not theirs.

"I know you do," he assured. "And you know I love you. Call me when you get a chance. I'll see you when you get back."

"Okay." She sniffled. "I will call you to let you know what day it will be."

"Okay. Love you, T."

"Love you." She dropped the phone on the lawn, dropped her head to her knees, and cried. How was she ever going to break up with him?

Colin had watched her from the living room. He closed his eyes, knowing very well that it was all his fault. Her tears were his to carry. If they could make it through this, they would be great together forever. The fact that she was with Matthew Taylor made all this so much worse.

After a few minutes, he walked out the back door. Kneeling, he picked up her phone and ran his hand softly over her head.

"Tess, come inside. It's starting to rain." Colin's voice was very soft, sympathetic.

Tess looked at him through a cascade of tears. Her breath hitched as she tried to stop crying. She nodded her head, and he gave her a hand getting up. Putting his arm around her, he guided her back into the house. Going to the kitchen sink, she splashed water on her face, and dried it off with a small towel. With a deep breath, she spoke, "You packed me some clothes, right?"

"Yes, I did." He pointed upstairs.

"Give me ten minutes." And she walked out of the room.

Tess went upstairs, pulled on some jeans and a cardigan, and put her hair up in a ponytail.

"You do pretty good picking out my clothes," she told him as she walked back into the living room.

"Would you expect anything less?" He raised his eyebrows.

"Nope," she replied. "I don't know why I'm so emotional. I'm not a crier, and you know that."

"It's fine." He took her hands in his. "It's my fault anyway."

"Yes, it is." She pulled his lips down to hers. "I'm starving."

"Let's go take care of that." He gave her a long hug. "I'm hungry too."

✳ ✳ ✳

When the call with Tess ended, Matthew had an uneasy feeling. Something was going on with her, and it was going to affect them, and he did not like that at all. With his phone still in his hand, he called James, one of his best friends for years.

"Hey," James smoothly answered, knowing it was his friend. "What's up?"

"I think I need to hire you for some investigative work," Matthew began. "I'd do it but I don't have time. I've got this deal I'm in the middle of trying to close."

"No problem. What is it, I'm listening?" James leaned against the railing of his deck at the house in Maine.

"You know I've been seeing this woman for the past three months," he began. "Don't give me any shit about this, but I don't even know her last name. Tess means the world to me."

"Since when do you not know who you're sleeping with?" James asked, very surprised.

"One thing just led to another. Anyway, she left today while I was at work, and I have a feeling something bad is about to happen. Can you please check into her for me? I talked to her earlier, and she was crying. I just don't feel good about this, James," Matthew sighed, closing his eyes a moment.

"You've got to give me something here to work with, like a number or a picture or something," he suggested.

"I have her cell, and I think I have a picture. Let me look through my phone when we are done here. I will send it to you."

"I'll be waiting," James noted and ended the call.

Matthew scanned through the pictures on his phone and found one of them on his boat. He forwarded it to James, along with her cell number. Knowing he wouldn't hear back from him for at least a day, he headed back to his office.

When the picture came through, James sat back and shook his head. He knew Matthew was seeing someone, but he didn't know how these two could have possibly met in Chicago of all places. With a sigh, he called his cousin, Jack.

"James?" Jack's voice came over the phone. "I haven't talked to you in a while. What's going on?"

"Jackson, you really need to come visit me. I don't want to have lunch with your brother by myself," James joked.

"Harrison's not that bad," Jack responded, defending his brother.

"I know. It's just been a while since we've seen you," James reminded him.

"I know," Jack admitted. "I'll make some time."

"I have a problem," James started.

"What is it?"

"Where's your girl?"

"Damn." Jack sighed deeply. "She should be with Colin. What has she done now?"

"Why has she been in Chicago for the last three months with Matthew?" he asked. "He doesn't even know who she really is."

"That's a two-way street because Tess doesn't know who Matthew is either," Jack educated him a little on this tidbit. "It is purely coincidence that they met and clicked. I told her if she liked him to go with it because Colin wasn't giving her what she wanted. Colin is supposed to be telling her who Matthew is as we speak. There is so much more to all of this than either of them knows."

"Matthew hired me to look into her," James told him. "What do you want me to tell him?"

"Can you stall him for twenty-four hours?" Jack asked.

"Yes, but only twenty-four hours. Otherwise, I will tell him what I know. He is my friend—just like McGowan is yours. Besides, this is Matthew we're talking about." James knew Matthew's skills were nearly as good as his, in research and combat.

"I know," Jack agreed. "I need to touch base with him to see how it went with Tess."

"I'll wait to hear from you, Jack, but after twenty-four hours, Matthew will know I'm holding back info."

"Got it," Jack replied. "I will call you."

CHAPTER 5

Rain was pouring by the time Colin and Tess arrived back at the house. They had eaten out and stopped off at the grocery store. With only a few bags of food to put away, it went rather quickly.

After, Tess turned to Colin, touched his stomach with her fingertips, and closed her eyes.

Colin slipped his hands behind her neck and over her shoulders. When she looked up, he leaned over and kissed her slowly. He felt her hands slip under his shirt. Reluctantly pulling his lips from hers, he kissed her on the forehead.

"Let's lock up down here," he suggested.

Upstairs, Colin started a fire in the fireplace in the master bedroom. Tess found a bunch of candles in the hall closet, brought some in the room, and began lighting them.

"I'm going to take a quick shower." Tess glanced around the room, then began taking off her clothes as she walked to the bathroom.

Colin wasn't far behind as he took off his clothes and followed her in. That was where the long, lingering kisses, soft, sensual touching, and intense love began.

Well before sunrise, Tess woke. The fire was still simmering with a mesmerizing red glow. The rain dancing on the roof made the whole experience cozy. They fell asleep on the floor before the fire amongst all the linens from the bed. It was soft and warm and safe. Tess was wrapped up tightly in Colin's arms, and there was no way she was moving without waking him up. As carefully as she could, she lifted his arm only to have him clamp it back down on her.

"Don't leave me," he mumbled.

"I'll be right back," she whispered. "Just let me go to the bathroom."

"Promise to come right back and slip into this same position?" Colin asked with his eyes still closed.

"Yes," she answered.

"Okay." He gave in and released his tight lock on her.

After Tess got up, Colin rolled to his back and opened his eyes. He needed to tell her about Matthew, but he wasn't positive about what her reaction would be. He didn't want to lose her, but he didn't want to keep this from her either. Knowing he needed to be completely honest for them to move forward made him wonder if he could handle her leaving him for good?

Tess came back a few minutes later and slipped back into his arms.

"I love you, T." Softly, he kissed her neck.

"I love you too," she replied, turning to face him. "I know there is something you want to tell me. I don't know what it is, but if you want us to be us, you need to learn to talk to me."

Colin looked deep into her intense blue eyes. "How do you know me so well? How do you know I need to tell you something?"

"Jack taught me how to read men." She shrugged without thought. "And you were one of my studies."

Colin laughed a little and shook his head. "Great, you and Jack hung out way too much together."

"Why did you let me bring Jack into our bed?" She sat up.

Colin took a deep breath and sat up as well. "Couple reasons. First, if I hadn't let you, I would have lost you to him. Jack and I are as close as brothers. He knows how much I love you, and you could say I trusted him to not take you from me."

"How did you know he wouldn't do that?"

"I know the way Jack's life was before we met. It wasn't as bad as yours, but they struggled. My father and Gina welcomed him into our family like they did with you and your sisters after his mom died. In his head, he probably figured that to be with you, he would lose the family."

"Would he have?"

"Never." Colin shook his head. "I would've missed the hell out of you, but I wouldn't forsake him the family because of it. I'm not twenty-five anymore. I made a mistake with my brother, and I won't repeat that."

"We talked about that at one point."

"I know." He took a deep breath, releasing it slowly. "Jack and I talked about it when he decided to go on the mission for six months."

"You know a lot more than you ever let on," she noted.

Colin smiled.

"And the second reason?"

"There was this wild sexual side of you that you needed to explore. I didn't want to have us married, and ten years later, you're thinking you wish you would have … you could say it was a compromise on my side. I, hopefully, wouldn't lose you to someone else, but you had the freedom … to play. Does that make any sense?"

Tess nodded.

"Although, there was a time when I thought I was going to lose you to him."

"Carina's." Her eyes filled with tears. "When I lost the … baby."

"Yes." He nodded this time. "I knew you two had been spending a lot of time together while you were working the Markenna case, and I really thought I was going to lose you."

"I loved him." Tess wiped away the tears. "James told me I had to let him go."

"Really? James?"

Tess nodded.

"Interesting," he replied. "If you hadn't lost the baby, what would you have wanted to do?"

"I don't know," she said. "But I do know that I couldn't have imagined my life without you."

"We made things so complicated back then." He gave a half smile. "And speaking of complicated things, I have a question for you."

Tess wrinkled her forehead, intriguingly.

"If you were curious about who Matthew Taylor was, why didn't you ask me?" Colin asked, dreading this conversation.

"You never said anything nice about him, and I didn't want to bring his name up and have you irritated. We were already having issues," she answered with a shrug.

Colin released a deep breath. Taking her hand in his, he spoke. "Matthew Taylor is my brother. And for some reason, I thought you knew that. He changed his name after we had our fight and permanently relocated to Chicago."

"No fucking way," Tess muttered, shook her head, then buried it in the pillows, and cried feeling his hand on her back, rubbing it gently.

"I would apologize to you for this, but I'm not certain what I would be apologizing for," he softly told her.

Tess lifted her head and wiped her eyes. "I did what Kate did to you." Tears filled her eyes again.

"No." Colin adamantly shook his head. "You and Matthew had no idea who each other were. Don't ever compare yourself to Kate. You're nothing like her."

"I feel sick." She rolled herself up, closing her eyes. "This explains why he never wanted to talk about his family. You have nothing to apologize for. You didn't tell me to go to Chicago and stalk him like I did. He really has no idea who I am."

"If we didn't have our fight, you wouldn't have left. It comes back to me putting business before you." He brought her hand to his lips. "I love you, always you."

"I know." She nodded as more tears fell. "We can't keep doing this. Things are great for a while, and then it's back to being crappy. I want to be married one day and have babies, a nice home, and a wonderful husband. But we are so up and down. I don't want to be raising kids by myself and living at your dad's house in Savannah."

"Come here." He reached over and wrapped a blanket around them. Then, his fingers pushed away a couple strands of hair on her face. "I've been tossing around the idea of moving to Portland with you. I can work from the office there, and we can start fresh—away from family, no other distractions, just you and me in a new city and a new life … together. I want all the same things you want, and I want them with you."

"You'd be willing to move to the other side of the country—away from your family?" Tess wanted clarification.

"Yes, but only if you'll come with me." He kissed her forehead. "You are my family."

"I don't even have to think about that." She smiled. "Yes, I will go with you."

"Thank goodness." He hugged her tightly. "I put a lot of thought into this before approaching you with it. We will fly out there together and find a place to live. I must tell my father my plan first."

"He's been wanting you in the Portland office for years," she reminded him.

"I know. That's why I think this will be an easy sale." He slipped his hand behind her neck. "I've missed you."

"What do you miss?" she asked. "The warm body next to you in bed? A dinner companion? What?"

"I miss coming home to you every day. I miss your cooking. I miss all your makeup crap in our bathroom. I want to go into work late because we're making love all morning. I want long lunches with you. I want you … just you. I don't want anyone else in our bedroom. I don't want to do any more contract work, and I don't want you having sex with anyone else. I'm done with all of that. I want to be a normal couple that goes to dinner on Friday nights and visits our families on holidays. I want to take vacations with you to romantic places. I love you, and I know I'm awful at sharing my emotions, but I'm trying to get better at that."

Tears fell down her cheeks. "That was really good."

"That's the way I feel," he admitted. "I love you, Tess."

She smiled. "I love you too."

Colin kissed her softly as they rolled back down in front of the fire.

"You want babies?" he asked.

"Your babies," she answered.

"Let's work on that." He nipped her lip and rolled on top of her.

A new passion ignited between them, taking their love to a new level. Maybe it was having full emotional exposure to one another that opened the feeling that brought them closer.

They woke, again, around noon. Colin woke before Tess, and he realized how lucky he was that she loved him like she did. It was a big relief, and he didn't realize how much it had been weighing on him. He planned on marrying her soon, and he couldn't imagine his life without her. The past three months had been hell, knowing she was sleeping with someone else—and when it turned out to be his brother, that was even worse. He didn't want her to go back there, and he didn't want his brother to have a chance to sweet talk her into staying with him. Colin knew he had to trust her and let her do it however she needed.

Tess sighed deeply as she woke up. She felt Colin's hand on her stomach, and she felt happy.

"Good morning, beautiful." He kissed her.

"Good morning." A wide smile crossed her lips. "Why do I feel like something changed between us?"

"Because something did." His fingers traced the hairline on her forehead. "Something good this time. I love you, and I promise to tell you that every day forever."

"Who are you?" she asked with a slight grin.

"The man who is going to marry you. That event will all happen the right way. It all starts with the ring, and I haven't found the right one yet." Leaning down, he kissed her lips.

"You've looked?" she asked.

"Yes, I have. It's a very frustrating task because it must be perfect for you," he shared caressing his thumb across her temple.

"I love you."

Colin leaned down and kissed her again slowly, softly.

"I'm so hungry." She admitted sitting up.

"Me too." He sat up with her. "Let's go make breakfast."

As they got up, Tess heard her cell phone vibrating on the nightstand. Seeing who it was, she tossed the phone to Colin.

"Hey, Jack." Colin watched Tess as she dressed.

"It's about damn time one of you answered," Jack stated, frustrated.

"What's wrong?" Colin asked.

"Matthew's running Tess," Jack began. "What do you want him to find out?"

"Hold on," he said as Tess had put his shirt on. "Tess, Matthew's running you, what do you want to do?"

"Put Jack on speaker," she directed. "I'm so angry with you, Jack, for not telling me who Matthew Taylor was the first night that I called you. Would it have really been that hard to tell me he was Colin's brother? Seriously, what the hell? Did you think I would never find out? Who's running this for him?"

"James," Jack said, unaffected by her irritation.

"Really? This is a smaller world than I thought." She held Colin's hand as they sat on the bed.

"James will tell him whatever I ask him to say." Jack sighed. "What do you want it to be?"

"How come he called you?" she wondered.

"Matthew gave him your picture," Jack explained. "As soon as he saw it, he called me."

Tess looked at Colin who simply shrugged. "I will be flying back today. I will talk to him tonight. Please ask James to stall until I get there."

"Okay," Jack replied. "Tess, we will have our argument later in person." And abruptly, ended the call.

CHAPTER 6

Close to eight that evening, Tess and Colin walked down the surprisingly busy street to Matthew's building. He had her hand in his, which was tucked into his coat pocket. It was very cold and windy, typical Chicago. After she was done breaking Matthew's heart, they were going back to Atlanta. She was dreading it, but she couldn't just disappear and let Colin tell him. No, this was a relationship that she was in; she would be an adult and tell him the truth.

They turned the corner and stopped at the entrance. Colin stood before Tess and placed his hands on her shoulders. "Are you sure you don't want me to go talk with him first?"

"No." She shook her head. "I am breaking up with my boyfriend. You can't do that for me."

"I know. It's just that I know this is hard for you—and it's my fault." He rested his head on her forehead. "I'm so sorry, Tess."

"I know." Her hand caressed his cheek. "You don't have to wait out here for me. It's way too cold."

"I'm going to be over at that coffee shop across the street. Just come over when you're done," he told her.

"Okay." She took in a deep breath and looked up at the building.

"I love you," he reminded her.

Tess looked back at him and smiled. "I love …" Her breath was taken away in a split second, and the impact pushed her against Colin.

It only took him a few seconds to register that Tess had been shot. He scooped her up and took cover inside the building. Colin yelled at a guard inside to call 9-1-1. Chaos surrounded them and people were screaming, but all he heard were muffled sounds as his soulmate was bleeding to death. He took off her coat and scarf and rolled her over to see where the bullet entered. Her back was covered in blood.

"Tess, baby." His face was directly in front of hers as tears filled his eyes. "Ambulance is almost here. Please fight. Don't give up."

Tess coughed up blood as her eyes rolled.

"Don't try to talk," he said as the paramedics ran over to him. "I love you."

✳ ✳ ✳

After five days, Colin mustered enough nerve to go talk to his brother. It was eleven in the morning when he walked up to Matthew's assistant.

"May I help you?" she asked.

"Yes, I'm here to see my brother. Is he available?" Colin asked.

The woman had worked with him for four years; she didn't even know Matthew had a brother. "Is he expecting you?"

"No." Colin shook his head. "But it is important. Tell him it's about Tess."

The woman nodded slowly, came around the desk, and opened Matthew's office door. "I have ... your brother here."

Matthew stood up, instantly knowing that his brother being here meant something bad had happened.

"What would you like me to do?" she inquired.

"Let him in, Anna." Matthew gestured. "Hold my calls, please."

Anna turned, motioning for Colin to go inside.

Colin stood before his brother for the first time in eight years. Both just stared, unbelievingly.

"Are father and Gina okay?" Matthew asked first.

"Yes." Colin nodded.

"Then what in the world could have possibly brought you here?" Matthew walked over to pour himself a drink.

Colin's eyes glossed over as words were elusive.

"Damn it." Matthew shook his head, closing his eyes for a moment. "Whatever it is, I know it's bad because you are the most cold-hearted son of a bitch I know. Just tell me what it is."

Colin squeezed his eyes together to push back the tears. "My … my girlfriend was shot downstairs five days ago."

Matthew stared emotionless. There was a catch here, but he wasn't quite sure what. "And I care about this … why?" Matthew cocked his head sideways as his eyes narrowed.

"Because she was living with you for the last three months," Colin admitted.

Matthew chucked his glass past Colin, and it shattered against the door. Walking over to his brother, standing no more than an inch away, he pointed his finger at his chest. "Eight years … eight fucking years I've stayed away, stayed out of your life, and you let your fucking girlfriend play me like that? You're still an asshole!"

"It's not like that, Matt." Colin put his hands up in his defense.

"What are you? Bored?" Matthew paced. "Is Father's company not enough for you to keep yourself busy? You still must plot and plan and manipulate me!"

Matthew paused when his door opened, and James stepped in.

"I'm hiring you to kill him," Matthew stated and turned to look out the window.

"That's not happening," James simply replied, glancing at Colin.

"I told you and Father that I was the wrong person to talk to him." Colin shook his head.

"Matthew." James positioned himself between the brothers with plenty of distance between each. "Tess didn't know who you were, and Colin didn't know she was here. This is not his fault, believe it or not. I've known Tess since she was sixteen. Your father took her and her sisters in ten or so years ago."

Matthew turned to James to look him in the eye. "She's one of those girls?" Matthew cocked his head at James.

"Yes."

Matthew closed his eyes for a moment "Is she … alive?"

"For her safety." James turned his attention to Matthew. "I'm going to tell you no. You're going to mourn the loss of your girlfriend. And no one outside of this room will think any differently."

"How long?" Matthew asked his brother.

"Five years," Colin answered.

"Why the hell didn't you marry her? She is perfect," Matthew told him, pouring himself another drink.

"She's been through a lot in her life." Colin shrugged. "I should have."

James's eyes went from one brother to the next, watching for any sign that they would strike out at each other. When Matthew poured another drink and handed the glass to his brother, he knew they would get through this.

"Does Father know?" Matthew asked.

"Yes." He took a seat on the couch opposite of Matthew. "He's with her now—with security—or I wouldn't even be here."

"Was it random?" Matthew asked.

Colin shook his head. "Single shot. Missed her heart by millimeters."

"I take it this is where you're stepping in, James?" Matthew asked.

"Yes," James stated firmly.

CHAPTER 7

Three Years Later, Day 1

On Thursday morning, Colin walked into his father's office at the plantation home. He had been up since six o'clock the previous morning. All he wanted to do was talk to his brother and go take a nap before flying home. But upon walking into the room, he knew sleep wasn't coming anytime soon. There were three other men in the room: his father, his brother, and Jack.

"Aw, hell," he muttered, shaking his head. His father was standing against the credenza, so he sat in a comfortable chair behind the desk since the other two chairs were occupied. "As if I haven't had the worst twenty-four hours of my life already. I know all three of you in one room only means one thing: bullets are going to start flying relatively close to me."

"Anything you want to talk about?" Matthew asked. "I didn't know you were going to Chicago—or I would have stayed there another day."

"Let's do this—and then we can talk." Colin looked at Jack. "I assume there is chatter?"

"Yep," Jack replied. "The link has been made with Tess to Morgan, and a picture was posted this time. I don't know who, how, or when. I just know it has been done. There is now a three-million tag on her head. It's privately funded out of a dummy account overseas. We're watching the account for activity. I have a computer guy trying to find the trail. Wherever you have her, she needs to be brought back here with 24/7 surveillance. I would go pick her up myself, but I don't know exactly where she is."

"Let me ask you something, Jack." Colin smiled. "Have you truly tried to find her?"

"Of course, I have," Jack answered. "I know you have moved her at least twice since she got out of the hospital, and I am pretty sure she is on the West coast. It wouldn't be LA since her parents died there, so it's probably the Northwest. And I will tell you why I think that. You started flying to Portland every month when she was first put under. It was always two weeks at the office there, then two weeks in Atlanta. Three years ago, you always complained about going there for work, so Jonathan did, but suddenly you decided to divide your time between both offices evenly. And eventually, you are there permanently. You give no reason to anyone; you just go. You don't have to explain yourself because you are Colin McGowan. Rich, powerful, and no one would question you, but everyone knows you have a secret. My theory, actually it's more than a theory is this: you tucked her away somewhere close to Portland, and you two are … still together. The only thing I haven't done is follow you to prove my theory is correct, but you know I would never do that to you unless your life was in danger."

"Wow, Jack. You never disappoint me." Colin looked from him to his father and smiled. His father knew what Colin was doing, but he was the only one in the family with that knowledge.

Jack laughed, knowing he was right.

"This leaves only one question, Colin," Jack began. "When are you going to pick her up because I am coming with you?"

"Well, pack a bag, my friend." Colin stood. "We leave in half an hour."

Colin's eyes went from his friend back to his brother. There was a question he knew Matthew wanted to ask but didn't dare. Colin knew the last three years had been hell on his brother, and he felt bad for him most of the time.

"Matthew, could we have that word?" Colin asked.

Matthew nodded, and the two of them walked out of the room. They went out the front door to speak on the massive porch that surrounded the home. They walked a few paces away from one another before turning back.

"What's on your mind?" Matthew asked, leaning against the white railing.

"I want to merge our companies," Colin started. "I know it's very random, but you'll understand why I want you in Portland as soon as I finish explaining this."

"Portland?" Matthew shook his head with a sour look. "I love Chicago. You move."

Colin smiled. "I thought about that, but my company is bigger— and the expense to move would be twice as much. There are three floors above mine that are available. In your complex, there's none."

"You've been doing your homework on this?" Matthew inquired, but already knew the answer.

"Extensively." He took a deep breath. "We've been trying to find a way to have you in Portland so you could be in your daughter's life."

Matthew froze. "Daughter? Tess had my child?"

"Yes." Colin shrugged. "Tess had Savannah nine months after she left."

"So, I have lost three years with my own child?" Matthew said aloud but it was more to himself.

"Well, she's almost two and half, not quite three. I took the paternity test," Colin said. "And she wasn't mine, but it was from the same gene pool. Which would be you."

"Are you two a couple now?" He needed confirmation of that.

"It's a little bit more than just that." Colin sighed, not wanting to venture that far yet, but wasn't going to have a choice.

"What is your definition of 'a little bit more than just that'?" asked Matthew.

Colin's eyes drifted off to nowhere and then back to his brother. "We are married."

Matthew held Colin's stare for a moment and put his hands on the railing. "So, you married the woman I loved—and you have been raising my child?" He shook his head. "In times like this, I wish I was a smoker."

Colin didn't speak this time knowing what he just dropped on his brother was a lot to process.

"Wow," Matthew breathed out. "Do you love her like you're supposed to?"

"I do, Matthew." Colin leaned against the house. "I wouldn't have married her if I didn't. And I wouldn't have married her just to get back at you. What happened between us had been coming for years—before you even met her—and you know that."

Matthew inhaled a deep breath this time, giving his brother a genuine smile. "Well, congratulations." He gave his brother a hug. "At least you know I like this one, and she's not a gold-digger."

"No, she is more of a gravedigger." Colin wrinkled his forehead, unable to remember the number of people she had killed.

"Aren't we all?" Matthew grinned. "You're a very lucky man, my brother, and she is very lucky to have you."

"Thank you, Matthew." Colin nodded. "That means a lot to me."

"They've been very safe then?" Matthew asked.

"Very." Colin nodded. "At first, when I wasn't with her, James was. He has one of his top men in Portland with her. When I'm not there, Grey is, every day."

Colin handed Matthew a small photo of Tess and Savannah from a few months before. Both had wonderful, happy smiles.

Matthew looked at the picture for a long time. Tess was still beautiful, and her smile said she was happy. Her daughter was just a smaller version of her: same dark brown hair and incredible blue eyes. Memories of her flooded his mind and his eyes filled a bit. "I shouldn't miss her like I do. First Sarah leaves, then Tess. Sorry." He glanced at his brother. "I know you don't want to hear this."

"Now you know why I have been thinking about this conversation for three years," Colin reminded him. "It's okay that you miss her. She misses you too."

"And that doesn't bother you?" Matthew asked.

"Of course, it does, but she met you because of something I did.

There's this void because she was never able to say good-bye to you. I know there will always be something between you two, especially having a baby. Tess and I are good, in an honest, solid place together, and nobody can come between us."

"I would never do that to you with her," Matthew defended. "I missed having you in my life all those years. There will not be a woman that comes between us again. Just make sure she's happy."

Colin nodded slowly. "I do my best every day, but I think we will be happier when I'm not constantly worrying about her being safe when I'm not there. It's one thing to put an adult under, but when you have a baby too, it's a whole new set of worries."

"So, when you bring her back here, you don't mind if I pull her aside for a conversation?" Matthew asked.

"Tess is a big girl, and this is something big between you and her." Colin eyed him. "I will not interfere. She knows this also."

"Father and Gina are going to spoil the hell out of that little girl," Matthew chuckled at the thought.

"Nobody else knows about Savannah, yet—nobody," Colin admitted.

"Nobody? Not even Father?"

"No." He sighed. "Dad knows where Tess is, but he doesn't know about the baby. Would you mind getting the room across from my old one ready for her? She likes pink and purple and sailboats."

"Me? I don't know anything about kids—young kids, old kids, middle kids. Did you say she likes sailboats?" Matthew's eyes popped up to his brother's.

"Yes," Colin confirmed with a smile. "She stares out the slider every afternoon, watching the sailboats on the river. It's very cute. Like father, like daughter."

Matthew smiled a proud father moment, and he hadn't even met her yet.

"Gina will help you." Colin grinned. "I'm sure she would love to help once you tell her why."

"Thanks. I see what you're doing." Matthew couldn't help but grin. "Let me be the bearer of this news. Gina has been hinting about grandchildren for a while now. This will make her day."

"Colin?" Harper turned the corner and spoke in her soft voice.

"Harper?" Colin tilted his head. "Did you just hear everything?"

"Yes. Please don't be mad." She walked slowly to Colin and Matthew.

"I'm not mad." He assured her, shaking his head.

"I want to go with you if you're bringing Tess home," she stated.

Colin's eyes went from Harper to Matthew and then back again. "I don't think it's safe enough."

"You're taking Jack. Why can't I go?" Harper's forehead creased with frustration.

"I'm taking Jack because we are bringing back our daughter. One on one. This is nothing new; you should know how this works."

"I miss her so much," Harper placed her hands on her hips, pushing back the tears. "I don't want her to die. If that happened, I would be stuck with Taryn, and she's not a nice person."

Colin and Matthew both smiled knowing she was right.

"I think everyone is aware of that." Colin gave her a hug. "We won't let anything happen to Tess. I promise you."

Harper was the youngest of the Monroe children. She was thirteen when her mother and stepfather were murdered in a home invasion. Her older sisters were sixteen, and her brother was nineteen. Harper was quiet and shy. After his father brought the girls here, Harper stayed close, even with college. Jonathan told her to pick the college of her dreams. She chose Savannah State, and she lived at the main house. After graduating with honors in business administration and premed, she still chose to not leave.

Colin vividly remembered the day he found out that she was his biological sister—same father, different mothers. They were sitting on the porch and chatting about school when his father brought it up. Harper already knew, but it was the first time Colin heard the news. Normally, he would have been a smartass with some snarky remark; instead, he smiled and hugged her tightly. He told her he knew there was a reason why they were the best-looking McGowan kids; the two of them took after their father, and the others looked like their mothers.

Harper had shoulder-length, light brown hair. She was built like her sisters, one was a model the other very athletic, and Harper fell somewhere in between. Colin always thought she was cute as a little sister should be with a demeanor that was 100 percent like their father's. Her mind was brilliant. Everything she did was fully calculated for the best outcome. What everyone had come to learn was that Harper had an uncanny ability to know things before they happened.

Matthew spoke, "Harper, I must fly to Chicago for a day, but I will be coming back here to fix that room for Tess's daughter. Would you like to help me with that? I could certainly use a female perspective on this. You could fly up to Chicago with me too if you want."

"We won't be seeing Taryn if I go with you?"

"No." He shook his head. "Absolutely not."

"Okay," she perked up.

When the front door opened, Jack stepped out smiling the moment he saw her. "Hi, Harper."

"Hi, Jack." Harper walked past Colin as if he didn't even exist. "I hear you are going to pick up Tess with Colin."

"I am." He nodded, placing a hand on her shoulder. "Stay here at the house while we're gone, okay?"

"Matthew's taking me to Chicago for a day, and then we will come back here," she told him.

"Just stay close to him please." His hand slid down her arm until her hand was in his. "Be safe."

Matthew and Colin looked at each other and smiled. They saw what was happening and wondered if Jack and Harper were aware.

"Pilot's ready. Time to go." Jack squeezed Harper's hand and let her go.

CHAPTER 8

The busy sidewalk café sold simple foods and specialty coffees and teas. Tess would have to guess that they did rather well with their revenues. The café in Pioneer Square had become her favorite place in Portland to sip tea and read in the early afternoons. Umbrellas protected the few customers who actually took breaks from their busy lifestyles.

A cool breeze blew off the Willamette River, through the towering buildings, to keep things rather pleasant on the early September afternoon. Faithfully, she read her book as she did every day while Savannah napped in her stroller or in Grey's arms. Occasionally, she would put it down and watch the people who walked by. Many businesses were in the area, and everyone seemed cloned with the same goal in mind: money.

For Tess, each endless day was followed by another, heading in no particular direction as she had no goals at this point in her life. The only thing changing was her age. She was a mother. Would that count as a profession now? Knowing her actions had put her in that situation, she would continue to make the best of it until it changed. With a sigh, she watched the faceless people, but she wondered how many of them had stories of tragedy, love, and misfortune. Were any of them happy? She sighed deeply, knowing the answer would never drop from the sky into her waiting hands.

As she watched Greyson Parker holding her daughter, a calmness always settled in knowing they were safe with him. Savannah had her head on his shoulder, and he rubbed her back softly as she slept. It amused her every time she saw Grey with Savannah. He was 6' 3" and all muscle. He was James's number one man in the field. When he wasn't working with James, he was a contractor. When James first put her under, Grey was finishing up a row of townhomes on the outskirts of downtown by the river. Even though Grey had a beautiful home on the hills overlooking Portland, he occupied the one beside her to remain close when Colin was back East. After three years, Grey had become a permanent fixture in their lives.

Glimpsing at her watch that Colin gave her last Christmas, she marked her place in her book and began to finish her tea. With her eyes wandering through the busy streets, someone tapped her on her shoulder. Surprised, without delight, she turned.

"Ms. McGowan." Jack smiled at her and felt the butt of steel against his rib cage.

"Jack." Tess popped up out of her seat. "Grey, it's okay. Jack is James's cousin."

Grey eyed Jack up and down.

"Your look of intimidation might work better if you didn't have a baby sleeping in your arm," Jack stated with a grin.

"I can take you out just as easily with or without baby girl in my arms," Grey told him, taking a seat at the table.

Tess hugged Jack tightly. It had been three very long years since seeing him.

"You had a baby?" Jack asked, stunned.

Tess nodded. "Savannah Grace. Not that I don't love the fact that you're here, but why?" She looked around for anyone suspicious. "Am I in danger?"

Jack nodded. "Time to come home. Colin dropped me off and went to park. He said you would be in the area."

"Oh my goodness." She sighed, sitting down. "I've become predictable."

"No, you haven't." He looked at the child in Grey's arms.

Tess smiled as she looked at her daughter.

"Wow," Jack said. "I can't believe he kept this from me."

"Yes, well." She shrugged. "We've done what we've had to for her safety."

Jack sat across from her. "You look great. How have you been?"

"Good, considering the circumstances." She smiled as an instant pang of emotions hit her. "I still can't believe you are here. Did you get married yet? Girlfriend, anything? You're still as handsome as ever."

Jack smiled and caught the look she gave him. It was that needing and wanting look that he hadn't seen in a long time. Their eyes hooked and didn't leave each other for a moment. Without a word, Jack watched her stand and walk over to him. Leaning over, she hugged him tightly.

"I've missed you so much," she whispered.

Jack felt a lump in his throat as he raised her head and caressed her cheek. "I've missed you too. Colin's coming."

Tess took a deep breath before taking her seat.

"That's a mighty big ring on that all-so-very-important finger. And since you aren't the one to wear jewelry, mind sharing?" Jack asked.

She smiled and looked down at her hand. "He didn't tell you?"

"He apparently hasn't told me anything." Jack shook his head slowly.

"I am surprised." She looked at the beautiful diamond on her finger. "Colin."

"Engaged or married?" Jack asked as Colin walked up to them.

Tess felt Colin's hands rest gently on her shoulders. She tilted her head, watching Jack as Colin gave her a kiss on the cheek. He pulled a chair up and sat to her left, taking her hand in his.

"Hi." Tess smiled at him.

"Hi, baby. How's everything been?" Colin glanced at Grey.

"Quiet," Grey replied for Tess. "Most of the time."

"Did you tell him yet, Tess?" Colin brought her hand to his lips, kissing it softly.

"He just asked if we were engaged or married." She raised her eyebrows.

"Well, maybe this will answer that question." Pulling out his wallet, he took his platinum band from the inside, and put it on his left hand. "Married."

Jack smiled. "Finally. How long have you been married?"

"Three years," Tess answered.

"She was four months pregnant," Colin added.

Jack thought back in time. "That makes sense. Wintertime?"

Colin nodded. "Why do you think that?"

"A few years ago, you were gone for three weeks in the winter. That's the longest time you've ever been away without any communication with your father. When you came back, you were different. I knew it had something to do with Tess. A few months after that, you came back after one of your two-week stints with a wedding band. No one else caught it but me, and I still remember you slipping it off inconspicuously during the meeting with your father. Right or wrong?"

Colin laughed a little as Tess answered. "Right." Tess glanced at the time. "When do we leave?"

"Sunday," Colin replied.

"Let's go Saturday after the four o'clock service," Tess suggested.

"That's fine."

"Are you going to church again?" Jack asked.

"Yes." She nodded and looked at Grey with a smile. "Grey's family reminds me a lot of Jonathan and Gina. I miss them, and you know how they were with church on Sundays."

Jack smiled. Jonathan and Gina always went to church on Sundays and sometimes in the middle of the week. They encouraged all their kids to attend; it gave them a sense of peace to know God was always there.

"We'll take Jack with us so he can meet them." Colin kissed her hand. "And this way, you can let them know you'll be gone for a while."

"We'll come back when it's all over though, right?" This was a question she asked knowing they hadn't spoken about the future.

"Absolutely," he began. "This is our home. We're not raising Savannah in the South. At this point, our baby is going to melt in the humidity."

Colin picked up Savannah from Grey and sat back down. He liked to cuddle her up in his arms. Kissing the sleeping child on the forehead, he looked over at Grey. "I was wondering if you would like to fly back with us until this is over? You and Tess have protected Sav down to an art. I would hate to break that up before this is done."

Grey smiled. "I'm not going to know what to do with myself when this is over. Of course, I'll go with them. James called me a couple weeks ago about all of this. Change was coming."

"Thank you." Colin nodded. "I was hoping for that answer."

"No wonder you are happy to come out here." Jack looked at Colin. "You two have the whole family thing going on. This I didn't expect."

"Not exactly what we expected in the beginning either, but with James's help and Grey, it's worked out." Colin rubbed Savannah's back gently.

"James knows about all of this?" Jack asked.

"Yes, he's helped us since she was shot. He gave her the new identity and took care of everything," Colin answered, catching a slight irritation in Jack's voice. "Can you give us a minute, Tess?"

Tess nodded and walked off with Grey.

"Do you want to know why I didn't tell you?" Colin asked.

"Yes." Jack admitted, shaking his head.

"It was too close to the baby she lost," Colin said the words his friend wouldn't. "You took that one hard. And I don't know if it's your own intuition because that baby was yours or not. I have no idea. I didn't want to ... hurt you. I already know how hard it was for you to walk away from her when you did and leave her with me—the one who kept taking her for granted. I figured it was just easier if we left Tess out of our conversations for a while."

Jack nodded. "Three years of not talking about her?"

"Yes, three years," Colin confirmed. "I had to do what I thought was right to keep her safe. That is why Matthew just found out about his daughter. If someone should be pissed, it should be him."

"The baby's not yours?" Jack asked.

"Nope, I thought he could use a couple days to absorb that information."

* * *

95

After Colin tucked in Savannah, he made his way to their room. Tess was drawing a bubble bath and lighting candles as she slowly took off pieces of clothing. She was down to her shirt and panties when he walked in and leaned against the door. Tess hadn't changed much since he first met her ten or eleven years ago. He couldn't really remember how long ago it was. Her mousy brown hair went down to the small of her back. She was always styling it a different way. Tonight, she pulled it up into a bun. Since she had Savannah, her body had more curves, which he found incredibly sexy. Living in the Northwest, her skin had just a hint of summer glow, nothing like it used to be in Atlanta. She was nearly 5' 10", which worked perfectly with his 6' 1", especially when she wore heels. Without any hesitation, he slipped his hands around her waist and pulled her close. She smelled so sweet and sensual. He closed his eyes as he buried his head into the nape of her neck.

"Mmm," he mumbled. "You are so beautiful, my wife."

"Mr. McGowan, will you loosen your hands long enough so I can turn around and kiss you?" His hands relaxed enough for her to spin around and face him. "I love you."

"I love you too." Their lips met with a passion that grew more and more with every encounter. He helped her out of the rest of her clothes, stripped off his, and slipped into the bath.

The kissing and caressing continued for half an hour. Tess leaned back against his chest as they soaked in the bubbles. With her hair pulled up, he kept nipping and kissing her neck, which she loved.

"How long have you been awake?"

"Working for almost forty hours." With a deep sigh, he leaned back and closed his eyes.

"At least you can sleep well tonight and sleep in tomorrow." She turned her head up and kissed him.

"I always sleep better when I am sleeping next to you." He kissed her neck softly.

"Jack is good," Tess noted. "He has that look, like he knows."

"Mmm." Colin was still nipping at her neck. "Speaking of Jackson, what exactly was that I saw when I walked up today?"

Tess turned to face him. "I don't know, but there was this

overwhelming feeling of … something. When I saw him, I think all these feelings of missing him came back all at once and hit me … hard. You know how I felt about him, and you know the last time we spoke I was so mad with him. All those old feelings resurfaced when I saw him."

"Should I be worried about this?" Colin asked.

"Seriously? Like you even have to ask that question." She shook her head. "I'm in love with my husband—you know that. Jack and I have an unfinished conversation."

"I don't want to repeat four years ago with him and you." Colin took her hands in his. "Bad things will happen, and you know I haven't hurt anybody in years."

A smile crossed her lips, and she kissed him softly. "Nothing's going to happen between Jack and me. I promise you."

"You are mine and only mine. My vows to you remain solid—till death do us part. And I'm hoping it's a long way away because I want a normal life for us and our children."

"Me too," she agreed.

"Speaking of children, are you pregnant?" Colin just popped that question out of nowhere.

"Damn it, Colin." Tess pursed her lips. "I don't know. I was going to see Jo next week and have a test, but now we are leaving. I wanted to surprise you if I was. How do you even suspect?"

"I know your body very well." He jetted his brows upwards, running his fingers over her stomach. "And you have this little poochy tummy thing happening that wasn't there a month ago."

"A huge part of me doesn't want to go back. I like our life here. Everything gets complicated when you add family." Tess ran her hands down his thighs.

"Tess, whatever happens, when you are feeling vulnerable, unsure, or scared, remember that I am there for you. You are my wife now, and I will go to hell and back with you—just like before. As long as I am still breathing, you will never be alone."

"I love you with every inch of my being." She turned, gently touching his face.

"I love you and Savannah." He kissed her. "And you're avoiding the baby talk, which I will let go—for now."

"Thank you." She kissed him. "Let's get out of here so I can have my way with your body."

Colin grinned, never denying her what she wanted.

✳ ✳ ✳

At one in the morning, Tess went downstairs. Jack was on his laptop. First, she went to the kitchen, poured herself a glass of water, then sat beside him on the couch.

"I heard you get up," he said without looking at her.

"Of course, you did," she replied, watching the screen. "What are you doing?"

"Just checking in with my men. You know." He stopped and looked at her. "That is a huge glass slider. It doesn't seem safe to me."

"It's bulletproof," she apprised him. "Grey and Colin added a few extra safety measures. He struggled so much in the beginning with this mess. He did not like leaving me at all, especially pregnant. Having Grey around helped ease his anxiety a little."

"So, Matthew's a father?" Jack asked her.

"Yep." Tess nodded slowly. "How has he been?"

"He's okay. He loved you very, very much. It hasn't been easy for him since you left, but he's managing."

"Not the answer I was hoping for." Tess felt a heaviness in her heart.

"It is what it is, T." Jack took her hand in his. "You know the one good thing that has come out of all this?"

Tess shook her head.

"Colin and Matthew have made amends. And that is a very good thing."

"Have you seen Taryn at all?" she asked.

Jack laughed. "You know I try to distance myself from her at all costs. She is nothing but trouble. From what I do know, your sister had been sleeping with Matthew for a while there."

"What?" Tess felt nauseated at the mere thought.

"Yep," Jack confirmed. "I don't think anybody in the family knows. Hell, they both live in Chicago. I don't know how they met, but I went to see Matthew one day at his office—and she came strolling in like they had been together for years. It was really fuckin' weird. I didn't investigate it any further because I just didn't care enough. I figured if Matthew was stupid enough to tap that shit, he gets to deal with whatever crap she brings."

"She has been a pain in my ass since our parents died." Tess shook her head.

Jack looked at her without speaking. She looked exactly as he remembered. The last visit at Carina's flashed through his mind: the kissing, the touching, the morning she was sick, laying in bed with her curled up in his arms as they talked.

"Are you okay?" Tess asked.

Jack nodded. "This whole mess with you has been very … stressful and frustrating. The way we left things was horrible. I heard from Gina that you had been shot and were being put under. Jonathan disappeared for a couple weeks, and then Colin was gone too. James wouldn't return any of my calls for three weeks. It was awful."

"It was like nothing I'd ever experienced," her voice was soft. "The pain was … let me just say that I was glad when I passed out."

"I never wanted you to have to experience anything like that."

Tess pursed her lips, put her head on his shoulder, and whispered, "I missed you."

"I missed you too." He closed his eyes and kissed the top of her head.

CHAPTER 9

Saturday Night, Day 3

Tess was curled up in the corner of the couch in Jonathan's library thumbing through a small photo album. They had arrived at the Savannah plantation just before midnight. Thankfully for Tess, only Jonathan and Gina were home—along with the dozen or two security guards who were strategically placed around the property. She thought Harper would be there, but she learned that Matthew had taken her into Atlanta for some shopping and wouldn't be back until tomorrow. It was weird for her to think of Matthew hanging out with her little half-sister.

She remembered sitting in this room every Sunday morning, after church, with Jonathan as he read the paper and she studied. It was a much simpler time. Tonight, she wanted to catch up with Jonathan. Colin offered to put Savannah to bed so she could take this time with his father. Part of her, admittedly, was a little bit nervous.

"Ah, Tess." Jonathan strolled in with a glass of wine for each of them. "Here you go, sweetheart. I've missed you very much."

Tess gave him a hug. "I've missed you too." She took her glass back to the couch. "It has been a long three years."

She studied Jonathan's facial features. For a man in his early sixties, he still looked charming, radiating an upper-class demeanor that only Colin had come to compare with these days. His hair was a charcoal gray, receding slightly at the temple, and hung around the back of his neck. Dark eyebrows lined perfectly over his signature dark blue eyes. A few wrinkles creased his forehead—she was certain they came from her after he received custody—and two more outlined his mouth. His lips were thin, yet warm, and his skin was as tan as Colin's.

"So." He sat back in his chair. "I want to know about you and my son."

As the smile emerged from her lips, she sat back in her chair, leaving one hand fidgeting with her glass. "I don't know what to say. Something happened, something changed after I was shot. I love Colin very, very much. And I hope you are good with that."

"My darling, Tess." Jonathan smiled. "I didn't bring you in here to tell you I disapproved. I wanted to speak with you because I have noticed the difference in my son since you went away. And now I know that the difference in him was because of you. He is happy again—happier than I have ever seen him before. I am thrilled."

"Thank you." She breathed out relief. "I was a little concerned that you might not approve, given my history with Matthew."

"My sons were in a very bad place with each other, but I have to say—given the current situation—they have begun to mend their relationship a bit. And as a father, that is all I can hope for at the moment."

"How's Gina?"

"Busy, but good. She missed you. She is thrilled to have a grandchild around."

"May I ask you something personal?"

"Of course."

"How did you and Gina meet?"

"That's not personal." He gave her a silly look, and she shrugged. "Well, we have Colin to thank for that. I had a very important merger I was working on in Atlanta when Colin was sixteen. It was back in the days when I had my little four-seater Bonanza plane. I was flying myself every day to the city for work."

"Why didn't you stay there during the week like you do now?" Tess pulled her legs up, wrapping her arms around them.

"I didn't want Colin and Matthew going to the schools in the city. They did well in the public schools here, and I made the choice years before to not uproot them during the school years. Once they started, I wanted them to continue with the same kids, same atmosphere. My work came second. I had an afternoon meeting that continued past seven-thirty this one night. I called Colin and said I wouldn't be home until ten or eleven. That was fine with him because he was going to the movies with his friends and wouldn't get home until eleven-thirty. Matthew was already in his second year of college.

"Lieutenant Donnelson called a few minutes after I got home to tell me there was a car accident. Colin had wrapped his '67 Mustang around a tree. Gina was the surgeon that night. Colin had a ruptured spleen, broken ribs, and a concussion that caused swelling on his brain. He was not in very good shape. He was in surgery for five hours, ICU for three days, and finally went into a regular room for ten days. I didn't leave the hospital for the first five days. Gina would go off shift, come back ten hours later, and I was always there. We just clicked.

"I finally got up the nerve to ask her to dinner, but she declined. She was working from three in the afternoon until three in the morning, five or six days a week. So, I asked her to breakfast and picked her up from work at three-fifteen in the morning. Within four months, we were living together and married within a year. When that call came in from Adam, Gina was right beside me."

"I remember." Tess bowed her head slightly. "She didn't seem too certain about how to handle us. I know she didn't want to overstep her boundaries. She wanted to mother us, but with what happened to our mother, she seemed to recede. I still think she's great."

"So do I," Jonathan agreed.

"May I ask what happened to Colin's mother? I know Matthew's mother died when he was almost three years old, but Colin never speaks of his mother."

"Adalyn Crandall is his mother's name." Jonathan took a sip of his wine as he thought back. "Addie decided when Colin was three and Matthew was almost seven that this wasn't the life she wanted—being a wife and mother. I came home one day from work, and the boys were with the babysitter. Addie had packed up and left while the boys napped. Colin only remembers bits and pieces of her, but Matthew remembers much more. He had a hard time with that. She was the only mother he knew. He and Gina have gotten close over the past ten years—but not in the beginning. Colin is fine with Gina but not as close as Matthew is with her.

"After she left, I really didn't have any desire to meet anyone else, so I didn't. I didn't want to put the boys through something like that again, especially being so young and impressionable. They deserve better. For years it was just the boys and me. And it worked out pretty good."

"Thank you for sharing that with me. Can I ask you something else?" she asked, tipping her head to the side a bit.

"Anything." He took a sip of his wine.

"Are these pictures of Matthew's mom?" She pointed to pictures in a photo album.

"Yes," he replied with a smile.

"She was beautiful," Tess said softly, looking at the pictures again.

"Yes, she was," Jonathan smiled. "Isobelle had this very subtle accent that Matthew has as well."

"I noticed that." Tess smiled. "Who is the other little boy in the picture?"

"Nicholas," Jonathan answered. "He was six months old when I met her. I raised him as my own until the accident."

"Oh my goodness." Tess looked up at him slowly. "He was in the car?"

"Yes." He nodded. "Matthew had been sick, so he was home with me that day. Isobelle had picked up Nicholas from school and was on her way home when it happened. They thought his little body had washed out to sea."

"I'm so sorry." She felt a tear fall at the mere thought of losing her own child. "I had no idea. What do you mean they *thought*?"

"He's still alive," Jonathan began watching her closely. "Kidnapped by his biological father, Marcos Markenna."

Tess froze.

"When you came to me years ago about Dominic, the name was too much of a coincidence. His birth name is Dominic. Isobelle changed it when she left South America to Nicholas. I've been having it all investigated for the past four years."

"I loved my time with him," she admitted softly. "He was very ... good to me, better than I was to him. I truly loved him."

Jonathan nodded. "I know. I could tell when you spoke to me about him. I'm sorry for asking you not to ever see him again. I wasn't sure how much his father had influenced him over the years, and I wouldn't risk your life until I knew."

"I understand." She grinned. "I still spent a few days with him afterward. It wasn't to defy you. I just needed to close things between us somehow."

"I understand. I was just concerned for your safety. You know all a parent wants—"

"Is for their children to be happy and safe." She smiled, finishing his sentence.

Jonathan smiled as he nodded. "And you now know this because you are a mother."

"Yes, sir." She nodded. "Although I want Savannah happy, her safety is my first concern."

"As it should be given this situation," Jonathan said.

* * *

Day 4, Sunday Morning

The strides were long and solid with her breath steady, even. She focused on each breath, taking in the cool, crisp morning air. The trees were just beginning to change color. Hundreds of oaks were on the McGowan property, and the grounds were mowed regularly to give the illusion of a lawn. It worked, she thought, noticing how it looked like a lawn for as far as she could see. She ran on a running trail by the fence. Everyone in the house used the trail for either running or riding bikes. The thick, black, iron fence was ten feet high. It sometimes felt like she was in prison. Today, it made her feel safe, especially with the guards every two hundred yards.

Tess rounded the long turn and came upon the main gates. Jonathan had two security guards at the main gate 24/7. They had an office that was housed on the perimeter, accessible from both sides of the gate with a key code only. The office was made of brick and bulletproof glass. It always reminded her of the fairy tale about the three little pigs with a twist. They could huff and puff, but that building wasn't coming down without a rocket launcher.

Tess stopped near the gate, noticing the black Audi that was waiting for the gates to open. Carefully, she walked closer wanting to get a look at the driver, but she stayed slightly tucked behind the corner of the building. Matthew had a car just like that. When the car pulled inside the gates she saw him, and their eyes connected. Her heart stopped, and they stared at each other.

It had been three years, yet she still felt a pull toward him in her heart. She wanted to walk up and hug him, but would he hug her back? Or was he angry about everything that had happened?

Matthew got out of the car, and Jack watched them cautiously, noting that Tess and Matthew had not taken their eyes off each other.

"T," he whispered, and she began to walk toward him.

When they were directly in front of each other, both hesitated.

"I've missed you," she whispered, wrapping her arms around his shoulders tightly and felt his hands come around her back as he hugged her.

Harper got out of the car and watched the reunion with Jack.

"Jack, who should she be with?" Harper was curious about her sisters' love life.

Jack took Harper's hand and began, "Tess always belonged with Colin. Matthew is something that happened before Colin could figure out just how much he loved her. Even though he married Tess, he gets to live with the fact that she loved his brother at one point—and Savannah is Matthew's daughter."

Colin's voice came over Jack's radio.

"Yes?" Jack answered not surprised that Colin was watching on a screen.

"Do I need to be worried?" Colin asked, watching his wife and brother on the surveillance camera on his tablet.

"I don't know." Jack grinned to himself. "Keep watching. It's like one of those chick flicks. I'm not certain what's going to happen next. Will it be the older brother or the younger brother?"

"Thanks," Colin replied with a chuckle. "I feel so much better now."

"Stop stalking her," Jack reminded him. "And trust her."

Tess pulled back, wiping the tears from her cheeks and eyes.

"I never liked it when you cried." Matthew released a held breath.

"I know." She grinned slightly. "Sorry. I wanted to tell you myself, but I never got the chance. I'm sorry it had to come from your brother."

"It doesn't matter," his voice was a mere murmur as his hand caressed across her cheek. "You're still alive, and that's the only thing that matters."

"I've missed … oh my gosh." She put her hand over her mouth, ran behind the guard house, and vomited.

Jack ran over to her before Matthew and Harper even registered what was happening. As she continued to vomit, he waved off Matthew and Harper.

"Harp?" Jack called her. "Will you get a bottle of water from inside and a towel?"

"Can I do anything?" Matthew asked.

"Yep." Jack nodded. "Get your brother down here."

"Is she okay, Harper?" Matthew asked after calling his brother.

"Yes." She smiled. "I'll bet you lunch that she's pregnant."

"Okay." He returned the smile. "Although you're probably right."

"And I want lunch somewhere like in Paris."

"Paris?" He shook his head. "How about Italy instead?"

"That would be even better. Let's go to Rome. I've always wanted to go there and see the ruins."

"As you wish, sweet Harper." He gave her a one-armed hug and a kiss on the forehead.

Colin drove up in his jeep and went straight over to Tess and Jack.

When he was certain that she was through being sick, he helped her up. She rinsed her mouth out with the water and wiped her face with the towel.

"You didn't have to come down here," Tess stated with slight irritation.

"Really?" Colin smirked.

"I'm throwing up," she said softly. "It's kind of embarrassing."

"I don't care." Colin cupped her face gently. "I saw you give birth. This is nothing."

"Very true." She smiled at him. "This is very weird."

"I know." He hugged her. "I've been watching you on the camera."

"Nice." She looked up at him. "I've got myself a stalker husband."

"Sorry." He ran a hand over her hair. "My brother with you is my only insecurity."

"That is an insecurity that you need not have," she reminded him.

"I try not to." His hand rested on her shoulder.

"Trust me, like I trust you."

"I do." He eyed her. "I really think you're pregnant."

She looked at him for a moment and shrugged. "That's the only time I throw up." Tears filled her eyes, and she shook her head.

"Baby, what's wrong?" he asked, pulling her close.

"Timing." She rested her head on his shoulder. "Can we not talk about this right now?"

"Let's go take a shower together before Sav wakes up," Colin suggested.

Tess stepped back and rested her hands on her knees and breathed out slowly.

Jack knelt before her. "Tess, what's wrong?"

"Everything is spinning," she answered.

"Okay." He looked up at Colin. "Take her back to the house. I'll follow. My medical bag is there. I'll check her out."

"I'll come with you," Harper interjected.

Colin scooped her up in his arms. Jack opened the door on the jeep, Colin put her on the seat, and closed the door. He looked over at his brother and shrugged.

"One second, Colin," Harper said, walking over to Matthew. "Are you okay?"

"Of course," Matthew replied.

"I'm going to ride back with Tess and Colin. You can just leave my stuff in the car. I will get it later. I don't want you to have to deal with it. Okay?"

"Harper," Matthew began. "It's not a big deal. Jack will ride back to the house with me, and we'll take care of it. You just go catch up with Tess. Don't worry about anything else."

"Thank you," Harper said, giving Matthew's hand a squeeze. "And thank you, Jack." She gave his hand a squeeze and held his eyes for an extra moment.

"I didn't do anything," Jack noted.

"But you will." Harper smiled and went back to Tess and Colin.

Matthew shook his head as they drove off. "Harper is definitely different from the others."

"I have been around that girl for the past ten years, and I still can't figure her out," Jack stated perplexed.

"You know Harper likes you," Matthew tossed out there curious for Jack's answer.

"I like her too." Jack shrugged.

"Okay." Matthew faced him. "We're not going to do this like we are sixteen. Harper is in love with you. She all but directly said it when we were in Chicago. And I know you like her too. I've watched you watch her."

"She is like your sister though." Jack shook his head.

"She *is* my sister." Matthew grinned. "You probably didn't get that memo. Do you really think I would be telling you this if I didn't want you to be the one by her side?"

Jack gave him a sideways glance. "Between you and me, I've been in love with Harper for a couple years."

CHAPTER 10

Tess stood in the shower with the hot water running down her back. The dizziness had gone away by the time they got back to the house, and all she wanted was a shower. As Colin joined her, she closed her eyes as a small smile emerged. Running her hands along his arms, she enjoyed feeling every muscle tighten as their kiss heated up and he pulled her body against his. She moaned, feeling every hard part of his body.

Colin cradled her face in his hands prompting her eyes to open. "I'm ready to go back to Portland now."

Tess grinned, shook her head, and pulled his lips back to hers.

The shower lasted until the water started going cold. Quickly, they washed up and got dressed.

"I'll go check on Savannah and meet you in the kitchen." Tess went across the hall to Savannah's room. Not wanting to wake her, she was surprised to find her bed empty. She sighed and went downstairs to find her daughter. "Colin, Sav isn't in her room—"

Much to her surprise, she saw her daughter sitting on Matthew's lap at the kitchen table.

"Mommy!" Savannah happily called out. "Daddy has a brother. His name is Matthew."

"Really?" Tess replied with a smile as Colin handed her a cup of coffee.

Savannah asked, "Can I have one too?"

Tess nearly choked on the coffee and looked at Colin with a smile. "Absolutely." Tess picked up Savannah, gave her a kiss on the cheek, and handed her to Colin. "Matthew, let's go for a walk."

Matthew followed her out on the patio and closed the doors behind them wanting a little privacy. He sucked in a deep breath, closed his eyes for a moment, and ran his fingers over his dark hair. "A daughter?" he asked.

"Were you wanting a son?" she asked.

"No—but I wasn't expecting a daughter."

"So, in your head, is this a good or bad thing? We can leave this with Colin being her father," she told him.

"No, no...this is very good." He smiled. "I needed something like this in my life. If I can't have you, at least I got to have a child with you." He tilted his head as he looked at her.

Tess smiled and hugged him tightly. "I missed you."

"I missed you too." He stepped back, taking her hands in his. "You are even more beautiful now than before. Being a mom has changed you."

"Being pregnant changes you." She smiled.

He looked at her tummy. "Are you?"

"Yes." She smiled.

"You love him?" He had to ask, dropping one of her hands as they walked down to the pier.

"I do." She pursed her lips. "I did for a long time before we even met. He just had commitment issues to work through. I had reached a point where I was done waiting for him to figure it all out, and that's when I went to Chicago. I needed time away from him, and when I met you, you gave me everything I was wanting in a relationship."

They stood on the pier and looked out at the water.

Matthew looked at her. "If he hadn't picked you up, would you have stayed?"

"Yes." She nodded, sucking in her bottom lip to keep from crying.

"You know you've changed him?" Matthew stood in front of her.

"That's what Jonathan said too." She looked down at his hands.

"He is a better man because of you." Matthew pulled her into his arms and buried his head into the nape of her neck.

Her eyes could barely see over his shoulder. As she gazed across the lake at the tree-lined water's edge, she caught a glimpse of something reflecting off the sun. "I want you to be in Savannah's life as her father," Tess said, pulling back slightly to look at him. "But Colin is her father too. This is something you both will have to learn to share—and not for your sake or his but for her."

"I know." Matthew nodded. "We'll make it work."

"So, have you known Jack as long as Colin has?"

"Yes," Matthew answered. "You know Carina?"

"Yep, Jack was my best friend." She shrugged. "We would do a job and then go hang out with Carina for a few weeks all the time. I met Harrison and James too. He saved my life once before."

"Harrison's my attorney," Matthew stated. "And friend. How did James save your life?"

"Four years ago, I had a miscarriage and hemorrhaged badly. We were at Carina's, and he was the only one there to help me."

"I had no idea." Matthew ran a sympathetic hand over her arm. "James and I are good friends and have been since college. He never said anything about knowing you when I called him that night. Wait until I see him again. Colin never said anything about losing a baby."

"He handled it pretty well," Tess stated.

"You never ran into James or Harrison when you were in Chicago with me?"

"No." She shrugged. "It's kind of surprising because that would have opened everything right then and there. At least I know why I was so attracted to you."

"Why?"

"You two are so much alike." She grinned. "The only difference is that you weren't afraid to tell me how you really felt."

Matthew looked out on the lake and realized they shouldn't be out on the pier. It was too open. Anyone could be watching them from across the lake.

"I saw something reflect from the other side." Tess stood behind him.

"We shouldn't be out here ..."

A shot rang out, and an incredible burning sensation ripped through his chest and into Tess. Lunging forward, he gathered her up in his arms before she fell. Then, he felt another burning sensation a bit lower on his back, but he wasn't sure if it hit Tess. With her tucked in his arms, he jumped into the water. They ducked under the pier for cover since it was closer than any of the trees.

Colin witnessed the entire event as he was watching them through the kitchen window. Running out the back door, he was yelling orders to the guards.

An incredible pain seared through Matthew's body as he tried to focus on Tess. He lifted her chin. "Are you okay, Tess? Talk to me. You know how this works, baby."

Tess was so dizzy. "Matt—"

"Hey, stay awake!" He lifted her chin again, but she dropped it down. "Just a couple minutes, and we'll be out of here. I promise. Stay awake, T."

Once her head dropped again, she was out.

"Colin!" Matthew yelled.

"Matthew!" Colin ran toward the pier. "Tess!"

"She was hit," Matthew yelled. "Is it safe yet?"

Colin didn't wait for the jeep to get there. He told the guards to cover him, and he dove under the pier.

"Take her," Matthew said, handing her over. He was on the verge of passing out too.

"Jack," Colin yelled. "I'm coming out. You better have a cover."

"I do. Move!" He watched Colin's head come out from under the pier. Tess was unconscious in his arms. "Where's Matthew?"

"Right behind me!" When he looked back, he wasn't there. "Take her." He passed her to Jack, went back under the pier, grabbed Matthew by his shirt, and turned him over. "Damn it. Don't you even pull this shit!" Colin dragged him up the water's edge, and two of Jack's men helped carry him to the safety of the other side of the jeep. Colin felt for a pulse ... nothing. He looked for breathing ... again nothing. He ripped Matthew's shirt open and began CPR with Jack's help.

After two sets of compressions and breaths Matthew, finally, coughed up water, Jack turned him to his side. When he was done, Jack rolled him onto his back. Matthew's eyes opened for a brief moment and then rolled back. He was out again, but at least he was breathing.

"Load him up," Jack directed, noting Colin hadn't moved. "Get them to the front of the house to Gina." He rested a hand on Colin's shoulder. "Let's go. They aren't out of danger yet."

Colin nodded and got in the jeep.

Grey stood behind a tree with his scope, scanning the area across the lake. When he saw the sudden reflection of a tiny object, he pulled the trigger and waited for five more minutes. When there was no more movement, he went to check out the area. Maybe he got lucky and killed the sniper.

Gina, Harper, and Jonathan were waiting at the door. They had cleared off the dining room table and instructed the men to put Matthew there. Jack walked in with Tess in his arms and took her to the kitchen table.

Gina rested her hand on Colin's arm, "Colin, Savannah is up in her room. Go to her and let me do what I do best. Okay?"

Colin nodded but followed Jack into the kitchen. Jack had already ripped off her shirt and was inspecting the wound.

"Jack," his voice was soft. "She's pregnant. No drugs that will hurt the baby, please."

"I know." Jack placed the stethoscope on her lower abdomen. He moved it slightly and listened. His eyes slowly looked up at Colin, and he smiled. Holding the scope on her stomach, he let Colin listen to the fast pace of his baby.

Jack grinned, again, and focused his attention on the wound.

Gina directed her attention to Matthew. She did a quick analysis, made sure his pulse was steady, and had Harper start an IV. They turned him onto his stomach to get a better look at the wounds. One was straight through, which must have been the one in Tess, but it was bleeding badly. The other was on his lower left side. There was no visible exit, and she knew that was where she was going to start.

Harper stood beside her. "Gina, I can take care of this one." She pointed to the one without the exit. "You've trained me well. I can do this. You do the bleeder."

"You're positive?" Gina asked.

Harper nodded and Gina ran into the kitchen for Tess. "What do you have, Jack?"

"One shot into her upper chest. Her breathing is normal—so the bullet didn't hit her lungs and there are no major arteries. Going through Matthew the bullet slowed. I should be able to fix Tess while you take care of Matthew."

Tess stirred a bit, and her eyes fluttered open. "My ba—"

"Relax, Tess." Jack ran a hand over her cheek. "Let me take care of you."

"Jack, I am worried about the water causing infection. Push an antibiotic before you start."

"Okay," Jack agreed as Gina went back to Matthew. "Colin, pull out the tablet and look up this drug." Jack tossed him a small bottle with a long name on it.

Colin typed in the name, pulling up all the information on the medication. "Here." Colin handed the tablet to him.

Jack scrolled down to see if it was safe for pregnant women. It took a moment to find, but he nodded and filled a needle with the drug. "Now look up this one." He tossed him another bottle.

Jack used long forceps to pull out the bullet while Colin found the information on the other drug. He put the bullet on a piece of gauze, set it on the counter, took the tablet, and read the information. "Hmm." He pulled another small bottle from his medical bag and pulled the information up himself. Satisfied that this one was less of a threat to a pregnant woman, he filled another vial and gave her a small dose to help with the pain.

"You can go to Savannah and let me finish up. She'll be fine," Jack advised.

Colin ran his hand over her wet hair, kissed her lips softly, and whispered *I love you* before leaving.

* * *

Colin popped his head into Savannah's room. He was still dripping wet, but he wanted to check on her. "Hey, sweetie. Are you okay?"

Savannah nodded. "Grandma said to stay in here until you came. Can I come out yet?"

"Tell you what." He gestured for her to take his hand. "Why don't you come and watch cartoons in Mommy and Daddy's room while I take a shower. Sound good?"

She grabbed her small blanket, took Colin's hand, and went across the hall. He tucked her into the center of the bed, turned on cartoons, and grabbed some clean clothes. "I'll be quick. Holler if you need me."

Savannah nodded and directed her attention back to the cartoons.

Colin rested his hands on the tile and dropped his head under the stream of warm water. This was not how the morning was supposed to go. With all the things he had done in his life, this was the most intense. His brother had died, and they brought him back to life. It was clockwork the way they worked together. It was as if Jack could read his mind. Colin knew Tess would be fine in Jack's hands.

Jack had done a year of humanitarian aid with Gina about seven years before and another six-month stint with Gina and Harper four years ago. With his medical training in the service and the work he did in the field with Gina, he was as good as some surgeons. Colin trusted him with his life, and he certainly trusted him with Tess's.

And he heard his baby's heartbeat.

After the shower, he dressed, laid by Savannah, and fell asleep. The adrenaline rush had exited his body.

An hour later, Jack knocked on the door waking him up. "You seriously fell asleep? That is having a world of trust in me. I feel complimented. Thank you."

"Oh, shit," Colin mumbled under his breath. "How's Tess?"

"She's fine. I want to bring her up here. We need to clean up the kitchen before someone wants to come down." Jack glanced at little Savannah who dozed off beside him.

"Okay." Colin slipped out of the bed. "I'll come get her."

Colin followed Jack down the stairs. In the dining room, Gina was still working on Matthew. The place looked like a hospital in a war zone.

In the kitchen, Tess was asleep on the table. There was gauze, blood, tweezers, bandages, and wrappers strewn all around. And blood. There was no way Colin would let Savannah come down here.

"She's pumped full of antibiotics and a low dose of painkiller. When she wakes up, we will just give her ibuprofen—and maybe Harper has something in her magical garden that will help with pain and healing." Jack flashed a smile and laughed.

"Harper and her garden." Colin shook his head. "Thank you, Jack."

Jack smiled. "She will probably sleep the rest of the day and tonight. Maybe wake up tomorrow. But she'll be fine. I will be checking the baby's heart rate off and on."

Colin scooped her up in his arms and carried her upstairs. After peeling off the wet clothes, he tucked her into bed beside Savannah and headed back down to help clean up and see how Matthew was doing.

Colin stood at the doorway of the dining room. "How is he, Gina?"

"The bullet that went straight through clipped an artery. He has lost a lot of blood. He really needs a transfusion." She leaned against the wall, taking her gloves off.

"Have you ever done a human-to-human transfusion in the field?" Colin asked.

"Yes," she said slowly. "That's not my issue. He is AB-. He can only get blood from AB-, A-, B-, and O-."

Colin smiled. "I'm A-. Hook me up, Mom."

"Are you serious?" Gina looked at him sideways. "I thought you were A+."

"Nope, that's Jack and Tess."

CHAPTER 11

Tuesday, Day 5

Dominic leaned against the long window and looked at the city around him. It had been four long years since he saw her, and he never gave up on trying to find her. All he had to work with was her first name and the brief history she gave him about her parents being murdered when she was sixteen. Every time he thought of her, his mind wandered back to their last night together. Making love with her was always passionate and intense, but that last night was amazing. And there was no way any other woman would compare to her. How was he supposed to move on after having her, after loving her? In a way, he guessed that he hadn't because every time he was with someone else, he thought of her, which wasn't fair to the current love of his life.

Lost in his thoughts, he was surprised when he felt her arms come around him from behind. He smiled, placing one hand over hers.

"Darling, I was watching Connor so you could get some sleep this morning."

"And I did." She hugged him. "It's eight o'clock. This is the latest I've slept in two and half years. Thank you."

"You're welcome." He turned around and put his arms around her. "You're so beautiful."

"I'm the same as I was yesterday and the month before that and so on." She grinned, wrapping her arms around his shoulders.

"No." He shook his head. "You've changed since I first met you. I love you, and I don't want you to do this. I have a very bad feeling."

Taryn stepped away from him, sighing. "I'm not having this argument with you again. This has been in motion for years, and I'm almost done."

"What about Connor?" he asked.

"I've already made arrangements with the Devereaux's," she told him.

"I'll keep him," he offered.

"No." She shook her head. "He's not your responsibility. I will not burden you with him. You are in and out all the time anyway with work. We've already been through this. I'm not doing it again."

"I think of him as my own son. Don't tell me he isn't my responsibility," he insisted. "Let me stay with him. I don't think pawning him off on the Devereaux's is a good thing. Besides, have you forgotten that I sold my company?"

Taryn shook her head in frustration and walked into the kitchen for a cup of coffee.

Connor was watching cartoons on the floor.

"Come here, buddy." Dominic held his arms open. "Sit with me?"

Connor smiled and climbed up on Dominic's lap. Leaning back in his arms, the child continued to watch television.

Two years ago, he was thumbing through a magazine and saw what he thought was Tess. With the help of his investigator, he found her twin. Taryn lived in Chicago, and he managed to work his way into her life, never letting her know about his intimate knowledge of her sister. He learned everything about her from her sister's point of view, which he found to be very cruel. There was never a kind word out of Taryn's mouth about Tess. And after he had been seeing her for about a year, he learned that Taryn had shot her in the back. And when she heard that didn't kill her, she put a mark on her. Taryn was more than a little pissed when she realized that someone, other than the family, put Tess under—a new identity, a new life, and a new city. If Colin or Jack hid her, she would have been able to find her, but without them knowing, she was at a loss. She had hoped that by putting a mark on her and a million bounty with it, some ruthless, heartless person would find and finish her off. Every year that Tess continued to breathe, her sister added half a million dollars to the pot.

Dominic knew that if he could just hold out long enough, Tess would have to resurface, and then he could see her again and warn her. His time with Taryn was a bit rough in the beginning, but over the past couple years, he softened her quite a bit. She had a college education with a degree in accounting. Taryn always said that she lived off a trust fund, which allowed her to not work and stay home to raise her son. When he investigated her accounts, he could see that ten thousand dollars was deposited into her account every month on the first. Six months ago, he realized he truly loved her and was willing to abandon his hopes of rekindling a relationship with Tess if Taryn would just stop with this revenge plot.

"I'm sorry, Dominic." Taryn sat on the couch beside him and her son. "I don't want to fight with you about any of this."

"I don't understand why you can't just let this go." He kissed Connor's head. "You have a son and me. Let it go and live your life with us."

"I will, but not until this is over," she insisted. "I'm sorry if you don't understand, but this goes way back with her."

"What happens to him if something happens to you?" he asked.

She ran a soft hand over her son's arm. "Should something happen you are first for guardianship. If you don't want it, Harper would probably take him."

"What about his father?"

"What about him?"

"Don't you think he should know?"

She shook her head slowly. "He left me for another woman. He doesn't deserve to be a father to my baby."

"I will keep him." He hugged the little boy on his lap. "And I will keep him while you are gone. He's not going to the Devereaux's. He can go with me to Virginia."

"I'm not going to win this one with you, am I?" she conceded.

"Nope, so stop fighting me," he advised.

"I love you," she whispered.

"I love you too." He kissed her. "How's that nasty cut on your thigh feeling?"

"It hurts." She shrugged. "The doctor told me to come back if it wasn't feeling and looking better in a couple of days. Gina will hook me up when I get to Savannah."

"I wish I could make it better for you." He kissed her again.

"My own clumsiness." She shrugged. "It'll be fine."

Dominic sold his company when he learned that a few of the investors were filtering money gained from the sex-trafficking trade. Knowing he couldn't just fire them as clients without suspicion, he decided to sell. He wanted no ties to trafficking.

Having the money from the sale of his business, he wanted to invest it somehow—with someone he could trust. Who fits that description better than his half-brother? Matthew had developed a highly respectable reputation in the finance world, which he admired. He did find it interesting that he went back to their mother's maiden name years ago. He wondered if Matthew ever spoke to his father. Did they have a falling out? Was it just to separate him from McGowan Industries and make a name for himself?

Dominic's memories of Jonathan McGowan were all good. He remembered him as a very kind, loving father who took the time to teach his children things that their curious minds wondered about. There was always laughter and play. They were happy back then.

Then, somehow, he ended up with his biological father. He had no memory of how it happened. His father said his mother was dead, and Jonathan didn't want him anymore. Dominic believed him until he was an adult and investigated his mother's death. He was even more surprised to find out that he was dead as well. His father had lied, yet again. His memory slowly pieced itself back together over the years, and after he finished graduate school, having severed his ties with his father when he was seventeen, his life was rather good, with the exception of his obnoxious brother, Dimitri.

Dominic took her hand in his. "Tar, make sure you come back because we are getting married."

Taryn looked at him rather surprised.

"Is it so hard to believe that I love you that much?"

"Yes." She nodded, swallowing the lump in her throat. "No one has ever treated me the way you do. I keep waiting for you to walk away and be done."

"I'm not walking away." His hand caressed her cheek. "But you need to tell me who his father is, and I need to tell you a few things about my life. Are you sure you still must go?"

"Jonathan is expecting me," she answered with a sigh. "He never asks anything of me, and he has requested that I go to Savannah."

"You just got back Sunday night, and you're leaving again," he said. "Take us with you."

Taryn shook her head. "Not this time. It won't be safe. That family is full of mercenaries, and my sister is an assassin. There's no way I would take Connor there. If you're not 'in,' you're not protected. I've always been on the border, and if I show up with him, some will be fine with it, but some won't. Just keep him safe for me … please."

"I don't want you to go." He brought his arm around her shoulders, pulling her closer.

CHAPTER 12

Wednesday Evening, Day 6

Matthew's eyes slowly blinked open. He felt heavily drugged, but the events of being shot were very clear in his mind. As he tried to sit up, pain quickly announced itself in his back.

Gina came to his side. "Finally, you are awake."

"I love your voice, Gina. It reminds me of Sarah," he said with his eyes closed. "Have you heard from her at all?"

"Nope." Gina sighed. "It's been over six months since our last conversation. I wish she would come back to the States. I worry about her in those other countries."

He opened his eyes. "When this mess is over, maybe we should go visit her."

"Wouldn't that be a surprise?" Gina smiled.

"How long have I been out?" he asked.

"Just four days." She held his hand gently. "You developed a fever as I expected. We have been very worried."

"How's Tess?"

"Good actually." Gina sighed. "She spiked a fever like you. The bullet was lodged above her heart, but it missed everything vital. The lake water hurt you two the most."

"Help me get up."

"Of course, slowly though." Gina went to the bedside. "You know you coded on Colin down at the lake. If your ribs are cracked and hurting, that would be from your brother doing CPR."

"Doesn't feel too bad at the moment." Matthew took a deep breath. "Did he breathe for me too?"

"No." Gina smiled. "That was Jack."

"Great, another man's lips have touched mine."

"You don't remember anything?"

"Just handing Tess to Colin, and then … everything went black."

"Colin pulled you from the lake and started CPR. You're going to love this part even more. You have his blood pumping through your veins. We did a field transfusion between you two. It was pretty cool—if I say so myself."

"Wow." Matthew stood up slowly with his arm around Gina's shoulders. "Are you trying to tell me that my brother saved my life?"

"Something like that—twice." She smiled, and they carefully walked to the kitchen.

Matthew took a seat at the table and noticed Taryn slicing vegetables in the kitchen. Their eyes met for only a moment.

Jonathan took off his glasses. "You look like hell—but better than yesterday." He patted his arm carefully. "You've had us worried."

"Thanks, Dad," Matthew said. "Did anybody find the shooter?"

"No," Jonathan answered. "Grey pulled off a shot in that direction and actually wounded someone, but they got away. There was blood pooled in a couple places—enough for him to pull for a DNA test. Other than that, there was nothing left."

Matthew heard little feet running down the hallway. He completely forgot everything else except that beautiful little girl and her adorable giggle as she came up to him. "Hey, pretty girl." With ease, he pulled her onto his lap.

"I'm not supposed to touch you." She scratched her nose. "Daddy said you were hurt like Mommy. Are you better now?"

Matthew smiled. "I'm working on it."

"Mommy is still asleep." She leaned her head against his chest. "She's been sleeping a lot. Daddy let me sleep by her earlier."

"Mommy will be fine." He ran a soft hand up and down her back. "Sleeping is good for her. She will get better faster."

Colin walked into the kitchen. "Sav', what are you up to? Matthew isn't 100 percent better yet."

"She's fine," Matthew told him. "I actually picked her up."

"I'm hungry." Savannah looked up at Colin.

"I got it." Taryn was making dinner. "Here, she can nibble on some carrots."

"Thank you." Colin set the small bowl of carrots in front of Savanna and Matthew. "Jeanette Crandall from your office kept calling, like close to stalker calling, so I spoke with her. The Fetterly Corporation's stocks took a dive, and she wasn't sure what to do." Colin smiled at his brother. "So, Harper got on the phone with her and told her exactly what to do. They put a price on the buy."

"How much did the stock drop?" Matthew asked.

"About 41 percent," Colin answered.

"Wow," Matthew smiled. "This is going to be a steal. At least something good is happening out there. What price did Harper put on this?"

Harper walked into the room during the conversation. "I told her to start at $6.5 million but not to go above $8 million. You'll still make a decent profit off this. That company has been mismanaged for years. If you turn it around, it could be very profitable." Harper sat down at the table.

"Harper, I think you need to come work for me," Matthew suggested.

"Thanks, but I don't want to live in Chicago. That is way too close to her," Harper stated, eyeing her sister in the kitchen.

"Don't worry, Harp," Taryn said with a little sass. "I feel the same way."

"Did you call James?" Matthew asked.

"Yes, he is aware of everything and said that he must pick up something in Idaho before he heads here. It's weird that Jack is related to him ... and Harrison," Colin added.

"Those three men would do anything for Tess." Matthew smiled.

"Yes." Colin's eyes got wide. "I am very aware of that."

Matthew grinned and ran his hand through Savannah's soft hair, remembering how he used to do that with Tess and then Taryn. He laughed to himself. "This is such a fucked-up family we have."

Taryn's eyes shot up, listening to every word.

"Hey, language," Colin warned motioning to his daughter.

"Sorry, Sav," Matthew smiled. "Look at the conversation we are having at the kitchen table. Families don't do this. They don't have hit men at the table, twins that are drop-dead gorgeous with one who's afraid to pack on a pound and one who packs a 9 mm. And Harper is just mystifying. Our friends are mercenaries. Then we have this beautiful little girl." He lowered his voice. "I slept with Tess, I slept with Taryn, and now Tess is sleeping with, hell, married to my brother. Seriously, we need to get our stuff together and try to be somewhat normal because what we do will now influence little people." He gestured toward Savannah.

"Are you having a pre-midlife crisis?" Colin asked. "Savvy, come here, honey."

Savannah climbed down from Matthew's lap and went over to Colin where he picked her up with ease.

"How's my girl?" he asked, nuzzling her close.

"Rock me like a baby," she asked.

"Like this, my little snuggle bug?" He smiled at her, wrapped her in his arms, and rocked her back and forth.

Savannah nodded.

"Dinner will be ready soon." He kissed her forehead and looked back at Matthew.

"The only consistent thing in my life is my firm. Everything else is a mess or a lie." Matthew looked over at Taryn.

Jonathan glanced at his eldest son. "Matthew, what makes you happy? And it's not a question I want an answer to. It's a question you need to ask yourself. If you know what makes you happy, embrace it. Your life will be fine. I know you have your solid foundation, but happiness is the anchor. Tess touched your soul three years ago, and you've been broken ever since she left."

Matthew knew his father didn't interfere in their lives much, but when he had something to say, it was always good advice. And, as usual, he was right again. He needed to find out what made him happy. He looked over at Taryn. They had been seeing each other on and off for the last two years, but he just didn't feel for her the way he did for Tess. He couldn't bring himself to go further than dinner and sex. Seeing her tonight was the first time in almost a year.

After dinner, Matthew headed back to his room. He'd liked his room at his father's house since his father restored the home. The room was private and quiet with an attached sitting room that he turned into an office when he was younger. After ten years, his room was exactly the same.

Taryn walked in. "Hey."

"I'm sorry, Tar," Matthew rested his hand on her shoulder.

"Don't. I'm a big girl, and I know it was just sex. It doesn't matter anyway. I've been seeing someone else. It seems to be serious," she shared.

"Good." Matthew ran a hand down her arm. "You should be happy."

Taryn smiled, leaned over, and kissed him then left the room. "Thank you."

Matthew was completely exhausted and sat on the bed after she left. Taking a slow deep breath, he fought through the pain. This was the reason why he stopped the contract work years ago. After being shot in the shoulder and the pain associated, he wanted to avoid bullets flying around him. Besides, James ended their work association due to his own carelessness.

"Matthew?" Tess opened the door slowly and peeked in. "Mind if I come in?"

"There must be something with twins tonight." He waved her in. "You can stay and talk, but I really need to lie down."

"Of course." She walked over to help as he struggled to take off his shirt.

"Can you help me take off this shirt?" he asked.

Tess unbuttoned the shirt. Their faces were within inches of each other. Her fingers fumbled a moment, and she placed her hands on his cheeks. "I'm so sorry," she cried. "This is all my fault. If I hadn't—"

Matthew put his hands on her cheeks and wiped away her tears. "Don't. This is playing the what-ifs, and we don't do that with the past because it won't change anything. Besides, look what we have between us now: a daughter and a bullet." He kissed her forehead, put his arms around her shoulders, and hugged her.

"I loved you so much, Matthew," she told him softly. "I should have told you more."

"You didn't have to say it." He looked lovingly into her eyes. "I knew you did. You don't make love like we did, with so much passion, and not love each other. You just don't."

Tess nodded and pulled his sleeves down.

"Would you mind getting Gina? I really need something for the pain," he asked.

"Of course." Tess went back to the kitchen to find Gina.

A minute later, Tess came back as Matthew closed his eyes. Tess laid on the other side of the bed, holding his hand as she drifted off into a light sleep.

Gina came into his room ten minutes later and felt Matthew's forehead. "Looks like you're running a fever again."

"Just do what you do best, please." He couldn't even keep his eyes open.

"I'm going to check the wounds on your back," she said, opening her medical bag. "Sleep. I will take care of you."

"You always do," he mumbled, rolling to his stomach. "I wish you had been my mother when I was a kid."

"I wish I had been too." She slowly peeled a bandage off. "I am here now, and I don't have to be blood related to love you like my own son. Rest and I'll make you better."

Matthew felt her stick him with a needle twice, and he was out again.

A few minutes later, Gina noticed Tess's eyes fluttering open, "Hey, Tess. How are you feeling?"

"Tired, mentally," Tess replied as she stood and yawned. "How is he?" Her hand slowly ran down the length of his arm, stopping on his hand.

"His fever is back to 103." She pulled out her stethoscope and listened to his lungs. "His lungs actually sound better than this morning. This fever needs to break and be gone. It concerns me."

Gina left him on his stomach and covered him with one of the blankets. "Let me have a look at you, Tess." She took her temperature and listened to her lungs and heart. When she pulled the bandage off the wound, she was stunned. "Tess, what have you been putting on this?"

"Some weird thing that Harper made," she shared. "How is it?"

"Almost completely healed," Gina answered, shocked. "And you feel good?"

"Yes, good enough." Tess shrugged.

Gina got up and called for Harper.

"Yes?" Harper came into the room with a smile.

"What did you put on Tess?" she inquired, amazed with the healing.

"Oh, it was just this herbal concoction I whipped up." Harper looked at the wound. "Wow. That was some good stuff."

"Harper, it is almost completely healed," Gina stated with enthusiasm.

"I know," Harper humbly agreed. "Can I put some on Matthew?"

"Absolutely. Go get it," Gina beamed.

"Cool," Harper replied.

"Tess, I know Colin and Matthew have had their issues, but underneath Matthew's hard exterior is a very gentle soul. Before I knew you were the woman he was with those months, he talked about this amazing woman he loved. That was the happiest I had seen him since Sarah left. Then when you left, he wasn't the same."

"Gina, I'm so sorry."

Colin walked into the room hearing the conversation as he walked from the hallway. "Gina, it wasn't Tess. It was my fault, and I am sorry."

"Understand this," Gina began. "You and your brother and you and your sister are my kids, blood or not. I have been there through some really bad things in all your lives. Fix this mess and the danger that the family is in—and do it without anybody dying. I don't want to lose any of you. This contract killing stuff is done after this. You two are married and have a daughter, and I want more grandchildren."

Colin smiled.

"And I want Matthew to be happy again." She walked over to Colin. "You two are done with your past issues. I'm damn sure you both are even. You were both right, and you were both wrong. Move on. I would like to start having a holiday where everyone is there, everyone gets along, and everyone is happy. That is all I want, and I have never asked for anything from any of you. You two are so good together; everyone can see it. Expand that with this family, please."

Harper walked in with a small bowl. With Matthew still on his stomach, she pulled the bandage off each wound and applied the mixture. He stirred a bit and then slept soundly again.

"It works best if you let it have open air." She set the bowl on the end table and fixed the blankets around him, making sure to leave his back exposed. "Need anything else?"

"No." Gina smiled at her. "You've got to tell me what you put in that. It's amazing."

"Come with me to the greenhouse, and I will show you," Harper said, taking Gina's hand.

Colin stared at Tess knowing she was feeling guilty for the state Matthew was in.

"Don't shut me out," he reminded her, pulling her into his arms. "I know he still loves you."

"I know." She bit her lip.

"But he doesn't get to have you." He lifted her chin so their lips could meet. The kiss was slow, full of love.

"I love you so much it hurts," she whispered. "This is so much harder than I thought it would be. Can we not talk here? Kinda weird."

"Yeah, it is. Let me make sure everything is locked up." He brought her hand up and kissed her palm. He checked the doors and windows, closed the blinds, and pulled the curtains before they left the room.

Colin took her hand, guiding her to the kitchen. "Dad, will you watch Savannah for me?"

"Of course," he answered.

"We'll be back in a bit."

In Jonathan's office, he put in the code for the safe and took out two Glocks and a couple clips, giving one to Tess.

"Where are we going?" she asked.

"It's a surprise." He kissed her and took her hand again.

It was a warm night, and the top was still off the jeep. Leading her to the passenger side, he opened the door and she hopped in. Then, he slid in the driver's seat. After Colin started the jeep, he pulled out his phone, and headed to the gate. "Jack, open the main gate. I'm going out."

"What the hell are you doing?" Jack asked as he put in the code for the main gate.

"I'm taking my wife out for a little. Track my phone so you know where we are. I will call if I need you."

"Be careful please." Jack waved as they drove through the main gate.

"We will be." Colin smiled to himself. "Take care of our baby girl."

Ending the call, he took her hand in his. For twenty minutes, he observed their surroundings and didn't notice anyone following them. When he found the side road to the beach, he felt comfortable taking it. Growing up in this area, he knew all the secluded beaches that only the locals knew about. He drove out on the beach and stopped.

"It's such a nice evening," Tess indicated as Colin got the backpack from the backseat.

"Yes, it is." He tossed a blanket to Tess. "Give me your gun, honey."

Tess handed it to him, and he put it in the backpack. They walked down the beach, and Tess laid out the blanket. Colin put the backpack on it and took his wife into his arms. His lips dropped to hers instantly.

There was no rush, no time crunch, and no one to walk in on them. Tess moved her hands under his shirt and pulled it off. Her hands slowly moved over his shoulders, to his chest and abdomen, finally resting on his hips. She kissed his chest as she felt his hands running through her hair then kiss the top of her head.

"I love you, T," he whispered.

"It's been so long since I've been to the beach with you," she softly spoke.

"I know," he replied. "Let's go swimming."

They stripped down and went into the water. There was more touching, kissing, and holding for the next hour until they ended up wrapped up on the beach in the blanket, listening to the waves.

"I forgot how much I liked the beach," Tess said as she leaned back against his chest.

"It's been years since I've been here." He kissed her neck. "I thought with what's happened lately, we could use this. What I find challenging is sharing you with everyone. Before it was just the three of us—no one else. I didn't realize how much I liked that."

"Yes." She tilted her head to look at him. "But at the end of every day, you're the one I want to crawl into bed with and kiss." She kissed him. "And touch." She turned her body around and straddled him. "And make love to." She ran her hands over his shoulders, feeling his strength beneath her fingers.

Colin nipped her lip as he slipped inside her. She held her arms tight around his shoulders and moved slowly, taking in all of him. His hands moved up to her shoulders, and she dropped her head back.

"Tess," he whispered. "I love you so, so much."

Tess couldn't speak. She was close to the edge. She opened her eyes and smiled as she peaked.

Colin kissed her, held her hips tightly, and came just moments after. He kept her wrapped in his arms as they both came down from the passionate moment.

"I love you," she said with a smile.

"I know." He kissed her and gently placed his hand on her stomach. "I love being married to you. I don't love the fact that we haven't talked about the baby."

Tess looked down as her hands rested on top of his. "I imagined telling you so many times, but the right time never seemed to happen."

"Don't cry," he softly spoke, noting tears were filling in her eyes. "I know we have wanted this for a long time."

"I just wish the circumstances were different." She stood naked, and her hands instinctively rubbed her stomach. "This wasn't supposed to happen yet."

"Sometimes it's not a choice we get to make." He stood with the blanket wrapped around his shoulders and pulled her close. "How far along are you?"

"I'm not sure, to be honest with you." She shrugged. "I'm thinking about three months or so. All I know is this belly is getting harder to hide."

"We're going to have another beautiful baby." He grinned. "I heard the heartbeat."

Tess smiled oddly. "How do I not know this?"

"It was when you were shot. I told Jack that you were pregnant, and he confirmed it by listening to the heartbeat. He let me hear it too. I didn't want him giving you any medication that would be bad for the baby. Nobody else knows."

"I'm really excited." She finally admitted.

"Me too." And he kissed her deeply, one more time.

CHAPTER 13

Friday, Day 8

James walked barefoot to the front door when Harrison knocked. Harrison was his attorney and his cousin. Standing about his height, Harrison's frame was slightly smaller than his, but James preferred his cousin's muscles to be in his brain. So far, he hadn't been disappointed. His hair was combed perfectly back. Harrison's suit was nothing less than $10,000, and his attitude was nothing short of spectacular, self-assured, and confident, definitely a family trait.

"Harrison." James shook his hand as he opened the door for him. "Come in."

"James, you are the only client I do this for. Why don't you move to the city? This doesn't suit you and your financial status."

"I like it out here." James took him back to his office. "You have a driver; why are you complaining?"

"Because I can." Harrison sat in one of the chairs in front of the desk as James sat behind it. "Did you review the paperwork?"

"Some of it." James picked up the folder on his desk and placed it in front of Harrison. "Why does attorney jargon have to be like a foreign language?"

Harrison laughed. "James, I am here for you. I would never steer you wrong. I may not agree with some of your decisions, but I write up everything the way you want. You have got to give me a name for the beneficiary of your estate."

"Tess McGowan." James watched him carefully for his response.

Harrison looked at him without speaking for a minute.

"Why Tess?" Harrison asked. "Not that I oppose, I just want to understand your thought process here."

"She is a finance major," James began. "And she knows what I want done with my money upon my death. We've talked in great detail about this."

"Last I heard, there was a mark put on her head," Harrison said. "And she was put under. Hasn't surfaced in three years."

"I put her under," James admitted. "And she has been brought in for round-the-clock protection since someone posted a picture of her on the Internet. Adam has been trying to get the site down for weeks now, but he can't seem to crack it. When it surfaced, I called Jack to let him know. He had Colin bring her in, and Jack beefed up security at Jonathan McGowan's estate in Savannah. I filtered a few of my men in the mix. You know she has a daughter?"

Harrison grinned. "Who's the father? You?"

"I wish." James smiled. "Matthew."

"Holy shit." He shook his head. "He didn't know, did he?"

"No." James shrugged. "He just found out. He and Tess were shot a few days ago. Colin said Tess's wound wasn't life-threatening, but Matthew coded on him and is having a difficult recovery."

"You live in such a fucked-up world," Harrison commented. "I don't know how you do it. I wouldn't like bullets flying around me all the time."

"Doesn't bother me." James grinned. "I make great money doing it."

"If Tess survives this assassination attempt—and you are able to let her live a safe, worry-free life—I will put her on here as the beneficiary."

"I suppose the responsible thing to do would be to put yourself on there." James smiled. "I'd say Jack, but he's in the same business as me. I need to make sure we all make it out of this alive. Who does Jack have as his beneficiary?"

"Harper McGowan," Harrison answered.

"Wow." James was surprised. "Did something happen that I'm unaware of?"

"Not yet." He nodded. "But it's coming. As if Harper isn't going to inherit enough with Jonathan being her biological father, she now gets Jack's estate too."

"Yes, but she is sharing that with the McGowan boys," James noted.

"Doesn't matter." He grinned. "Jonathan McGowan is worth so much, dividing it three ways won't hurt any of them. But you know what I find interesting?"

"What's that?"

"They don't act like all the spoiled socialites out there," Harrison stated. "Matthew works his ass off, Harper is just so humble and smart, and Colin would be the only one who is a bit extravagant."

"He changed when Tess almost died on him," James shared. "That rocked his world."

"Good." He smiled. "Something needed to give him a wake up call. He could be such an ass."

James laughed knowing the truth behind that statement.

"So, put yourself in there for now—with the stipulation for Gran's expenses."

"Jack and I will take care of her too. She isn't just your responsibility. We love her just as much as you. And I go see her on the third weekend of every month."

"Wow, so super specific." James cocked his head.

"I don't have the luxury of doing one job and then wandering the globe for six months. I must go into the office every day and work."

"Your name is on the door." James shrugged. "You can do what you want."

"My name didn't get on the door because I was absent all the time."

"I know." James smiled. "I just like messing with you. I want Gran to be able to stay in the house until she dies or wants to move."

"I know." Harrison nodded. "And she will get to do whatever she wants. Jack, you, and I are on the same team. I promise you."

"Okay, then." James sighed. "You should put in there that I want this house to go to you."

"Smartass." He shook his head. "I would sell it."

"I'd be dead. I wouldn't care." He grinned. "Just make sure you get everything out of the basement before you sell it."

"Why don't you just get married, have some kids, and let them inherit it?"

"Why don't you?" James asked.

"I'm not the marrying type." He smirked. "You could be."

"The one who suited me went and married someone else because I let her go. Can't say I have found anyone close to her since then."

"Stop comparing everyone else to her, and you will. Cut your loss, move on, and don't let the next one go," Harrison advised.

"Is that your professional opinion?" James stood.

"No, if it was, I would charge you extra." Harrison cocked his head.

"When I get back, I will take you to dinner—and I will even wear a suit."

"Do you even have one that fits anymore?"

"Are you saying I'm fat?" James smiled.

"I'm saying you probably haven't put one on since you were twenty," Harrison reached into his pocket and handed him a business card. "Call him. He will come here and fit and style you right down to your tie. Bring Jack with you. I haven't seen him in a while. Make him get a suit as well."

"You've always been a bossy big brother," James reminded him.

"I know." Harrison smiled. "I'm good at it. I know you are heading out on another adventure. I expect to have dinner with you when you return. I'm going to ask you something, and it's going to seem like I have a hint of compassion in me, but don't think it will become a common emotion."

"Okay." James grinned amused with his cousin.

"How are you, given what you've been doing for the last couple years?" Harrison asked.

"It was hard, Harrison," James admitted. "Seeing the various situations, all horrible, the children were in was difficult."

Harrison nodded. "Yes, but just think of how many you saved by bringing them to Brian. You did a very good thing, James. You eliminated a lot of very bad people. My firm placed most of those children you freed into good homes—with caring, honest parents."

"Not their biological parents?"

"Just a handful went back to their parents." Harrison shook his head. "Since they were young when they were taken, they can't identify them. Brian assembled a team to work on age progression to see if they can match the kids. They are beginning DNA processing. Most of the kids are better off with the parents we found."

"I would burn the world down if someone took my child." James stared into nothing, and then he snapped back to reality. "This makes me not even want kids."

"You need one to inherit this damn farmhouse." Harrison smirked.

"Ha." James shook his head. "I wasn't aware you were working on the other end of this. I'm glad it was you and your people. The unfortunate thing is that the list isn't even done yet."

"You don't have to go back to it," Harrison reminded him.

"Yes, I do. I must finish what I started. There's a little more than a dozen left, but I will help Tess first."

"Well, go save her." Harrison sighed. "And tell her I said hello."

"Will do," James said as Harrison walked off the porch.

Closing the door, he turned around and looked at his farmhouse. It was originally built at the turn of the century. He kept the basic structure and style, but the house was fully remodeled with a top-of-the-line kitchen and hardwood flooring throughout the home. The power was all solar. He wanted to be off the grid as much as possible. There was a well for water. Overall, it was a very efficient home by the time he was done.

The upstairs had four bedrooms, three bathrooms, and his master suite. He had lived there for seven years. The only woman who ever saw his home was Tess. He hoped to have a family someday, but finding the right woman was damn near impossible. Then there was his job. He knew he couldn't have a family and continue to do the work he did. It wouldn't be fair; he would have to retire from that line of work. The question remained; was he ready to retire? No.

Turning on the sound system, he went upstairs to pack. His next job was going to keep him out of town for a while. As he packed, he thought of the only true friend he trusted over the years: Matthew. With years of working together, they developed a mutual understanding and respect. But like all good things, it would come to an end if Matthew or Colin found out about his minor indiscretions with Tess. He wondered if Tess would let him name Savannah as heir to his estate. Maybe Harrison would get off his ass about the whole family thing.

With a sigh, he stopped packing and looked out at the vast fields of wheat. This was his land—all nine hundred acres. When he moved there, he was looking for flat land and privacy. He wanted the flat land so he could see anyone coming. Privacy was a given with his profession. He leased his land to some farmers for a modest fee, as he didn't need the money, and liked watching the fields grow.

To the west of his house was the airplane hangar. There was comfort knowing his private jet was right there for his convenience anytime he wanted it. The runway was in between two fields, one corn and one wheat. It looked like it hadn't been used in years, even though he flew out every month. Learning to fly was like learning to drive—second nature. He managed to get certified before he turned twenty. Knowing the direction he was taking for his career choice, he knew it would be a plus.

As he took a deep breath, he wondered what it would have been like if she had stayed with him. Not a day had passed in three years that he hadn't thought of her. He visited her a lot the first year—but only twice since she had the baby. His work took him all over the world; his list held some of the worst people who did horrible things. The list was very long, and he didn't have many left, but Tess was his first priority. He would help her—and then finish the list.

✳ ✳ ✳

James landed at a small private airstrip in Misty Falls, Idaho. His ride showed up just as he exited the plane. Opening the truck door, he tossed his duffle in the backseat, and stepped up into the passenger seat. This was a lifted 4x4—dark blue exterior with tan leather inside. Top of the line. A gun rack was in the back window with one single-barrel shotgun and one double-barrel shotgun. On the seat, there was a 9 mm.

"I love this state," James chuckled.

"Me too," the driver replied. "How was your trip?"

"Considering last time? Pretty smooth. That summer storm you had here a few months ago was a bitch. Thought for sure I was going down. Craziest ride yet. Are you ready to copilot this time?"

"Yep, legally licensed as Theo Jacobs." He laughed and rolled his eyes. "I have to say this whole name thing is such a pain in the ass. I've been doing it for nearly fifteen years—it should be a breeze."

James picked up the 9 mm because he loved the feel of a gun in his hand. "Better than the death penalty. And everyone knows, in California, you sit on death row for fifty years."

"Yeah, yeah," Adam replied, turning down a remote dirt road. "Shouldn't have to do the time since I didn't do the crime."

"If you wouldn't have acted so sketch, they wouldn't have tried to pin the murders on you." James reminded him.

"Weird how everything works out. I like my 'sketch' life." Adam grinned at James and continued to drive.

They pulled up to a modest A-frame cabin. Adam had lived there for eight years. It was the longest he had stayed in one area in fifteen years, and he wasn't willing to move anytime soon. Over the years, he had learned computer coding and hacking. The money was good, considering it was all under the table and untraceable. He liked being anonymous, and his best friend, James, helped him keep it that way.

They would head out together in the morning. James needed all the information that Adam had on the three parties interested in the bounty on Tess. All information shared between them was in person—not on any electronic device—unless an urgent situation arose. That had only happened once when James's ride out of Honduras was killed, and he required alternate transportation. Adam had him picked up within an hour.

"This one is personal for you," Adam stated as they reviewed the information he gathered. "You are breaking your own rules."

"Thanks for pointing out the obvious." James stopped reading and took a sip of the whiskey in his hand. "It's your damn family."

Adam laughed. "You have seen and spoken with them way more than I have in the last fifteen years. Not to mention a few other things." Adam raised his eyebrow.

"I did not plan that," James defended.

"I still can't believe a man with your self-control fell victim to her." Adam laughed.

"Yep, me neither. In my defense, she isn't like any other woman I've ever met." James stood up. He had been reviewing the information for two hours and needed a break. "Show me the weapons you're bringing."

Guns were their hobby. James knew Adam's arsenal was stocked with nearly as many guns as his own. They ventured around the world, collecting guns and weapons of all sorts. Once a year, they would go on a hunting trip for a few weeks to keep their skills sharp. Africa was James's favorite hunting ground. There were bigger game and fewer rules, and money talked over there and he had plenty of lengthy discussions.

CHAPTER 14

Sunday, Day 10

Tess closed her eyes in the warmth of the sun. She had on her cutoff shorts with a couple buttons undone and a loose tank top. The gunshot wound was healing quickly, and she felt pretty good. A slight breeze rustled the leaves in the big oak trees every few minutes. Not wanting to be in any open areas again, she stayed close to the porch. Savannah was coloring and singing to herself on the patio. Grey was with her, which made Tess feel completely at ease.

"Tess." Jack walked up to her.

"Yes?"

"You know I do not like you being out here." Jack knelt to her. "It's not safe."

"We're close to the house," Tess pleaded. "I need fresh air, and Savvy needs it more than I do."

Jack sighed and sat beside her. "So, another baby?

"You would know." She grinned.

"It was pretty cool hearing the heartbeat," Jack admitted.

Tess took his hand in hers. "It's amazing, but it doesn't change the fact that I will do whatever I have to do to protect myself and my family."

"I know." He shook his head. "Damn stubborn is what you are."

Tess simply smiled.

"Do you remember those days at Carina's after the Markenna job?" Jack asked.

"Do I remember the couple of days we had incredibly passionate sex over and over again until you left?"

"Regrets?"

"Absolutely not." She shook her head. "I loved my time with you. Do you have regrets?"

"Never." He smiled. "I have secrets because of my profession and the security work I do, but you know me best—even better than Colin. You and I have done some crazy stuff that's nearly killed us, and we've done some very intimate things, which ... gives you a very special place in my heart. I love you, which you already know, and I want you to know that I ..."

"Jack." Tess took his hand. "You can tell me anything, and it will stay between us. You know this."

"I know." He looked her in the eyes. "I'm in love with Harper."

Tess nodded. "I know."

"How do you know?" He was perplexed.

"Everyone here knows." She covered the back of his hand with her other. "We're all just wondering if you and Harper were aware."

"So, you're okay with this?"

"Of course I am." She turned toward him. "What has happened between us stays between you, Colin, and I. Harper knows you're a well-traveled man. I don't want her to know about me."

"Okay." He nodded. "That's what I wanted to know. I just wasn't sure how you felt about it."

"I love you, Jack." She grinned. "My sister would be very lucky to have you love her."

"Thank you." He hugged her. "How's the chest feeling?"

"No pain, a little tight with really deep breaths." She shrugged.

"Good." He yawned but continued to keep an eye on the lake. "Colin and Matthew should be back soon."

"Yep," she replied, sitting up. "Makes me nervous that they both went out there together."

"They didn't just go by themselves. Harper went with them." Jack pursed his lips. "At least those two are capable of taking care of themselves and their sister." Jack stopped talking when the front gate came over his radio. He pulled his phone out and called them. "Yes, okay. Don't let them in until I get there."

"What is it?"

"An unexpected visitor at the main gate." He wrinkled his forehead as he stood. "Grey, can you take Savannah into the house please? Take her upstairs. I'm not quite sure what this is going to be about."

"On it," Grey replied, kneeling to Savannah. "Come on, sweetheart. We need to take this inside."

Savannah helped Grey pick up her coloring books and crayons without complaint.

"I'm coming with you," Tess announced standing beside him. "Don't even think about saying no because I will find my own ride there if you don't take me with you." She pulled her 9 mm from her waistband.

"You fucking stay behind me, Tess—or I will shoot your ass myself."

They drove to the gate in Colin's jeep and parked behind the brick building. He hopped out of the jeep and waited for Tess. Pointing to the empty space behind him, he warned her to stay there.

Around the corner, three guards pointed rifles at a man outside of the car. Another man sat perfectly still in the passenger's seat.

The guard spoke to Jack, "These two men say they have business with Tess, but they wanted to see you first."

Jack walked cautiously closer, knowing Tess was right behind him. He smiled when the man raised his head. "Really? You couldn't just call me?"

"Colin called, but I was on my way already. I just figured it was easier this way, Jackson."

Jack gave him a hug, leaving Tess exposed. And that was when he saw her. James stopped, and his attention was completely diverted. What was it about this woman that mesmerized him? She looked like an incredibly sexy Southern belle. "What is it with a woman and a 9 mm that is so damn hot?"

Jack moved aside, and James walked over to Tess. She slipped her gun back into her waistband and gave James a huge hug.

James picked her up off her feet, burying his head in her shoulder. "Lord, I've missed you. I've thought about you every single day since I saw you last."

"Why didn't you call?" Tess said when he set her down.

"I like to be spontaneous and unpredictable." He smiled, taking her hands in his.

"Let's walk," she said, turning away from the guards and Jack.

"Okay." He looked back at Jack. "Will you take care of my friend in the car? He's the computer guy I hooked you up with last month." James took Tess's hand, and they began to walk along the fence line.

Jack turned back to the SUV. "You, out."

The passenger door opened, and a man stepped out. He had short, dark blonde hair that had no rhythm or reason to it. Looking about five ten and 210, Jack figured he could easily take him down if necessary. Jack let the guards keep their weapons aimed at him. "What's your name?" Jack asked.

Scratching his head, the man grinned. "Adam. I'm not going to shoot anyone. That's not really my thing. Well, honestly, that's a lie. I'm just the computer guy ... who has been helping you, by the way."

"How do you know James?" Jack replied, not moving his eyes from his.

"Really?" he replied.

Another car pulled up, and Colin hopped out. "What's up Jack?"

"Do you know someone named Adam?" Jack asked.

Harper got out of the back seat.

"Only one." Colin walked over to Jack and the guy who didn't turn to let Colin see him until he was beside him.

Harper jetted past Colin.

"Harper, stop!" Jack grabbed her by the waist and swung her behind him. "What are you thinking? You don't know this man."

"Yes, I do." She looked at him meekly.

Colin looked at Jack. "Meet the girls' brother—Adam Monroe."

❋ ❋ ❋

"Where've you been?" Tess asked as they walked.

"Working on the list." He pursed his lips and looked down at the ground as they walked.

"It has affected you?" It was more of a statement than a question.

"Yes." He stopped and put his hands on her shoulders. "It was a deep, dark, hideous world that I had to go in, and I don't want to think about it right now because you are its opposite."

"Have you been to Carina's?" Tess asked.

"No. I haven't had time. Everything with the list moved quickly. When I wasn't working on that, I was working on this predicament you're in."

Tess stopped. "If you need to talk, I'm here. After everything you've done for me, that would be the least I could do for you."

"Oh, no, it's not." He smiled. "You can cook for me."

Gently, his hands cupped her cheeks as he gazed into her blue eyes.

"Don't do it," Tess said with a cautionary smile. "There are cameras everywhere on this property, and besides that, I'm married. Remember?"

James kissed her forehead and hugged her tightly.

"All I've wanted to do is kiss you," he sighed disappointed.

She pulled back from him. "You can't."

"Are you telling me the only intimate memory I get to have of you is at the beach that week in Oregon—and a few of those other times?"

"Yes," she answered with a grin.

"Well, that blows." Clearly disillusioned, he half grinned.

James remembered his time with her as if it was yesterday. The second month she had been put under; Colin had to be in Atlanta for about a month. James had no other work pending and offered to stay with her until he was able to return. They had been bouncing around in the Northwest since she was able to travel. They were working on getting her in a safe, permanent place, but it wasn't quite finished yet. After a week in the Dalles, James told her to pack up, he was taking her to the coast for a while.

"*I kind of like hanging out with you,*" James admitted at a little seaside restaurant.

"*I don't know why.*" She put her fork down and looked at him. "*I throw up randomly throughout the day, I sleep all the time, and I cry a lot. I don't even like hanging out with me.*"

James laughed, resting his hand over hers on the table.

Tess raised her fingers intertwining them with his.

"*You're just pregnant. All that stuff will pass. Try this.*" James gave her a bite of his crab salad.

"*That's really good,*" she commented.

"*I know.*" He nodded. "*The most off-the-wall places can have the best damn food.*"

"*Can we walk on the beach when we're done?*" she asked. "*It's not raining yet.*"

"*If you want.*" He shrugged. "*It's cold out there, though.*"

"*I don't mind the cold.*"

"*How's your back feeling?*" he asked.

"*It's okay,*" she replied, popping a shrimp in her mouth. "*Want one?*"

James nodded, and she popped one in his mouth. "*Lung capacity?*"

"*Sucks,*" she answered, giving him another shrimp. "*I'm a runner, and it feels like I will never be able to run again.*"

"*You're dramatic when you're grumpy.*" He gave her another bite of his salad.

"*I know.*" She looked up at him. "*I'm sorry. Honestly, I am. You've been so good to me.*"

James raised her hand and kissed her palm. "*You've been through a lot. It'll get better. Let's get out of here and walk on the beach.*"

Tess looked out the window and shook her head. "*It's raining again. Let's just go back to the room and watch a movie.*"

James managed to get them a room overlooking the ocean. The rest of the afternoon was dark and stormy, perfect for sleeping. As soon as Tess laid down on the bed, she was asleep. James turned on a movie, curled up behind her, and wrapped her in his arms. They slept for a couple hours before his cell phone woke him up.

"*Hello?*" James' voice was grumbly.

"Hey," Jack began. "How's it going?"

"Good enough," James replied.

"Is she doing okay?" Jack asked.

"She's okay." James ran a hand through his hair. "She sleeps a lot, and breathing is still a little difficult, but every day, she is a little better."

"Okay. I just—"

"I know you miss her, and I know it's eating you up that you're not here taking care of her." James stood. "I promise you, Jack, that she will be fine and will make it through all of this."

"I just ... thought it would be easier by now," Jack sighed sorrowfully.

"Jack, you know I've never loved a woman the way that you loved her. I have no great words of wisdom for you." James sighed. "Gran always said everything seems to get better with time."

"I know. I need to get going. Hug her for me, please."

"If you insist." James smiled, watching Tess rub her eyes as she woke.

Jack laughed and ended the call.

Looking down at her, James sighed. She was a mess from the inside out, and he loved everything about her. It was with only complete control over his physical desire that he had been able to avoid making love with this woman. He just hoped that he could maintain that control, but he truly had his doubts. "I didn't mean to wake you," he said lying before her.

"No biggie." She yawned. "How much sleep does a person actually need?"

"With your wound and a baby inside? A lot."

"Can I ask you something without it getting weird between us?" She touched his chest.

James eyed her for a moment. "I'm confident in our ... odd relationship here, to know that it wouldn't get weird. What's on your mind?"

"Why haven't you tried to sleep with me?"

"We do sleep together," he reminded her.

"Let me rephrase that. Why haven't you tried to have sex with me?" Tess was a bit more specific this time.

"I battle with that every single day I am with you." His hand rested on her hip. "It is only with great restraint that we haven't. I certainly want to, but you are carrying a McGowan baby. At this point in time, you will

147

either be with Colin or Matthew, and whether or not you love either one is irrelevant. I don't know if you realize how powerful the McGowan name is, but that baby may as well be the heir to a king. I guess what I'm getting at is there is no future for you and me as a couple. Do I want to step into that arena, knowing it's just an affair?"

Tess didn't say anything.

"For the life of me," he began. "I don't understand why he hasn't asked you to marry him yet."

"That's a question I ask myself all the time." Her eyes drifted to her hand on his chest. She ran her hand softly over his hair, down his neck, and to his chest. She kissed his lips softly and felt his hand tighten on her hip, pulling her body closer. The kiss deepened, their bodies pressed against each other, and their legs tangled. Her hand slipped under his shirt, feeling the warm skin.

"Damn it, Tess." James rolled away and sat up. Taking a deep breath, he stood but turned around to glance at her. After a few seconds, he straddled her thighs, pushed up her shirt, and brought his mouth to her stomach.

"It was a really great affair." She smiled remembering all the details.

"Yes and leave it to Colin to marry you so soon after it began." He ran a hand through her hair. "It began and ended so quickly."

"It wasn't that quick."

"It was." He shrugged. "I know why Jack had such a hard time leaving you. You are vibrant with emotion when you don't turn it off. Remember our conversation at Carina's?"

Tess nodded.

"You talked about that all-consuming love." He took her hands in his. "I had never experienced that until you. I had never made love like you spoke of until we did. The only thing that kept me grounded when I was working on the list was reminiscing about my time with you. I will always love you, and I will always be there for you and your family. I will get one last kiss."

Tess smiled and hugged him tightly.

"Does he make you happy?"

"Yes. He isn't like he used to be at all. Since I was shot, he completely changed. I think his life without me flashed as mine did. Thinking I was dying, he realized what was important and reprioritized his entire life. He is a wonderful husband and father. You will see that while you're here."

James kissed her forehead again. "I'm happy for you then. If you ever leave him, you better call me first."

Tess laughed a little. "I know I haven't seen you in a while, but I really missed our conversations."

"Me too." He grinned as they started walking again.

"I wanted to tell you that Jack was a little angry when he found out you knew about the baby and didn't say anything to him. I think Colin defused that, but I don't know how your relationship with him is. So, this is my heads-up to you."

"How has it been seeing him?" James asked.

Tess stopped. "I don't think it will ever be easy being around him. I missed him so much, but I haven't said anything. Nobody knows except you. Besides, he says he is in love with Harper."

"How do you feel about that?" James wondered.

"Well, it's not like I can tell him who he can and cannot love." She pursed her lips. "I just keep thinking I know what she's getting into bed with him. And I should not be thinking that way. I think that way with you too."

James laughed. "You know that is what every man that you've been with thinks when they see Colin. That bastard gets you. It's not fair."

Tess smiled.

"We should head back to the house. Colin will be back anytime, and I don't want him worried any more than he already has this week."

"Yes, where is your war wound?" James asked.

She pulled her top down just a bit to show him the scar.

"Looks pretty good." He looked around. "I just don't know who the fuck it was. I have tracked every possible person who could pull this off. There was no one in the area a week ago."

"And there is now?" Tess asked.

"Yes," he answered "You're popular. Let's get back. I need to work on this."

149

Tess walked in the front door with James. The large foyer was empty, but she heard voices in the great room.

"Mommy?" Savannah called from upstairs.

Colin walked down the spiral staircase with Savannah.

"Hi, sweetie." Colin put her down at the bottom of the stairs, and she ran to Tess. "How was your time with Grey?"

"He colored with me." Savannah twirled a piece of Tess's hair in her fingers.

"Did he color as good as you?" Tess asked.

Savannah nodded.

James watched every move the little girl made. Savannah looked like Tess, absolutely beautiful. "She has grown so much since I last saw her," James surmised.

"She's like a weed." Colin shook his hand. "Glad you're here. Thanks for coming."

"Like you could keep me away after all we've been through. And as for payment for my services, Tess must cook. I've missed her cooking."

"I love her cooking too, but in all honesty, all the women here, except Taryn, can cook like her. Even Jack gets thrown into that mix."

"Hey." James smiled. "Did you like my surprise?"

"I'm not sure yet." Colin glanced at Tess.

"What surprise, James?" Tess asked.

"Do you remember that time at Carina's you told me I had a secret—and I told you one day it would be presented to you?"

"Of course, I remember." She cocked her head wondering where this was going.

"Follow the voices." James smiled and looked over at Colin.

"Come on." Colin took Savannah and walked down the hallway to the family room.

Gina was sitting with Jonathan on the small sofa. Matthew was in a recliner with a drink in his hand, while Taryn and Harper were chatting away with her brother.

"Adam?" Tess walked in slowly. "Seriously?" She hadn't seen her brother since she was a teenager.

"Yes, ma'am." Adam stood and walked over to her.

"Oh my gosh." Her arms wrapped around him in a tight embrace as tears filled her eyes.

James took a seat on a barstool and watched. He loved reunions, even if it was someone else's family. His eyes kept going back to Savannah. He wanted to hold her, and he didn't even really like kids. This was the child who made him want a family of his own. Watching her grow in Tess's stomach for nine months—and then being there for the birth—made that desire more prominent. Once he started working on the list and seeing all the children who had been abused and hurt, quickly squashed the desire for children of his own. Savannah changed that thought again. Randomly, she popped her head up from the sofa and looked at him.

He smiled.

Savannah slid off the sofa and walked over to him. "Who are you?" she asked.

"My name is James." He slid off the barstool, kneeling to her level. "I met you when you were a baby."

"I'm still Daddy's baby." She touched his face. "Your face is pokey like Daddy's."

"Yes, it is." He laughed. "Be glad your face isn't pokey."

"Mommy says my face is as soft as a baby's. Feel." She took his hand and brought it to her face.

James gently touched her face. He felt something tighten in his throat as that familiar feeling from long ago began to surface. "Your face is very soft. Mommy is right."

She nodded. "Yeah. I like Mommy."

"I like your mommy too. You're pretty like her. How old are you now?"

"I'm almost three." She held up three fingers.

"You are well spoken for an almost 3-year-old," he said with a smile.

"Mommy says I'm smart like Daddy." She continued to touch his face softly.

"Yes, you are." He nodded.

"Do you live here too?" Savannah asked.

"No, just visiting. Do you live here?" James asked knowing the answer but was completely taken with this child.

"No, we live by the boats. I like watching the sailboats." Savannah smiled and turned her body back and forth while standing in one place.

Tess placed her hand on James's back and leaned down. "Sav." She smiled at her daughter. "Are you getting hungry yet?"

"Yes. Do you know James?" she asked her mom.

"Yes, I do. And I know that he has had a long trip today. We should let him rest. You and I are going to make dinner for everyone tonight."

"Oh, goody." Savannah clapped her hands together.

Tess picked up Savannah and looked at James. "You okay? Let me give her to Colin, and I will show you your room."

"No." James headed out of the room. "I just need some air."

"James, wait." Tess handed Savannah over to Colin and followed him to the foyer. "Don't leave."

"Really? Just let me go for a drive, clear my head, refocus because that was ... like a three-year throwback."

Matthew came up behind Tess. "James, you're not going to get through the gate without one of us. Pick someone."

"Seriously! You know who I am! I don't need a fucking babysitter." He grabbed the door handle and turned around. "Colin. Let's go, McGowan."

Colin glanced at Tess, handed Savannah back to her, and followed James out the door.

"Hope you don't mind speed," James stated as they walked towards his rental.

"If you're wanting speed, I have something a little better than that rental you have," Colin remarked with a mischievous grin.

James stopped and chuckled. "Of course, you do."

"Come on." He motioned for him to follow.

Colin punched in a code on the side door of the six-car garage. It was more like a shop than a garage. Colin always worked on his cars here. His house in Atlanta had a three-car garage, but he didn't have the space for all his tools. His father's place in Savannah was always a quiet refuge for him to escape to. They walked over to a covered car.

Colin pulled the cover from the front corner of the car to reveal his fully restored 1967 Mustang.

"Sweet ride," James whistled and ran his finger along her side. "What's inside?"

"351 Cleveland." Colin tossed him the keys. "Jack and I rebuilt the engine. Actually, we rebuilt the whole car after I wrapped it around a tree."

James eyed him and shook his head. "Jack is good at this stuff. He helped me with mine," he said as they got in the car. "I have a '68 Camaro. Love her."

"Yep." Colin nodded. "I remember seeing that car at your house. Tess and I would race along the coastline. I was in this, and she was in her 911 turbo. That was fun."

"Surprised you're not dead," James stated with a sideways glance.

"Should be." He shrugged. "We had some close calls. But, damn, we had fun."

James started the engine and listened to it roar to life and purr like a tiger waiting to run. He closed his eyes to soak in the perfect sound of the engine.

Colin pressed a remote to open the garage.

James put the car in gear and pulled out of the garage slowly. They went past the house and hit the main driveway.

Colin called ahead, telling the guards to have it open. "She is built for speed." He raised his eyebrows.

That was all James needed. His foot went down on the gas, and they were gone.

Knowing all the back roads, Colin directed James to the ones where he could really open her up, test the speed and feel how well she gripped the corners. This was the car that Colin crashed when he was younger. The car nearly killed him, but that was all it took for him to have a new respect for this car and the power behind the wheel.

CHAPTER 15

Sunday Evening

The sun had been down for a couple hours by the time James pulled into a little honky-tonk bar and grill off the main freeway. They got out of the car, and James tossed Colin the keys.

"You should call someone to pick us up," James advised.

"Why?" Colin asked as they walked into the dive bar.

"'Cause we're drinking," James said as a cute barmaid walked up to them. She wore shorts and a tank top that read "This Girl Is Made of Gunpowder and Lead."

"Holy crap," Colin mumbled thinking this was going to be a bad idea.

"Sit wherever you'd like, gentlemen." She gave a friendly smile. "What can I get started for you?"

"Umm." James leaned on the counter, amazed by her mystic green eyes. "You're beautiful."

"Thank you." She giggled with a smile. "You're not so bad yourself."

"Not so bad? Would that be a compliment?" James asked Colin.

"Seriously?" Colin laughed a little. "How do you ever get laid?"

They sat up at the bar. There were only six other patrons in the place, and they all looked fairly harmless.

"We will start with two shots of tequila each and then a couple beers—and keep them coming." He looked at Colin to make sure he was good with this and laid a hundred-dollar bill on the bar. "Don't let us run dry, and you will get an amazing tip."

"You got it," she stated. "Want any food with this?"

"Sure." James shrugged.

"What would you like?"

"Surprise us." He gave her a wink and a twenty. "That's to get the music playing."

The barmaid brought them their shots and beer, turned on the jukebox, and put in a food order.

James lifted his first shot up to Colin. "A toast. To that beautiful ride out there."

"I'll drink to that." Colin clinked his glass.

"You do the next one." James put one shot glass down and picked up the other.

Colin began, "This one's easy—to you for all your help back then."

"You're welcome." He nodded. "But you don't have to thank me for that. I'd do anything to help her."

"You helped me too." Colin raised his eyebrow.

James nodded. They drank, and the barmaid refilled the first one.

"How's Matthew been?" James asked. "I haven't talked to him in a while."

"He's been out of sorts a little since he was shot. He was pretty sick for a few days, and it seems to be taking quite a while for him to bounce back."

"I have all interested parties tracked right now. No one was in town a week ago. So, that means I missed someone."

"All of us need to sit down and share the information so we are all on the same page." Colin raised his glass. "Your turn."

"This one's for not wrecking your car on that one turn where it slid out a little under me." James lifted and drank, and Colin did the same.

Colin took a swig off his beer. "You wreck her, and you are rebuilding her back to the way she is right now."

"Fair enough," James replied. "Did you make sure we had a ride coming? We're kind of far away."

"Yep, I texted Jack and said to track my phone because I don't really remember where we are. I said to bring another driver. My car is not staying here without me." He nodded, and the barmaid came back with the tequila.

"How are you guys doing over here?" She refilled the empty shot glasses.

"Gotta name?" James asked.

"Jesse," she answered. "You gotta name?"

"James." His forehead wrinkled in thought. "That would be weird." He was talking to himself.

"What's that?" Colin asked, feeling a good buzz.

"If I hooked up with her, it would be like Jesse James."

Colin shook his head and rolled his eyes at his odd humor.

James directed his attention back to Jesse. "Would you go to dinner with me?"

Jesse smiled and shook her head. "Why would a guy like you want to go out with me? I may be working in this dive, but that doesn't mean I do one-night stands, especially for rich men like you."

"Oh, punished for being rich." James leaned back. "I'm not like most rich men."

"Prove it." She smiled, giving him a wink.

"Oh my." He watched her walk away to get their food. "She will be a challenge."

"Hmm." Colin watched her walk away. "A challenge? Are you planning on coming back here?"

"Yep." James shifted his eyes from Jesse to Colin. "You ever miss being single?"

"Nope." He shook his head. "I like my ring on her finger and going home to her every day. The last few years have been pretty damn good with Tess."

Jesse brought them their food, and they moved to a booth where there was more room. She brought their beer and asked if they still wanted shots.

"Absolutely," James answered. "Just bring the bottle. I will pay you for it."

"You got it." She brought him the bottle of tequila and he gave her a hundred-dollar bill for it.

"It's not that much." She shook her head. "I will get you change."

"No," James said before she walked away. "No change. Keep it."

"Well, thank you." She smiled. "I'll be by the bar. Give me a holler if you need anything else."

When she left, James looked up at Colin.

"For the love of God, what are you wanting to say?" Colin took a bite of the fried chicken.

"Things are good?" James asked and continued to eat.

Colin laughed and shook his head. "Ah, yes. At least until we came back here."

"How do you never talk to anyone about her?"

Colin sat back in the booth. "What's there to talk about?"

"Really?" James shook his head. "You're supporting, literally, another family, and there's nothing to talk about."

"I haven't seen her since I've been married, and I had no idea about the kid." Colin shook his head. "Should we all survive this mess with Tess, I will go after custody of my son with or without Tess by my side."

"Would you give up your wife for a kid?" James asked.

Colin shook his head. "No, that's not what I'm saying. I can't very well make Tess stay with me if she wants to leave after finding out I've slept with her sister and had a son, but I will not abandon my son either. Being a parent changes everything. I will be like my father is with his kids—blood or not. I will never be like my mother."

"You certainly get yourself into interesting predicaments." James poured them each another shot. "Here's to you not being quite as big of an asshole as you used to be."

Colin laughed as they raised their glass and downed another shot. They talked about cars, guns, and some of the jobs they'd done. They shared their work wounds and women woes throughout the years. By the time Jack showed up with Taryn, they had finished the bottle of tequila and half a dozen beers. The music was loud, more people had filed in, and it turned out to be a hopping joint.

Taryn sat beside Colin, across from James.

James waved down Jesse. "Can I get three more shots and then cut me off?"

"Of course." She grabbed another bottle of tequila for him and poured three shots.

"Ah, the little devil twin," James said with a slight grin.

Taryn gave him a wicked flash with her eyes. "Still following me?"

James nodded. "Always. I know what you've been up to."

"No, you don't," she replied. "If you did, I wouldn't be allowed at Jonathan's house."

"Damn. You're feisty." James slipped his hand behind her neck and whispered, "No wonder Colin liked to fuck you. I bet you're the same way in bed."

Colin picked up one of the shot glasses and held it up. "Who's the third one for?"

"The feisty little twin across from me." James handed her a shot glass.

"I'm a driver," she reminded him.

"Can't you handle one?" James eyed her.

"I can handle more than most men think." She looked at him with one raised eyebrow. She picked up the shot, gave him a salute, and downed it. Then she took his and did it again. "I've been locked up in that house way too long. Waitress!"

James looked at Colin with a grin. "I bet she fucks like a porn star."

"You will never know." Taryn cocked her head sideways. "Which one of you has some cash on you?"

They both pulled out their wallets.

"How much?" Colin asked.

"What do you have, Mr. McGowan?"

He handed her a hundred-dollar bill.

"That's a good start." Taryn went to the bar and got Jesse's attention. "Got another bottle of tequila we can buy?"

"Absolutely." Jesse grabbed a bottle from under the counter and handed it to her. "Are you his girlfriend?"

Taryn looked at the men at the table. "Which one are you talking about?"

"I'd say the good-looking one, but they're all damn fine."

"The one in the corner is my new brother-in-law, so he is way off limits. Next to him is the bodyguard, and the other sexy-ass-looking one is a contract killer, but he can be kind of a dick. Take your pick. Between you and me, I would fuck all of them." Taryn gave her a smile, dropped the bill in her hand, and walked back to the table. "Jack, you should call another driver." Taryn poured another round of shots. "Cheers, gentlemen!"

Jack shook his head and sent a text to Tess. "Not to put a damper on this party, but this isn't exactly a controlled environment."

"Thank goodness for that." Taryn stood up. "Come on, Colin." She pulled him to the dance floor.

Jack swung around to the other side of the table. "How are you doing, James?"

"I'm good." He laughed a little, feeling the serious effects of the alcohol. "As long as I just sit here."

Jack shook his head with a smile, sat back, and watched the people.

Colin had his arm around Taryn's waist as they danced slowly. She rested her head on his shoulder and had to remind herself that she couldn't kiss him like she wanted to do.

"We shouldn't be doing this," he whispered in her ear.

"I know," she said, but neither moved.

"I'm supposed to be mad at you." He turned his face into her hair.

"I know," she agreed. "Can you just give me this moment before you go back to being an ass?"

Without having rational thoughts of his own, Colin tilted her head up and kissed her softly. Slowly, the kiss became deeper until they weren't dancing anymore. They made their way to the other side of the room and down a dark hallway. Colin pressed her body against the wall as her hands slipped under his shirt and then moved down to his pants.

"Oh my God," Colin whispered. He lifted her up, and she wrapped her legs around his waist.

"Colin." She closed her eyes as his hands slid up the sides of her skirt.

"Want me to fuck you right here?" he whispered.

"Yes," she answered as he kissed her neck.

Colin stopped, instantly bringing a hard stare to her. Catching his breath, their faces were only inches from each other.

"I bet you do." His lip twisted up a little. "I wouldn't fuck you if you were the last woman on earth. I told you the rules in the beginning, and you just had to break them."

"Fuck you and your rules, you bastard," she said regaining her composure as he put her down.

"I told you the consequences if you broke the rules," he reminded her.

"You're really going to kill me?" Taryn was unphased by his threat.

"Nope," he replied. "I want my son."

"You will have to kill me to get him," she firmly stated. "Besides, what do you think Tess is going to do when she finds out I had your son?"

"She's going to support me in getting him away from you." He smiled wickedly. "And you know that. She can't stand you."

"She's going to leave you," Taryn smirked.

"Nah." He shook his head. "She won't. I'm better at this than you. Don't forget that."

"I hate you," she muttered. "I've kept your secret all this time."

"And I pay you very well to keep that secret. Besides, you're not going to have that secret to hold over me for much longer."

"This could work out so much better if you could just stop being such an asshole," she spat.

"You did this," Colin reminded her, again. "You knew the rules. Damn it, Tar."

Taryn felt tears surfacing, and she didn't want to give him the satisfaction of knowing he made her cry, so she turned her head away.

Colin knew he was mean. Part of him felt bad, but the other part didn't. Touching her shoulder softly, he turned her back to him. "You need to bring Connor here, and we can try to work this out amicably. We need to make this work. If we end up in court, I will make sure you don't even have visitation rights."

"You better kill me." She stared coldly at him. "Before I kill you."

"What the hell are you two doing?" James asked, walking up on them.

"Well, making out—and then we had a little discussion about our son. By the way, she does fuck like a porn star."

James tried his best to not smile.

"Your friend is an asshole," she stated and walked away.

Colin turned to the wall, hitting it with his fists. "I can't fucking believe I just said that to you."

"You were kissing her?" James was puzzled by the man's behavior.

"No." Colin felt woozy. "Yes, but I stopped. I'm so damn drunk. I want to go home."

"Is Tess not enough for you?" James asked.

"Since we've been married? Yes! Taryn was the kinky fantasy type. You could do almost anything to her, and she would do almost everything to you. Tess is the one you make love to. I haven't been with anyone else since we've been married. I hold true to my vows."

"And Tess holds true to hers," James noted. "Can this be put on the back burner until we get this mark off Tess?"

"Absolutely. Tess is my priority. I'll deal with that little bitch later." With a sigh, Colin ran his hands through his hair.

"Think she'll say anything to Tess before you?" James wondered.

"No. She has her badass attitude, but it's all show. She's still afraid of me. Besides, I give her ten grand a month to shut the hell up. I dare her to say something." Colin fumed at the mere thought of Taryn.

"Okay, then." James sighed.

"I gotta sit down before I pass out." Colin swayed a little.

Colin walked back to the table, and his mind drifted to his last night with Taryn.

Colin walked into the apartment unannounced. He owned it—so why should he have to knock? There was only one other time that another man was there when he showed up. As soon as he said that he was her husband, the man quickly left. This time, he just needed to tell her one thing, pay her off, and leave.

The place was clean considering her housekeeping skills. The slider was open, and the sheer curtains were blowing in the breeze. She was standing against the railing with a cup of coffee and staring out over the city. She didn't notice him until he was nearly three feet from her.

Seeing him, she smiled. He was her best-kept secret. Even though he was incredibly handsome, she knew what an arrogant bastard he could be.

"Mr. McGowan, you didn't call."

"I wasn't planning on staying long."

"Oh?"

He ran his hand down her arm. "However, you look … different."

She smiled. "I feel … different." She shrugged. "And if you came here to fuck your little whore, turn around and leave. That girl is gone. I don't want your money. And don't worry, I will still keep your dirty little secret from your family."

Colin smiled, took the cup from her hand, and set it on the table. He placed his hands softly on her cheeks and kissed her.

"Damn it." She sighed. "I can never say no to you."

Colin walked her back into the bedroom. He didn't treat her like a whore or a mistress this time. Instead, he made love to her just like he would Tess, slow and with deep affection. Afterward, even though it was early afternoon, they both fell asleep.

Colin woke around five and looked at her. Sleeping, she was as beautiful as Tess, but as soon as she woke up, her smartass attitude didn't make her so attractive. He wondered if he was going to miss any part of this. The secrecy of their sexual relationship added a bit of excitement to it. Even though they were both single, Colin knew he was spoken for—even if they weren't official.

"Hey," she whispered softly as she woke.

"Hey," he replied.

"I like this side of you," her voice still low.

Colin grinned. "Since this is coming to an end, I thought we should do this a little bit differently for a change."

She sucked in her upper lip. "What's changing?"

"My life," he answered softly.

"And I'm not going to be a part of it anymore." She leaned up on her elbow.

Colin slowly shook his head. "No. I have to make a change because I keep messing things up with Tess, and I don't want to do that anymore."

Trying her best to hold back the tears, she nodded. "How long are you here for?"

"I'll be leaving in the morning," he answered.

"Okay," she murmured.

"Let's order some dinner and make the most of our last night together." He leaned over and kissed her. "I want you to know that I will still take care of you financially. I'll still give you ten grand every month."

"I don't care about the money," she exclaimed, sitting up.

"You'll care if you don't have any," he said, getting up.

"Damn it, Colin." She stood and put on her robe. "I hate you sometimes."

Colin pulled on his pants and walked over to her. "What's the matter? You are usually a coldhearted bitch, and you are so far from that right now. I'm not sure what to do with you."

"You don't have to do anything with me since you are leaving me." She shrugged his hands off her and walked away.

Colin took a deep breath and followed her into the large master bath. She was brushing her hair before the mirror. He spun her around, picked her up, and placed her on the counter. With his hands on each side of her, he had his face within inches of hers. "You knew what this was when we started it—no emotions between us."

"I know." Her eyes reddened. "But I have seen you every month for the past four years, except when you two were being exclusive. It's kind of hard to not feel something. I'm not part of your posse, where all of you turn off your emotions to kill people. I'm just a real girl with real feelings."

"I know," he acknowledged. "But it's not going to change anything. You and I were never an option for marriage because of your past. You know the type of woman I must marry, and your addictions are documented along with your arrests and two stints in rehab. You know who I am and the reputation I must maintain for business."

"Go to hell." She tried to push him back.

"Don't be like this right now. You know I care about you—or I wouldn't have given you this place to live in and support you."

"Am I going to need to move?"

"Absolutely not." His hand moved to her cheek. *"The only reason it's not in your name is for tax purposes. This is your home."*

✳ ✳ ✳

Couple hours later, Jack watched Tess and Grey walk in the door. She looked hurried, on edge and highly irritated.

"Come on, Colin." Jack got up and pulled Colin upright. He knew he'd been in and out of consciousness for hours. "Tess, take him. I will get James and Taryn."

She grabbed Jack by the shirt collar. "I think we were followed."

"Got it," he noted. "Grey, go with her."

Tess draped Colin's arm over her shoulders, and she began taking him out the door with Grey's help. She had her gun in her waistband and hoped her sweatshirt didn't hike up and expose it.

Colin stumbled along with her. "Baby, I'm sorry."

"It's okay. Let's just get out of here," she said, trying to keep him upright.

Taryn and James were talking at the bar drinking coffee. Jack put his arms around them like they were in a huddle. "Let's go. Tess and Grey are here, and they were followed. Instant sober right now."

James stood, looking around as he felt for his gun. Then he remembered, he'd left all the weapons in the other car.

"Let's get outside." Jack moved them to the front door.

"I'll be right there," James said, waving down the barmaid. "Jesse, thank you." He dropped ten hundred-dollar bills on the counter. "I will be back in a few weeks to take you out to dinner. I promise."

Jesse shook her head, but he was gone before she could tell him 'no'.

"Colin, give me the keys," Tess said as she tried to get him in the vehicle.

He fumbled around his pocket and pulled out the keys barely able to stand.

Tess quickly unlocked the Mustang door and put him in the passenger seat. When she went to the other side of the car, a dark shadow lunged at her. Her hand fisted around the keys and put one right between her knuckles. When she brought her fist up for her first hit, the key jabbed into the man's chin. The man stumbled backward, and Tess kicked him as hard as she could in the lower chest. The man stepped back, again, nearly falling.

James caught him in a headlock, gave a sharp twist to the man's neck, killing him instantly. "Get out of here!"

"Tess," Jack hollered. "You take the lead."

"Got it." Tess raised her hand, and a bullet hit her forearm, just missing her head. Then more shots rang out hitting her back. The force of the impact pushed her body against the car as all air escaped her lungs for a moment rendering her unable to catch a breath. In seconds, she dropped to the ground. Knowing she knew she needed to muster up enough strength to get in the car and drive away, she pleaded with herself to push harder.

With a deep, painful breath, she tried to lift herself up, but the pain seared through her back. With her eyes closed, all sounds were muffled except her breath which was back but ragged. *Come on, she told herself, you can do this. Just get in the car.* Glancing to her left, James was crouched down, making his way over to her. He was trying to say something, but she couldn't hear him. She couldn't hear anything as the pain was overwhelming. Her eyes wanted to close so badly but James kept trying to talk to her.

Suddenly, the gunfire stopped—or she blacked out.

James was beside her as Jack ran over and unzipped her sweatshirt and found the bulletproof vest. Jack felt behind her neck and lower body to make sure she wasn't shot anywhere else. Taking the keys from her hand, he gave them to James.

"Hope you're sober now. You get to drive," Jack told him.

James nodded as Jack scooped her up, putting her in the backseat of his SUV. Somehow, they managed to drive off before the cops showed up.

About twenty minutes down the road, Tess moaned in pain from the back seat. Knowing he needed to pull over and help her, he called James and Grey to let them know that he was going to stop. A few minutes later he found a fairly secluded spot off the freeway. He got out, as James pulled in behind and Grey continued back to the house with Taryn.

"Jack, the pain is horrible," Tess cried as he ran his hand over her head.

"Let's take off the vest and have a look," he said with his calm, empathetic voice.

"Okay," her voice hitched in reply.

Jack and James helped her stand. Jack unzipped her sweatshirt and took it off, revealing her bulletproof vest.

"James, would you mind getting the medical bag from the back? It's red. You can't miss it." Jack placed his hands on her face. "I'll make this better, Tess. You know I will."

"Make sure the baby's okay?"

"I will," he said.

He kissed her forehead, ripped the Velcro from the sides of the vest, tossed it behind the seat and lifted her T-shirt off. Having her turn around, Jack saw the bruises.

"Damn, baby." James looked at the two well-formed bruises. His hand instinctively caressed her head, stopping at her neck.

"Damn it, James," Jack spoke with gritted teeth. "I told you not to sleep with her. Whose baby is she carrying?"

"Baby?" James dropped the medical bag and opened it.

"Yes, baby. You didn't know?"

"What do you want first?" James asked, ignoring his question.

"Stethoscope." Jack placed the stethoscope on her lower stomach. "I think there's two heartbeats in there."

"Seriously?" James asked with surprise.

"Yes. It's like mirrored. It could be an echo."

"Wow." She sighed. "Okay. Something for the pain please. I feel like I'm dying."

"James, hand me the syringe with the yellow label and then the one with the red label. Get ready to grab her because she is going to sleep."

In less than thirty seconds, Tess passed out. Gently, James put her in the back seat and turned to his cousin. "I don't need a lecture."

"Not giving you one." Jack put the syringes in a plastic container.

"Don't be an ass," James said frustrated and began to walk away.

"What the hell do you want me to say?" Jack stood with his hands on his hips.

James walked back to him and pointed at his chest. "You dumbass! She still loved you. It was always you—not Colin. But you walked away from her, and she let you because she didn't want you to lose the family. Both of you are fuckin' idiots. And now there's no way she would ever leave him because he became ... you."

Jack stared at him in disbelief.

"I probably should have never told you." James stepped back.

"It doesn't matter." Jack shook his head. "Nothing's going to change. Is that Colin's baby or yours?"

"His." James sighed. "I haven't seen her in almost two years. I started the list, saw her only once after that, and have purposely stayed away since. I loved her before I even met her—and you know why."

"We need to get her back." Jack began to walk away but glanced at his cousin. "It's a bitch once she gets inside your heart, isn't it?"

James smiled and headed back to the car.

CHAPTER 16

Monday, Day 11

Tess woke at nine the next morning. Her head hurt, her arm hurt, and her back hurt—but not as badly as the night before. Rolling out of bed, it was easy to ascertain that she was grouchy.

Colin was snoring. It had been years since he drank like that, and he would certainly feel the effects when he woke up.

Quietly, she dressed in her running clothes and headed downstairs. In the kitchen, she found the aspirin and took four. "Good morning, Gina." She gave Savannah a kiss on her head. "Sorry I overslept. I don't mean to be an intrusion with her."

"Seriously, Tess." Gina smiled. "She is wonderful to have around. I didn't mind bringing her down. I know things were a little tense last night. Besides, I truly love being a grandma."

"Thank you so much for all your help since we've been here." Tess leaned over the couch and gave her a hug. "Do you mind hanging out with her a little bit longer if I go out for a run?"

"Not at all, but you're not going for a run. Your back is bruised, and your arm may begin to bleed again if you get your heart rate up too much. Pilates or yoga instead—doctor's orders. Harper is out there already. You should join her." Gina ran a soft hand over Savannah's head. "After we are done here, I am going to take her up to my painting room to let her paint."

"She will love that. And thank you. I will not be long."

"Be careful, Tess. Your chance of having another miscarriage is a little higher because you've had one before."

Tess walked back to Gina. "I'm assuming Jack told you?"

Gina nodded, taking her hand. "I'm worried about you. You can't keep taking the hits you take without it affecting the rest of your body. Please be careful."

"If Taryn wouldn't have started drinking last night, this wouldn't have happened. I was content in my bed sleeping." Tess paused to hold back the tears. "I can't stand her, Gina. She irritates me just by the sight of her and I don't understand why."

"Your gut is telling you something." Gina gave her hand a squeeze. "Be careful with your body. Don't take any chances, please."

Tess nodded in agreement before she went out to the patio. With her arm throbbing, she went down the steps.

"Good morning." Harper's voice was pleasant as usual.

"Morning. I'm going to join you if that's okay," Tess asked.

"Of course, just like old times," Harper gave her a smile. "When we finish here, I have something that will help with the bruising on your back."

"I was hoping you'd say that."

The morning was cool and quiet. Tess placed her 9 mm on the lawn beside her and began mimicking Harper's moves. They were slow, precise, and perfectly executed even though her body was very sore. She needed to clear her mind of the aggravation that festered like a splinter.

"Are you happy married to Colin?" Harper randomly asked.

Tess smiled. "Yes, why do you ask?"

"Just wondering," she said as Jack walked up behind them.

"Harper, one thing I know about you is that you don't *wonder* about things, especially things like that."

"I want to be married," Harper admitted. "Not immediately, but within the next couple years."

"Do you have a man in mind that you want to marry?" Tess looked at Jack.

"Yes, I've waited so long for him, but I know he's the one." Taryn continued her moves staring straight ahead.

"Who?" Tess asked.

"Jack Keene," Harper answered with a smile as she turned to her sister. Instantly, her face turned bright red when she saw Jack beside Tess. "Oh my gosh."

Jack walked up to her, put his hands softly on each side of her face, and brought her lips to his. It was a slow, lingering kiss that had been years in the making.

Tess quietly picked up her gun and walked up to the porch. She knew that would happen eventually, but she wasn't sure how long it would take Jack to build up the nerve. Which was surprising, as Jack wasn't shy with women.

* * *

That afternoon, Tess took a walk around the garden while Savannah napped. Harper and Gina grew many strange things for lotions and antiseptics. Given it was fall, the garden was beginning to change colors and die off, but she still found beauty in the change. She took a seat in an old wooden rocker, closed her eyes, and soaked in the sun.

Jack sat on the porch and kept an eye on Tess and the lake. If someone was going to gain access to the property, it would be through the lake. He asked Tess to stay within his sight today.

"Hey, Jack," Harper walked up to him with a glass of sweet tea. "Here. Made you this."

"Thank you." He took the glass from her. "Sit with me?"

"Okay. It's such a quiet day. I love it here."

"I know you do. You never want to leave." He put his hand out across the table for her to take.

She smiled and slipped her hand in his. "Why leave? There's nothing out there that interests me that isn't here."

"Do you think I could get you to leave here so I could take you out to dinner?" Jack asked.

Harper grinned. "Are you talking like a date?"

"Yes, ma'am. I think it's about time," he stated. "Are you okay with that?"

Harper smiled. "You know I am."

"Good." He sighed. "I've wanted to ask you out for a long time now."

Jack glanced at Tess just as Taryn walked over to her. Knowing Tess was already irritable, this could certainly escalate into something critical.

"Harper, would you get Matthew or Grey for me please? I don't think your sisters should be in the same space alone."

Tess opened her eyes as Taryn approached and wondered if her shooting skills were still as sharp as they had been three years ago.

Taryn began, "We haven't really talked much since I got here. What did you think of that place? Actually, what do you think of James? I never cared for him before, watching me all the time, but after last night … he's an interesting, sexy man! I think the waitress kind of liked him. Although, who wouldn't? He's damn hot … kind of like your husband. You know all the women like your husband, and he does nothing to deter them. I think his sadistic mind feeds off it."

It must've been the snarky comment about Colin that made the shot ring out. Just one shot and Tess kept her gun in her hand when she stood. Glancing over to Jack who was now, slowly making his way over to her shaking his head. She noticed he was speaking over his radio to his men letting them know it was just a misfire of Tess's gun.

"Really, Tess?" Jack asked as he walked up to her.

Tess shrugged, unenthused.

"You shot me! You are fucking crazy!" Taryn yelled.

"Shut up, you self-centered bitch." Tess knelt to her sister. "I can't really say that I find it a blast when I get shot three times because I am in a dumpy little bar that I shouldn't have had to be in in the first place. If you would have just done what Jack asked you to do, picked up Colin and James, none of this would have happened." Tess raised her forearm. "Now you know what it feels like."

Jack put his hand up to Colin and Matthew when he saw them on the porch and started to walk down to them. They stopped, trusting Jack, and waited.

"It is your fault that I am here in the first place." Taryn gritted her teeth.

"True." Tess agreed. "And it is my fault that I don't want the person or persons who are trying to kill me to be able to kidnap, torture, and rape you to get to me. Sorry I wanted to keep you alive and safe. But let me assure you, Taryn, your actions ever risk my family again," Tess grabbed Taryn's wrist, jerking it down, "I will not hesitate to put you on the other side of that gate and let them do whatever they want to you." Tess let go of her arm and stood up. "Do we have an understanding?"

Taryn nodded as tears filled her eyes, and Jack helped her up.

"Now we have matching scars." Tess flashed a sinister smile. "I think it is only appropriate given that we are twins. There is the bullet wound on my chest that you don't have ... yet. And, by the way, James is off limits. Do you really have to follow behind me and fuck every man I have?"

Taryn's eyes narrowed and she began to speak, "You don't scare me, you don't get to control me, and you don't get to say who I can and cannot sleep with. I am here because Jonathan asked me to come here—not because I wanted to be all cozy and friendly with you. I was glad you were gone for the last three years. You're a bitch, and I don't care if they kill you."

"If you don't want to be here, then leave." Tess pointed to the main gate.

Jack eyed Tess to stop.

"Come on, Tar." Jack kept pressure on her forearm. "Let's fix this up."

While Jack walked Taryn up to the house, Colin came down to see Tess. "Give me your gun." He demanded and she turned it over to him where he tucked it into his waistband. "You cannot shoot your sister, Tess. What the hell are you thinking?"

"She irritates me so much," she stated walking away, but he followed.

"If your hate for her in any way brings any harm to this family, you will have to deal with the other me—and he's an ass."

"Fine." She rested her hands on her hips. "Sorry."

"You didn't shoot me," he reminded her.

"You want me to apologize to her? Go to hell!" she hissed.

"What do you know about her? Have you even asked what she's been up to for the last three years?" Colin asked.

Tess shook her head. "I don't really care."

"With the exception of our kids, I love you more than anyone else in this world," he began. "You have been so inward focused, which you know I understand, but don't forget about your sisters, your brother, and our parents."

"All I want to do is stay alive," she reminded him. "She was not thinking last night, and I would be dead if I didn't have the vest. You don't get to do this to me. You don't get to make me feel guilty."

Colin grabbed her arm as she turned away from him, again. "Don't walk away. I will do this to you because everyone else is afraid of you and won't say anything."

"Are you not grasping the fact that we wouldn't even be having this conversation if I hadn't put on my vest?" Tess turned on him with a rage. "I would be dead, our baby would be dead, and you would be planning our funerals."

"I'm sorry for coming down on you." Colin sighed, giving her a hug which she promptly pushed him back. "We have enough bullets flying around us. We don't need to be shooting each other."

"Then keep her the hell away from me," she snapped.

"I don't trust her, Tess," he spoke softly. "Call it a gut feeling, but please don't be alone with her—and don't let Savannah be alone with her either."

"Is there something I need to know?" she asked, eyeing him.

"Just a gut feeling, baby," he replied.

CHAPTER 17

Monday Evening, Day 11

Jonathan sat at the head of the table, waiting patiently for everyone to sit down so the discussion could begin. Only the main players were sitting in on this: Tess, Colin, James, Jack, and Adam. He figured Matthew would come in just to listen, but he didn't expect him to participate in anything more than research. The two gunshot wounds to his back were causing more problems than he really wanted to let on. Jonathan knew his son and knew he wasn't feeling 100 percent.

Being semi-retired worked well. Colin ran most of the day-to-day operations. The investment firm had produced solid profit margins for the past thirty years. Due to this and extensive research, he opened an office in the Northwest eight years ago. He divided his time between both offices each month because Colin didn't show much interest in the Northwest. When the incident with Tess happened three years before, he suggested that she be put under in Portland. Colin could manage a schedule where he was in the Portland branch a couple weeks every month allowing them to maintain their relationship, which seemed to work perfectly.

Colin walked in the formal dining room and took a seat by his father. "Tess will be down in a few minutes. She is finishing up a bedtime story."

"That is something I never thought I would hear." Jonathan smiled.

"I'm sorry I didn't tell you that we married sooner," Colin began. "It was all very emotional when we first moved her, and then things started happening between us. Next thing you know, we're married—and three years have gone by. My only regret with all of this is that we would have liked to share the day we got married with our family."

"We would have loved to have been there," Jonathan said as Tess walked in.

"Gina thought you would like this." Tess handed him a glass of red wine.

"She was so very right." He took a sip. "Thank you."

"You're welcome." Tess took a seat next to Colin.

Colin took her hand and kissed the top of it. "Sav asleep?"

"Yep." She nodded as Jack and Adam walked in with their laptops.

Jack sat across from Tess. "Gina and I think you should go in for an ultrasound to make certain all is well with the baby and to see how far along you are. We all have a bet going."

Tess shook her head. "A bet?"

"Yep." He smiled, pulling up the security cameras on his tablet. "I think you're fourteen weeks, Gina says sixteen, Harper thinks thirteen, and Matthew says fourteen with twins."

"Are you in on this, Colin?" Tess asked.

"Nope." He squeezed her hand. "Let's hope Matthew is wrong."

Tess smiled as James walked into the room, tossed a manila folder on the table, and sat down.

"Where've you been all day?" Tess asked.

"Dealing with a bad hangover and working on this mess you're in. You seriously shot your sister?" He cocked his head in her direction and connected with her eyes.

Tess looked at Colin then James.

For the first time in his career, James wasn't certain how her actions would affect the outcome. "Dominic Markenna sound familiar ... to all of you?" James slid the folder to Tess.

Tess turned pale, and her hand trembled. Closing her eyes for a moment, she tilted her head down praying that Dominic didn't have anything to do with this.

"I know this family isn't shy." James pursed his lips. "So, don't all speak at once."

Tess pushed the folder back to James and shook her head. "I'm not opening that. I already know what's in it. I lived it, so I don't need to see it again."

"You looked stunning in those photos," James' brows raised as he stated that known fact. "I can't believe you were with him of all people! He's on my damn list!"

Tess glanced at Jonathan.

"What list?" Colin asked him.

"The last couple of years, I've been working on a list of 128 marks." He took a deep breath. "Every person on the list plays a part in the trafficking of minors."

"What part does Dominic play?" Jonathan asked.

"Finance," James answered. "He has certain investors that run the money through his firm."

"He sold his firm three years ago," Matthew chimed in from the doorway.

"And you know him how?" James asked.

"I invested his money from that sale," Matthew said. "And he's my brother."

An eerie silence fell across the room as Matthew's eyes connected with Tess.

"Did you know this?" James asked.

"Not until I came back here. Jonathan told me a couple weeks ago," she admitted.

"Brian put him on the list," James firmly noted.

"Brian is wrong," Tess adamantly insisted. "Dominic wouldn't be involved in something that would hurt children."

"He's the third." He looked directly at her. "Isn't he? You can tell by the way you look at him."

"It doesn't matter." She eyed him. "He wouldn't knowingly be a part of this."

176

"You just don't want to think he would," he smirked.

Tess grabbed Jack's tablet, stood up, and slammed it down in front of James.

"A little emotional, don't you think?" James asked knowing he was pushing her to the edge.

"No, this is." She picked up the tablet and swung it at him.

James popped up quickly, stopping the tablet with his arm as he laughed a little.

Colin grabbed his wife. "Tess, stop!"

"Why? You took my gun, so I'm not shooting him!" Tess raised her voice.

"Holy shit." James was stunned with that comment.

"Who are you?" Colin asked her with an unusual calmness.

"He's wrong," Tess was furious.

"Okay, but it doesn't mean you have to hit him with the computer," Colin remarked.

"He wasn't listening." She defended.

"You've always been so calm and levelheaded." James tossed the tablet over to Jack. "I always wondered what it would take to get you riled up ... and now I know. Dominic Markenna."

"Will you please stop?" Colin asked him.

Jonathan took her hand. "Tess, remember our conversation about Dominic when you first came back?" Jonathan asked and she nodded. "I'm going to share that story with the ones who don't know it. Do you want to hear it again or would you rather go see what Gina's up to?"

"I don't need to hear it again." She stood up, wiping her eyes dry.

"Will you do me a favor please?" Jonathan asked.

"Of course," she replied.

"Stay inside the house," he requested.

Tess rested a hand on Colin's shoulder, leaned over, and kissed his lips softly. Knowing James watched the kiss, she eyed him on her way out.

Matthew walked up to the table after she left the room. "What was her name when she worked on the Markenna case?"

"Morgan Kellas." Jack tried to get his tablet to work right.

Matthew looked at James. "Dominic was on the search for the woman who was taken from him. He said her name was Morgan. He doesn't want her dead. He's in love with her."

James looked over at Jack. "What was this job anyway?"

"It was personal because of Taryn," Jack began. "She damn near OD'd on this street drug that Markenna was producing. When Tess gets her mind set on something, you either go along with her—or she'll do it herself. We even brought in your friend Brian. The drug was in the beginning stages, meaning small quantities were made in only one place, and there was only one chemist with the formula. That's why it was so expensive and sold mainly to the *elite* drug users with deep pockets. In Tess's head, it wasn't getting the addict away from the drugs—it was getting rid of the drug all together. The addict had no supply … anywhere.

"When Tess laid this out for Colin and me, it made sense. The only thing we should have done differently was kill Markenna. We didn't due mostly to extenuating circumstances. Brian needed somebody alive. Markenna had a chemist at one of his homes. The location was in Dominic's safe at his office. Tess inserted herself into his life as his girlfriend for three months. The night we pulled off the job, she got into the safe, pulled the address for the house, and left some other stuff because she knew Brian was getting a search warrant.

"After Tess relayed the address to us, Colin and I got there before the info was given to Brian. We took out security and the chemist and blew up the house. It was all clockwork until he showed up at her place and found out his brother was killed. After Markenna was arrested, she got Jonathan to call in a favor and got him released. Tess told Brian that she planted the evidence in the safe and how it was his brother. She pegged the wrong Markenna. The Markenna who was producing and distributing was his brother, Dimitri Markenna. The house was in Dominic's name; therefore, she thought he was the one making it."

"Are you kidding?" James crossed his arms and shook his head. "He is the third person on the list. And he's not the only Markenna on the list. Did she not know who she was messing with?"

"She knew," Jack easily admitted. "It just took too long for her to get the information she needed. He got into her veins, and she fell for him. When you met her at Carina's, we were coming off that job."

"The baby?" James asked.

"Was not his," Colin interjected. "She was pregnant when she started that job."

"She had a lot of losses back then." Colin shrugged as he glanced at Jack.

Jack knew he was one of her losses. Feeling frustrated, Jack walked outside and flung the tablet against an oak tree. Was it possible to love a woman too much? With all the mixed emotions he had since she came back, Jack knew he needed to turn it off and focus. Taking a deep, cleansing breath, he walked inside.

In the foyer, Harper was getting ready to walk up the stairs. "Are you okay?"

Jack cupped her face softly, bringing his lips to meet hers in a slow, needing kiss. He felt her hands on his waist, and her mouth parted. The kiss made him forget every other emotion. "After this is over, I'm taking you away—and we're not coming back for at least a month."

Harper grinned and kissed him.

"I love you, Harper." Jack kissed her again.

"I love you too," she said softly.

"Can I use your tablet?" Jack asked.

"Sure, it's in the kitchen. Where's yours?" She wondered.

"In pieces against the old oak," he told her honestly.

"Nice," Harper remarked with a simple nod.

"I have another one, but it's at the main gate."

She handed hers to him. "No problem. I only use it for shopping anyway."

"What do you shop for?" Jack asked curiously.

"Why don't you look at my history." She raised her eyebrows in a mischievous way. "Maybe you can help me pick out something."

Jack smiled, hoping it was something sexy. He thumbed through her browsing history and pulled up the last page she was on. Letting out a slow whistle, he glanced at her. "You should order one of everything. You can try on each one, and we can see which one we like best."

"Pick a color," she asked.

"Pink." He leaned over and kissed her again. "I love you. Thank you."

Harper smiled and watched him walk back to the dining room.

Jack walked into the room, sat down just as Jonathan began to share the story of Dominic's early life.

✳ ✳ ✳

Matthew left the room when his father began talking about Dominic. He knew the story, and he didn't need to hear it again. He wanted a glass of wine and perhaps a conversation with Tess if she was up to it. Walking into the kitchen, he poured himself a glass.

In the family room, Tess was laying on the couch with Gina. Matthew walked into the room and knelt before Tess. It was simple to ascertain that she'd been crying. "Come chat with me?" he asked. "Hopefully, we won't be shot at, this time."

"Okay." Tess grinned and gave Gina a kiss on the cheek. "Thank you."

Matthew took her hand, and they walked down the hall to his room.

"Make yourself at home." He walked over to the double French doors. A storm was blowing in from the sea, and she could hear the wind from the quiet confines of his room. He sat on the floor in front of the door and leaned against a dresser, "I love the warm storms that come through here in the summer and fall. When I left, I missed that the most. I used your sister, hoping she could be a replacement for you, but I was very wrong. You two are yin and yang. I don't mean to be rude or mean, but that is the way I feel. She lacks a certain something that you have."

"Would that be class?" Tess sarcastically asked as she sat opposite of him.

"I think so." Matthew nodded in agreement.

"Tar and I have always been opposite. What did you know about my life before your father took us in?" Tess wondered if Jonathan had told him anything at all about her.

"My father told me everything after you were relocated," Matthew admitted. "I wanted to know what the hell had been going on, and Dad told me everything from the moment your brother called him. Do you remember when you said you were running away from your life?"

Tess grinned. "Yes, I remember every moment with you."

"What were you running away from?" he asked.

"Your brother," she answered. "He would get so wrapped up in work that we would go weeks without seeing each other, and that wasn't the kind of relationship I wanted. We had a huge fight before I came to Chicago, and I didn't talk with him for months after I left. When I met you...well you know what happened after that."

"I should've asked you more questions." He shook his head. "I didn't even know your last name until Colin came to see me after you were shot. I never date anyone without having a full background done on them. For some reason, with you, I didn't want to know. Maybe it was intuition. I knew it wouldn't last because it was so good with you, and we clicked so well together. I loved you so much. And I know I still do."

"I was very happy with you." It was easy for her to admit.

Matthew nodded.

"I didn't mean to hurt you." She reached for his hand. "I'm so sorry. I should've left you alone."

Matthew smiled. "If memory serves, I was the one who approached you."

"Yes, but I had been watching you for about three weeks."

Matthew laughed, shaking his head. "Seriously?"

"Yes. Colin would speak your name every now and then, and I was intrigued."

"Interesting." He chuckled a bit.

"I didn't understand this before, but it makes perfect sense. Colin always watched your company and the other companies you'd buy and sell. It was the only way he was able to know what you were up to. He missed you, but he was too proud to humble himself and make amends."

"Until you were shot," Matthew added.

"No." She shook her head. "Actually, he was going to come talk to you after we talked in Aspen. He was on a mission to fix the things he'd messed up in his life. You were at the top of the list with me."

"We were best friends until Kate happened." He leaned his head against the dresser as those memories surfaced. "I missed him all those years."

"Well, if it matters any, he missed you too." Tess pursed her lips.

"He loves you so much," Matthew stated the obvious.

Tess nodded. "I know. There is this connection between us. I swear that he can read my mind."

Matthew grinned. "If someone had told me years ago that he would be raising my kid, I never would've believed it. But seeing the change in him the last few years, I wouldn't want it to be anyone else. He is very good with Savannah."

"I know he was disappointed when he found out she wasn't his, but he loves her as if she is." Tess pursed her lips a bit.

"I like watching him when he snuggles her in his arms," Matthew began. "It's the cutest damn thing. Look at you. In the last week, you've had a bullet in your chest and another through your forearm, you beat up some guy, you took a couple shots to your back, and you shot your sister. You're always so calm. That is one of the things I like about you. And you are the only girl I know who always walks around with a 9 mm."

Tess couldn't help but grinned. "Colin tried to get me to carry a .357, but I was more comfortable with the 9."

"I actually have a .357." He reached under the bed and pulled out a black leather case.

"Why aren't you packing this? It hasn't exactly been safe around here." She opened the case, checked to see if it was loaded, and handed it to him.

"I do when I have to." He held the gun in his hand easily remembering the old days when he worked with James. "Like when Colin and I went into town the other day. Besides, we have a mini army around here. This isn't my life anymore."

"Do you miss it?" she asked.

"I miss the carefree attitude when I was in my twenties, but as I have gotten older, I prefer research and data. I like seeing how people tick, what makes them behave the way they do. This is going to sound bad, but I really like to mess with people's minds. It's amazing how easy it is to manipulate people," he said with a smile.

Tess nodded in agreement having watched Colin do that for years.

"My brother is very lucky to have you as his wife," he admitted.

Tess smiled.

"I'm not sure how I feel about … this." He finished off the bottle and set it on the floor between them.

"About what specifically? Savannah?" she asked knowing they needed to finish their conversation from the pier.

"Yes." He looked back out the window. "Little Savannah. She is such an innocent, beautiful child. How do you keep all the bad things out there from touching her life?"

"It's one day at a time." Tess shrugged. "I just do the best I can."

"You've done a great job with her." He reached over and took her hand. "I ask myself if I am being selfish if I want her to be a part of my life or should I let her go and let my brother be her father. I don't want to mess this up."

Tess swallowed a small lump in her throat. "There is no right or wrong with this. She is your daughter. I have no problem with you being in her life. I think we have a problem with distance. You live in Chicago, and Colin and I live in Portland for the most part. Short of one of the companies moving, I don't know how to make this work."

"We've already been talking about merging the companies," he shared. "I could move to Portland."

"We talked about that a little, but I didn't know how much thought he actually put into it," Tess noted.

"Let me tell you." He raised his eyebrows. "He's put a lot of thought into this, merged numbers, talked with the attorneys, and done some serious research. You know what I did to him years ago?"

Tess nodded. "He had come clean for us to move forward. He had to be honest."

Matthew shook his head. "I was wrong for what I did."

"Yes and no," she grimaced. "Colin's stubbornness was wrong. Your delivery was wrong. With that said, you did the only thing left to save him from financial ruin, at the time, and heartbreak. There would have been a divorce down the road had he married her. So, it is what it is."

Matthew nodded, humbled by her understanding. "I must tell you that I am glad Colin was with you through everything. I know we had our falling out, but he deserves every bit of love that you give him. It is very apparent how much the two of you love each other."

"Thank you, Matthew." She picked up the top of the bottle and twirled it between them. "Can I ask you something personal about what happened between you two?"

"You can ask me anything, and I will always be honest with you," he answered.

"Every story has two sides. Would you mind sharing yours with me?"

"Kate was a gold-digger," Matthew began. "And everyone knew the McGowan boys were very rich and very single. Kate made up her mind that she was going to marry one of us. I met her a couple months before Colin in Atlanta. She was one of those one-night stand party girls. We had fun one night, and I walked away the next morning. She tried to call me a couple of times, but I was done with her. I honestly didn't even know her name. The next thing I know, Colin met someone named Kate and they started *dating*. We were working in Chicago and Atlanta, and I didn't meet her for four or five months. By then, they were getting serious. As soon as I met her, she knew I knew what she was doing. She all but threatened me to keep my mouth shut.

"I don't take threats kindly. I told Colin that she was only after the money and he needed to get rid of her, but he wasn't hearing it. He proposed to her a few weeks later. And wedding plans commenced. I knew if I pushed him hard enough, he would stop talking to me altogether and still marry the bitch. It was too important to not risk it. All it did was push him further and further away. A few days before they were supposed to get married, I asked her to come over to my place so we could remedy the uncomfortable situation between us. Colin was supposed to come over about an hour after Kate. It was easy to get her into bed. She told me I was the one she originally wanted."

Matthew's memory served him well as he remembered every detail of that life-altering day. Kate was half-naked and straddling him on his bed.

Her kisses were aggressive and demanding. Matthew let her think she was in control. She guided him inside her and rocked her hips intensifying the feeling.

Matthew heard the downstairs door close easily and knew his brother was looking for him. It would only be a moment or two before he came upstairs and found his fiancée on top of his brother.

Colin knew Matthew was in the shower, and he went to let him know he was there. To his complete surprise, he walked into Matthew's room to find Kate riding his brother like a porn star.

"Are you fucking kidding me?" Shock emanated from his facial expression.

Kate's eyes flew open in horror. She quickly got off the bed, pulled her shirt down, and searched for her pants. "This isn't what you think. He did this on purpose to manipulate me. I love you!"

Matthew caught the murderous look in his brother's eyes. There was no love—only hate and disgust. Sitting up, he pulled the sheet up over his waist.

"He manipulated you to sit on his dick?" Colin laughed. "Kate, my brother has been warning me for a long time about you. Guess he was right."

"Colin, please," she begged. "Can we just go home and talk about this privately?"

"Nope." He pulled out his gun. "Because the only place you are going is to hell."

Colin fired one shot into her temple, and she dropped to the floor. "This is yours to clean up." He put his gun back in his waistband. "I don't care how you spin it. I will wait for you to finish, and then I am leaving town. And you and I are done. Stay the hell out of my life."

Colin walked out of the room, and Matthew put his jeans on and went after him. "Colin, she was going to fuck you over, and you wouldn't listen to me. What else was I supposed to do? You really think I wanted to fuck that bitch again?"

"Well, I guess you got what you wanted." Colin turned and walked out the door.

"And he was gone," Matthew sighed looking at Tess. "We didn't start talking again until three years ago."

"Why didn't you just do a hit on her without Colin knowing? You certainly had the ways and means to do that."

"Nope." He shook his head. "I'd prefer Colin to be pissed than have a broken heart."

She took his hand. "He was both."

"I know that now." He took a deep breath and released it. "I couldn't get him to listen to me. I'd never seen him be so stubborn as he was with her. And it's not that I was jealous or anything like that. I wanted him to be happy with a woman—just not her."

"Mission accomplished." She picked up the empty wine bottle. "It's just too bad you two lost so many years with each other."

"I used to think that, but I see him now with you—and he is happier than ever. It was worth it. You are his world." Matthew sighed knowing she had been his whole world at one time.

Tess grinned as the bottle shattered in her hand. Instantly, they rolled away from the French doors. Matthew had a dresser between him and the outside wall, and Tess had the closet.

"What the hell?" Tess shook her head frustrated.

Matthew pulled out his phone. "Colin, shots fired into my room from the north side of the house. Sniper shot. Be careful." He looked at Tess. "You okay?"

"I'm fine but hanging out with you seems to be dangerous to my health." She joked.

"I think it is the other way around," Matthew noted. "When I said you were going to be the death of me, I meant sexually—not literally."

"Remember when you said that?" she asked as she laughed a little.

"Yes, I do." He grinned mischievously. "In the foyer, your legs wrapped around me and your hands unzipping my pants. That first time was not what I wanted, but it was damn hot."

"Yes, it was." Tess smiled.

The perimeter lights of the property suddenly lit up the grounds like a small city.

Jack shouted orders to the guards outside. As soon as he came to the French doors, Tess and Matthew stood up.

"I need to check on Savannah." Tess ran from the room.

"What happened?" Jack asked, and Matthew relayed the information. "You and Tess are not allowed to be together."

Matthew laughed. "Do your thing, Jack. I'm going to check on Tess and Savannah." Matthew patted Jack on the shoulder, went back inside, and headed upstairs.

CHAPTER 18

By the time Tess got to Savannah's room, Colin had her in his arms.

"She's still asleep," he whispered softly as they walked into their room. "But I want her sleeping in here with us tonight."

"Absolutely." Tess took a pillow and an extra blanket and made a bed for her on the chaise—far from the window.

Colin made certain the windows were locked and the blinds were closed. Sitting on the edge of the bed, he watched Savannah sleep as Tess put on shorts and a T-shirt.

Matthew knocked on their door, even though it was halfway open. "I just wanted to make sure they were okay?"

"I relayed your call to Jack and James. I figured you and Tess could manage." Colin ran his hand over his short hair. "When the two of you need to have a conversation, go to the wine cellar. There are no windows, no doors, and no access. This isn't working for me."

"I'm sorry." Tess took Colin's hand in hers. "He could have hit me easily from where we were sitting. That bastard is just toying with us now."

Matthew nodded. "Yes, she's right. He had the perfect shot."

Tess's phone rang, and her heart nearly stopped. An unsettling chill ran through her body as nobody called her except the family, and they were all there. To top it off, she didn't recognize the number.

"Answer it," Colin told her.

"Hello?"

"Tess?" Dominic sighed, relieved to finally hear her voice. "Do you know how long I've waited to hear your voice again?"

"What are you doing?" Tess asked.

"I told you I would find you," he said in a voice that was soft and smooth. "I've learned a few things since I last saw you. I've missed you so much."

"Dominic, are you doing this to me?" Tess asked as James walked in.

"No, I would never." He sighed wondering why she would even think that. "But with the company you're keeping these days, I would think one of them would have figured it out by now."

"You know who called the hit on me?" she asked.

"Yes, I do. I've never been around someone with so much hate for another in my life," he stated exasperated.

"Who?"

"You won't believe—"

The phone was cut off.

"Dominic? Damn it!"

Hitting redial, she sighed when she got a busy signal. "He knows who called the hit," she relayed. "But we were cut off before he could tell me."

"Mind if I take your phone?" James plucked it from her hand before she answered. "Thank you."

"I am going to leave this one to you, Colin," Matthew remarked, following James out.

"Who would he know that we know? It sounds like it was a mutual connection." Tess wondered.

Colin scratched his forehead. "Let's see if James can get a trace. Come on."

They left a light on in the bathroom for Savannah and went down to the living room.

Colin turned on some music and sat on the couch. "Come here."

Tess straddled his lap and rested her head on his shoulder. They didn't speak for a while as he held her tightly, just being in the moment.

"I love you," he whispered in her ear.

"I love you too." She lifted her head up.

Colin wiped the tears from her cheeks.

"I don't want to die." She easily admitted.

"You won't—and neither will any of our people. We are the best at what we do, and we have a small army: Jack, James, Matthew, and me. I trust all of them. This will be okay. We will be okay. I promise you."

Tess kissed him slowly as he rolled her onto the couch. As her legs wrapped around his body, her hands ran through his hair, over his shoulders, and back again. They were lost in the sensual arousal of each other, and the music prevented them from hearing anybody walking in.

James walked past the living room catching a glimpse of Colin and Tess wrapped up with each other. Wishing Tess to be in his arms instead, he pushed his desire to eliminate Colin out of his system, again, and walked to the kitchen. "My favorite McGowan." He took a glass from the cupboard and filled it with water.

"You're drinking water," Matthew noted. "That means you are going to work."

"I always liked you best," James smirked.

"Past tense, did that change?"

"Actually, not for me." He shrugged. "I always liked you best—until I met her. You are lacking that whole female perspective that is so hot on her."

"I can't even go there." Matthew took a sip of his wine. "When did you start your list?"

"About a year after we put Tess under," James shared.

Harper walked in and sat down by her brother across from James.

"How did you even come across a list like that?" Matthew asked.

James eased back in the chair. "Our friend, Brian. He ran a special task force for missing and exploited children. He had to run things within certain limits of the law, but I didn't. We had a conversation after I got back from taking Tess to Portland, and he accidentally left a list of names of people in the sex-trafficking trade. I started with the last name on the list and didn't stop until … I haven't stopped yet. Tess is my priority—over anything else. I needed to be here to help with this."

"Damn," Matthew let out a low whistle. "Harper, would you like a glass of wine?"

"No, thank you." She looked at James as she wanted to understand him better. "Finish your story, please."

"Jack worked on some of it with me. I never broke so many necks in my life. There were men and women on the list, and I did not discriminate. The places were shitholes. I can't even tell you how many children were freed from that. This has been the most disturbing job I've ever done. But it's also the most rewarding and I'm not talking about monetary value."

"I don't even know what to say," Matthew sighed. "I raise my glass to you. That is a whole new level of respect, my friend."

"I would think about Tess having the baby, and I remember thinking that the child would never experience the darkness I had seen during the last couple years. That kid's mother and father would rip out the throat of any person who tried to harm her. Wouldn't you, Matthew?"

"Absolutely." Matthew raised his glass taking another sip.

"Does it bother you at all?" Harper asked curiously.

"Killing people? Nope." James assumed that was the question she was asking.

Harper grinned knowing James worked off that preverbal gut feeling. "I've seen Tess detach from emotion, actually, I watched all of them do that. There is something I think I need to tell you, James. Matthew, I don't want you to get mad at me when I say what I have to say because it has to do with Taryn."

"I would never get mad at you. You have the most genuine heart," Matthew told her.

"Yes, but you had a thing with Taryn—and I'm not sure if it's over or not." She looked down for a moment. "I really hope it is because she was using you. You are too nice to be seeing her."

"Well, it was mutual. What do you know? What do you want to tell James?" Matthew asked.

"I know you don't know me, James, but I know things about you. I know you can do things that they won't do here because you aren't emotionally attached."

James leaned over the table. "Do you want to speak in private—without Matthew?"

"No. He needs to know. Tess will kill her—and you can't let her do that. I don't want her living with something like that."

"Matthew and I won't let her do that." He reached out for her hand. "Tell me."

"I've been listening to you and Adam when you are working your scenarios and probabilities with Jack. You missed someone. You need to run a check on Taryn. She's been seeing a man named Nick for a few years. I heard her on the phone after Tess shot her. She told Nick this job needed to get done because she wanted her dead. She used a few other words that I am sure you can imagine."

James's eyes connected with Matthew's, and neither spoke for a full minute as they processed the same thoughts.

"How did I miss that?" James asked as he recollected what she said at the bar.

"We all missed this," Matthew admitted. "We need to get Adam to pull her finances. I bet she funded the first million on the account. Dominic is my brother, and I can't imagine him wanting to hurt Tess."

"Why does everyone in this family have blinders on?" James asked. "Think about it. Tess worked a job on him, and he fell in love with her. Jonathan forbids her to see him after she asked for that favor to get him released. Who would you want revenge on if that was you?"

"My father," Matthew answered.

"Exactly," James agreed. "It's no coincidence that he's hooked up with Taryn. He probably found her out of dumb luck in one of her modeling ads. Find Taryn—and you find the rest of the family. What you don't find in the past three years is Tess. Taryn posts Tess's picture, knowing she would have to be brought in for around-the-clock babysitting. The safest place is here, and Jonathan asks Taryn to come here for her own protection. Now Taryn is on the inside. She can access Tess at any time, and Markenna can access your father when the time is right."

"Sounds logical," Matthew agreed, processing this new scenario.

"But what if we're wrong about Dominic? He keeps trying to warn her, but he gets cut off every single time. I need to talk to him."

"And how do you plan on doing that?" James asked.

"I don't know," Matthew replied. "I'll call my assistant in the morning and have her pull his file at work. We'll see what kind of contact information there is."

"Okay." James pulled out his phone and called Adam and Jack. "Harper, how long ago did you hear her talking to Nick?"

"I heard her again tonight, around five or six," she answered.

"Can you do me a favor?" James asked.

"Of course," she replied.

"Is Savannah in her room?"

"No. Colin moved her into their room."

"I want you to stay with her," James told her. "Lock the door and pull a dresser or something in front of it. Do not open that door for anyone except who you trust. Okay?"

"Okay."

"Go—and be quiet about it. I don't want Taryn to think anything is up. I will let Tess and Colin know what's going on." James put his hands on her shoulders. "Are you okay with this?"

"Of course." She went to Tess's room and did as instruct.

CHAPTER 19

Monday Night, Day 11 into 12

Matthew leaned on the back of the couch, as Tess and Colin were wrapped up in each other. "When you two are done acting like teenagers on mom and dad's couch, we're meeting over in the gym."

"Okay," Colin mumbled as he kissed his wife again.

"Harper is up with Savannah." Matthew headed out the door.

"Okay," Colin repeated.

In the gym, Adam set up two laptops. One was doing a search on Taryn's finances for the last three years, and the other was working on a cell phone search. He would have never imagined Taryn as being involved in any of this, but with the way she had been behaving, perhaps she could be. It was easy for him to detach since he really didn't know her. It all made sense if she was involved.

James and Matthew were talking too fast for anyone else to keep up. Every sentence one started the other finished. Stopping before Adam, they both looked at him.

"Anything yet?" James asked.

"Nope. You will be the first to know when there is." Adam looked at the computer screens.

Jack walked in with his hands up. "What now? This has been a very busy evening."

"Did you see Colin or Tess out there?" James asked.

"No." He shook his head.

"Remember when I told you I was missing something?" James asked.

"Yes." Jack stood with his hands on his hips. He had a rifle slung over his shoulder and a .357 holstered.

"Taryn." James knew saying the name was enough for Jack to know his thoughts on the current situation.

"She's in the house," Jack stated with an urgency. "We need to … kill her."

"Whoa." James looked at him with a wrinkled forehead. "We need to make sure we are right, but I know we are."

"She is in the house with Tess, Colin, Savannah, the parents, and Harper. If she is capable of putting a hit on Tess, imagine what she would do to them in the house given the opportunity. We need to be in there doing this without her knowing somehow. Figure it out, James." Jack headed back to the door.

"Hey, Jack." Tess smiled as she nearly collided with him. "What's going on?"

"Colin, come with me." Jack pointed to the house. "Tess, go see James."

"What is it, Jack?" Colin asked as they walked briskly to the house.

"Got your .45?" Jack asked.

"In my hand." Colin put his hand on his shoulder when they reached the porch. "What?"

"Taryn," Jack simply said her name.

Colin's heart skipped a beat, and everything fell into place for him.

Jack put his hand on the door. "You go to Harper, and I will go to your parents." Jack turned the knob. "She doesn't know that we know."

Colin nodded, and they went into the house. Jack headed to Jonathan and Gina's room, and Colin took the stairs to get Harper and Savannah.

"Harper." Colin knocked on the bedroom door. "It's me. Open the door."

Harper pushed the chaise from the door and unlocked it.

"Where's Savannah?" he asked.

"I made her a bed in the bathtub." She shrugged. "I figured it was safer, and she didn't wake up when I moved her. I hope that is okay?"

"That was perfect." Colin gave her a hug. "That is exactly what I would have done."

"This is scary, Colin." Harper's eyes filled. "I don't like this at all. I didn't know telling James and Matthew what I heard would cause this. I'm so sorry."

"Harper, it's okay. We needed to know so that we can keep anyone else from getting hurt." Colin gave her another hug hoping to calm her.

There was a knock at the door. Colin motioned for Harper to be quiet and hide in the bathroom. When she was safely behind the bathroom door, he went to the bedroom door. "Yeah?" he asked.

"It's Jack."

He unlocked the door and let him in.

"Just checking on everybody before I close down for the night." Jack stood in the doorway.

"Yeah." Colin nodded. "Everything is good here. How are Dad and Mom?"

"Good," Jack answered. "Locked in and loaded."

Colin nodded as Harper came out from the bathroom.

"Harper." Jack's voice was soft as he knew she'd been crying.

"Jack." She walked over to him, touching his chest.

"Don't cry," Jack spoke barely above a whisper, wiping away her tears. "This will all be fine."

Harper touched his cheek, and their lips met. Their kiss was soft, simple, and needed. He pulled her body against his as their kiss deepened.

Colin took a step back, crossing his arms. He knew Jack hadn't been serious about anyone since Tess. So, seeing him with Harper kind of surprised him.

"Wow, Harper." Taryn was standing in the hallway. "I didn't think you had that in you."

Jack turned around with his gun in his hand.

"And Jack?" Taryn smiled. "You're jumpy."

"I thought you were asleep, Tar," he stated.

"I was." She sighed. "But my arm hurts really bad. I was wondering if you or Gina could give me a shot to kill the pain."

"Of course," Jack replied. "Let me go get my bag. We should probably change the dressing also."

Jack looked at Harper. "Let me take care of Taryn, and then we need to finish our conversation."

Harper nodded sucking in her lower lip.

Colin walked over to Taryn, as Jack went down the hallway, and motioned for her to go back into her room. Slipping his hand under her hair at the base of her neck, he wished he could snap it.

"Where's Connor?" he demanded.

"Somewhere safe," smugly she answered with a smirk. "Your wife shot me, and you wonder why we don't get along."

"That shit is between you and her," he said between gritted teeth. "Don't mix Tess and me up. If it had been me, I would have shot you in the head. I want my son. You have twenty-four hours to get him here—or I will kill you and find him on my own."

"I don't even care what you do to me," she sneered. "Without me, you won't find him."

Jack met Taryn in her room and was surprised to find Colin in there, standing unusually close.

"Am I interrupting something?" Jack asked.

"No." Colin released his grip smoothly and turned to Jack. "I'm done."

"Okay, Taryn. Sit on the bed," he requested. "I am going to give you two shots. One for the pain—and one that is an antibiotic."

"Whatever you think is best, Jack." Taryn looked him in his eyes. "I trust you."

Jack smiled. "I hope so after all these years." And he gave her two shots.

"Thank you, Jack." Taryn's eyes drooped.

"The painkiller will help you sleep—just like earlier today."

"Okay." She yawned, and her eyes closed.

"What's going on between you and Colin?" Jack asked as she was close to being submerged into sleep.

"Connor …"

When she fell asleep, Jack put his things back in the bag. He took her pulse, checked her eyes for dilation, and went back to Colin's room. "She should sleep for the night. I need to get some sleep while I can. The rest of you figure out whatever you need to figure out and let me know in the morning. Nobody is to be alone with her. I will pull two guards to be up here tonight. If she takes someone because she can't get her hands on Tess, it will be Savannah or Harper. They aren't like the rest of us, and she knows they are the only ones we would fight for. Tonight, you are with Savannah. And Harper, you're with me. Good?"

"Yep." Colin nodded as Harper went to the hallway with Jack.

Jack called Grey and Thomas to guard Taryn tonight.

"Lock your doors. And will you let your dad know that she is out for the night," Jack apprised him.

Colin put his hand on Jack's shoulder. "We can handle this. Go get some sleep."

"I know." Jack shook his head and took Harper's hand. "I'm missing something here between you two. And all I have to say is that you better know what you're doing."

Colin watched them walk down the hallway to Jack's room. Sighing, he went back into his room and closed the door. He needed to tell Tess about Connor, but for the first time in his life, he wasn't certain of her response.

Jack walked Harper into his room and closed the door behind them, locking it. He placed his hands on her hips. "I wasn't done." He locked his eyes with hers. "Before we were interrupted."

Harper placed her hands on his chest as he brought his lips to hers. His kisses were soft and gentle and slow. Harper felt strange, but good feelings ran through her stomach. She felt his hands move to her back and then up through her hair.

"Harper, I want you to sleep in here with me tonight, but as much as I want to make love with you, we can't." Jack's words were soft as his lips kissed her down her neck.

"Why? Is something wrong?" she asked, concerned.

"I have waited for you for years." He took her hand, and they sat on the bed. "And I want to do this right for you. I want your parents' blessing and a ring on your finger. I want you to know that I am fully committed to you and only you for the rest of our lives. I can honestly tell you that I have loved you for many years."

"I know." She ran her hand over his cheek and through his short hair. "I've been waiting for you to ... what would Tess call it ... make your move."

"Have you?" He smiled at her. "I wasn't sure if you felt the same way or not. Matthew told me you did. I'm not good at any of this. Sorry it took me so long."

"I wasn't going anywhere." She kissed him. "Now you know why I stay here and don't like to leave. You're always here."

"Really?" Jack grinned as now it made sense to him.

She nodded. "I've liked you since I was fifteen. At twenty-six, I can tell you that I love you."

Their lips met again with more passion. They nipped, kissed, and tasted each other as they fell back on the bed. Jack's hands roamed her body, and it was difficult to not undress her. Harper's hands slid under Jack's T-shirt, allowing her hands the opportunity to explore his firm and fit body.

"Mmm, Harp." Jack rolled to his back, taking a deep breath. "We need to sleep. I need my A game tomorrow."

✳ ✳ ✳

Tess walked back to the house with James at twelve thirty in the morning. They stopped on the porch, and she put her hand on his arm. Their eyes connected, as if speaking silently. "Does Jack know?" she asked.

"Yes," he answered with a sigh. "I messed up and called you baby and kissed your temple that night, and he knew right away. I'm sorry."

She placed her hand on his cheek, giving a soft smile. "I'm sorry about the computer thing earlier. You made me so mad."

"I shouldn't have done that." He shook his head. "I guess I was ... mad at you."

"Mad at me? For what?"

"Doesn't matter." He smiled and kissed her forehead.

"It matters to me." She rested her hand on his arm. "Tell me."

"It's completely selfish." He smiled, feeling guilty for his thought. "Having another baby."

Tess grinned sympathetically, knowing he wanted a family.

Thinking back, Tess remembered walking along the riverfront in Portland with James. Savannah was sleeping in the stroller, and she knew he had an odd sense of wanting a family.

"You're quiet." Tess stopped and looked at him. "And I can tell something is weighing you down."

James smiled. "We need to clone you. That way, every man who falls in love with you can have you."

"You laid out the circumstances for us before it even started," she reminded him. "And I work very hard to keep my feelings in check with you. I struggle with it constantly, but I don't tell you about it because you made it clear what this was in the beginning."

"I never really cared for this before." He leaned on the railing. "My life was good, free, and perfect—or so I thought. We can disappear—you and me and the baby. I have complete access to do that, but there is this sense of responsibility that says we can't. We have Carina and Matthew to consider. Your husband has become my friend—and look what I've done to him. He trusts me completely with you, and I was sleeping with his wife right up until he married you. You're my best friend."

Tess had tears falling down her cheeks. "I'm so sorry, James. I should've never let it start."

"There were two of us there." He gave her a small grin.

"Yes, but I wanted you. I wanted to feel your lips on mine and to touch your body. I knew how to get what I wanted. You really didn't have a chance. We would have ended up together at Carina's when we first met, if I hadn't had a ..."

"I know." He ran his hand over her shoulder. "Do you think I wasn't fully aware of what was happening between us? I knew. Hell, Jack knew.

I let myself give in because I wanted the same thing you did. You know me better than anyone else, and you know that if I want something or someone, I will get it. Do you know how many times I have thought about pulling a hit on your husband just so I can have you for myself?"

Tess's eyes got big, and she shook her head. "Don't."

"Really?" He tilted his head. "I would never do that ... to you. I know how much you love him. I just can't figure out why you would take the chance of having an affair with me. If he found out, you would lose everything."

"I haven't slept with you since I've been married." She scrunched her forehead. "I don't think the definition of an affair applies."

"Perhaps we haven't slept together but seeing each other without him knowing is just as bad. I still don't understand why you would risk it."

"You really don't know?"

He shook his head.

"I love you," she said softly. "I love him too though."

"Isn't that confusing for you?" he asked, taking her hand in his.

"Nope." She grinned. "I don't sleep with men I don't love."

"You realize that I am in the same position Jack was with you?"

"No, you're not. You're in a worse position. Colin knew about Jack."

"True." He wiped a few of her tears away.

"If you need to end this, we can. I don't want it to end, but I know our secret rendezvous can't go on forever. I love you but I cannot say good-bye to you like I did with Jack. It needs to just be something that slowly happens. Just make it so I see you less and less."

"Remember that job I was telling you would take me all over the world?"

"Yes." She nodded.

"It starts in three days." He leaned over and kissed her forehead. "I will be gone for months at a time."

"I guess that's when the end will begin."

James slipped his hand behind her neck and kissed her forehead, again, softly. "I love you," he whispered.

Tess sighed at the memory, slipping his hand into hers. "I can't even say sorry for that because I have wanted to have a baby with Colin for years. I wish I could give you what you want also."

James wrapped his arms around her shoulders, held her tightly, and kissed the top of her head. "I love you, little mama," he said softly. "As much as I want you, I know you and Colin are perfect together." He held her eyes. "He loves you so very much."

"I know." She nodded. "And you know how I feel about him."

"You should go in and get some sleep." He gestured toward the front door.

Tess nodded, stood on her toes, and kissed his cheek. "I've missed you."

* * *

"Damn, Tess." Colin pulled her into their room when she finally showed up.

"What?" She grinned with eyes wide.

He pulled her into his arms, giving her a long kiss. "Guess who's in Jack's room tonight?"

"I don't know." She shrugged as she thought. "Wait ... is it Harper?"

"Yes, ma'am." Colin smiled. "I am pretty sure they shared their first kiss in our doorway."

"No, not their first. They've been sneaking around behind corners," she shared. "And you watched?"

"And just where was I supposed to go?" He looked around their room.

"I'm excited for them. I hope he knows ... Harper has never been with a man before."

"Oh." Colin kicked the door shut, and they moved to the bed. "I just can't get enough of you."

With his lips upon hers, he took her clothes off and started on his. When she pushed him over and got on top of him, she smiled as did he. Colin liked it when she took control of these moments.

"Whoa there." Her hand moved from his neck to his waist. "Where's Sav?"

Colin smiled. "In the bathtub."

"Why is our daughter in the bathtub?"

"Harper put her there." One of his hands slipped between her legs, making her breath hitch.

"Why?" She closed her eyes, enjoying the pleasure that he was giving her. "Oh my gosh."

Colin watched her eyes and body knowing the moment when she would peak. He slipped two fingers inside her and let his thumb rub the little nub that would bring her to orgasm.

Tess grabbed his wrists as she came.

As her body shuddered, he smiled.

"Damn." She grinned. "I love that you know my body so well."

"I do." He pulled her down for a kiss. "And I'm not done with you yet." He rolled her over on the bed, taking off the rest of his clothes.

CHAPTER 20

James, Adam, and Matthew worked on their laptops at the kitchen table. Matthew was tracking Taryn's finances, Adam was working on the cell phone tracing, and James was contacting all his men in the field to begin eliminating the parties that wanted to collect on the bounty. After that process began, he would start a backtrace on Taryn and everywhere she had been in the last three years—and who she has been with. He would have no problem putting a bullet in her head if the need arose.

"Where is Jack?" Matthew asked.

"Sleeping," James replied, not looking up. "He's had maybe five hours of sleep in the past fifty hours. Figured we could pull all the data we needed and then we could all conspire in the morning."

"She's been skimming from someone's account for the past three years," Matthew noted. "Last transaction was five months ago. All in the amount of 10k. She took that money, put it into a dummy account, and transferred it overseas. Adam, what was the account number you took the $3 million from?"

Adam rattled off the number, and Matthew laughed to himself.

"I haven't taken that money yet," Adam apprised. "I was just waiting to see if there was going to be any more activity on it."

"Pull it," James directed. "This will be ending within the next twenty-four hours."

"Okay." Adam ran his fingers across the keyboard. "I distributed it evenly between your three accounts in Switzerland."

"Give it to Matthew," James whined. "I don't want it."

"I want it," Matthew chimed. "I want some of that money, at least. Hell. Guess who funded the hit on Tess? Tess, Colin, and me. That bitch hacked my system at work and at home. And it was easy enough for her to get Colin and Tess's info."

Matthew laughed. "That's why she slept with me. I'm such an idiot!"

"Was she worth that million?" James grinned.

Matthew nodded with a deep sigh and a smirk. "Every damn penny."

"You're such a whore," James joked.

Matthew glanced at Adam and spoke, "Can I get a refund, Adam?"

"What account do you want it in?" Adam asked. "Cayman or Swiss? I won't bring it back into the States."

Matthew thought for a minute before speaking, "I don't even want to know how you know what accounts I have. This should bother me— it really should. Cayman."

"You can let Colin and Tess know you have their money," Adam stated as he moved the money.

"What information did you have on me?" James asked.

"Just a phone number," Matthew sighed. "That's all she would need to start."

"One bullet," James said, focused on the computer screen. "One kill. You know how this will end?"

Matthew nodded.

"Will there be repercussions from the family—any of them?" He glanced at Matthew.

"Not from me, but I can't speak for the rest of them."

"My accounts look fine." James looked back down. "You should check your father's."

"Why?" Jonathan asked as he walked in the kitchen.

"Taryn has skimmed millions from Colin, Tess, and me over the last three years. She has played me from day one. I don't know what she has done with you, Dad, but I think your books need to be thoroughly audited."

"I will call Milla Jacoby in the morning and get things rolling. Matthew, you should have your business accounts audited as well. Your accounts run hand over fist with profits. Colin said Jack drugged her for the night?" Jonathan inquired.

"Yes," James confirmed. "And he put two guards upstairs."

"Is everyone playing this off as business as usual?" Jonathan asked.

"So far," Matthew answered. "Yes."

Jonathan stood up. "I'm concerned about the money but not as much as her desire to call a hit on her own twin sister. That's disturbing. Gentlemen, I'm requesting that she not be harmed, unless it's unavoidable, until I get to speak with her."

James spoke, "Please understand that I am here for one purpose—and that is to take out the threat against Tess. I will kill her without any hesitation."

Jonathan placed a hand on his shoulder to explain, "I purposely gave you a loophole. And I fully expect you to use it—but only you. The rest of them are emotionally attached to her."

"I understand." James nodded in agreement.

CHAPTER 21

Jack woke at seven, and Harper was tucked safely in his arms. Their bodies were aligned perfectly, and she smelled so sweet. After a few minutes, Taryn came to his mind. She had to be stopped. He couldn't imagine putting a bullet in her after all these years. She would have to be threatening one of them in order to do it. How would he live with the fact that he had killed Harper's sister? Would she forgive him?

Jacked eased his arm from under Harper and sat up. Would there be bloodshed—or would everyone make it another day. What did Markenna have planned with Taryn? Many questions floated in and out of his mind as he dressed and quietly left the room.

Grey and Thomas were in the hallway chatting softly.

"Anything?" Jack asked.

"Silent," Grey answered.

"After Colin and James wake, you two can go get some sleep. Thank you for standing watch last night. I really needed some sleep." Jack shook their hands and went to Taryn's room.

Taryn was nearly in the same position as he had left her the night before. He smiled, knowing he had pushed a heavier dose than normal. She was beautiful, but when she opened her mouth, a malicious woman appeared. He checked her pulse: slow and steady. The thought of giving her another barbiturate shot crossed his mind. If he did, they would have the morning to figure out their next moves.

Jack went back to his room and prepared another shot. Just before he walked back into her room, he ran into Colin in the hallway. "Give me a minute."

Jack injected Taryn again, which would buy them at least another six hours. He grabbed her phone from the nightstand and headed back out.

"What's up, Colin?" Jack asked.

"I was just about to ask you that same question."

"I just gave her a little bit more of the sedative. It will give us time to discuss how to handle this situation."

Colin nodded and they headed towards the stairs.

"So, you and Harper?" Colin asked as they walked down.

Jack stopped on the stair, looking at Colin. "Are you okay with that? I didn't even think about how you would feel with this."

"Really, Jack?" Colin shook his head. "I have no problem with it. Did you two like, you know … last night?"

"Seriously?" Jack smiled. "You're not asking me that question."

Colin grinned, and they started down the stairs again. "Tess was just telling me that Harper hasn't done that yet."

"I didn't know, but we didn't do … that. Not that it is any of your business, thank you. You can tell Tess that Harper's virtue is still intact. I want to wait."

Colin stopped on the stairs prompting Jack to stop again.

"What?" Jack asked.

"Wait? For what?"

"I don't know—maybe for all this other stuff to be over. I would like to have your parents' blessing. I want to do this right with her. Harper's not like the rest of them. I love her, man."

"That's very cool of you." Colin patted him on his back.

In the great room, Adam was asleep on the couch. James was sprawled out on the other couch, and Matthew was in the recliner.

Colin went to the kitchen to make coffee, knowing the sound of the coffee grinder would stir up the masses. After he got the coffee brewing, he opened Matthew's computer to see what he had found.

Jack took James's computer and asked him for the password. He mumbled it to Jack, then rolled over to keep sleeping. The two of them sat up at the counter, reviewing the recent information.

"Holy crap." Colin rubbed his unshaved chin. After a few minutes, he grabbed a cup of coffee and went back to the information.

"Look at this." Jack turned the computer to face Colin. "It's the security camera in the lobby of her Chicago apartment. Didn't you have a place in that building?"

"Uh-huh," Colin muttered. "Is that … Markenna?"

"Yes, he hasn't changed much," Jack noted as Markenna looked directly into the security camera. "Cocky fucker."

"What was the date on that?" Colin asked.

"A week ago on Tuesday—the day Taryn flew in."

"Is that a kid he's carrying?" Jack asked.

Colin looked back at the picture a little bit closer, and sure enough, Dominic Markenna was carrying his son.

"Asshole," Colin mumbled under his breath.

"What?" Jack looked at him sideways.

"Nothing." Colin shook his head. "I do not like him."

"That makes two of us," Jack noted. "If he's carrying a kid, is it his and Taryn's? Did she have a baby? If she did, how come no one in this family knows about this?"

"Because she kept him a secret from everyone, including his father," Colin answered softly.

Jack looked sideways at him. "Whose Connor—and what aren't you telling me?"

Colin explained his relationship with Taryn and asked him to not tell Tess. He wanted to do it himself after this other issue was dealt with.

"When I left Tess at Carina's to do that six-month mission," Jack began. "I was thinking what a mess I was in with her pregnant and not knowing if I was the dad or not. I had no job, nothing. Our relationship was not right, and I kept thinking how I had messed up everything. However, you have fucked up way worse than I could ever imagine. Good job." Jack grinned, giving Colin a pat on the shoulder.

"Thanks, Jack," Colin muttered. "Love the support."

"Anytime," he replied. "Seriously, if I can help you with anything, let me know. I'm here for you."

"I'm having a harder time wrapping my head around the fact that it's Taryn behind the trigger. It's unbelievable, knowing her the way I did." Colin released a long, deep breath trying to understand where Taryn lost her edge.

They continued reviewing the information as everyone else began to wake up and filter into the kitchen for coffee. Tess and Savannah, apart from Harper, were the last ones to arrive.

"Daddy," Savannah bubbled as she came into the room. "I slept in the bathtub. Mommy said Auntie Harper made me a bed in there."

"I know." He picked her up. "Crazy place for you to sleep, but we thought you would like it."

"It's silly." She rubbed her nose to Colin's.

"Yes, it is. Are you hungry?" he asked.

"Yes, can I have the cereal with the tiny raisins in it?"

"Yep." He set her at the table. "Hang tight. I will get you a bowl." He handed the computer to Adam.

Savannah slipped off the chair, walked over to Matthew, and climbed on top of him.

"Savannah," Matthew mumbled with a yawn. "What are you up to?"

"I slept in the bathtub last night," she enthusiastically shared.

"Really?" He smiled as he woke.

"Yes, Auntie Harper made me a bed in there. Daddy said it was crazy. Where did you sleep?" She touched his face delicately with her tiny fingers.

"I fell asleep right here in this chair," he answered.

Colin called to her, "Sav, scoot on over here and eat your cereal."

"Okay."

Colin sat her on his lap as he drank his second cup of coffee. Carefully, he watched Tess for any kind of reaction to the information she was reading. There was none. She was in perfect control of her emotions. After ten minutes, she closed the computer and joined them at the table.

Jack handed Adam Taryn's phone.

Adam downloaded all the numbers, texts, and pictures he could pull from it. After five minutes, he handed it back to Jack.

Jack grabbed a cup of coffee and sat in front of the computer, again.

James had taken notes and made a timeline that showed her meeting Dominic Markenna a couple years earlier. "She's damn good! I will never underestimate another woman."

"You know who told us to look at her?" Matthew asked and Jack shook his head. "Harper."

"Serious?" Jack was surprised.

Matthew nodded this time.

Jack eyed Tess, "Are you hiding anything?"

Tess answered with a slight chuckle, "Nope."

"I would never have seen this coming." Jack went into the kitchen and pulled out the sausage and biscuits.

"Jack, make enough for me please." Tess walked into the kitchen for more coffee. "Actually, do you want help?"

"Sure." He tossed the sausage package to her with a smile. "You make the sausage gravy. I'll make biscuits."

"Not exactly what I had in mind." She pulled out the big frying pan and turned on the music and moved to the rhythm as she cooked.

Jack turned it up, and they danced as they prepared breakfast for everyone.

Jonathan and Gina came in and watched Jack and Tess dancing.

"I knew those two were in the kitchen." Jonathan grinned at Gina.

James rolled over and sat up. Glancing over, he smiled seeing Tess and Jack. Being around this big family was different than what he was used to. Normally he was by himself at home or with his Grandmother. Part of him found comfort in these surroundings, but another side missed his solitude. Gesturing to Matthew he asked, "Is it always like this around here?"

"Honestly, this is all new for me," Matthew answered. "Tess wasn't here before when I was."

James stood and stretched. "You got a cool family—a little fucked up, but cool."

∗ ∗ ∗

Jack headed upstairs to wake up Harper and see if Grey and Thomas wanted to eat. "Breakfast downstairs," he said to the two men. "Go eat. She's not waking anytime soon."

"Thanks Jack," Grey stated.

"No, thank you. After you eat, sleep. I got this." Jack went to his room, but Harper was not in bed or in the bathroom. He walked down the hall to her room and knocked lightly on the door, but there was no answer. When he opened it, steam was pouring out of the bathroom.

Harper walked out with nothing more than a towel held to her chest.

"Jack?" She was startled briefly then smiled.

"Harp." Jack looked down. "I'm sorry. I just wanted to let you know breakfast was ready."

Harper walked over to him. With one hand still holding the towel up, her other touched his chest, making him look at her.

"This is cruel and unusual punishment." He smiled trying to maintain control.

"Kiss me, Jack Keene," she whispered, rising on her toes.

"Harp," he breathed out looking down at her.

Harper moved her hand to his neck, pulling his mouth to hers. Jack kissed her slow and carefully, keeping his hands on her bare hips. She used her foot to close the door behind him.

"What are you doing? I only have so much control in me, Harper," he mumbled as his hands ran over her bottom.

Harper dropped the towel, wrapping her arms around his shoulders as their kiss deepened.

Jack pulled her closer. His hands roamed from her butt back up over her hips to her shoulders, then back down. The kiss deepened, and she pulled his T-shirt over his head. He picked her up, with her legs wrapping around his waist, and they fell slowly onto the bed knowing

Harper was going to get what she wanted from him as he could not resist her anymore.

Jack took his time and kissed every inch of her soft body. His hands went everywhere his lips did and her body responded to every touch and every kiss. Finally, his fingers slipped between her legs, making her breath hitch. Jack continued to kiss her as he slipped two of his fingers in her tight opening. Working her slowly, he gave her an orgasm. As her body tightened, her breath stopped. She pulled his lips back to hers as she trickled down from the heightened moment.

Rolling his body into hers, he slowly inched his way inside her tightness as he gazed into her eyes. "I don't want to hurt you," he was barely able to speak as she felt incredible. "Do you want me to stop?" he asked.

"No." She smiled. "You feel exactly as I imagined ... perfect."

"Tell me if I need to stop."

"I want all of you, Jack." She kissed him. "Don't stop."

Jack gave her all of him—every ounce of strength, vitality, and love.

After they were expended of all sexual energy, Harper turned on her side and rested her hand on his chest.

Jack pushed back her hair and kissed her softly. "It will be better for you next time."

"Are you kidding? I thought that was amazing."

Jack kissed her slowly. "I love you, Harper."

She smiled. "I love you too, Jack."

"So much for doing right by you." He ran his hand over his shaved head.

"I wanted you like that for so long. There was no way I could wait any longer," she confided.

Jack pulled her back on top of him and kissed her. Which started things all over again. This time, he let her be on top. As he guided himself inside, her breath caught just as before.

"Just slowly roll your hips until you find that place that feels really good for you," he suggested as her hands pressed on his chest.

"I feel awkward," she admitted. "What about you?"

Jack smiled. "Don't worry about me. Do what feels good to you, and—trust me—it will feel good for me too."

When she found that place, her mouth opened slightly with surprise.

"Breathe," Jack whispered, placing his hands on her hips, keeping that steady motion.

"Oh my gosh, Jack." Harper's eyes closed as the orgasmic feeling rushed over her.

As soon as his body realized that she had climaxed, he joined her and felt her body tense all the way down to her toes. Laying on top of him, Jack languidly ran his fingers over her bare back. Feeling her heartbeat on his chest, he knew when she fully relaxed.

Harper finally rolled off him and onto her side.

Jack propped himself on his elbow looking down at her. "You felt amazing."

Harper ran her hand over his face. "That was better than I imagined it would be."

"Have you been waiting all this time … for me?" Jack ran his hand over her stomach.

"Yes." She bit the inside of her lip.

"I'm sorry it took me so long." He kissed her again.

"I knew it would happen when you were ready." Harper pulled him down to her as their lips met again. "I like the feeling of you on top of me."

"I like the feeling of being inside you." His forehead rested on hers as her hands roamed his body. Their bodies slowly rubbed against each other.

"Can we do it again?" she innocently asked, biting on her lower lip.

"I don't know," Jack teased. "Have I created a little sexual monster?"

"I think so." Harper tried to look innocent as she brought his lips to hers.

CHAPTER 22

Colin, Tess, and Adam were talking at the kitchen table. Matthew joined them with coffee in one hand and Savannah in another. The four of them looked sideways as Harper and Jack walked into the kitchen. Both appeared freshly showered and were unusually quiet as they made their plates and popped them in the microwave. Jack poured the coffee, and Harper grabbed their plates.

Colin spoke first, "So, Jack, that conversation we had on the stairs this morning?"

Jack shook his head. "Blown all to hell, thank you."

Colin laughed.

"What's on the agenda today?" Matthew asked.

James walked in and spoke, "Plotting, conniving. Perhaps a little murder to wrap the day up properly. Can Sav hang out with Gina for a bit?"

Matthew stood up. "Come on, Savannah. Let's go see what Grandma's doing?"

"Okay," Savannah replied in a soft voice.

"I kind of like Matthew being around her. He's like a father-nanny." Tess glanced at Colin with her little grin.

"Enjoy it because you're not going to be able to just scoot the next one off on his father." Colin smiled.

"I am going to work on a lotion that we can rub on your tummy to make you have twins or even triplets. Wouldn't that be fun?" Harper was bright eyed with her idea.

Colin responded, "No, Harper. That would not be fun. You are not allowed to touch her stomach—ever."

Tess simply laughed.

Matthew came back and sat down next to James.

"I think this is all of us. Adam do your thing." James gestured to him.

Adam ran a hand through his hair. "I think all of you know the basics. That list of contributors that Matthew wanted-it's you, Colin, and Tess—nobody else. All the money was filtered from your accounts to a dummy account and then to this particular one. Her phone is packed with calls to and from Markenna. His number is to a burner. We all know those are almost 99 percent trace proof."

"What do you mean 99 percent?" Tess asked.

"You can ping that phone if all conditions are right and he is on the phone long enough, but it's hard to do. I tried it once, but I was only able to get a general location within a mile. She hid nothing and didn't delete anything in regard to this hit on you, Tess."

Tess smiled. "She wants me to know it's her and that she is smart enough to pull all this off."

"We can't lock her in a room and toss the key," Matthew stated. "What do we do with her?"

"You don't do anything," James began. "I will take care of her. The hit is planned for here. She has given him all the information about floor plans, security detail, everything. They know how many men Jack has posted at all times and where they are posted. Let them come here—on your turf. No matter how much they know about this place, you guys know it inside out. You still have the advantage."

"We can't let him come here." Tess shook her head. "We can defend ourselves, but Jonathan, Gina and Harper can't. I won't put Savannah at risk."

"Jonathan said the wine cellar is set up just like a safe room." James shrugged. "Put them in there. Put Adam with them. He's always done the research and helped with plans, but he can shoot a target with perfection if need be. We'll put him in the room with them. Make sure they have plenty of ammo and food."

"There is a whole computer set up down there too," Jack added. "Adam can do all the surveillance from there and control the cameras, lights, and locks. The radios and cell phones work there too."

"That makes me incredibly nervous." Tess ran her hands through her hair. "I want her with us. But, if we send her away, they might follow her."

James covered Tess's hand with his. "If she was my child, she would be here on this property with me. No one will fight harder for her safety than her parents. I can't tell you what to do with this, but I strongly suggest always keeping her here—with one of you. When things go down, put her in the cellar with Adam and the others."

Matthew took a deep breath looking at Tess. "This is what James does for a living. He's never done wrong by me, and his calls are dead on. If this is what he suggests, I agree with him. But you two must agree. This isn't just a one-parent decision—it's all three of us."

"Come on." Colin pulled her up from the chair. "Give us a minute, James."

They walked into the living room, and he wrapped his arms around her waist. He let her cry for a few minutes as he knew her emotions were all out of whack. "You know he is right," Colin finally spoke.

"I know." She wiped her eyes. "It's just hard making this decision because she can't defend herself. She's so small and innocent. I would die if anything happened to her. With every one of my actions since I've had her and been married to you, I wonder what the reaction will be for the two of you. I don't want to make the wrong call and lose either of you. Would it be easier to confront her so no one else gets hurt?"

"Absolutely not!" Colin took a step back. "I will put a fucking gun to her head before I let you do that. And do not do that behind my back. It will be bad for us."

Tess smiled. "Can I finish?"

"You weren't done?"

"No. I wouldn't do that to you. I know you love me the way I love you, and we both love Sav the same. She stays with us, Matthew, Jack, or James always. Matthew needs to start carrying his .357."

Colin hugged her again. "Okay."

"I have the best men in the business here to help me. Do you really think I would go at this alone? Three years ago? Probably. Now? Absolutely not. I have too much to lose."

"Let's go work this out."

Colin and Tess rejoined the group, and James looked at them for an answer.

"Sav will stay here with all of us," Colin explained. "I know you don't like to carry anymore, Matthew, but you need to start carrying your .357 so you can protect Savannah when she's with you."

James sat back in the chair at the table. "Do all of you trust me?"

"You wouldn't be here if we didn't," Colin simply stated the obvious.

"Good." James grinned. "I'm taking the lead on this. Let me do what I do for a living. My sole purpose for coming here was to make sure Tess and her little girl lived and the threat against her was eliminated. That hasn't changed. As of thirty-three minutes ago, one of the teams my men were watching was taken out. Tonight, the other two will be eliminated. That will leave just Markenna and Taryn."

"I don't think he is part of this, James," Tess relayed, holding firmly to her belief. "I think it is all her."

James raised his eyebrows. "If he's been fucking her for the last two years, he's playing a part in this."

"How many men do you have on the ground here?" Tess asked.

"Twelve," he answered. "Five are in the field, and the other five are mixed with Jack's men. Two are a secret. All my men have white bands on their right arms. Don't take them out if it's dark. None of them wear masks. If you see someone with one, it's not ours. Jack's men follow the same protocol, and their bands are yellow.

"Adam is still trying to triangulate the location on the call Markenna made. Until then, everyone needs to be prepared. I will be taking Taryn for a little interrogation. If anybody has a problem with that, stay away. Tess, I'm not that much of a dick. I realize she's your twin, and this is not easy to digest. That is why I will deal with her and none of you."

"I know." She nodded. "I'll be fine."

"As soon as Adam gets some sort of location, Grey and I will check it out. Until then, someone needs to stay with Harper and Savannah. I will let Jonathan know what's going on. Questions?"

"I'm going to town." Colin stood up. "Who wants to go with me?"

James said, "I'll go with you. We need to talk."

"Fine. But there will be no alcohol involved."

* * *

Colin drove. Both were silent for the first few miles, deep in thought. Colin was continuously processing his conversations with Taryn years before, wondering if he missed a vital key that would have alerted him to her abnormal dislike for Tess. The only thing unusual was her look the last time he was with her. Something in her had changed and he had no idea what it was.

When they were a couple miles from town, James asked, "Where's your head with this?"

"I don't know." Colin answered honestly. "I don't get it. I gave her everything: money, a nice place to live, and a child. Why does she want to kill my wife?"

"You gave her everything but yourself," James reminded him.

"If that's her reasoning, this is all my fault. I'm nothing special."

James shook his head. "Apparently, you're everything she wanted but didn't get to keep you. Women are wicked mean. I was contacted by a woman who wanted me to take out another woman. It really wasn't the kind of work I did, but she was persistent. I had Adam pull up all the info on both women. The woman wanted the wife of her lover taken out. She was crazy."

"What did you do?" Colin asked as they pulled into a parking lot.

"I shot the cheating husband and the mistress." He smiled. "Made it look like a murder-suicide, so the wife got the life insurance."

"Seriously?"

"True story." James grinned. "Didn't charge the wife. I don't know what the husband was thinking because she was hot. I spent a weekend with her, and that was enough payment."

"You surprise me every time you speak."

"I've traveled everywhere." James grinned. "I have lots of stories."

"Tell me the one about you and my wife." Colin looked at him.

James took a deep breath. "What do you want to know?"

"I want to know if you have slept with her since we've been married," Colin asked straight up.

"No. The moment she said 'I do' to you, she changed—just like you did. I am surprised given the past both of you have. She loves you more than anyone else in this world. I hope, for both of your sakes, that you both make it through this hell that is quickly coming upon us."

"You love her though?" Colin asked.

"She is my best friend in the world," James answered in a round-a-bout way. "All I ask is that you don't take that from me."

"I won't take that from you." Colin shook his head. "I can't stand the secret stuff."

James looked at him rather surprised. "I have more secrets with you than her—and you know that. I have known about you and Taryn for years. I knew about her kid before you did. The thought of telling Tess never crossed my mind. That is your business, your mess. You deal with it. If you need help dealing with Taryn, I'm there. You want me to put a bullet in her head, say the word—and it's done. We can go back to the house, and I will do it while she's sleeping. I've no problem with that. I will protect Tess from physical harm, but I can't protect her from emotional harm. That is your job."

"I still don't know what to do."

"What's your gut instinct?" James asked.

"Shoot her," he said without hesitation.

"Then that's what you should do," James told him.

"But she's the mother of my son." Colin shrugged. "I don't even know where he is. I'm so pissed that I can't even bring myself to talk with her about it."

James opened the door. "Lose the damn compassion—or she's going to fucking kill you and Tess."

✳ ✳ ✳

After Tess cleaned up the kitchen, she took Savannah out to the garden. Tess pointed out different flowers and told Savannah stories about them. Jack shadowed them, hanging back a little so she could spend time with her daughter.

They went back inside after Savannah picked a few of the flowers that hadn't wilted and put them in a vase. Tess made Savannah lunch and gave Jack a glass of sweet tea. As Savannah ate, Tess read her a story and Jack listened.

"Ready for your nap?" Tess asked, noting she was done eating.

Savannah nodded.

"I'm going to put you in Mommy and Daddy's room, okay?"

She nodded again.

"Jack, can Grey watch her? I want to go work out."

"Yep." Jack cleared the plates. "He's up there already watching Taryn's room. I'll go up with you two."

"Let's go, baby girl." Tess scooped her up in her arms.

"Stay with me until I fall asleep?" Sav asked.

"Of course." Tess kissed her cheek and laid down with her until she was asleep. Afterwards, she changed into workout clothes and found Grey and Jack talking in the hallway.

"I'm going to have Grey stay in your room with her. Thomas will stay in the hallway," Jack said. "I'd feel better that way."

"Okay," Tess agreed. "Colin will be back soon, and he can watch her. Thank you, Grey."

"No need to thank me." Grey took a seat on the chaise in the corner. It had a decent view of the hallway toward the stairs. "Just close the door halfway please. And, Tess, nothing too strenuous. You know how Jo was with your last pregnancy."

"Yes, sir, Dr. Grey." Tess kissed his cheek and walked out of the room with Jack.

Jack asked, "Do you have your phone and your gun?"

She smiled, shaking her head. "I have my phone, but Colin took my gun from me."

"Here." Jack handed her his 9 mm. "I'm going to stay here until Colin gets back. I'll see if Thomas will go over to the gym with you. I don't want you to be alone."

"I'm going to head over. He'll find me."

Jack stopped her before she walked away. "I changed the code on the door."

Jack gave her the new code, and she took off.

Tess wore spandex running shorts, a sports bra, and a zip-up hoodie. She walked to the weight equipment, turned on the music, and began stretching. After ten minutes, she began her regimen with the weights.

The music was loud, and she didn't hear James and Jack come in. She was doing twenty-five pull-ups when Jack walked over.

"They're back, and Matthew is with Sav. You can do ten more," Jack told her. "Get your ass up there."

Tess rolled her neck, jumped up to the bar, and did ten more. "Happy?"

"I guess." Jack pulled off his tank top and tossed it on the bench. "My turn."

Tess grabbed her water bottle and drank as Jack did seventy-five pull-ups.

"Stare much?" James asked.

"At Jack? Of course." She smiled. "I wouldn't be a woman if I didn't admire the perfect physique of the male body, especially the ones around here." She winked. "If my memory serves me right, you aren't lacking in that department either. Show me what I can't touch."

James took off his T-shirt, tossed it in the corner, and stood in front of her. "As you remember?"

"I remember touching every single inch of your body." Tess released her breath remembering her hand caressing over his abs.

James laughed. "And I remember kissing every inch of your body."

"Shh—that's our secret."

"Your turn." He grinned.

Tess unzipped her sweatshirt, took it off, and tossed it over by Jack's.

"Shit." James let his eyes skim down her body. "Damn. Colin gets this every night. Even pregnant, you're hot."

"Think you two could quit undressing each other and be productive?" Jack asked, dropping from the bar. "Tess, want to hit the mats?"

With a nod, she followed him.

"Do you want shoes on or off?" Jack walked over to the floor mats.

"Off," she answered.

Their stances mirrored each other. Jack nodded for her to take the first hit, and she did. They went at it for thirty minutes while James worked with the weights. Every now and then, James would glance over to watch them. Being in the business he was in and knowing he would like to work a contract or two with Tess, he wanted to observe her skills. When he finished on the weights, he walked to the mats and watched from the sideline.

"How is she doing?" Colin asked as he stood by James.

"She's good," James admitted. "You guys taught her well."

"Jack taught her," Colin spoke honestly. "I learned from him."

Jack put his hands up to stop Tess and motioned for James to come over. "Your turn. She needs someone other than Colin and me. Upper body only—and don't lay her out."

"Why are there restrictions?" James asked.

"Baby." She pointed to her stomach.

"That's right." James looked her up and down, dropped to his knees, and placed his hands on her stomach.

Tess shook her head and put her hands on his shoulders. "James, what's wrong?"

"You're the only one I've known who is pregnant, and I missed seeing the last one grow." He stood up. "You know I'm going to hang around just to watch your stomach grow with this one."

"That's kind of like watching grass grow," she sighed with a shake of her head.

"I have all the time in the world." He smiled. "Are you sure you should be doing this?"

"It's a baby," she noted. "I've done this before, and I kept working out."

"She's doing fine," Jack interjected. "I've monitored her and the baby since she was shot."

James took a deep breath and smiled. "Be careful, and if I need to stop, tell me."

Tess wiped the sweat from her face. "I will."

The second James hit stance, she lunged. She managed to avoid his fist a few times, and then one connected with her jaw. She turned away from him, spun around, and kicked him.

James stepped back a few feet, but he didn't fall. "That was good," he remarked.

"I know," she replied with full confidence in her skills.

"What are you doing?" Grey asked when he walked in seeing her sweaty and red-faced.

"Just a little workout," she defended.

Grey shook his head. "You know what Jo would say."

"Ugh." Tess was instantly deflated.

Grey glanced over at Colin. "You know she shouldn't be doing this."

"Tess is going to do whatever she wants. She knows her body and what she can handle." Colin knew this and couldn't control her if he tried.

"I didn't come here to watch her lose the baby." Grey snapped his fingers and pointed at Tess. "Go, it's my turn."

James laughed and took formation against Grey. They had worked out together off and on for twenty years. They knew each other's moves, weaknesses, and favorite hits.

"He's right, Tess," Colin spoke softly as he rubbed her shoulders.

"You know how I love being told what to do," she reminded him.

"I vividly recall you telling me that you wanted to have babies—my babies. And now you have my baby growing inside your belly. Why would you risk losing him or her?" Colin asked, placing a kiss on her cheek.

Tess turned and brought her hands to his face. "I love you—and I know what my body can handle. I would never risk losing our child. Maybe I shouldn't be doing the floor work, but I did work out with Grey the whole time I was pregnant with Savannah."

"Jo and Grey monitored you weekly," he reminded her this time.

"And look who I have here watching me … daily?" Tess glanced around the room.

"I'm not going to debate this with you." Colin shook his head. "I'm not going to hover over you either—unless it's in bed. We've been through too much to risk the slightest mishap."

Tess wrapped her arms around him and buried her head into the nape of his neck.

"Colin, have you ever watched these two spar?" Jack asked.

"No," he answered, wrapping his arms around his wife.

"Grey will lay James on his ass," Jack gleamed. "Keep watching."

James and Grey sparred for fifteen minutes. They were evenly matched—until Grey took a cheap shot and split James's lip.

James wiped the blood on his pants and eyed Grey. "What was that for?"

"You know exactly what that was for," Grey stated unapologetically.

James swung his fist and hit Grey in the abdomen.

Grey laughed. "You are so emotionally involved. You know the repercussions of bringing that into a job."

"She's not a job," James breathed out.

"She's a job that I've been in for three years," Grey rested his hands on his hips. "I'm not losing her because everyone is so damn emotional about this. Detach, focus, and do what you are famous for."

"Are you going to tell me you feel nothing for T and Sav after all these years?" James asked.

Grey motioned for Tess to come over to him. "How do I keep you and Sav alive?"

"Diligence in keeping emotions in check," she answered.

"Would I die for you and Sav?"

"Yes. Our survival is not an option. Savannah is first, then me, then you."

"Do I love you and Sav?" Grey looked at Tess.

"Yes. We're family, but safety is first: Savannah, me, and then you. There is no place for emotions when your primary focus is keeping us alive. That separation is imperative to keeping us alive."

"Did you brainwash her?" James asked.

Grey shook his head.

"No," Tess answered for him. "That process has worked for us for three years. Grey has kept us safe and alive. Suppressing emotions has kept us focused. Being focused keeps the error rate down. This would have never worked any other way. The focus quickly changed from just me to an innocent child. I will not lose focus on keeping my child alive—no matter the cost."

Colin nodded in agreement when Tess glanced at him.

CHAPTER 23

Savannah rested her head on Colin's shoulder while he swayed to the music that played softly. This was how he always put her to sleep at night. It became routine, replacing the typical bedtime story. Every now and then Tess would put her to bed and read, but most often this was his time with her. He loved her small, innocent hands on his shoulders. Tonight, he wondered how he would incorporate Connor into their routine. Tess would know how to do that, as he was confident in her skills when it came to the children.

Glancing up, he saw Tess watching him, leaning against the door frame. Colin motioned for Tess to come over, and he kissed the top of her head. They continued to slowly dance as if nothing else in the world mattered.

James walked into the house, passing the living room. Inside, he saw Colin, Tess and the baby all swaying slowly to the soft music. That is when he knew he was in the right place doing the right thing. The love they shared was peculiar at best, but solid and impenetrable.

Walking into the kitchen, James sat down next to Adam. "I need something personal."

"All of this is personal to you," Adam reminded him as he stopped typing. "Could you define that a bit more please?"

James sighed wondering why everyone was on his ass today. "Will you run a background check on a girl named Jesse from the bar?"

"Yep," Adam answered. "Do you remember the name of the bar?"

"The word *sand* was in it somewhere," James said thinking back. "It was next to the beach, about an hour and half south of here. That's all I got. If you bring up the satellite, I can tell you yay or nay."

"I've worked with less information." Adam's fingers flew across the keyboard. He narrowed the search to a five-mile radius. When he narrowed it down to two places, he spoke, "Which one?"

"The one on the left. The Sand Bar and Grill. I snapped that guy's neck about five feet from the entrance."

"Thank you for sharing that unnecessary detail." Adam pulled up the information about the bar and went into employee records. "Jessica Anders."

"Got a pic?" James asked.

"Yep. Wow! She's beautiful. Why is she working in a bar?" Adam wondered.

James smiled. "Yes, she is."

"There's gaps in her history," Adam sighed, knowing this wasn't good.

"Seriously?" James sighed. "Why can't I find a normal woman?"

"Were you thinking Tess was normal?" Adam asked.

"Normal enough for a man like me." James shrugged.

"Only you would think a female assassin was normal." Adam pulled up her bio, browsed the history, and went into the Witsec database to research her identity change. "She's been through some bad shit, James," Adam turned the screen so he could read it. "Her real name is Emma Anderson. You need to make her life better."

James read about her entire life. How was it possible that—out of billions of women on the earth—he found one with a tie to Marcos Markenna. What were the odds? Didn't matter though, something about her intrigued him enough to want to get to know her better. Tess was the only woman he'd spent more than a few nights with. No one else even came close. Jesse was different—he knew it the moment she came over to them that night.

"Adam, not a word about the Markenna name coming up in here

to anyone. Can you get me a number for the bar and the owner's name? I have an idea."

"I'll forward it to your phone," Adam told him.

"Thanks." James glanced at his watch. It was almost time to meet Jonathan. He went to his room to change. He had certain clothes for certain jobs, and the one with Taryn would require black cargo pants, a black T-shirt, and steel-toed boots with a knife built into the sole. He personally designed the boots and had them made overseas. He could pull out the six-inch knife in any situation. Since he wasn't sure when this thing with Dominic Markenna was going to play out, he wanted to be prepared.

James strapped on his watch, popped his neck, and twisted his back. He was ready. It had been coming for a long time, and he was ready to kill someone. His shoulder holster held two guns and four extra clips, but all he needed was his Glock. He would have to be dead for someone to take it from him. He put a five-inch switchblade in his pocket. The cord to his radio was discreetly hidden under his collar. He put the radio in a pocket on the outside of his thigh and pressed a button on his collar. "Testing, two?"

"Two, confirmed," Grey responded.

"Testing, three?" he said next.

"Three, confirmed," Thomas replied.

Tess walked into his room without knocking and closed the door behind her.

James cocked his head as he finished confirmation with his men. "What's up, T?"

"I can't say what I want to say because I know you're not supposed to say those things in this business." She slipped her hand behind his neck and pulled him close to her, touching her forehead to his. Quietly, they remained like this for a couple minutes before she pulled back.

"Don't." He wiped away her tears. "Let me work and do what I do best. This is already very emotional for all of us. You've got to let me focus."

Tess nodded. "Sorry."

"Don't apologize—just don't cry." He smiled. "It's interesting how a moment like this is enough. It's all work. Keep your hair up in a bun so my men don't confuse you with her. Stay with Colin and stay safe. Do not leave his eyesight."

"Okay." She nodded again and turned to walk away, but James grabbed her arm pulling her back to him.

"Only God knows how much I love you," he said before letting her go.

"I noticed you lied in the gym."

"About?"

"Not seeing the last one grow," she reminded him of his words.

James smiled. "No one needs to know our secrets."

Thinking back, James vividly remembered Tess curled up in arms. Her head was nestled into his neck as her fingers fidgeted with a button on his shirt. She was six months along and had been married for two months.

James couldn't stop himself from seeing her when Colin was in Atlanta. He kissed her head as his hand rubbed her stomach. "After you have the baby, I will be gone for a while."

"How long is a while?" she asked.

"A year or two," he answered with a sigh.

"Why?"

"There's a list I'm going to be working on." His hand caressed her cheek. "It will take me all over the world. Grey will be here with you when Colin isn't. If he needs backup, he knows who to call. I wouldn't leave if it wasn't important—and I wouldn't leave you if you weren't in capable hands."

"I know." She touched his jaw.

James closed his eyes as he absorbed the simple touch of her fingertip and thought of how Colin McGowan could come to an untimely demise so he could have her all to himself. "I love you." He gave her a soft kiss on her forehead.

"I know," she whispered.

James sighed, pushing the memory to the back of his mind. It was time to work. Heading out of his room, he called Jack on the radio. "Where are you at, Jack?"

"South side, two hundred yards down the driveway," Jack replied.

"Meet me in the front," James requested but it was more of a command.

"Okay, two minutes." Jack turned to walk back up the driveway. He had just finished position confirmation with all his men on the property. Everything was quiet, but Jack had a feeling and things were going to change. The sun was setting when he met James in front of the house. "I see you're in your work clothes."

James nodded, handing Jack a small radio and earpiece. "It's time. No matter what happens, this radio will keep working. Adam worked on these so there could be no interference of any kind. And he always has one on when I work."

Jack put the earpiece in his left ear and slipped the radio into his pocket.

"Test, thirteen," James spoke into his microphone.

"Thirteen, confirmed," Jack stated.

"Listen up." James pressed his button to speak to all his men. "Jack is thirteen. If I go silent, Grey is second to me. Jack will be able to listen and assist if needed. Copy?"

Everyone copied in perfect order.

"Well-oiled machine," he remarked.

"Only the best with me." James raised his eyebrows.

"Yeah, yeah." Jack laughed. "You're just missing a couple of the best of the best."

"Yep," James chuckled, turning back to the house. "The sacrifices I make."

Jack scanned the grounds meticulously as a cool wind blew through the dying oak leaves, making brown blankets beneath the trees. The clouds had broken up a bit, but there were some dark, menacing ones lingering. Jack was feeling disturbed, just like the weather. With an uneasy feeling, he dialed Harper's cell. "Where are you?"

"Kitchen," she replied. "Cooking supper with Gina."

"Can you do me a favor?" He asked looking at the damp ground.

"Of course," she replied.

"Stay in the house." His eyes shifted down the driveway thinking he heard something. "Stay with one of your brothers."

"Okay," she softly replied.

"I love you."

"I love you too, Jack. Be safe out there."

Jack went to get the jeep as uneasiness settled deep within.

CHAPTER 24

Taryn knocked on Jonathan's office door after supper. He requested to speak with her. So, she figured she would amuse him with her presence for a little bit. She had slept most of the day, which she figured was good since she would be up all night. Finally, she would get to see Dominic. It had been a week since she had seen him and found it odd that she missed him.

Jonathan opened the door and gestured to her to take a seat in front of his desk as he walked back to the other side and sat down.

Taryn turned around when she heard the door close behind her. "Why is James in here?"

Jonathan leaned back in his chair and spoke, "Well, he works for me."

Taryn sat back in the chair keeping complete control over her emotions. It was at this moment that she realized they *knew*.

"You know the type of work he does," he reminded her.

"You have a family full of assassins—why would you need to hire him? Save your money and use one of your sons or Tess. Is he here to kill me or rough me up?"

"Which would you prefer?"

"That's a stupid question, even for you Jonathan, golden Patriarch of the McGowan family."

"You stole money from your sibling and my sons and opened an account to fund the hit you put on your sister. Given the family you have stolen from, do you think he should kill you? All I must do is give him the okay."

"Not yet." She smiled. "I want to see her die first—and then you can do whatever you want with me. I really doubt you—or James—will get the opportunity to kill me because he will stop you."

"This *he* you speak of is your boyfriend, Dominic Markenna? That is having a lot of confidence and trust in a man who was in love with your sister." Jonathan figured she didn't know that little bit of information.

"Bullshit," she said, not believing that for a moment.

Jonathan smiled. "You didn't know. I'm betting that he found you and said all the right things to gain your trust. His end game is simply to find her. He probably didn't know her real name until he saw you and thought the resemblance was too much of a coincidence. Your sister asked me to call in a favor for him once, and I did. The price she paid was to never see him again. I wasn't certain how he was raised by his biological father." Jonathan sighed. "His father murdered his mother— my wife and Matthew's mother, Isobelle—and kidnapped Dominic. I thought he died in the accident."

Taryn stared blankly at the desk as she comprehended this turn of events. Thinking back, she remembered Dominic saying he needed to tell her a few things about him. Was this one of the *things*?

"I understand sibling rivalry—I dealt with it with my sons—but I don't understand how you could hate your sister enough to call a mark on her."

"That's between her and me," Taryn smirked.

"So be it." Jonathan grinned realizing there was no compromising with Taryn. "Your trust is so misguided. For a moment, I wondered if that was my fault. Did I raise you differently than the other girls—or is it just you?"

"Would you rather I trust Tess?" Her eyebrows jetted up.

Jonathan laughed, stood, narrowing his eyes. "I don't give a damn who you trust. You can't do this to *my* family. I don't know who has set you up so nicely in Chicago, but let's hope you don't mess that up. I don't think you will have much family left after this. You stepped on the wrong side of the line. We already have the money, and all interested parties were eliminated last night—except for Dominic. We are saving him for last because I have a few questions for him." He walked around the desk and sat beside her. "You think you are so smart with the way you manipulated everybody all these years, but your biggest mistake was turning me into your enemy. There are two sides to every person." His hand rested on her forearm that Tess shot yesterday. "You saw the side of me that picked you and your sisters up from a horrific event, brought you here, gave you everything I could possibly give you, and loved you as my own." His hand slowly tightened around her wound. "And this is the side has no boundaries to stop me from protecting my family at all costs."

Jonathan held her eyes as the wound began to bleed beneath the pressure. As she began to scream, James covered her mouth. Only after a few moments did Jonathan release her arm, pulled out a handkerchief, and wiped away the blood.

"The man I speak of ... isn't Dominic," she growled through the tears.

"Sure," Jonathan shook his head.

Taryn's lip curled. "Kill me—and you will never find your grandson."

Jonathan looked over at James. "Let me make sure Savannah isn't around. Take her over to the gym and tie her up. I want a guard on her. Cover her mouth. I don't want her to be able to speak to anyone."

"Yes, sir." James sat beside Taryn as Jonathan left. "I would have snapped your neck two days ago if given the choice."

"So, you slept with her too?" Taryn smiled between the tears.

"You say that as if it's in the past." James grinned and leaned closer. "Colin can't save you from me."

"If he ever wants to find his son, he will," she dared.

Jonathan walked into the family room and found everyone except Jack. "Do any of you know where Jack is?"

"Outside," Colin replied. "On patrol, checking in with his men. Harper is with him."

"I am requesting that all of you stay in this room until I return. No questions, no comments, no speculations. Just stay here please. Colin, give me five minutes—and then I want to speak with you in the study."

* * *

"Come on, little terror." James put his hand on Taryn's neck. "Make one slight move and I will snap your neck like a twig."

On their way to the gym, Tess called out to them from the porch, "Wait." She jogged over to meet up with them by the door of the shop. "Let her go for a second."

Against his better judgment, James released his hand on her neck but remained close.

"Why?" Tess asked.

"You should know why," Taryn replied.

"I don't know what I did to you to make you hate me so much." Tess was inches from her face. "We don't like each other—that is no secret—but I would never call a hit on you. Just stay the hell out of my life. It didn't have to come to this."

"Fuck you, Tess." Taryn struck Tess across the cheek with her fist.

Stunned, but only for a quick moment, Tess balled up her fist and hit her a dozen times before James pulled her off.

"You're lucky," Tess yelled. "I would have beaten you until you were dead."

Taryn smiled with a wicked laugh. "For all your education, you aren't very smart."

Colin walked up behind Tess, taking her arm. "Tess, let's go back to the house."

"Okay." Tess turned back to Taryn, balled up her fist, and hit her one more time. Then she turned and kicked her in her chest hard enough to make her lose her breath. "That's for Chicago, bitch."

Colin glanced at Taryn. "James, give me a minute?"

"You let her go—and I will shoot you in the head." James firmly eyed him and walked a couple paces away.

Colin pushed her against the door and put his hands on the sides of her head. "Why? I gave you everything you could possibly need."

"Except you," she told him. "All of this is because of you. You bear this blood. You bear any death that happens here. You bear the fact that if I die, you will never find Connor."

"You truly underestimate me," he snarled between gritted teeth. "I will find my son, and you will never see him again—if you live."

"Thank God for tiny retributions." Wickedly, she smiled. "I see you haven't told Tess."

"Done here," he spoke to James with his eyes on Taryn. "She's all yours, James. Do as you please."

"Something you need to tell me?" Tess crossed her arms as Colin walked over to her.

"Yep. I met her six months before I met you. Ending things with her was part of my twelve-step program back then," he began honestly. "She lives in my apartment in Chicago, and I give her ten grand a month to keep her mouth shut. The last time we were together, she got pregnant and had my son, which I just found out the day before I brought you here. Paternity results came in yesterday. Now she's hidden him from me. If something happens to her, I have no idea where to begin to look for him. I haven't spoken to her in three fucking years. I'm a little pissed right now, Tess. I know you want to lay into me right now as you rightly should, but you need to put it on the shelf and save it for later."

"Don't tell me what to save for later." Her voice was soft but daring as she placed her hands on her hips.

"Tess?" Colin reached out for her, and she pulled back.

"Don't fucking touch me." She warned and turned to walk away.

"Please don't walk away. You can't tell me you don't have a secret affair that you haven't told me about."

Tess shook her head. "Don't you dare turn this back on me. Matthew wasn't a secret affair for four years."

"Maybe Matthew wasn't—but James has been."

"Go to hell," she said and walked off.

* * *

Jonathan went to his office, shut the door, and paced for a few minutes. For the life of him, he couldn't figure out where he messed up with her. What did he do differently with her than with Tess? There had to be something, some tiny incident that would turn her viciously against her sister. His thoughts were interrupted by a soft knock on the door.

"Dad." Harper walked into his arms.

"My sweet, sweet girl. I love you, Harper." He kissed her on the head.

"I love you too, Father." She gave him a simple smile. "I have a request."

"Okay." He leaned back against the desk. "What is it?"

"I know you have her." Harper looked down for a moment. "Please don't torture her. Make it quick and painless. Given her betrayal, I know it must be done, but please make it fast."

"As you wish," he said, giving his daughter false hope. Taryn's fate was in James' hands.

"This might make you feel really bad," she continued. "If you know of a way to avoid it, try. You're too good of a father to feel bad. I've tried to think of ways to avoid this, but nothing seems plausible. She would just keep coming back for revenge."

His hands cradled her face. "Harper, of all my kids, you are the most compassionate, kindhearted, selfless one. I have adored you from the moment I picked you up. Thank you for being a beautiful light in my life. I love you."

Harper smiled and kissed his cheek. "I love you too. James is waiting for you. I should leave you two to tend to business." She walked out the door.

James was standing in the hallway waiting for Harper to leave, so he could finish business.

Harper grinned and placed her hands over his. "I know you don't really like people and trust them even less but keep me here." Her hand covered his heart. "You're almost done with this business, and when you are—and you're ready to talk and ask me all the questions you want to ask—I will be here waiting. I will never lie to you, cheat you, or judge you. Don't forget to go see Jesse when you're done here. She is the key to your future."

"How do you know Jesse?"

"You were calling her name the other night when you were sleeping." She smiled. "And saying some other things that I won't repeat."

"Harper, I don't know why I like you so much. You are so strange—in a good way."

She smiled.

James gave her a hug. "Stay pure of heart, Harp. Jack is very lucky to get to marry you."

Harper pulled back, eyeing him. "We haven't talked about the *m* word."

"You will." He gave her a wink.

Colin walked down the hallway, and James grinned, finding odd pleasure in Colin's troubles. "I've never seen your father pissed. I am curious about how this will go down."

"Thanks." Colin shook his head. "I think you should wait out here." He walked into his father's office and closed the door behind him.

"Son, is there something you need to tell me?"

"No. The conversation I needed to have was with my wife."

"You're the one who has her set up nicely in Chicago," Jonathan concluded.

"Yes," he finally admitted.

"Have you been seeing her since you've been married?" he asked.

Colin sighed. "No. I ended things with her a few days before Tess was shot in Chicago. I didn't know about Connor until I showed up here. It was dumb luck that I happened upon her walking down the street with him."

"Why didn't you tell me?" Jonathan asked.

"I couldn't even figure out a way to tell Tess." Colin stood up and paced. "I want to put a fucking bullet in her head, but I don't know where my son is! She has ruined my life. I didn't want a kid with her! I want the baby that is growing in my wife's belly. I don't want to lose my wife over this. Tess and I have been so happy for the past three years. I don't want to lose that, but I don't know what to do. I just don't know."

"Is Tess aware?"

"She just found out." Colin leaned against the wall. "And she's not talking to me."

"This is unreal." Jonathan sighed. "We will find the boy with or without her alive."

Grey knocked on the door and walked in with James. "Sorry to interrupt, but the DNA results came back from the shooting of Tess and Matthew a few weeks ago. It's a match for Taryn."

Jonathan nodded.

✳ ✳ ✳

Tess left Savannah with Matthew and changed into her running capris, a T-shirt, and tennis shoes. Jack gave her another 9 mm, and she slipped it into her waistband. She also strapped a four-inch switchblade to her ankle. She needed quiet time to think. With the tension like a visible wall everywhere, she really wanted to go for a run, but that certainly wasn't happening tonight.

Jack was out patrolling with Harper. James and Colin were out by the shop, and Tess decided to sit in a white rocker on the porch.

A breeze blew through the trees, making an eerie rustling sound. It sprinkled here and there, and the winds were picking up. When she closed her eyes, she could hear Colin's jeep, in the distance. Within five minutes, Jack parked in front of the house.

Jack and Harper walked up on the porch. "Why are you still out here, Tess?" Jack asked.

"Just listening," she answered. "Colin and James are right over there by the shop. I got my gun. I'm listening to everything." When her phone buzzed, she looked at the caller ID. "It's Taryn."

"Answer it," he said, stepping closer.

"Hello?"

"Tess."

"Dominic, I've been waiting for you to call back," Tess spoke his name as his voice was distinct.

"I've missed you so very much."

Tess closed her eyes and walked away from Jack. "Tell me what you know—please. I am fighting for my life and the life of my daughter."

"She has a small army," he began. "I'm not exactly certain where, but they will be coming."

"When?"

"The last I heard they were assembling on a property close to your father's," his voice was hurried. "It's tonight. Just get somewhere safe—please."

"Dominic," Tess whispered. "You know who Jonathan is, don't you?"

"Yes, I know. I hope to sit and have a conversation with him someday. There are a few things I still don't understand."

"Please don't come here until this is over," she nearly begged. "I don't want you to be hurt."

"Don't you mean *killed*? He asked. "My life has been hell since you left. I don't really care if I live or die. That's a lie as I would prefer to live."

"They already have her locked up," she advised. "She won't hurt me. Please stay away because they aren't certain of your intentions."

"I want to talk with you," he told her. "You know I would never hurt you, but you have information that I need. I need to put the pieces together."

"Dominic, we can talk, but you need to wait until this other mess is over. I don't want them to kill you—and you know they will."

"Tess, she has a son, but I don't know who—"

"Dominic?" Tess gritted her teeth. "Damn it."

"Tess?" Jack put his hand on her shoulder. "What the hell are you thinking? Let him come here. Why are you warning him? You don't know what his intentions are."

"He's not going to hurt me," she replied with full confidence.

"You don't know that. We're trying to keep you alive. All of this is for you."

"Maybe you should have left me in Portland," she stated flatly.

Harper slipped into the house as she knew a fight was coming.

"Damn it, Tess," Jack fumed. "Since when did you become so trusting? You don't know him like you think you do."

Tess's eyes hardened. "I do know him, and I was the one in bed with him—not you."

Jack backed her up against the house and put his hands on each side of her head. "He isn't an amateur. There were 128 people on a list that James was working, and he killed 106. Markenna is no saint. He slipped through with James, and you know how good he is at this. He finances human trafficking. I don't want you talking with him until we know his intentions. Understand?"

"You don't want me talking to him?" Her eyes were wide with fury. "I trust him—like I trust you."

"Can you just wait until one of us can figure out what he wants?"

"Gut instinct, Jack," she dared him to argue with that point.

Jack caressed her cheek, held her eyes for a moment, and was so close to kissing her but stopped himself.

Tess pushed him away almost instantly when she caught the look in his eyes. "You can't do that anymore."

"Damn it." Jack stepped back and placed his hands on his hips frustrated with himself.

"You walked away from me," she whispered. "And I loved you so much. You just walked away."

"I know." He stared blankly at her. "And it was the worst thing I ever did back then. If I could take it back, I would."

"Well, you can't. I lost our baby, and you still left," she reminded him.

"You didn't want me to come back," he reminded her, this time. "I would have been on the first plane back there, but you said no."

"Come on, Jack. You know me better than that. I needed you, and you left. Colin and I had our problems back then, but I knew if I needed him, he was there—or on his way. You walked away from me to save your relationship with him, and it's shit anyway."

"You know I would have walked away from all this to be with you. All you had to do was say the word. I kept waiting, but you never said it. I left because I figured you had made up your mind and loved him more. I left because it was way too difficult to be around you and not touch you and love you the way we were so good at doing. I think about how things would be very different had you not lost the baby, but you did. It wasn't just difficult for you. I can't tell you how many times I cried about it. If you don't believe me, ask Gina. She is the one who helped me get through it."

"Gina knows?" she asked.

"Gina knows everything," Jack lowered his voice. "You had Colin. I had nobody."

"I'm sorry." She softly wiped a tear away. "I was so broken from losing you—then the baby—I didn't think about what you were going through. I'm so sorry."

Jack shook his head. "It doesn't matter anymore. It was so long ago."

"It does matter." She crossed her arms. "Every minute with you mattered. Our baby mattered. All of it mattered."

"I'm struggling here." Jack shook his head. "You've got to give me a break. I haven't seen you in three years. You almost died, and I couldn't come see you. Do you know what that was like?"

She nodded as a few tears slipped out. "I wanted you to come and tell me everything would be alright—just like you always did."

Jack shook his head, and his eyes filled with tears. "Why didn't we have this conversation before?"

"Because he got it right, or so I thought, and I'm not supposed to still love you like I do."

Jack wiped his eyes and hugged her. "We messed this one up. There's nothing we can do about it now. You know that don't you?"

"I know. Married, baby, and he's not the same man he was back then. I'm not sure who he is at this moment. Besides, you have our sweet Harper. She waited for you, and that means everything to her."

"I know. I really do love her, Tess. It's so simple, and we were so intense. I know that's because of the circumstances we were in, but I will marry Harper," he told her knowing she would understand.

"Of course you will." She grinned. "If not of your own accord, I'm sure we could find a shotgun around here."

Jack laughed. "Damn, I've missed you. I miss just sitting around and talking like we used to do."

"If we all survive this, we should sit down and catch up," she suggested.

"Yep. I need to give this to Colin," he said, running a hand down her arm. "I hope he won't beat the crap out of me for almost kissing you."

"Did you know he was seeing Taryn all those years?" she asked.

"No. And I wouldn't lie to you for him either. I'm sorry for what you're going to be going through with this. Had I known I would've never left you."

Tess ran her hand down his arm. "I missed you so much."

"I need to give your phone to them." He kissed her forehead. "Love you, T."

"Love you too, Jack," she replied.

✳ ✳ ✳

James sucked in a little bit of air when he saw Jack nearly kiss Tess knowing Colin saw the same thing he did.

"I don't know what the hell he's thinking right now," Colin said, irritated.

"Not sure, myself." James glanced at Colin wondering just how angry he was about that near kiss.

"Here." Jack tossed the phone to Colin and said, "I'm sorry about that."

In one swift move, Colin punched Jack in the jaw. "Sorry about that."

"Damn it," Jack muttered rolling his jaw.

"She's my wife," Colin reminded him. "Not just my part-time girlfriend."

"I'm aware of that," Jack replied. "And I said I'm sorry."

"Was that Markenna?" Colin asked.

"Look." Jack pointed to the phone.

"Well, well." Colin chuckled. "Taryn called her. How the hell?"

"Impossible," James spoke this time. "Adam has her phone. I left it with him tonight."

Colin hit redial.

"I knew you'd call back," Dominic sighed. "I don't know why the call keeps dropping."

"You are causing issues in my life, and I'm starting to get pissed," Colin thundered. "What the fuck do you want?"

"Tess," Dominic remarked.

"You realize she is married, right?" Colin asked.

"I don't care," Dominic bluntly stated. "None of you gave a damn when she put herself in my life."

"Stay away from my wife—or I will kill you. And I want my son. If you have him, it would be in your best interests to bring him to me," Colin advised firmly.

"How much do you love that little girl you've been raising?" Dominic exclaimed and hung up.

Colin nearly threw the phone at James and ran to the house. Pain rooted in his heart deeply as he panicked with the thought of something happening to Savannah. Running up to Savannah's room, he stressed a bit more when she wasn't there. Double stepping down the stairs, he nearly collided with Tess at the bottom.

"What's wrong?" she asked but he didn't answer.

"Matthew!" Colin yelled running to the family room.

"What?" Matthew stood up with Savannah in his arms. "What's wrong?"

Colin took Savannah from his brother's arms and held her tightly. His knees buckled, and he sat on the floor with her knowing she was safe in his arms.

"Daddy, you're squeezing me," her small voice squeaked.

"Sorry, baby girl." He loosened his grip.

"Daddy, are you sad?" Savannah creased her forehead.

"No. I'm just glad that you are safe with Matthew." Kissing her forehead, he sighed relieved.

"You have tears," she said, touching them with her tiny fingers. "I wiped them away like you do with mine."

"Thank you." He kissed her cheek. "I love you."

"I love you too, Daddy." Giving him a squeeze, she kissed his cheek.

Colin breathed a sigh of relief and cradled her in his arms. "It's late for you to be up."

"Matthew was rocking me like a baby—like you do."

"Want to go back to Matthew so he can rock you like a baby and put you to sleep?"

Savannah nodded.

"Okay, then." Colin handed her back to his brother and watched him sit back down. "If she's not with you she's with Tess or me."

"Yep," Matthew agreed.

"Let's go, Colin," James hollered, walking into the room. "Adam has a trace."

Colin turned to Tess but didn't speak. Nothing he would say, at this moment, would fix this problem between them. With their problem aside, he noted Morgan was behind her eyes. He hadn't seen this side of her in years. Knowing nothing he said would penetrate through Morgan, he opted to kiss her forehead and leave the room.

Tess walked over to Matthew. She laid a soft hand on her daughter's cheek wondering if this would be the last time she would see her. Would tonight be the night that she died? Her skills weren't as sharp as they were three years ago.

"Keep her safe, Matthew. If something happens to me, make sure she knows how much I love her." Tess gave Savannah a kiss on her soft cheek, then kissed Matthew on the forehead and left. As she passed the dining room she glanced at Colin. "I'm going back outside."

"Here." Colin handed her his phone. "You got the other 9 mm Jack gave you?"

"Yep." She walked out the door.

"She shouldn't be going by herself." James glanced up.

Jack explained, "In case you didn't notice, that is not Tess. Morgan is alive and by the looks of it not too happy."

James handed Tess's phone to Adam.

"Markenna's call showed up like it was from Taryn's phone," Adam began to explain. "I'm thinking he just bounced the call since her phone is right next to you."

James stepped away from all of them and went out on the front porch. He knew Tess was out there somewhere, preferably close, but he needed to make sure. Closing the door behind him, he spotted her in a rocker with a 9 mm in her hand. Out of habit, he pressed the button on the radio to speak with his team. "Everything quiet inside, six?"

"Yes," Purcell responded.

"Copy that, six." James looked over at Tess. "Are you going to sit out here all night?"

"Shh." She held her finger to her lips and continued to listen.

James walked over to her and knelt on one knee.

"It sounds like a jeep," Tess whispered. "Colin's is right here in front of us. I thought I heard a shot, but it was muffled by the wind. I think it is coming from the east end of the property. It's all wetlands over there. A jeep wouldn't make it through."

"Jack ran a patrol there an hour ago," he told her.

"James, there's something out there. I can hear it," she insisted.

"Okay," he conceded, resting a hand on her knee. "I will get Jack to run patrol again, and we'll check in with everyone. My other five men are at the airstrip with the chopper, waiting for instructions. If we need them, they will be here in two minutes."

Tess nodded.

"If you're staying out here, stay low—otherwise, get your ass inside," he instructed.

Tess got out of the chair, sat on the porch, and leaned against the house.

"Don't leave this spot unless you're coming inside." James gave her a firm look.

"I got it, okay?" Tess fired back with eyes wide.

James put his hand on her shoulder. "I don't want to lose you," he began. "If I am being mean, that is why. I don't even like you out here alone."

"Short of someone pulling a sniper shot, I'll be fine right here. I have no intention of leaving the porch. I promise you."

"You know how I feel about promises."

"Yes, I do." She smiled. "Sometimes it's all we have in this world."

"Are you doing okay?" He took a moment as he was concerned.

"I don't know. And I don't want to talk about it." Tess directed her eyes to the long row of oak trees that lined the long drive, she was done talking.

James kissed the top of her head, stood, and went into the house.

In the dining room Jack, Adam, and Colin were pinpointing a satellite image of the property next to this one.

James did another radio check again.

"Why did you do that again so soon?" Jack asked.

"Would you mind doing a patrol again on the east side?" James asked. "She swears she hears something over there."

"Tess said that?" Colin popped his head up.

"Yes, is there something with her and this listening thing?" James asked.

"Yes." Colin nodded. "What did she say she heard?"

"She said it sounded like a jeep and a gunshot," James relayed.

Colin went and sat on the porch next to Tess and listened. A few minutes later, they popped their heads up and opened their eyes at the same time.

"Did you hear that?" she whispered.

"Yes," he answered. "To the east?"

"Yes." She nodded. "I keep hearing a vehicle. It stops and goes about every ten minutes or so."

Colin buzzed Jack. "We heard a shot—just like a handgun and not a rifle—on the east side."

Jack walked out the front door with his rifle in hand and his Glock on his hip as he wore a bulletproof vest.

James followed Jack to the jeep, and they headed to the east side of the property. Jack drove and told his men he was doing another round. They had to give the right-hand movement, or they would be shot. They drove the fence line slowly. James used the spotlight to thoroughly check things. When they reached the wetlands area, James got out and walked the line.

James kept the searchlight straight out with his gun in hand, ready to shoot. He scanned the water for unusual ripples and the water's edge for footprints. Jack drove alongside him as he carefully checked out the area. There were about three hundred yards of wetlands on that side of the property, and James walked the entire line. He stopped a few times to watch for movement of any sort, but there was nothing. Jack stopped by the iron fence at the end and picked up James. They finished the patrol of the perimeter before going back to the house.

Tess and Colin stood up when they came back.

James got out of the jeep. "Nothing. There wasn't even a ripple in the water."

"Maybe my direction is off." Tess questioned herself.

"We drove around the perimeter." Jack shook his head.

"I'm sorry." Frustrated, Tess walked inside the house.

Jack looked at Colin and held up his arms.

James sighed in his own frustration. "I don't think any of us thinks she is lying. What are we missing? If I were the one infiltrating the grounds here, I'd use a long-range rifle to pick off the men from the remote perimeter. From there, I'd form my own perimeter within the gates, so you don't have to watch your back, and then bring it all in, surround the house, and take it. Or create a distraction over there and come in on the lake."

James opened the front door, and the three men walked in.

Adam waved James over to the computer. "The call on Tess's phone came from this area," he announced and pointed to a map. "It's within a one-block radius on the property beside this one, which is owned by the government. If you bring up the satellite image and zoom in, you can see the iron fence around more of the wetlands. Jonathan's fence didn't cross the entire area because it is just too marshy to make it stick. It can be crossed with a boat. I don't think it can be crossed by foot. It's like quicksand."

Colin couldn't focus on protecting Tess knowing they were not in a good place with their relationship. Finding Tess on the couch, he simply looked at her for a moment. "Sit up for a minute, baby." He sat down, as she curled up to him. "I'm sorry. At some point, we need to talk about this."

"I know." She looked up at him. "I saw you hit Jack."

Colin pursed his lips. "I saw him almost kiss my wife."

"Did you also see your wife push him away?" she wondered.

"I did, but it was a guy thing." Colin shook his head with a shrug.

Tess looked up at him with a small smile. "Sometimes I get so mad because I love you when I'm angry with you. And I'm so angry at you right now."

"I know," he conceded. "And I was out of line earlier. I'm sorry for what I said about James."

"And that is my dilemma." She sighed with a small shake of her head. "How can I be mad at you for her when I never told you about him? I think any other girl would have been okay, but her? How did you even know about James?"

"There's a way you look at him. I don't know. I just know that look is a look that you give me." Colin couldn't clearly explain how he knew, he just did.

"The thing with him was a long time ago." Tess rested her hand on his cheek. "I married you because you're the one I love. Yes, I love them—but not like I love you, and you know that."

"I never doubt your love for me," he admitted.

"And I don't with you," she sighed. "I just don't understand how I didn't know you were seeing her ... and for so long."

"You were always gone when I saw her," he answered honestly. "I met her before I met you. I cared about her—but not like you did with Jack. I never loved her like I love you. It was just sex—not someone I could spend my life with. Do you understand what I mean?"

"It doesn't make me feel any better. I never expected something like this, especially with my damn sister."

"I know." Colin kissed her forehead. "I never expected the son I apparently have with her."

"Well, that makes two of us." Tilting her head, she kissed his lips softly.

"Do you two want some privacy for this conversation?" Matthew asked. "I'm thinking this is something you don't want us hearing."

"No." Tess looked back at Colin. "Does your father know?"

Colin looked at his dad. "Yes, I talked to him after I told you. The only other person who knows is James because he, apparently, knows everything."

"Might as well tell your brother and Gina," Tess suggested.

After a deep breath, he looked at Gina and his brother. "I have a son ... with Taryn."

Matthew grinned with a low chuckle.

"Oh boy," Gina said, not surprised. "How old?"

"About the same age as Savannah. She's hidden him. I haven't spoken to her in three years, so I have no idea where to begin to look for him."

Matthew smiled and shook his head. "Dominic."

Colin nodded. "I already told that son of a bitch that he better bring him to me, if he is the one who has him."

"I don't think being an ass to the man who probably has your kid is the way to go," Matthew suggested.

"I don't want to worry about this stuff," he easily admitted. "I want to take care of my wife and our daughter and our baby growing in her tummy and nothing else. I didn't want a child with anyone else, but ethical responsibility tells me I need to step up and be a father to a child I didn't even know existed three weeks ago."

Tess cupped his face. "We will take care of him as if he's ours—regardless of the circumstances. Remember, he is just an innocent child."

"I don't want to lose you." Colin's eyes filled with tears.

"The only way you will lose me is if she lives by your doing." Tess was as honest as she could be.

"James said he would take care of her," Colin stated. "I'm trusting him to do just that."

James walked into the room. "Grey and I are going to check out this place on the other property. Jack and Purcell will be on the west side of the wetlands. One of us will call you to let you know if we find anything."

Tess followed James to the foyer. "James, I have a terrible feeling about this."

"I don't. The end is near. It's time this is done." James didn't have time to deal with her emotions.

"You ready, James?" Jack was surprised to find Tess with him. "What's all this about?"

Tess wiped the tears from her cheeks as James left the room. "Someone is over there, Jack. I heard it. Please be careful."

"This is what we do, and he does this for a living. We will be fine. I promise you. Okay?"

"I can't lose anybody," she pleaded.

James waved Colin from the family room. "Do something with her. We need to move."

"Okay." Colin walked into the foyer with James. "Come on, Tess. Let them go."

Tess nodded as her eyes filled, again. Taking his hand, she let him lead her upstairs to their room where she curled up in bed beside him on the bed.

"What's wrong besides the obvious?" he asked.

Tess looked at him with reddened eyes. "I have a very bad feeling, and I don't want to lose them."

Colin wiped her tears. "It's okay to feel emotions."

"I hate the emotions I have when I'm pregnant," she reminded him.

"I know you do." Pulling her closer, he held her safely in his arms.

Tess lifted her head and kissed him slowly and maneuvered her body so she could unbutton his pants. With that move she felt his hands push hers off her hips. Their lips never left one another as they undress each other. She needed the feel of him on top of her, inside of her.

"Colin?" She whispered his name as she kissed his neck.

"What, baby?" he mumbled between the nips on her ear lobes. Colin closed his eyes, absorbing the incredible feeling of the moment. His movements were slow and perfect as their kisses were endless.

Feeling her breath catch when he first entered her body, made her unconsciously hold her breath. Tess lost her words as he brought her to the edge quickly and held her there for a moment before they both went over together.

"That was way too fast." Colin rested his hand over her belly as they lay facing each other.

"I know you like to go slow." Her finger trailed down his chest. "Sometimes I just need you to take me to that edge fast."

"It seems like all of it's been fast lately—except the other night. That was intense."

"Yes. That has got to be my favorite position." Tess remembered straddling his lap.

"Which one? We were in several," he reminded.

"You sitting and me straddling you," she described. "I like the feel of your chest against mine, your lips on my neck, and your hands all over my backside."

"I like that one too," he agreed. "You know that was the third time in the last sixteen hours?"

"Are you complaining?" She pulled his mouth back to hers.

"No." He mumbled between the kisses. "Just an observation."

"That's good." She straddled him. "Because we are about to go for the fourth time."

✳ ✳ ✳

"What the hell were you thinking on the porch, Jack?" James asked.

"I don't know." Jack shrugged. "I don't want to talk about it."

"You're lucky he didn't pull out his gun and shoot you," James shook his head, not understanding why his cousin nearly kissed Tess earlier.

"I don't really care." Jack looked at him. "I should have stayed four years ago. Maybe none of this would be happening."

"Yes, but maybe both of you would be dead," James tossed that idea out there.

"I thought she was out of my system."

"Focus on Harper, there is less drama with her. And you know there are no other men because she's a virgin."

"*Was* a virgin," Jack muttered.

James chuckled and put his arm around Jack's shoulder. "Jack, my brother, are we going to get an heir in the family?"

Jack shrugged. "Maybe, because there was no protection used."

"Good. That'll get Harrison off my ass." James took in a deep breath and sighed.

"I love Harper, but it's different than with Tess. It's simple. Do you know what I mean?"

"Yes, I completely understand because I have so much experience with this thing you call love."

"You do." Jack eyed him.

"No, I don't. We knew it was only an affair—never anything more." James smiled as Jack got in the jeep and took off.

Grey came up within seconds in another jeep and picked up James. They headed out to the airstrip. James found his other five guys at the hangar, waiting. They gave him a vest and a hip holster. Grey handed James an AK with extra rounds, which he slipped into his pocket.

"I'm not sure what we will be walking into. Be prepared for anything. Jack's men have the yellow band," James told them as he looked at each one of his men who nodded in response.

"What about the family members? They aren't going to end up in the line of fire where we're not sure if they are good or bad?" Javier asked.

"All of you have seen the pictures of the family. Colin, Matthew, and Tess will work with us. They know how to distinguish you guys and Jack's men. I told them no masks. If they have their faces covered, they aren't friendly. Tess's twin is responsible for this. They look very similar. Tess has her hair braided or wears it up in a bun. I asked her to keep it that way so you guys could identify her. Her best identity marker is the 9 mm she carries. I'm fairly confident you will know her if you cross her path."

"How are we going in? Bold or silent?" another one of the men asked.

"I was originally thinking silently, but I'm leaning toward bold now." He looked at them with a grin. "What do you guys want to do?"

"Bold," one of them said and the others agreed.

"Bold it is," James confirmed with a smile. "Get her in the air. Grey and I will go in with the jeep. Light it up."

James got back in the jeep as the chopper blades started spinning. He pressed his radio button to let Jack know they were going in bold and to be prepared if anything happened. He called his other men and told them to join Jack and Purcell on the east side of the wetlands.

CHAPTER 25

Adam walked into the family room with a concerned look upon his face. "Matthew, I just lost all my electronics. Try your phone."

Matthew pulled out his cell. It was dead. "Nothing." Standing, he handed Savannah to Gina.

Colin woke up Tess and went to the kitchen, opened the computer, and brought up the cameras.

"Circular feed," Adam muttered as they watched the screens. "Look at number three. See that glitch? Someone's in the system, and there's a jammer on the phones. There's no communication with Jack's men. James has it with his men, but that's it."

Matthew went into his father's office and punched a code that opened a hidden door. He grabbed two rifles, two handguns, and extra ammo and went back to the kitchen. He handed Adam a rifle, a handgun, and some ammo and gave his father the other set.

"Let's move them down to the wine cellar," Matthew commanded as he scooped Savannah back up.

Jonathan took the lead with Gina behind him, and Matthew followed with Savannah. The area had a sofa and chair in one corner, and wine racks lined the walls. Matthew laid Savannah beside Gina and covered her with a blanket.

Matthew put in another code that opened a smaller room that

housed the computer guts for the house and property. "Adam, think you can get us back online? We need cell phones."

"I'll work on it." He took a seat at the expansive computer setup. "This is very cool." His fingers started flying over the keyboard. Adam put on his headset to the radio that went directly to James and contacted him. "No communication. Okay ... I will." He went to his backpack, pulled out another radio, and handed it to Matthew. "James said to put this on Tess. They're under heavy fire. It's the second scenario that they were talking about the other night—watching the lake."

Matthew nodded. "You know what to do, Father. Take care of her for us please."

"Number one priority," Jonathan declared. "Go kill these bastards."

"That would be my number one priority." Matthew closed the door and waited until he heard the click of the dead bolts. Knowing they would be safe; he could focus on keeping Tess safe.

Upstairs, Tess and Colin were strapping on their vests in Jonathan's office. Tess took two handguns and extra ammo from the closet and moved out of the way so Colin and Matthew could get what they wanted. Then, Tess wrapped her hair up in a bun as per James' request.

"Here, Tess," Matthew hooked the radio around her neck and gave her the earpiece to put on. "Press here, hold, and you can talk to James and his men. All of them will hear you, but James will be the one to answer. If he can't, it will be Grey. Colin, James said the second scenario."

"Got it." Colin nodded and walked up to Tess. "Protect the baby. I will have your back."

Tess nodded. "I will."

Matthew looked at them. "Are you sure about going? Maybe you should stay here?"

"No." Colin shook his head. "She stays with me. Besides, she's an expert shot."

"Your call." Matthew shook his head not agreeing. "Not mine. I'll take the lead. Let's go out the back and head to the shop. Let's make sure Taryn's still in there."

Colin nodded.

"Let's turn off the house lights and turn on the first perimeter lights," Matthew suggested.

"Okay." Colin went back to the kitchen with the surveillance computer and opened the electrical panel. He turned off the lights on the outside of the house and turned on the first perimeter, which was a hundred meters away from the house. "Let's go."

"Wait," Tess whispered. "Where's Harper?"

"Damn." Matthew ran up to Harper's room. She wasn't there or in Jack's room.

"Greenhouse," Tess suggested and headed in that direction. When Tess opened the door to the room, there was a broken flowerpot in the middle of the floor. Instantly, an uneasy feeling sank in her stomach.

Colin went to the door that led to the side of the house, and the glass above the handle was broken.

"They got her," Tess stated aloud a fact they already knew. "Let's go see if Taryn is gone too."

"Might as well go out this door," Matthew sighed as this was not good.

Matthew took the lead, Colin pulled up the rear, and Tess was in the middle. Once outside, they crouched and listened to gunfire in the distance as they scanned the area around them. The next open area was between the house and the shop. There was nothing to hide behind. Matthew had his rifle aimed forward with the butt resting against his shoulder. Colin was in the same position, covering behind them.

At the shop, the door had been jimmied open.

Two masked men rounded the corner, and Tess shot them instantly without hesitation.

Colin took one of their radios and the AK and went cautiously into the shop.

Each of them scanned the inside of the building, but they found no one around. They headed to the adjoined gym. The lights were on, and there was a body in the corner with a yellow band on the arm. By the chair, they found cut zip ties and blood.

"Back door," Matthew pointed in that direction.

The three of them leaned against the wall by the door once they made their way there.

"Where is everyone?" Matthew whispered.

Tess turned off the lights when a door opened. The three of them crouched down and listened. Someone banged into a tray of tools making a loud crashing sound.

"Jack?" she whispered softly.

"Tess." His breathing was labored, and he stumbled toward her with Matthew catching him. "Get my vest off."

Colin ripped the Velcro from the sides, and Matthew pulled it over his head. Four bullets were stuck in it. Colin plucked each one out, and Tess helped him sit on a stool. She pulled his shirt up to see how bad the bruising was.

"Where is everyone?" Colin asked.

"There were so many of them—like fucking ants." Jack shook his head. "Purcell and I took out a lot, but I know some got through. James and his men on the other side dropped into a war zone. James has radio contact with his men, but my wire was shot. I can't reach any of my men, and the cell isn't working. A few of James's men helped Purcell and me, but I was hit. I told Purcell I needed to get back here to tell you guys, but you seem to know. Do you have everyone in the wine cellar?"

"Everyone but Harper," Matthew explained knowing Jack wouldn't take kindly to this new problem. "We're pretty sure she was taken out of the greenhouse. Broken shit everywhere."

"Oh my God." Jack ran his hand over his forehead. "We have to find her."

"We will," Tess spoke in her calm voice.

"They used the wetlands as a distraction," Jack began. "They had to get to the house by the lake. It was the only way—unless they've taken out the guards at the gate. I need to get back to the house for more ammo. I'm out."

"How is James doing out there?" Tess asked.

"James and his men are good—damn good." He smiled. "Not one casualty on his side when I left. He had eight, and I had four. They know their kill zones."

"You have a casualty in the gym," she grimaced. "I'm sorry."

"Damn. I take it Taryn's not in there?"

Tess shook her head.

"Let's go back to the house and reload. I must find a way to check in with my men." Jack grabbed his vest and strapped it back on. "Let's do two in front and two in the back."

Colin nodded slowly.

"Colin's not letting Tess out of his sight. I will go with Jack through the front, and you two get the back." Matthew suggested.

"Okay," Colin agreed. "Ready for this, Tess?"

"Yep." She pulled her gun from the holster.

Matthew shook his head at her. "Be careful, little mama."

Tess smiled and followed Colin out the side door with Jack and Matthew behind them. They split in the middle, and Colin and Tess moved slowly along the side of the house. Instead of going through the greenhouse, they went to the back patio.

Colin peeked his head around to see if anyone was there. He counted three men with masks, and they weren't wearing armbands.

"You want high or low?" he whispered.

"Low," she lipped.

"On three." He counted down with his fingers. On three, they both rounded the corner. Tess shot one in the head, and Colin hit the other two in the neck.

Cautiously, they moved toward the French doors off the family room. Colin noticed a light was on and hoped to hell it was Jack and Matthew. Colin opened the doors without noticing anyone in the family room. He motioned for Tess to follow, and they both went inside.

Four men in black with masks jumped them. Colin's gun was kicked from his hand and the hand-to-hand combat began. Tess shot the first man who came at her, but he had a vest. Instead, she shot him in the head.

The next man punched her in the face and knocked the gun from her hand. She stumbled back against the fireplace. Feeling around, she grabbed a fire poker and swung it hard, piercing the man's skull, nearly making her vomit. She charged one of the two men Colin was fighting.

She hit one in the knee with the poker, and when he buckled, she hit him it the head.

Colin smacked the other man's head against the bricks and tossed him through the French doors. "You okay?"

Tess nodded, and they picked up their guns.

Then lights came on, and Taryn was holding a gun to Harper's head. Two masked men, standing just behind Taryn, pointed their weapons at Tess and Colin.

"All of you should know to have a backup plan for the backup plan." Taryn looked directly at Tess and smiled. "I take it that you know your husband and I slept together over and over and over."

"So what?" Tess smiled back. "He married me."

"Yep." Taryn shrugged. "But he was kissing me the other night."

"You mean the other night when he was drunk and thought you were me? He told me, bitch."

"You always think you're all that and then some." Taryn shook her head. "Do you know how gratifying it was to be sleeping with your boyfriend, having him give me his place in Chicago for free, and having him give me ten thousand dollars every single month?"

"Most men do pay for their whores." Tess raised her eyebrows.

"That doesn't bother me, Tess." Taryn sighed. "I just look at it as child support."

The two masked men took off their masks. One of them was Dominic. He raised his finger to his lips, telling her silently to be quiet.

"You know you are second best for Dominic. Didn't you see the pictures of us? I think James still has them on the table. He only found you because he was looking for me."

"Doesn't matter anymore." Taryn shook her head. "You can keep your bitch attitude, your husband, and this family. Oh wait—you don't get to keep your husband."

Before anyone could react, Taryn released three shots at Colin.

CHAPTER 26

James stood up cautiously and scanned the grounds slowly. No one was moving and the distinct stench of death was in the air. "Two, check?" he said softly into his radio.

"Two, copy, behind you," Grey replied.

James nodded and did roll call on the rest of his men. Everyone checked in except Jack. He motioned for Grey to follow him, as he damn near ran to the jeep. He needed to get to the house. He made a promise to Tess, and he was keeping it.

Grey drove as James gave his men orders. "Secure this area and bring it into the main house," he directed. "We take no prisoners." James closed his eyes. "Tess, check?"

"Check," she whispered softly.

"Where are you?" He heard voices over the radio, but they weren't his men. Listening, he knew she couldn't speak. "We're on our way. Do whatever you have to do to stay alive."

At the main gate, two of Jack's men were still standing guard.

"Do not leave this post for any reason," James commanded. "And don't let anybody in."

"Yes, sir," the man said as he opened the main gate.

James nodded and Grey drove them to the front of the house.

Matthew and Jack were engaged in hand-to-hand combat with

three men. Having no patience, James pulled out his weapon and shot two of them in the head. Grey shot the third.

"Why the hell aren't you shooting them?" James asked.

"We find gratification in beating them." Jack glanced sideways at him. "Out of ammo."

"Here." James tossed Jack his rifle. "Tess is inside, and she has company. She couldn't talk. Grey, let's go to the front. You two go in the back."

James and Grey crouched down in the darkness of the hallway. When James saw Dominic Markenna take off the mask, he knew Tess was right, Dominic wouldn't hurt her. Out of nowhere, Taryn fired her weapon at Colin.

Colin's body jerked back from the impact, and he hit his head on the fireplace.

"Colin!" Tess screamed and knelt by his side.

Colin took her hand and pulled her close. "Kill that bitch." He released her hand and passed out.

The silence in the room was eerie. Tess heard her own breath escape her lungs, then get sucked the air back in again. Closing her eyes, she made the transformation to Morgan, then stood.

Tess gave a wicked grin and walked toward Taryn. "So, you fell in love with him?"

"Have you ever been with a man for a long period of time and not fallen in love with him?

"You have a child," Tess reminded her. "Why are you doing this? Leave and be with him."

"Yes, I have a child who your husband plans on taking from me."

"I won't let him take your son from you," Tess told her. "But you can't behave like this and expect to keep him. Hell, if you make it out of here, what do you think will happen? Let me tell you what will happen. If you and Colin can't come to some resolution, he will hire an attorney and destroy you. You'll be lucky to have a weekend pass to see your son."

"He'll destroy me anyway," Taryn told her. "You know what kind of man he is. You just don't see that side because you choose not to. Let's be honest, he doesn't show it to you."

"Why kill me?" Tess asked. "Do you really want to be someone's second choice?"

"If you weren't around, I wouldn't have been a second choice. Why didn't you just stay with Jack?"

Harper backed away from Taryn. "You were with Jack, Tess?"

"Yes, she was," Taryn smirked. "For a few years—even got knocked up. We all know that it wasn't Colin's."

"Taryn, stop." Tess stared coldly at her.

"Hit a nerve?"

"No, you're hurting Harper—and she has done nothing to deserve this," Tess stated firmly.

"Where's the baby?" Harper asked. "And please tell me you didn't have an abortion."

"Harper, we can talk about that later." Tess didn't take her eyes off Taryn.

"Taryn?" Dominic's voice was soft.

"Dominic." Taryn looked at him with surprise. "I thought you were going to wait for me? What are you doing here?"

"Darling, Colin's the father and you're afraid of him. That's why you didn't tell me."

"Yes."

Dominic placed one hand on her shoulder while slowly pushing Harper away from her grasp.

"I won't let him take Connor from you," Dominic assured. "All of this can be worked out."

"No." Her eyes filled with tears. "He's mean, viciously mean. Tess is just as bad as him, but nobody seems to see that side of her."

"Maybe if you didn't act like a whore, he wouldn't have treated you like one," Tess sneered.

"And you have so much room to judge me." Taryn smiled. "You and Colin deserve each other. I'm surprised you had Savannah's father narrowed down to just two men."

"Are you done here?" Dominic asked.

"Just about." She smiled at Tess.

"Hmm." He ran his hand slowly down her arms and kissed her neck softly with his eyes on Tess.

"Mmm." Taryn's eyes closed momentarily with the distraction he was causing.

"I think you've made your point," he whispered softly. "Let's go."

"No. She has to die first." Taryn looked at her sister.

"No." Dominic was firm. "We're leaving. Put your gun down while you can still walk out of here. You will not make it out alive if you harm her."

Taryn looked to her left, and James Cordello had his weapon pointed at her head.

Jack made his way in the room and stood in front of Tess as Matthew knelt by his brother.

"Wow, if that doesn't make a statement." Taryn smiled. "Protecting your lover instead of your girlfriend. How do you like him now, Harp?"

By this point, Harper was hiding behind James.

"Are you working with them, Dominic?" Taryn asked, confused by his behavior.

"No. Your reasoning is wrong. You don't kill someone because you have a broken heart, especially your twin. Love doesn't have to be hidden and tucked away in the dark. Colin McGowan didn't love you if he was keeping you hidden and a secret. Walk away from this hate. You are so much more than this."

Tess rested her head on Jack's back.

"Why didn't you tell me that you knew her?" Taryn asked.

"The timing was never right," he answered. "Your vision of love is so askew. Love is soft and kind and mutual. It's tender and passionate. We were none of that when we met. You were so filled with hate and revenge that you wouldn't have known love if it was forced down your throat. Then, you started changing—and I know Connor and I made that happen. We love you. I don't want to lose you to this unnecessary mess that can be fixed."

"Did you love her?" she asked.

"There was a time, yes, but the circumstances surrounding us prevented her from staying with me."

"You used me," she stated.

"I used you," he admitted. "But after a few months, I began to fall in love with you."

"Jack?" Tess whispered. "Please make it end."

Taryn looked at James with a wicked grin. "Does Colin know about you and Tess? Or are you another one of her secrets?"

James smiled and shot her in the wrist. Her hand jolted, and the gun fired as it dropped from her hand. Then, he grabbed her by the throat and pushed Dominic out of the way. "Don't fucking move, Dominic, or I will shoot you too. Harper, get Gina now."

Grey took Taryn and spoke to his boss, "James, go help Jack."

Jack was on the floor, and blood was coming from his chest. Tess was applying pressure to help slow the bleeding.

"This is the first time I've ever been shot." Jack winced in pain.

"Seriously?" James smiled.

Jack closed his eyes for a moment. "And it hurts like a bitch."

"Well, I've been shot three times," James raised his brow. "I know the pain."

"Tess, I'm so sorry." Jack reached up to her cheek.

"For what?" she asked.

"I know the bullet went through." Oddly, he looked at her. "Did it miss you?"

"I ... didn't ..." Tess looked up at James, knowing something wasn't right.

Seeing a glazed over gaze from her, James pulled the Velcro from the vest so she could take it off.

"I hurt everywhere, James," her voice softly spoke.

"I know, baby. Let Gina work on Jack, and I will check you," he told her knowing she was hit somewhere.

James helped Tess over to a chair.

"Tess, look at me." James tilted her chin up as her head began to slowly drop.

"I'm so tired," she whispered as her eyes closed.

"Baby, stay awake." James had a terrible feeling but couldn't pinpoint where the bullet went through.

Tess rested her head on his shoulder.

When James put his hand on her head, he felt the damp, stickiness knowing it was blood.

"Oh my God, Gina, she was shot in the head!" he exclaimed.

CHAPTER 27

James rested his head on the back of the waiting room chair. They had been at the hospital for more than eight hours. He called Brian, shortly after they arrived, to have him deal with the local police department. Bringing in three victims with gunshot wounds would definitely bring attention that they could do without.

Gina had been in the emergency room with Jack, Colin, and Tess. Jack was admitted after his surgery to clip a bleeding vessel. Colin was admitted and put in a private room. He had two broken ribs—the two shots to his chest hit his vest—ten stitches on his head, and a severe concussion. There was still no word on Tess.

"How much longer do we have to wait?" James asked impatiently.

"Hopefully not much longer." Jonathan walked over to the windows.

"Do you know how many times I've waited in a hospital for news on Tess?" James asked.

"No, tell me," Jonathan said, leaning against the back of a chair.

"First time was when she had the miscarriage," James sighed. "Next time was when she was shot in Chicago—and then when she had the baby. That was a good memory. Now this. I loathe hospitals."

"How long were you and Tess seeing each other?" Jonathan asked.

James smiled and shook his head. "Um, well it started before she got married."

"And when did it end?"

"Why is it that I can't lie to you?" James wondered, eyeing Jonathan.

"Because I am the sort of person who knows things." He grinned.

"I guess you could say it ended when she got married and I started the list." He shrugged. "I was gone for months at a time, and then almost two years had gone by."

"Did you love her?"

James smiled. "Tess showed me how to love a woman. I never had before. And it was like nothing I'd ever experienced."

"She is certainly a special girl. I'm glad Colin didn't meet her until she was in her third year at college. He was … not ready for a woman like her. And Tess needed some time to heal after what happened with her stepfather."

"That was one of the best triggers I ever pulled," James told him with a wink.

"I hate to admit it, but it was," Jonathan remarked. "Thank God he got stopped. I can only imagine what would have happened to the girls had that incident not happened."

"This is my fault," James admitted. "I shot Taryn's wrist, and that made her trigger the gun. If she doesn't make it through this, it's all on me. I should've shot her in the head."

Jonathan placed a gentle hand on his shoulder. "No, son. All of this is a circumstance of events. Do not blame yourself. It is not your burden to bear. Out of curiosity, why didn't you do a headshot?"

"Dominic's head was aligned with hers. I couldn't without killing him. He wasn't there to hurt Tess, but it still doesn't make sense." James stopped speaking when Gina walked into the room.

"This is Dr. Morris," Gina explained. "He removed the bullet from her skull."

"Well, doc? Prognosis?" James asked.

"I removed the bullet and the skull fragments. There is a bit of swelling in the cranial cavity. She is being put in the ICU for close monitoring. Hopefully, the swelling will go down tonight, and she will be on the road to a full recovery. The next twenty-four hours are critical."

"And the baby?" James asked.

Gina beamed, "The *babies* are doing fine. She is fourteen weeks, and there are two little guys in there. Matthew wins that bet. The OB doc is monitoring them closely as well."

"Oh my gosh—twins." James smiled and shook his head. "Wait until Colin finds out. I need to see her."

"She is sedated," the surgeon stated. "She won't be awake for a while."

"I don't need her to be awake," James told him. "I just need to see her, please."

The doctor took James to see her in the ICU. She was hooked up to several different machines, and the doctor pointed out the screen that was monitoring the babies heart rates. The two lines went rapidly up and down in unison.

James took her hand and prayed. He didn't make any promises to God that he knew he couldn't keep. He just asked for her to get better and to have healthy babies and a happy life. Then, he apologized for not getting to her sooner and saving her from all of this. After ten minutes, he stood up and kissed her on the cheek. "I love you, Tess."

And she squeezed his hand.

"You rest and get better. I'm going to go deal with a few loose ends. I'll be back later to check on you."

Tess held his hand tightly for a moment and then released him.

In the waiting room, Jonathan and Gina stopped talking when they saw him.

"Okay?" Jonathan asked.

"Better." He grinned. "She squeezed my hand. It's amazing how such a simple thing can bring such relief."

Gina smiled. "She's a tough girl."

"Yes," James agreed with a smile. "I'm going to head back to the house to help clean up. Call me if anything changes."

"Of course." Jonathan nodded. "You can take our car if you need it."

"Thomas is coming to pick me up but thank you." Reconsidering a passing thought, he sighed. "I'm going to check on Colin before I leave. I'll see you two later."

Colin was sleeping peacefully when he walked into the room.

James stood at the end of his bed and softly spoke, "I'm sorry I didn't get back to the house sooner. I need you to wake up and tell me what you want me to do with her. You deserve to make this call after what she did to you and Tess. I still haven't found Connor. Dominic won't talk to me, and Matthew won't let me touch him."

Colin's eyes opened, and he stared at James.

"Did you hear me?" he asked.

Colin nodded slowly.

"And?"

"Tuck her away somewhere until I'm better." Colin took a shallow breath. "I will deal with her."

"Very well." James nodded.

"How's Tess?" Colin asked.

James swallowed the lump that formed in his throat before speaking, "The bullet went through Jack's chest and lodged in her skull. They removed it, but there's some cranial swelling. She's in ICU right now, and they're monitoring her closely. If she makes it through tonight without complications, she should make a full recovery."

"And the baby?" His eyes filled with tears.

"*Babies*." James smiled. "The twins are doing good. She's fourteen weeks along."

Colin smiled. "I can't live without her."

"I know." James nodded. "And we're not doing a repeat of Chicago. Get that shit out of your head. She'll be fine. I need to head back to the house. Rest and get better. I don't know how to take care of your family like you do. I'm very much out of my element with this."

Colin grinned. "It's the same as the way you approach your work—gut instinct, a dose of compassion, and a lot of love, especially for my girls."

* * *

A couple days passed, and Colin didn't mind the peacefulness of being in the hospital. He wasn't able to move very well, but if he made it through the day with just aspirin to control the pain, he would probably go home tomorrow. There was a little bit of hesitation with leaving since he wanted to stay for Tess. She'd been in ICU for three days, and he hadn't been able to see her. There had been one complication after another, but both babies were still alive.

"Daddy!" Savannah ran up to his bed, and Matthew was close behind.

"My beautiful girl," he grinned.

Matthew picked her up. "Which side do you want her on?"

"Left," Colin instructed. "I've missed you."

Savannah snuggled up in the crook of his arm. "I miss you and Mommy. Can I see her?"

"Not yet, honey." Colin kissed her on the forehead. "Soon though. Are you keeping Matthew busy?"

"Yes." She played with the IV in his arm. "When are you coming home, Daddy?"

"Soon, baby. I promise. I want to stay here for Mommy until she's better. Are you okay with Matthew?"

"Yes." She sighed and put her head on his shoulder. "I miss you."

"I miss you too." He covered her with the blanket as she snuggled in his arm.

With great detail, Savannah told her about her time with Matthew. As she chatted away, Matthew put his head back and closed his eyes. It didn't take long for her to finish her stories and eventually doze off in his arms.

Matthew opened his eyes when it had been quiet in the room for about five minutes.

"I was thinking she wore you out," Colin said looking at his daughter sleeping.

"No." Matthew stood up and walked over to him. "She's been a good girl the last few days. She just misses you and Tess. Dominic wants to talk with you. He says it is very important."

"Well, have him come in," Colin stated.

"He's actually here with Dad and Gina, hoping you'd be up for talking with him."

"Go get him. And, please, come back. I'm sure this will affect you in some roundabout way."

Matthew came back with Dominic in less than five minutes.

"I imagine you want to talk about her son," Colin suggested. "Or better yet, my son."

Matthew leaned against the wall.

"I know where he is if you'd like me to bring him here," Dominic replied.

Colin smiled. "I asked James to find him a couple days ago. Would you coordinate with James?"

"No." Dominic was firm. "I don't need a mercenary to help me with a two-year-old boy. Besides, I don't like him—and he doesn't like me."

"Fair enough." Colin nodded.

"I don't suppose you will let her go?"

"She shot Tess in the back and somehow didn't kill her. Then this whole mess at my parents' house—and you want me to just let her go so she can try it all again in a few years? I have a daughter, and my wife is pregnant with twins. Would you risk your family's life?"

"You treated her like shit, and she was afraid of you," Dominic reminded him. "What was she supposed to do?"

"Talk to me like an adult. I was angry with her for keeping this from me, and I understand why she was afraid of me, but she didn't even give me a chance. She didn't seem to mind the lifestyle I gave her. And you don't get to judge me. You weren't in our relationship."

"Fine," Dominic conceded. "Let me tell you a little something. I have been Connor's father for nearly two years. He calls me Daddy. Legally, with Tar gone, I am his guardian. Don't even think about having me killed because if something happens to me, do you think she would forgive you for that?"

"Why does everyone think Tess will leave me?" Colin shook his head. "Let me tell you a little something. First, don't ever threaten me. I have no intention of killing you. My father has waited too long to see you again, and you are Matthew's brother. Can I shoot Tar in the head? Probably not—but I need to talk to her. And you don't get to see her before I do. I will not rip Connor from you. You're forgetting that

I have a daughter his age, and Matthew and I are going through a very similar situation with her. I didn't want a child with her, but now that I seem to have one, I will love him as much as I love Savannah and the twins. Don't assume you know me based on my reputation outside of this family. I never mistreated her. If that's what she told you, go ahead and believe her. Most addicts are great liars. Everything she has in her life was because of me. I made it happen because I didn't want her to be a crack whore living out of a dumpster. Forgive me for giving her a better life."

Dominic stared at Colin. "Damn you! I want to fucking hate you, but even though you're an ass, you always say it straight. No bullshit."

"I don't have space in my life for bullshit." Colin glanced at Savannah. "I'm a father, a husband, and a businessman. And it's all pretty much in that order. You have my son, and I want him. Don't think you can hide behind Matthew on this because he's your brother. He's my brother too."

Dominic sighed. "I'll bring him to you when you're out of here."

"Thank you." Colin nodded.

Dominic walked out the door.

"I'm damned if I do and damned if I don't," Colin mumbled.

"I think the first thing you need to do is talk to Tess," Matthew remarked.

✳ ✳ ✳

When Gina walked into the room, Colin, Savannah, and Matthew were sleeping. She almost hated to wake any of them, but she walked up to Colin and ran her hand over his forehead.

Feeling a hand touch him, Colin's eyes opened slowly.

"Hi." her voice was soft, like a mother's.

"Hey." Colin blinked and glanced at Savannah. "How's Tess?"

"That's why I'm here," she began. "They are bringing her in to see you. They don't want to sedate her, but she's really stressed. One of the babies' heart rates is dropping. We need her to calm and relax, and we're hoping you can do that. I think she needs to see you and be with you."

"Okay."

"Do you want me to take Savannah?"

"No, not yet. I've missed her."

"I'm sure you have." Gina grinned as a nurse and doctor wheeled Tess into the room.

Colin looked at Tess and smiled. "My beautiful wife. Come here." He held out his hand.

The nurse helped Tess up, and the doctor watched her carefully as she laid beside Colin. The nurse pulled up the bedrail so she wouldn't fall off. Tess put her head on his shoulder and rested her hand on his stomach.

"She needs to relax," the doctor explained. "Baby number two is stressed, and it comes from the mother. Everything else is fine. We're hoping you can get her calm, perhaps even sleeping. This is very unorthodox, but I don't want to sedate her again. It's not good for the babies."

"Okay," Colin replied understandingly.

"I'll be back in a while to check on her," he noted. "Call the nurse if anything urgent arises."

Colin ran his hand over her shoulder and kissed her forehead.

"I missed you," Tess whispered.

"I've missed you too." He kissed her head. "It's like hell not being able to see you. Just rest, baby. You are safe with the best of care here. I won't let them take you from me. I love you and our babies."

Tess looked up at him. "Matthew was right: twins and fourteen weeks."

"How are you feeling about that?"

"I want to be excited, but I'm afraid to be until I'm released from the hospital and both the babies are fine."

"They'll be fine," he assured her. "And you'll be fine. And when we get out of here, I need to wrap up a few things before we go home to Portland. I miss the hell out of our calm, drama-free life. I want to buy you a house big enough for our growing family, and we need a bigger car. We need our normal."

Tess leaned her head up and kissed him softly. "Our normal is going to be a little different because Connor and Matthew are going to be in this mix."

"I know." He kissed her temple. "It's easy to bring Matthew in, but I'm still trying to grasp this concept of Connor."

"We'll work it out." She yawned.

"Three people have said that you're going to leave me because of this," he shared.

"Nope." She shook her head and closed her eyes. "I've put you through worse. We can handle this."

The three of them slept for a couple hours. Colin only woke when Matthew picked up Savannah.

"I'm going to take Savannah home," Matthew whispered. "I'll be back tomorrow."

"Thank you, brother," Colin lipped softly.

"Just get better so you two can come home," Matthew said as he walked out.

Colin scooted over to give Tess more room. With a long yawn, she moved her hand to his chest.

"Tess, lift your hand just a little—please," he asked as it rested on his broken ribs.

"Oh my goodness." She raised her hand. "I'm so sorry."

"It's okay," he assured. "Just be very gentle."

"Can you hit the nurse button? I need to move."

"Are you feeling okay?" he asked as the nurse walked in.

She nodded.

"I was wondering when you two would wake up," the nurse began.

"Can you help me get up?" Tess asked.

"Yep." The nurse put down the rail on the bed, took Tess's hand, and helped her upright. "How do you feel? Dizzy, nauseous?"

"My head hurts a little," Tess replied. "My back was hurting."

Tess rested her hands on her stomach and stared blankly ahead.

"Tess?" Colin knew something wasn't right.

Slowly, she turned to him with a small smile. "They moved."

"You felt them?"

"Yes." She leaned against the bed and held Colin's hand to her stomach. "I want to go home."

"Me too, but you need to be 100 percent, and I need to be able to move a little bit better," he told her. "We can't take care of Savannah in our current conditions."

"Matthew will help us," she reminded.

"I know." He gently rubbed her stomach. "He's done so much for us already."

The doctor walked in. "Good evening. We're moving both of you to a different room—with two beds. Tess, do you feel up to walking? It's just two rooms down the hall."

"Yes." She nodded. "Slowly."

"Of course. Once you're in there, I'll examine you and the babies."

"Okay." Tess kissed Colin and walked out of the room with the doctor and the nurse.

Within half an hour, they were settled into the new room.

Colin walked around the room a bit and held Tess's hand while the doctor did an ultrasound. The doctor pointed out each baby and their beating hearts. It showed a good, steady rhythm for both. When he was done, they were, finally, alone.

"Better?" Colin asked as he sat on the edge of her bed.

"Yes." She nodded. "I needed you. You're my balance."

Colin ran his hand over her cheek. "I know. You are mine too. Do you remember everything that happened?"

"No." She shook her head. "I only remember putting my head on Jack's back and ... is Dominic ... alive?"

"Yep." Colin sighed. "He paid me a visit. He doesn't want me to kill Taryn. He says he's in love with her."

"Well, that's weird." Tess closed her eyes. "I just want to be safe and have our kids to be safe. Do whatever you feel is necessary."

"I promise she will never bring harm to our family again."

CHAPTER 28

Two Weeks Later

Colin and James walked over the sandy knoll along the overgrown pathway. The dilapidated beach house was on a remote section of the Georgia coastline. The seclusion gave them the confidence that no one would hear her scream.

Grey was standing guard on the porch as they approached. "There's a rumor about you and this business," Grey chuckled.

"And what would that be?" Colin asked, checking his .357.

"*Ruthless.*" Grey smiled.

Colin shook his head, then pursed his lips. "My ruthlessness is about to be tested."

Grey pursed his lips, knowing what Colin was about to deal with.

Taryn was tied to a chair with her back to him. She was slumped over, and her eyes were closed. There were dried droplets of blood beneath her hands as the bandage on her hand that James shot was soaked in dried blood, he noted, as he walked around her.

Colin took out his switchblade and cut the rope that bound her wrists and ankles.

With the unexpected release of her arms, she jolted awake. When he removed the tape from her mouth, she cowered away from him. "Please don't kill me."

Colin knelt before her. "I don't want to but look at what you've done. Tess had a bullet lodged in her skull. You shot me, twice, in the chest. Me! What the hell is wrong with you?"

"I just wanted you to love me like you did her," she meekly responded.

"You could have married anybody else within reason and gone on with your life," he explained. "Instead, you chose this path, knowing how it would end. Did you not want to see our son grow up?"

"Yes. I do! I know I messed up really, really bad, but please don't let Connor grow up without his mom," she pleaded.

"You were willing to let him grow up without his father."

"He needs me," she told him. "He hardly knows you."

"And whose fault is that?" He stood up and stretched his legs, frustrated.

Taryn stood and noticed James by the door. "Why is he here?"

Colin's hands rested on her shoulders. "If I can't pull the trigger, he will."

"Please, Colin, put me in whatever crappy town you want. I will stay there. Just let me have my son. You will never, ever see or hear from me again."

"That was my first thought." He walked to a broken window that faced the ocean. "The problem is that I don't trust you. You methodically skimmed money from our accounts. You managed to put together a mini-militia—by the way, they're all dead—that infiltrated my parents' home. You shot Tess, Jack, Matthew, and me. I told you I didn't want children with you."

"You don't have to worry about him." She wiped the tears from her cheeks. "I will never tell him about you. Just let me have him and leave. You will never see us again. I promise."

Colin shook his head. "You don't understand how this works. You truly don't realize who I am." He placed his hands on the sides of her cheeks.

Matthew quietly slipped in the door standing by James.

"I'm Colin McGowan. I'm very rich and very smart, and if I make a mistake, I will cover it up and bury it. However, in this case, Tess and I will raise Connor as ours. People will think we have twins since the children are only a few days apart. Savannah looks like her mom, and Connor looks like his father. No one will ever know that you carried my son except the immediate family. You've been on the outs with the family since you were eighteen, and it won't even make a difference that you disappeared. Everyone knows you're an addict and have fought addiction since college."

Taryn shook her head as tears streamed down her cheeks.

"You tried to kill my wife and didn't give it a second thought that she was pregnant." His hand slipped behind her neck. "What you didn't realize is that I did love you. I adored you and your bitchy attitude. Even with all your bad habits, I liked coming to see you."

"I was good enough to sleep with—but not good enough to marry?" She sucked at her bottom lip as her breath hitched.

"Simply put? Yes." Colin brought his forehead to rest on hers as his eyes filled with tears. "I'm so sorry I did this to you. I never thought our being together would cause this."

Softly, he brought his lips to hers.

Taryn's arms came around his waist, and he pulled her closer.

After a few minutes of kissing, he noticed Matthew was standing by James. He kissed the top of her head, moved her behind him, and looked at Matthew.

"I'm not here to hurt her," Matthew stated. "You should know me better than that."

"I do know you." Colin eyed him. "You used to be just like James."

Matthew smiled, not denying something so true. "Will you trust me enough to let me help you with this?"

Colin stared at him. "I don't want her harmed."

"She is the mother of your son," Matthew explained. "I will not harm her, but she needs to realize that she can't harm Tess anymore because she is the mother of my daughter."

"I know." Taryn slowly came out from behind Colin. "I'm sorry. I will never try to hurt her or anyone else in the family. Can I please just have my son? I will leave, and none of you will ever see me again."

"You can't take Connor," Matthew said. "He needs to stay with Colin."

"Please! I'm a good mother, and he's my world."

"Everyone outside of this room needs to think you're dead," Matthew sighed raising his brow, not certain if this would work.

Colin put his hands on her shoulders and kissed her head. "This is the only way you live. As it is, if she finds out what we've done, we're dead, then she'll find you and do the same thing."

Taryn walked over to the broken window.

"Is this the right thing?" Colin asked his brother.

"If you want her to live, then yes. I've gone through this thoroughly with Dominic, and this will be the only way," Matthew answered.

"Is Connor with Dominic right now?" Colin asked.

"Yes," Matthew answered. "The boy knows him. They're waiting for us in town."

"Can I see him every now and then?" Taryn walked back over to Colin.

Matthew shook his head. "I will keep you updated on him and send you pictures, but you can't see him. You and Tess are almost identical, and it will confuse him. We can't have him seeing you and then telling Colin and Tess how much you look like his mother."

Tears filled her eyes again, and she nodded.

"Can you two give us a minute alone?" Colin asked Matthew and James.

"Sure," Matthew said as they walked out the door.

Colin wrapped his arms around her shoulders. "I know this is breaking your heart, but if this keeps you alive."

Taryn looked up at him. "Promise me that she will love him like her own. He's allergic to nuts, and he loves strawberries. I hope Dominic got his favorite blanket when he picked him up."

Colin nodded and kissed her forehead as he hugged her.

Quickly, Taryn pulled the .357 from his waistband and stepped back. With tears falling down her cheeks, she pointed the gun at him.

"What are you doing?" Colin glared.

"I will not be without my son," she told him, shaking her head. "And I'll be damned if you will get him and raise him with that bitch."

"What the hell is wrong with you? You can walk away," Colin roared.

"I will walk away." She pursed her lips. "I wish I had used a higher-powered rifle when I shot her in Chicago. Then, maybe, it would have gone through her and killed you. Live and learn. It worked better when I shot her through Matthew."

Colin shook his head irritated and stunned at the same time.

Two hundred yards away, Grey was watching through the scope. Seeing her wicked transform before his eyes, he pulled off one shot. It was the one shot that assured Tess and her children would live.

Colin's eyes went wide as her body dropped to the floor. His heart stopped for a moment as the shock rolled over him. Someone else pulled off the shot. Kneeling, he hung his head low remembering the first time they met.

❋ ❋ ❋

It was late fall, and he was in Chicago to speak at a convention for his father's company. These things bored him, but he had another agenda. One of the twins his father had adopted years before lived there. Knowing she liked to party hard, and his father had bailed her out of many situations in the past four years, Colin found himself curious.

Tracking her down was easy, and he smiled when he walked into the bar. Taryn was the center of attention at the other end of the dimmed room. Casually, he went up to the bar, ordered a scotch, and took a seat, knowing she would notice him at some point.

After ten minutes, she walked over and leaned against the bar with a sexy grin and seductive eyes. "Hi," she began. "You're new here. Did you just move here—or are you just visiting?"

Colin smiled. "Does it matter?"

Taryn thought for a moment and shook her head. "I guess it really doesn't." She took a seat beside him and asked the bartender to get her another beer. "I'm Taryn."

"I know." He nodded, taking a deep breath. "Taryn McGowan. I've seen you in some of those ads on TV. You're very beautiful."

Taryn grinned. "Thank you. Do you have a name?"

"I do." He nodded.

"Are you going to tell me?"

"No." He smiled, shaking his head. "Maybe later."

"You're not like the rest of them." She took a sip of her beer.

"No, I'm not." He shook his head.

"You come from money," she stated the obvious.

"Does that matter?" he asked.

"Yes. I'm not supposed to be hanging out with my old friends. They're apparently bad influences. You're different. I like you."

Colin laughed a little. "You just met me. How do you know?"

"It's easy." She smiled. "You're easy to read. Rich guy, family money. You have your own, but you came from money. You're very handsome, and you know it. You probably get whatever you want and whomever you want, but you're searching for something or someone. You don't know what, but you'll know when it happens. Under this dapper demeanor, you have a wild side that likes to play."

Colin eyed her. "I have to say that I'm a bit impressed. And it's not easy to impress me."

"Was I right?"

"Yep, not too far off." He sipped his scotch.

Taryn grinned. "I think we should get out of here and go do what both of us want to do to one another."

Colin grinned, pulled out his billfold, took out a fifty, and left it on the counter.

The bartender walked over to them. "Hey, Tar. You need to even up on your tab. It's been two weeks."

"What does she owe?" Colin asked before Taryn could say anything.

"She's at eight-fifty," the man replied.

Colin shook his head, opened his billfold again, and handed ten hundred-dollar bills to the man. "That should take care of that." Colin tucked his wallet back inside the pocket. "The extra is so you won't serve her again. She walks in—you call me."

Colin slipped his business card to the bartender.

"Will do, Mr. McGowan. Is she your family or wife?" the bartender asked.

"Something like that." Colin glanced over at Taryn. "Are you ready to go?"

"I guess so, Mr. McGowan," she replied, clearly disappointed that he was part of that family.

Outside, she stopped walking. "Jonathan send you?" she asked.

"No." He shook his head. "You have quite a reputation, and I thought we should meet. I have quite a reputation as well."

"What do you want from me?" she asked, touching his chest.

"I have a proposition for you." He leaned in and whispered, "I want to take you back to my place and have a night of uninhibited sex. If you like the way the night goes, we'll talk business in the morning. If you don't, you can leave and only see me on holidays at the family gatherings."

"Which son are you?" her curiosity peaked.

"The youngest," he answered. "And which twin are you?"

Taryn grinned. "The one who knows how to have fun."

They got in a cab even though his apartment was only three blocks away. He'd bought it on the twenty-third floor five or six years ago. He was finishing college and working with his brother—before the big break between them. Now, he only went there a few times a year for business, but he was willing to change that if Taryn was willing.

The next morning, he woke rather late. Taryn was sound asleep, and he smiled. She was sexy, uninhibited, and fun in the bedroom, and she enjoyed every single moment as much as himself. Putting his hands behind his head, he wondered how it was going to work out—or if it would even work out. All he wanted was to have his sexy play toy on the side. He could never marry her because of her past, and it would be in his best interests that no one knew they were sleeping together.

Taryn slowly woke and ran her hand over his chest and down between his legs. Feeling himself grow hard as she stroked him, he turned his head and looked at her.

"Good morning," she said with a smile. "Mind if I take a ride before you get up?"

"Do as you please," he said with his hands still behind his head.

Taryn wasted no time taking what she wanted from him, as he watched her enjoying his body, but mostly his cock.

When he knew she was close, he placed his hands on her hips, for he was close as well. "I want you as my mistress."

"And what's in it for me?" she asked, keeping a perfect rhythm.

"How about this place and ten grand a month?" He gripped her hips and stopped her motion.

"You're serious?" She caught her breath and looked around the room. "Can I remodel a little, update?"

Colin grinned. "Yes, I just don't want anyone else living here or in my bed. If you feel a need to fuck someone else, do it somewhere else—and get tested if you don't use a condom. I will kill you if you give me a disease or get pregnant."

"For some reason, I believe that." Her hands caressed his stomach.

"There are rules with this." He moved his hands to her breasts. "You have to be good with that or this won't happen."

Taryn began to move her hips again.

"No drugs, minimal alcohol." He rolled her nipples between her fingers. "If I take you to dinner, I like classy, not trashy—and tone down the makeup. You're a beautiful woman, you don't need that cheap whore look. Behind the bedroom doors, I want what we had last night. And nobody can know about us."

"Is that all? Are you done with the rules?" Taryn asked as she was getting bored with him talking.

"For now." He slipped his hand behind her neck, pulling her lips to his. "Now come for me."

✱ ✱ ✱

Colin dropped to his knees, but no tears came. Once she was dead before him, he realized how much he cared about her. Maybe he even loved her a little, but nothing compared to his wife.

Matthew and James heard the shot knowing exactly what happened. They waited on the porch until Grey rounded the corner with the rifle.

"Done?" James asked.

Grey nodded as Matthew went inside.

"Colin." Matthew put an easy hand on his brother's shoulder.

Colin looked over at Grey as he walked in and shook his head.

"It wasn't your choice," Grey said with no remorse in his voice.

"Colin?" Matthew spoke his name, again.

"I can't do this anymore," Colin whispered. "I should have been better to her—maybe this wouldn't have happened."

"Don't do this, brother. You were good to her. You gave her your apartment in Chicago—not to mention the money you sent her every month. You got her away from the drugs and alcohol. Don't think you didn't do anything for her. You did more than most men would have done."

"It wasn't enough." He stood up, wiped his eyes, and took a deep breath. "She needs to be buried on the property."

"We'll take care of it," James interjected.

Colin eyed him in disbelief.

"I promise," James added.

"Come on, Colin." Matthew guided him away from the house.

Colin leaned against the SUV, crossed his arms, and looked out at the sea.

"What are you processing in that brain of yours?" Matthew asked.

"I wanted it all," Colin explained. "I wanted Tess on my arm in public, and I wanted my mistress on the side. Men like us do that all the time. Hell, Tess got two men. Why couldn't I have two women?"

Matthew didn't answer as he only wanted one woman and he couldn't have her.

"I tried to do right by Tess," Colin began. "Ended my thing with Taryn before asking Tess to marry me, and then everything got fucked up. I should know better. My wife was shot because of me. You were shot because of me, and so was Jack. This whole damn mess is my fault."

Colin pressed his palms to his eyes then rested his hands on his hips. "I have a son. I still get a part of her through our son."

"Yes, you do," Matthew agreed. "Do you want to go pick him up? Dominic is waiting."

Colin was suddenly overwhelmed with a feeling to leave, get in his car, and go.

"Matthew, would you do me a favor?" Colin pulled out his cell phone. "Take this. I'm going for a drive."

"The only reason you ditch your phone is if you don't want to be found," Matthew reminded his brother. "Where are you going?"

"I just want to be lost for a little bit," he explained. "I need to … grieve before I can be there for Tess. She doesn't understand the depth of my relationship with Taryn. Can I just have a day or two before I go back to all my responsibilities?"

"The last time you did this was …" Matthew started but stopped midway.

"When I shot Kate," Colin finished. "I know. I was drunk for a week. I can't be gone that long now. Please trust me."

"At least take my phone," Matthew said, pulling it from his pocket. "I can check my messages and my missed calls from my computer. Only answer calls from me. I won't tell anyone else that you have it, and I will only call you if it's an emergency. If you don't come back, I will marry your wife."

Colin grinned. "Good thing I'm coming back. Twins? I won't walk away from that or Tess."

Matthew hugged his brother and watched him leave, heading south. Colin disappearing for a couple of days would be easy to explain, but he wondered if Colin would walk away from his family forever.

CHAPTER 29

Matthew walked into the foyer with Dominic and Connor. It would be the first time the family would see Connor, and Matthew felt like Colin should be the one bringing his child home. Since he wasn't here, Matthew would do it for him and let Tess know that he was taking a few days to process.

"Ready, Dominic?" Matthew asked.

"I guess so," he answered as he held Connor on his hip.

They walked down the hall and found Tess and Gina in the kitchen. Jonathan was playing with Savannah in the family room. Everyone stopped what they were doing when they saw the young boy in Dominic's arms.

"This is Connor," Matthew announced.

"Mommy." Connor held his arms out to her as a bright smile crossed his lips the moment he saw her.

"Hi, sweetie." Tess walked over and took Connor from Dominic. She knew the child was going to think she was Taryn, but it didn't bother her. "I've missed you so much."

"I missed you too, Mommy." Connor played with Tess's hair. "Are you going away again?"

"No." She shook her head. "You're stuck with me for a long, long time. Want to go meet your sister and Grandma and Grandpa?"

"I have a grandpa?" he beamed.

"You do." She walked him into the family room and introduced him to Jonathan, Gina, and Savannah.

Matthew pulled leftovers from the fridge and watched Connor play with his grandparents and Savannah.

Tess came back into the kitchen. "Where is he?"

"He needed a couple days to … process what happened," Matthew stated making himself a plate for dinner.

"He needs to process?" Tess looked at Matthew in disbelief.

Matthew took her hand in his. "She was shot in the head in front of him. He needs to work through the motions. Like it or not, he cared about her at one point in his life, and she was the mother of his son."

"She is still affecting my life even after she's dead." Tess wiped away a few tears. "I was always the one to take off—not him. I would always come back—except when I was with you. I was never coming back."

"Yes," Matthew agreed. "He came and got you because he loves you that much. He'll be back. I know he will."

"These damn emotions when I'm pregnant drive me crazy," Tess sighed, shaking her head.

"I'm here, and I won't leave until he's back." Matthew kissed her cheek. "Dominic and I will help you with the kids. I know you are supposed to take it easy."

Tess nodded. "Thank you. I'm going to rest. Would you mind putting the kids to bed for me?"

"Not at all," Matthew replied. "I'll check on you later."

Tess walked up to Taryn's room. She hadn't set foot in there since she'd been back to Savannah. Taryn's room was clean and tidy—so unlike what it used to be. She touched a music box on the dresser that Jonathan had given her for her eighteenth birthday. There were pictures of Paris and London from Taryn's modeling work. Her four-poster, queen-sized bed with white linens was beautiful.

Tears filled her eyes, wishing she could have just one more conversation with her twin. She just couldn't understand how she could risk her life with her son—and for what? Revenge? She curled up on the bed and put her head on the pillow with one hand underneath. Feeling something, she pulled out two pictures: one of Dominic, Connor, and Taryn and one of Adam, Harper, Taryn, and Tess when they were little. Seeing the photos made Tess realize that Taryn did have a heart beneath all that bitchiness. With tears in her eyes, she cried herself to sleep where the dreams began.

❋ ❋ ❋

Tess's eyes jetted open when she felt a hand on her shoulder. It was dark in her room, and she tried to focus.

"Tessy, wake up," Harper's voice was shaking.

"What, Harp?" she asked half asleep.

"Someone's in the house," she whispered. "I heard mom and Robert yelling at someone—and then a gunshot."

Tess sat up. "Are you sure?"

"Yes," she cried.

They jumped when they heard another gunshot in the hallway right outside her door.

Tess waved Harper over to her closet. Digging through a pile of clothes and shoes, she found the small door that went to the attic. Tess handed Harper a flashlight and told her to go. Just as Harper went in, Tess turned back around to grab a blanket and froze.

A masked man was standing in her room. He walked toward her with his hand out. "Don't be afraid of me."

Tess wrapped her hands around herself with her heart beating madly.

"Your mom and stepfather are dead," he explained. "Robert was into a lot of bad things—not to mention what he was doing to you. And your mother was a drug addict. You and your sisters deserve better. Your brother is calling a man named Jonathan McGowan. He will come here to pick you three up and take care of you. You can trust him."

"W-w-where is Adam?" Tess asked, her words stuttering from fear.

"Don't ask questions," he told her. "Just do as I said—and you'll be safe. And you and I never had this conversation." The man started to leave.

"Wait a second," Tess called out. *When he turned around, she spoke. "Thank you."*

The man nodded once and left.

✳ ✳ ✳

After a few hours, Tess slowly opened her eyes. When Adam arrived, she learned the man was James. Adam and James had met in college and were roommates for two years before James transferred to the East Coast. The death of her parents was James's first job.

The room was fairly dark, but a small lamp in the corner gave off a soft glow. She realized Dominic was on the bed, holding one of the pictures. "They're looking for you," he whispered.

"Oh," she simply responded. "I'm so sorry you lost her."

"Me too," he said as a tear slipped from his eye. "She knew what she was risking, and she was willing to do it anyway. I couldn't stop her—no matter how hard I tried. I even told her I wanted to marry her, but it didn't matter."

"Our fighting was not worth dying for," Tess whispered. "I just don't understand. And if she was afraid of Colin, why didn't she take Connor and go somewhere else. Jonathan would have never let Colin hurt her. There were so many other alternatives."

"I know," he agreed. "I tried so many times to get her to just leave with me. Money wasn't the issue, but she was hell bent on revenge. She hated you."

"It all started with our mother's husband," Tess began. "We had just turned sixteen, and Robert gave us an unusual amount of attention. Taryn loved it, but I wasn't comfortable with it. I think because I didn't *like* him like she did, he was persistent about changing that. One night, I ended up alone with him in that house. I stayed in my room and locked the door. He broke it down, slapped me hard, and told my mother I had been talking back. That was the first night he molested me, and he did it over and over and over for the next nine months. I fought him at first, and then he said if I continued to fight him, he would go after Harper. She was only twelve, so I stopped fighting.

"I knew he was doing the same thing to Tar, but she invited him in. I didn't. I think her hatred for me stemmed from the moment he stopped having sex with her and devoted all his attention to me. It was awful, and my mother did nothing to stop him. She was drowning herself in booze and any pill she could pop. Happiest moment of my life, with two exceptions, was when Robert and my mother were killed. Taryn was never the same after that. She inherited our mother's addictive nature. And she could be just wicked mean.

"I asked Grey to feel it out, and if there was another alternative, to try it. I didn't want her dead. I just wanted her to leave me alone. I wanted a normal life where I did not have to watch over my back every time I walked out the front door. I want my kids to be able to play in the yard and not worry about them being snatched or killed. It didn't have to be this way. I hope we can all move forward from this."

Dominic took her hand in his. "I'm sure we can. What are the two exceptions? If you don't mind me asking?"

Tess smiled. "The first is the day Colin proposed, and the second was when Savannah was born. I know everyone wonders why I stay with him after all the things he's done. People don't realize that I've been very challenging for him. He is the one who helped me overcome my past. He dealt with the days when I didn't want to be touched, the nightmares, the tears. Dealing with a victim of molestation is difficult, and he gave me space when I needed space, a shoulder when I wanted to cry, an ear when I was ready to talk, and love when I was ready to move forward. He broke down the boundaries within my life that were so limited and showed me how to live, take control of my life, and live every moment of every day without fear. Even when I want to be mad at him, it doesn't last long because I love him that much."

"He's lucky to have you love him *that* much." Dominic caressed her cheek.

"I loved you and our time together," Tess assured him. "Please don't think that you were just a job to me."

"I don't." He gave a half grin. "Our last four days together told me otherwise. I missed you so much from the second you left."

Tess placed her on his cheek, leaned over, and kissed him slowly.

Dominic's hand moved from her hip to her back, and the kiss deepened as their bodies pressed against one another.

Dominic pulled back first. "I can never have you, can I?"

Tess shook her head.

"Can I just have tonight?" Dominic asked. When her hand caressed his cheek, he had his answer.

* * *

It was nearly midnight when Tess checked on the sleeping children again as she couldn't sleep. Pulling the blankets up to their shoulders, she bent down and kissed each one on the forehead. She took an extra minute looking at Connor through the moonlight that crossed his bed. It was a bit uncanny how much the little boy looked like Colin. A paternity test wasn't even needed to determine this result.

Was this going to be her life? Tucking children into bed at Jonathan's house because she was raising them alone? Tess knew Colin would try and save Taryn somehow and she could have gone along with it, but she also knew her twin very well. If Taryn went to these extremes to kill her, she would continue until she succeeded. Her twin was a master liar and manipulator; more so than herself. It made her wonder, if she wouldn't have tried to save her life with her drug addictions, would any of this have happened? The drug Dimitri Markenna made did take her life and it was by pure coincidence that Tess and Jonathan found her passed out on her apartment floor. There was only a very faint pulse and her breath had ceased. If she wouldn't have been carrying the naloxone, like she always did after the first overdose attempt, she would have died that day.

Maybe Taryn wanted to die. Maybe she couldn't live with the horrors of their teenage years. Maybe deep down, Taryn really didn't like Robert coming to her room, but she didn't know how to stop him. Maybe she should have let her go because that was what Taryn wanted. Maybe that is why Taryn wanted her dead, so she would stop saving her.

After a moment, she released a soft breath and left the room.

Clad in only her tank top and some pull on shorts, she made her way downstairs. There were nightlights strategically placed throughout the house so she could walk without turning on any lights. With everyone in bed, she softly tapped on Matthew's door, then walked in without waiting for him to answer.

Matthew leaned up on his arm and turned on the lamp beside his bed as Tess walked in.

"Hey," he said barely above a whisper as she closed the door behind her and locked it.

Tess didn't speak, she simply walked to the other side of the bed as Matthew turned off the light, rolled over and pulled the bedding back so she could slip in. Climbing in the bed, Tess pulled the covers up as she sank into the comfort of Matthew's open arms.

"I've been waiting for this moment," he softly spoke before kissing her lips.

"Me too," Tess told him as their legs tangled and the kiss became deeper.

Matthew's hand slid down her hip and held as their intimacy took his breath away. He loved this woman, even after three years of not seeing her. When Colin said he needed to leave for a few days, Matthew was good with knowing Tess would be at the house waiting. Maybe not for him, but she would be there.

"Matthew." Tess pulled back slightly sucking in her bottom lip. "Maybe I was wrong to have Grey kill Taryn. Maybe I should have tried to talk to her."

With a sigh, Matthew rolled back, running his hand through his hair as he thought for a moment wanting the right words. "Baby, Taryn had this planned out for years. She was too far over the edge to bring back. It was proven when Colin offered her a way out and she pulled his gun and was going to kill him because she refused to let him and you raise her son. Grey did the right thing. Don't doubt yourself and the actions that were taken. You were working off a gut feeling and you know that is always right. You did the right thing. There was no alternative at this point."

"Do you think Colin loved her?" she asked, unsure of the answer.

"No, not the way you're thinking," he answered, knowing he was correct. "She was more of an outlet for him."

"Do you think he regrets marrying me?" she wondered.

"No, not at all. Colin played the field for a very long time. Women literally dropped to their knees for him. Then, you came along and were completely opposite of what he was used to." Matthew grinned as it was almost the same way for him. "He loves you more than anyone else I've ever seen him with."

"Then what are we doing?" she asked as her hand brushed over the wings on his tattoo as his chest was bare.

"I love you more than anyone else also," he answered, leaned over, and kissed her softly.

EPILOGUE

Colin woke to a vibration on the nightstand. Picking up the phone, he saw six missed calls from Matthew. With a sigh, he hit redial.

Matthew answered immediately. "Brother, it's been three days. Don't make me trace my phone."

"It's only been two days. Don't get dramatic." Colin yawned. "What time is it?"

"Noon," Matthew remarked, a bit irritated. "Where are you?"

Colin tried to focus and seeing Emma sleeping beside him prompted a deep sigh of drunken regret. "I'm about an hour and half from where we were the other day. Is everything okay? Tess okay?"

"There was a little scare with the babies. Gina took her back to the hospital this morning to make sure things were still good."

"Christ," Colin mumbled. "I'll be back in a few hours."

"If you're coming back, I'll fly back to Chicago today and take the kids. I have work I need to deal with."

"Want me to pick them up tomorrow?" Colin asked.

"No." Matthew sighed. "I'll be back in a couple days. I'm taking Dominic with me. You need to get back to Savannah and talk with Tess."

Colin was silent as he didn't like to be told what to do.

"I'm going to remind you of something," Matthew began. "Remember when you came to Chicago to pick her up when she and I were together? Three years ago? You were hell bent on getting her back.

Remember what it felt like when you didn't have her? You wanted her more than anyone else in the world. Don't fuck this up, brother. You have a great life with her, and you have 2.5 kids right now as well."

"Damn it, Matt." Colin sat up. "You piss me off sometimes."

"I only piss you off when you know I'm right," Matthew sighed, not understanding how his brother could do this to Tess. "Whoever is sleeping beside you right now needs to stay wherever you found her. Don't bring that shit here."

"Why do you always think the worst of me?" Colin asked.

Matthew laughed. "Brother, I love you, but I know you."

"I'll be home soon." Colin put the phone on the nightstand. "Fuuuuck," he muttered knowing he messed up badly. Glancing to his left, he sighed as Emma yawned.

"Who was that?" she asked in a soft voice.

"My brother," he answered. "I have to go."

Her hand touched his chest. "It was kind of nice hanging out with you and talking. I haven't been able to be honest with anyone in quite a while."

"I liked talking with you too." Softly, his hand touched her cheek. "Thanks for listening to me."

Emma sat up, guilt was brewing inside knowing his body belonged to another woman, *his wife*.

"Move to Portland," he suggested out of nowhere. "I'll help you out. Hook you up with a job. At least you would have more opportunities in a city than a place like this."

"No." Emma shook her head adamantly. "You don't get to buy me. It's bad enough you bought me a car."

"It's just a car." Colin shrugged, not thinking much about it as he stood.

"To you, it's just a car." Her voice was barely above a whisper. "To me, it's a safe form of freedom. I can take off and not worry about breaking down and wondering how I'm going to pay for repairs."

"I've never lived that way," he admitted. "I've been very fortunate."

Emma bit her lower lip. "I never had the opportunity to go to college and have that higher education to have a better life. Besides that, every time they found me, I was relocated. You can't have that type of life and end up with a successful career. The two just don't go together."

"Let me help give you a better life," he suggested as he pulled on his jeans.

"No." She shook her head slowly. "I would only let you do that if there was a future for us, but there isn't. I want my own. I'm not sharing. This is nothing more than an extended one-night stand which I'm already regretting that this even happened as I am not this type of woman."

"I'm sorry," he sighed, running his hand through his hair. "I wish it was different."

"No, you don't." Emma was blunt. "You simply want a replacement for your mistress. You love your wife, don't be looking for a replacement. That's just messed and what we've done is messed up."

Colin sighed, knowing she was only partially correct; he did love his wife. "I know we didn't talk about birth control before…this happened, and since, apparently, we didn't use any last night, will you promise to let me know if you are pregnant from this?"

"If I am, I won't have an abortion. And I don't need you around to raise a child," she explicitly reminded him.

"I know you don't." His brow raised. "I wouldn't want you to have an abortion unless that was something you wanted. I will support my child—if there is one."

Emma ran her hands through her tousled hair. "I don't want you around and I would not share this child with you, and I don't want your money."

Colin blew out his breath, she was more stubborn than his wife. It was probably better this way anyhow. With Tess, he had two kids at home, two more on the way, and a perfect life with her in Portland. What the hell did he do last night sleeping with Emma! The alcohol had to stop; it was making him behave like he was twenty again.

Leaving shortly after one, he drove along the coastline, stopping at a restaurant to eat. It was there that he realized how much *he* regretted his actions with Emma, but he couldn't go back and change it now.

Knowing he was going to tell Tess the truth, he drove slowly the rest of the way to Savannah to organize his thoughts.

When he arrived in Savannah, he took a seat in the rocker next to his father on the porch. For a few minutes, they just enjoy the silence of the pending evening.

"How are you doing, son?" Jonathan finally asked.

"Okay."

"James brought Taryn's body back," Jonathan looked out into the pending darkness. "I was waiting for you to return before we bury her. Tess is not doing well. Disappearing for a few days caused her a lot of stress. It's not been easy to keep her calm and relaxed."

"Is she resting now?"

"Yes. Matthew and Dominic took the kids to Chicago this afternoon. They'll be back in a few days."

"I needed to talk to someone who wasn't emotionally involved with this family in any way. Christ, Dad. Tess's sister called a mark on her because of me—and then she turns out to have my son. Everyone was put through hell because I had a mistress before I was even married."

"Who is this woman you've been with for the past couple days?" Jonathan asked, knowing his son very well.

"Emma is her name," Colin answered, rolling his eyes, as no one could hide anything from him. "She's a bartender a couple hours south of here."

"Did you sleep with her?"

Colin sighed and looked out at nothing not answering.

"Is she going to be Taryn's replacement?" Jonathan persisted.

"No. She's not that kind of woman."

"What about your wife? Have you given any consideration to Tess and what she's going through—and been through—with all of this? And you are going on a two-day hiatus and sleeping with another woman. You're married—do I need to remind you of this?" Jonathan shook his head in disappointment.

"I'm very aware that I am married." Colin stared at his father. "I had to get my head on straight before I could help my wife deal with any of this. This wasn't just difficult for her, it is for me, too. If you don't understand that, sorry. I'm not leaving Tess—ever. I will never divorce her, and I will never let her divorce me. We made that promise to each other as soon as we started trying to have children of our own, regardless of what happens. All of you think Tess is so damn perfect. Well, she's not. She's about as fucked up as I am. Christ, Dad, she was having an affair with James when she was first relocated, and we got married. Don't preach to me about faithfulness.

"I'm going to go see my wife, make amends, and help her deal with all of this—just as I always do. When we come downstairs in the morning, we will be fine. We will go back to being that undeniable happy couple that everyone is used to seeing."

"Colin—" Jonathan eyed him.

"Dad, I love Tess more than any other woman in my life. I know she feels the same way about me. We'll be fine once we get back to Portland. This life isn't our life. This place messes us up every single time we are here." Colin stood, shaking his head, irritated with himself.

Jonathan got up and gave his son a hug. "I don't agree with what you've done, but this is your marriage to Tess—not mine. I'm here if you need me for anything, anytime."

"Thanks, Dad." Colin hugged him. "Sorry I was such an ass."

"You are my son. You can tell me anything in confidence—as always."

Colin went inside to the family room, where it was unusually quiet.

Gina was reading in a recliner, glancing up when he walked in. With a simple smile, she pointed to the couch.

Lipping a thank you, he knelt before his wife and ran a gentle hand over her cheek as her eyes opened. He took one of her hands and held it tightly, as his other slipped behind her neck. He kissed her forehead and whispered, "I'm so sorry for leaving the way I did and for what I'm about to tell you." Then, he kissed her again. "Forgive me, please?"

Without speaking, Tess sat up, and they went to the living room for a little bit of privacy.

"I kept thinking I could let this go just once. I didn't want to be that woman—that bitchy, naggy, no-wonder-my-husband-fucked-somebody-else-because-I'm-a-bitch type of woman. But I can't. I'm just not engineered to let it go." Tess was furious with him.

"Tess—" Colin put his hand up in an attempt to calm her.

"I knew coming back here would cause issues between us," Tess began, again. "The only thing that kept me here was the simple fact that I can't fly yet. Otherwise, I'd be gone with both the children. Then you could go fuck your new little whore all you wanted."

"Tess, that's not what happened," he wanted to defend his actions, but she wasn't ready to listen.

"Bullshit. I don't know who you think I am, but I'm not ignorant to any degree. I know you better than you think. I may not have known about Taryn before we were married, but I know you now. And stop trying to calculate the best way to handle me. Why do you keep forgetting that I have a minor in psychology!"

Colin grinned and looked away from her for a moment as he feared daggers of fire were going to shoot from her eyes. "What do you want me to say?"

"Why? Why did you find it necessary to sleep with some other woman?" She demanded an answer.

"It was just sex and alcohol that encouraged, Tess, nothing more," his voice was calm as one of them had to be.

"So, when I tell you I slept with somebody else while you were gone and assure you that it was just sex and nothing more, you'll be fine with that?" She cocked her head and watched his face redden.

"You didn't?" his voice dropped low, and his eyes narrowed.

"Didn't I?" Tess retorted.

"Who?" A fire started burning in his stomach.

Tess shook her head slowly. "The feeling in your gut—that makes you want to vomit at the thought of me with another man—is exactly how I feel with you having fucked another woman you stupid, self-centered asshole!" Without thought, her fist zipped out and punched him on the side of the cheek.

His eyes widened as he rolled his jaw. "I'm sorry."

"You're sorry? I will find out who this other woman is, and I will kill her, too," Tess said with a sweet grin. "Then, if you go and do this again,

I will repeat said action, a third time. And you can live with the fact that every time I kill a woman that your dick slipped in, it's your fault."

"Jesus, Tess, just let it go." Colin shook his head not knowing how to calm her down. "She's nothing—no one compares to you. Leave it alone, Tess. Why do you have to act like a crazy person?"

"Why do you find it necessary to whore around? Am I not enough for you? It makes me feel inadequate as your wife." With arms crossed, she waited his answer.

"It's nothing like that. If you had heard her story, and the alcohol… you would've slept with her too," he added. "Was it my brother?"

"No!" Her eyes were wide.

"Will you tell me if I guess it right?"

"Does it really matter?" she asked, shrugging her shoulders.

Taking her hands, he gazed into her icy green eyes. "I will let it go if you do the same."

"Fine, but I will still find out who she is." She pulled her hands from his.

"Why?" he asked, tossing his hands up.

"I don't want to ever be around this woman." Tess's cold glare made him shiver.

"The only women around you are Gina and Harper," he reminded her. "I don't really think you're going to go to some offbeat, sleepy town and run into the woman."

Tess pushed on his chest, but he didn't budge. "Fuck you, just fuck you, Colin! I hate you right now." Tears were coming and she was doing her best to hold them back, but she felt defeated.

"If it makes you feel any better, I hate myself for what I did to you, too," he admitted reaching out to her and this time she didn't move back. First, he took her hands, then moved his hands up her arms to her shoulders as he knew tears were welling up behind her eyes. "I wish I could do a rewind, honey, I really do. I'm sorry."

Tess buried her head in the nape of his neck as tears cascaded down her cheeks. How could she be mad at him when she did the same thing? "Can we go home? I really don't like us when we're here."

"I was ready to go home when we were in the hospital," he reminded her.

"Why do we always get messed up when we're here?" Tess asked, sighing deeply as she pulled back and he rested his forehead on hers.

"I don't know. I just know how much I love you and our kids and our life in Portland. We have been here way too long. It's time for us to go. I don't want to keep having problems between us just because we're around everyone else. I fucking hate who we become when we're here."

"We're going to have four kids within the next six months. That's a lot, and it's scary. I've told you before that I didn't want to be raising these kids by myself."

"Tess, you're not." He kissed her temple. "Remember our promise when we decided to start having our own children?"

"We said we would always be together, never divorce, and work through any problems that came up."

"I'm still holding true to that," he assured her. "I know I'm not perfect, but you are the only woman I've ever loved. I love you with every inch of my heart and soul. I cannot—and will not—live my life without you ever."

"You hurt me, and you promised me you never would," she reminded him.

"I know. I'm sorry, and I will spend my life making it up to you." He tilted her chin up so he could kiss her, but she didn't allow it. "I love you and our family."

"I don't love you right now." Then, she thought for a moment. "No, that's not true. I love you but I don't like you right now."

"Fair enough," he understood. "I shouldn't have left you for the last couple days. Here, beside me, is my best friend, great lover, and mother of my children. I risked everything for alcohol induced sex with another woman. She didn't even compare to you. Matthew called me. Sometimes I forget almost losing you to my brother, to Jack, to the bullets that nearly killed you. Matthew reminded me of what I fought for. And even though the damage is done, for what it's worth, I am sorry. I hope, at some point, you will forgive me."

"This only works if we trust each other," she reminded him. "I knew coming here would be bad for us. I don't understand why we fall into such bad habits here."

"I don't know either." He shook his head. "I think it's okay to visit, but we've been here almost two months. That's a long time away from home." Colin kissed her temple as his hand rested on her stomach. "How are the babies doing?"

A smile crossed her lips, and her hand rested on his moving it to where they were kicking. "I didn't feel them move for almost twenty-four hours. That's why Gina took me back to the doctor's office. Everything is good."

"Aside from me being a pain in your ass, how are you feeling?" Colin truly did worry about her.

"Better now that you're home, surprisingly." She shook her head and rolled her eyes. "I'm so used to you always being around. When you're not around, it's hard for me. I miss you, damn you. Don't you ever do that again. I will leave you next time."

"I'm sorry," he said in a solemn voice. "I promise, it won't ever happen again."

Tess took a seat in one of the living room chairs, and leaned forward with her hands holding her head. Trying to hold back tears, she swallowed the lump in her throat, as he knelt before her.

"We can't do this anymore, Colin," her voice barely audible as she looked at him. "I don't want to fight with you."

Colin slid his hands down her thighs to her hips, then rested his head on her lap. "I know, baby. Let's get out of here and drive to our place in Atlanta for a few days. There are no children, no family, just you and me."

Tess wiped away the tears that were trailing down her cheeks and nodded.

BOUNDARIES WITHIN, THE SERIES COMPROMISED BOUNDARIES

Book II

James walked up to the house and knocked on the door. Grey was at the bottom of the steps, and Rick and Thomas were at opposite ends of the home. James always liked to be prepared. A man opened the door and eyed James, shaking his head. Stepping back, he gestured for him to come in alone.

"Do you realize how inappropriate it is for you to just show up at my home like this?" Brian walked him into the dining room, and they sat across from each other.

"Do you realize I don't care?" James remarked. "That family has been through hell the last couple of months."

"Tess is okay? She made it out of the hospital with the babies doing well?"

"Of course." James grinned. "You know who she was fighting for her."

"And the rest of the family?" Brian asked.

"Sort of fine. You know who called the mark?" James asked.

Brian shook his head. "We didn't get to talk much that night. I only had time to back off the local PD and organize a small team to clean up that mess."

"I know, that's why I'm here. It was Taryn, her twin," James shared. "She's the one who shot her in Chicago and started this whole damn thing. This is the part you'll love—it was all over a man. Robert Monroe was the festering wound, and then it was Colin McGowan."

"Colin?" Brian was shocked. "I know all about Robert, but Colin?"

"Colin kept her as his little dish on the side for years until he married Tess," James explained. "He still supported her, but he didn't see her again. The last time he was with Taryn, she got pregnant with his son. Now Taryn is dead, and Tess is alive. All the parties that were after the bounty were taken out as well. Tess is free."

"I know you didn't fly up here to tell me all that," Brian said. "What's on your mind?"

James looked around the meticulous room. "Dominic Markenna."

"I knew there was something bothering you. He hasn't surfaced in years." Brian shrugged.

"Are you positive he was involved?" James asked.

Brian took a deep breath. "His name hasn't come up since he sold his company. I'm going to leave a little room for possible misinterpretation, but he is a smart man. His father is a manipulative bastard—even from prison. One of my friends in the Justice Department, Meagan Trask, stood up for him when I arrested him after the incident with Tess. I cannot give you a definitive answer."

"Markenna is at Jonathan's home as we speak," James told him. "They won't let me touch him. I just don't trust him. I've worked the list with precision. If he's not supposed to be on it, you've got to tell me because I'm almost done."

"Where's Jonathan?" Brian asked.

"In Savannah," James answered.

"I'll fly down tomorrow and talk with him. Who else is at the house?"

"Gina, Colin, Tess, Matthew, the kids and Dominic," James answered. "I will be there until Jack gets back. Half of my men will stay close until I feel comfortable enough to release them."

"Where's Jack?"

"Taking a much-needed vacation with Harper." James grinned.

"What's he doing? He figured he couldn't have Tess, so he'd take the next best sister?" Brian laughed.

"Something like that," James chuckled. "My team and I are heading out tonight to follow a lead on a few people from the list. I should be back in Savannah tomorrow morning. I want an answer tomorrow—or I will put a bullet in his head regardless of his connection to the McGowan family."

"Fair enough," Brian conceded. "I'll wait for your return."

Made in the USA
Las Vegas, NV
17 February 2023